Scruples & Drams

Scruples & Drams

Cynthia Frank-Stupnik

NORTH STAR PRESS OF ST. CLOUD, INC.
St. Cloud, Minnesota

ISBN: 978-0-87839-796-9

First edition: May 2015

Printed in the United States of America.

Published by
North Star Press of St. Cloud, Inc.
P.O. Box 451
St. Cloud, MN 56302

northstarpress.com

Scruples & Drams

Preface

JENNIE PHILLIPS'S STORY began in my mind years ago. I am not sure when I first learned about her. She died before I was born or our family moved to Clearwater, but she was a model of what a woman could do at the turn of the twentieth century. A druggist and postmistress, Jennie was a respected leader in the village, which is obvious when I read the Clearwater newspaper articles written and edited by John Evans. While Jennie is the main focus, other people and other incidents also helped create this story.

Outside of marriage and family, women like Jennie Phillips cannot be categorized as simply ahead of their time; they were of the time. She and others had entered a new era where they were making conscientious choices and professional decisions about their futures. Although in most states they still couldn't vote, have custody of their children if they were divorced, own property, sit on juries, or have access to reproductive health information, women were getting educations and entering the work force.

This new generation of professional women often chose to postpone marriage or not marry all together, which went across the grain of women's roles at the time. In 1966, Barbara Welter wrote an essay entitled, "The Cult of True Womanhood: 1820-1860," (also referred to as the cult of domesticity) focusing on the expectations for women in the nineteenth century (Welter, Barbara. "The Cult of True Womanhood: 1820-1860." *American Quarterly* 18:2: Summer 1966). In a nutshell, true women embodied virtues of piety, purity, submissiveness, and domesticity. Their spheres were in the home, cooking, cleaning, baking, and keeping their families on the right spiritual track. Men were encouraged to look for wives who were religious because the other virtues would fall into place if they loved and listened to God.

Men, and even some women, regarded the female gender as the less intelligent and weaker, so they needed protecting. In fact, in some ways, women were physically weaker. Giving birth to an average of six or seven children, often when doctors instructed them not to have any more, countless women died in childbirth. In addition, the infant mortality rate was high; some women lost half of their babies in the birthing process or from childhood diseases.

To make matters worse, women's fashions caused health concerns. Women have always wanted to follow the latest fashion fad. Costumes often included heavy and weighty layers of fabric, slips, hoops, bustles, and corsets, which was a health hazard in itself. According to the time, the smaller the waist, usually women boasted of having seventeen to twenty inches, the more sex appeal they had. This stringed device constrained a woman and put immense pressure on her internal organs, which caused fainting, crushed internal and reproductive organs, and even broken ribs. But much of this changed after the mid-nineteenth century. Doctors and feminists began educating women about the health hazards of such cumbersome and dangerous clothing, especially the corset.

In addition, advocates for social change encouraged women to become educated. Many women took up the challenge with some earning more basic education than men. Woefully ignorant about their bodies, women also began educating themselves about their anatomies. When they had some type of reproductive symptom, they seldom went to doctors because they were too embarrassed to talk about their sexual issues. Instead, they sought out other women, someone specializing in plants and roots, or midwives, for help. They also studied pamphlets, books, magazines, and newspapers. If one were to believe the advertisements' claims, over-the-counter products could cure anything from gout to toothaches. To be fair, some of the ingredients were harmless, consisting mainly of herbs and roots. Because much of the patent market was aimed at female complaints, those who could afford these products sought out a druggist's stock which, up until the early twentieth century, was not regulated. Many contained either alcohol or opiates, or both, with the potential of causing addiction and even death. Often people were raised with the knowledge of what herb or root helped what ailment, and a lot are still used in the pharmaceuticals today. Women who were knowledgeable about the reproductive process, sought ways to control the number of babies they had, and yes, to even end a life. They found this information in pamphlets, books, and magazines, along with the patent advertisements; they bought the products in drug stores like the Phillips's store in Clearwater, Minnesota.

Although this is a work of fiction, most of the characters and events are historical and helped me weave this story together. I began my research in 2006 by reading the village's early newspapers, *Clearwater Herald* and *Clearwater News,* and many items in the *St. Cloud Times*. I re-learned my Minnesota history that I had to take in elementary school. I also realized that the village and Minneapolis had other connections besides the Mississippi River and Jim Hill's Great Northern Railroad. Simon Stevens, explorer, pioneer, and one of the owners and founders of Clearwater, was the younger brother of John Harrington Stevens, "Father of Minneapolis." Minnesota promoter, who founded other communities including Glencoe, John Stevens was also an owner of the steamboat the *J.B. Bassett* that paddled its way from Minneapolis to St. Cloud and made regular stops at Clearwater. He held office in the first state House of Representatives in 1858 and many other offices throughout his lifetime.

My sister and I read a wonderful handwritten story at the Minnesota Historical Society about the Phillips family written by Ruth Phillips, the youngest child in the book. Here Ruth relates stories about the village, an almost tranquil environment, and gives clues to her parents', brothers', and sisters' personalities, the fun, love, and tightness of the family, and the relationship between Pitt Colgrove and Jennie that Jennie breaks off. Pitt's father James did, in fact, invent the potato planter manufactured by Granite City Iron Works where my father, Harold Frank, worked for decades. James Colgrove was instrumental in helping local farmers get settled and improve their crop productions. D.D. Storms was also an influential farmer and teacher. According to many sources, he was a fun-loving, story-telling, and intellectual individual.

Anyone born and raised in Clearwater knew about Maude Porter. Born in 1862, Maude was one of the first white girls born in Wright County. She was the daughter of Tom Porter and Abigail Camp, both early pioneers to the area who had stories of their own to tell. Maude died in 1965 at the age of 103, the oldest living person in the county.

Alice Leonard, a teenager from Irish Town in Lynden Township was murdered in May 1893 after a flag-raising event. Her story can be found in the *Clearwater Herald, The St. Cloud Daily Times,* and other local newspapers around the vicinity throughout the summer of her murder. Although the case was never solved, I only mention names and circumstances that are documented in these papers. I do not point fingers at any of those involved, relaying only the facts documented for the period.

Minnesota Congressman Charles Townsend came to celebrate Decoration Day 1895, which packed the town. A fire took out the northern part of the village in May 1895, a week or two before the event was to take place. A set of burglaries took place. An object, which you will read about, actually was found in a mysterious place. Fiction couldn't make up that story. I also mention the burglars as they were documented.

Most of the characters that help move the story along are from the era, the whole Phillips family, Doc Edmunds, the Pecks, the Lyons, Louisa and Robert, Jennie's female friends, many in Lynden Township and Irish Town. I have changed some names to protect those whose families may still be living. Many characters and situations are simply that—fictional—to help move the plot.

Chapter 1

Spiritus vinosus (SV)

Ardent Spirit of Any Strength

CROWS CAWED NOISILY OVERHEAD. Jennie looked up at the small patch of blue sky and saw a dozen or so black birds sweeping onto bare branches.

She breathed deeply. The air smelled of damp peat and wet tree bark. This year, spring came on at a gallop, Jennie thought, as she felt the rising heat and humidity of the May afternoon. Only last weekend, a blast of cold sleet had blanketed the area around Clearwater. Thankfully, all that remained of the storm were puddles in the muddy road.

Luckily, the brief snow hadn't frozen the budding spring flowers. When Doc Edmunds had asked her if she had time to deliver a prescription to Anna McKey in what Clearwater folks called Irish Town out in Lynden Township, she had agreed, hoping to find a bouquet of wild flowers to put on the church altar for the morning services. And sure enough, Jennie saw a few purple sprouts in the ditch up ahead.

"Whoa, Solly," she said firmly, pulling on the reins. Solomon was the calmest of her family's horses. Jennie knew he would be content to nibble fresh spring grass while she gathered her blooms.

Hiking up her black skirt with one hand and holding tight to the handle of a wicker basket with the other, Jennie jumped down from the buggy. Her wire-rimmed glasses slid down onto her nose as her straw hat slid sideways, almost falling into the mud.

Robins chattered back and forth. How she loved spring! As she headed toward the clump of phlox, Jennie remembered a line of poetry from Tennyson: "But I must gather knots of flowers . . ."

She couldn't remember if "phlox" was Latin or Greek, but Jennie had recently learned that its leaves could be steeped into a tea and used as a blood purifier. She had excelled in sciences in high school, and yet, when she started Normal School in St. Cloud, she focused on her education classes. She had almost forgotten her early interest in biology and chemistry until she began apprenticing under her father in his drug store. Now she spent days compounding and dispensing whatever Doc Edmunds, the area's respected physician, ordered. She had to learn the medicinal values to roots, herbs, and stock pharmaceuticals, and how to measure each ingredient precisely. One small mistake, a scruple instead of a dram, could cause serious health problems for the patient.

Wishing she would find a few more wildflowers, Jennie looked ahead a few rods where she saw a small lavender garden. As she got closer, attempting to keep her hem from getting soiled, she felt clammy. She noticed that fog huddled over some of the underbrush. She assumed the Tamarack Swamp, the wetland that covered quite a bit of the township, had to be close by.

Jennie looked back at the buggy. Solly stood munching tender grass. As she bent and clipped flowers, she thought of how her life had changed this past year. Last May, she had been teaching at a country school near Atwater. She had enjoyed her students, but she missed her family. She really wanted a position closer to home. When her brother Carl had decided he no longer wanted to work as a clerk in the confines of the family store—he preferred to work outside—she had been surprised when her parents asked if she'd like to take Carl's place, at least until another teaching job opened closer to home.

She had come to love working at the drug store, and could not believe how much she had learned this past year. Unlike teaching where she knew far in advance what her students would be learning because of her strict adherence to the lesson plans, she never knew what the day would hold once she and her father opened up in the early morning. Doc Edmonds often met the two of them at the door because he needed an order made up as soon as possible. Almost all day long, a steady stream of customers wandered in to buy over-the-counter medicines, smoking tobacco, or anything else from toothpaste to horehound candy. She and her father kept so busy, Jennie seldom had a moment to herself.

She was thankful for today's rare outing. Early next fall, Jennie would have even more responsibility and even less time to herself when her father opened another drug store in Eden Valley. He would be home on the weekends, but the vast majority of the store's responsibilities would be hers.

A woman running a drug store? Some people in her small community might be skeptical of her ability, but Jennie had built up the trust of many women already, and with Doc's promise to help out when he could, she knew she was up to the task.

With her basket full, Jennie knew she had to leave the peace and quiet. As she straightened up, she felt an ache in her back. It had been a long afternoon, riding out the five miles from Clearwater.

After stretching, she started to head toward the buggy. Suddenly, she heard some rustling and then a loud "Snap!"

Probably a rabbit hopping over leaves, Jennie thought. Then the "Snap, crack!" came louder and closer. Maybe she was hearing a fox or a dog stepping on fallen branches.

Crows cawed more anxiously and began fluttering their wings again as they took flight.

Then she heard more crunching of leaves, but this time closer and louder.

"Yaaaauuuuuwwwwwww! Yaaaauuuuuwwwwwww!"

"What the . . . ?" Jennie asked out loud.

Was a child crying? Was someone in pain?

Even though she had a hard time seeing into the dark, dense woods, she scanned the low-lying shrubbery. Surely, a child would not be alone out here!

She pushed down scraggly branches as she stepped into the thicket. She stopped fast when she heard soft whimpering.

"Who's there?"

Hearing more whimpering, Jennie followed a narrow path that trailed deeper into the woods.

"Hello, hello?"

She had hardly taken more than a dozen steps before her right foot got stuck in the mire of a bog. As she pulled it out, her left foot sank. The wetness seeped into her new shoes, but she couldn't pull either foot loose. After finding a spot to set her basket, Jennie looked around for something to clutch onto for balance. With her right foot, she stepped off the path and up onto a pile of leaves. A couple feet away she was able to anchor onto a strong-looking tree limb. Gripping for leverage, she pulled hard and plucked her right foot free from the muck.

Her shoes were ruined. With a twig, she scraped off the mud. So much for her splurge on the newest spring fashions from Webster's Mercantile. And how many times her father had warned her about Webster's cheap goods.

"Yaaaauuuuuwwwwwww!"

Jennie jolted. Her heart beat so hard she felt the pressure in her ears.

"Who's there?" she hollered.

Not waiting for an answer, she seized her basket, pulled up her skirt, and scurried out of the thicket, barely escaping the bog again.

When she finally made it back to the entry of the swamp road, she realized Solly had run off, pulling the buggy behind him. He had come to a stop in the middle of a family friend's field. As she came up to the side of him, she heard him snorting and whinnying.

Not wishing to frighten him more, and trying to catch her breath, Jennie called softly, "Solly, Solly!" while reaching for the reins that had been dragged through the mud. Throwing her basket of flowers on the seat, she slowly walked closer, shushing and patting his side until she reached his halter. Once she got in front of him, she stroked his nose. He snorted again and shook his head. His large, black eyes showed fear.

"There, there boy," Jennie spoke soothingly. Had he heard what she had?

She led him slowly and gently across the corn-stubble field toward the Dorsey farm.

Earlier, on the way out to Lynden, Jennie had stopped to visit her friend Ida who, along with her new husband, Sherm Shattuck, lived with her parents, Orrin and Mary Dorsey. She and Sherm hoped it wouldn't be a long stay, just long enough to buy their own farm.

Jennie needed to talk to Ida about plans for the upcoming Decoration Day celebration, Jennie, Ida, and another friend Maude Porter had volunteered to decorate the town. This was a big event for her small community. Congressmen, former lieutenant governors, and other local and regional leaders were going to be in attendance, including Minneapolis founder John Stevens who was brother to one of Clearwater's founders, Simon Stevens.

Unfortunately, Ida wasn't home. Wasn't that ironic, her mother said. Here Jennie was out to see Ida, and she and Sherm had ridden into town to run a few errands and to see her at the drug store. After Mary Dorsey gave her a few instructions on where to find a few spring flowers near the Tamarack Swamp, Jennie left, promising she would stop again on her way back.

As Jennie and Solly came back to the Dorsey house, she knew she was a sight. Not only had she ruined her new shoes, but her skirt was splattered with mud. She hoped Ida had returned home from her trip into Clearwater, though she doubted she'd even have time to say more than a quick hello.

Ducks squawked, hens cackled, and Pepper, the black-and-dirty-white sheep dog, ran to greet them. Pepper must have sensed Solly's mood and stayed a few yards away, allowing Jennie to calmly lead the horse to the tree to tether him.

"My gracious, what happened? Did you fall in a puddle or something?" Mary Dorsey asked as her hand swept over her mouth

Short and thin, the older woman had been born in England and had come to America with her parents when she was a baby. Although she didn't have a thick English accent, she spoke so fast Jennie had to catch up with what she had said.

"Something like that," Jennie answered as she limped up the steps. She wasn't ready to talk about what she heard by the swamp. She pulled out her hanky from her sleeve and dabbed at the beads of perspiration on her forehead and the back of her neck.

"You're flushed! Sit down in this rocker. I'll get you some lemonade and a cool wash rag to wipe your face. Then we'll see what we can do about your clothes."

The screen door creaked and slammed as Mary Dorsey hurried into the house.

Jennie removed her hat, gathered up some of the strays of her light brown hair, and pinned them back into the bun.

"It sure turned warm this afternoon," she hollered sideways into the house, using her hat as a fan.

Mary Dorsey came out carrying a wicker tray with two sweaty glasses of lemonade. "Here, take a good long sip of this. It'll fix you up as good as new."

"Thank you." Jennie took a gulp of the sweet, cold drink. She hadn't realized how thirsty she was. "This is so refreshing, Mrs. Dorsey!"

She fanned herself again before she asked, "I suppose Ida and Sherm haven't returned yet."

The older woman handed Jennie a wet wash cloth before kneeling down to clean her skirt with another. "I have to tell you, Jennie, I'm beginning to worry about them. I would've thought they'd been home long before now. Surprising you didn't meet up on the road."

"I took the St. Augusta road. The Seven Hills road may be shorter, but I was afraid if I went that way I'd run into low, wet areas and get stuck." Jennie took another sip of her lemonade before setting the glass on the wicker table beside the chair. As she wiped her face, neck, and hands, she said, "I can't tell you how good this feels."

Mary Dorsey continued to dab at Jennie's skirt. She looked up and said, "Now that you say that, I think I overheard Sherm tell Ida they were going that way even if it were wet." She laughed before adding, "He's a man. They've more confidence than we women, but they can get stuck like we can. I hope that hasn't happened."

Jennie nodded. Although she was plain looking, Mary Dorsey's smile made her face light up.

"I wouldn't worry about them, Mrs. Dorsey. They could've run into friends to talk to or they could be taking their time. It's ironic, though. I'm out here, and she's in town."

"You're probably right, Jennie." After a few seconds, she noticed her shoes. "Why don't you kick those things off? I'll take them back to the old pump and try to clean them up for you."

"I know I'll have to throw them, but I'll still need something to get home in," Jennie said as she obediently followed Mary Dorsey's instructions. "My feet are literally swishing around in them!"

"You rest here, dear, and let me see what I can do to fix them up long enough to get you home. Otherwise, what size do you wear?"

"These are a five."

"Both Ida and I wear six, but if I can't clean them maybe I have some slippers that you wouldn't swim around in."

Mary Dorsey went down the steps, carrying Jennie's shoes, then walked out of sight around the hedges that ran around to the back of the house.

"Is Jennie all right?" Mrs. Dorsey's husband, Orrin, hollered as he walked up the path. "Did the horse throw her? I saw him running in the field like he was a frightened banshee."

Jennie tucked her feet under her skirt. "Hello, Mr. Dorsey. I'm fine. Mrs. Dorsey's in the back by the pump. I don't know what got into Solly. He ran off, and I had to run after him."

"Something frightened him. You sure you're okay?"

"Yes. I'm fine. A mess, but fine. I'm not sure if he heard the same thing I did, but while I was walking out there by the swamp picking some flowers, I could have sworn I heard a child crying."

Orrin Dorsey's eyes widened. "A child crying, you say?"

"What were you saying about a child crying?" Mary Dorsey asked as she rounded the corner of the house carrying Jennie's wet shoes.

"Jennie said she thought she heard a child crying while she was down by the swamp."

Jennie looked at Orrin Dorsey, who seemed to be staring at his wife. She, in turn, seemed to give him a "knowing" look—like parents gave each other when they had a secret they didn't want to share with their children.

He cleared his throat. "I was going to tell Jennie that Sam Stokes said he thought there might be a bobcat out there, maybe even a den with new cubs. They make a crying noise, especially if you get too close to the babies."

"Oh, no!" Jennie exclaimed. "I was close to a bobcat? Are they dangerous?"

"Not usually," he said, trying to reassure her. "But I'm sure if she thought her cubs were in danger, she might have pounced. Her cry did what it was supposed to do—warn you not to get any closer."

As if she knew that Jennie was even more afraid, Mary Dorsey said, "Now, Orrin, you're frightening Jennie. Here are your shoes, dear. I couldn't do much with them, though. I'll try to find slippers if they are too uncomfortable."

"I'm sure I'll be fine until I get home. Thank you." Jennie reached out and took the shoes.

"You could sure stay here tonight." Mrs. Dorsey offered, looking at her husband for some agreement.

"Thank you, but no. Father and Mother will be worried," she said as she slid her feet into the cold, wet shoes. She knew if she didn't leave now, she would be riding home in the dark.

Mary seemed to read Jennie's insecurity. "Orrin, if she won't stay, can't someone escort her into town?"

Jennie laughed a little. "Please, don't make a fuss," she said, trying to hide her fear. "Solly knows the way home. I'll be fine."

"You're right, Mother. Jennie, I'd never forgive myself if anything else happened to you. Besides your father would expect me to look out for you. If nothing else, I'll see if one of the Mooney boys can ride along with you."

Orrin Dorsey started walking back to the barn before Jennie could argue with him. Besides, she knew that it wouldn't do any good to tell him no. He had sounded firm, like her father when he made up his mind about something.

Jennie stood up. Her feet still sloshed inside her shoes.

Mary Dorsey walked with Jennie to the buggy. "I'm sorry your trip out here was a waste, Jennie. If you don't meet up with Ida and Sherm on your way back to town, maybe you two can talk tomorrow after church."

"Don't worry. The trip wasn't a waste. I had to come out anyway to deliver some medicine to Anna McKey. Doc's been so busy he didn't get out here today. I had a nice time picking wildflowers for the church altar tomorrow. The lilacs by the railroad tracks aren't in full bloom yet, but I saw some bordering the Colgrove farm. I'll stop on my way back and pick some."

"Colgroves?" Mrs. Dorsey asked, smiling coyly at Jennie.

Jennie knew what she was alluding to. She and Pitt Colgrove had dated for two years, but lately, they couldn't agree on where their relationship was going so they hadn't seen much of each other.

Jennie could still feel the strain between the two of them at their last meeting. After their New Year's Eve party, he had pressed her again to marry him, to "become my wife and the mother of our children."

She hesitated before answering. "I can't commit right now, Pitt. We've discussed this before. Maybe in a year or two, but right now, I want to help my parents. Besides, I really enjoy what I'm doing."

What Jennie hadn't told him was that she didn't have any of the romantic notions her friends had for marrying. The oldest of Stanley and Marietta Phillps's eight living children, she had been her mother's right hand in the care of her younger siblings. She had fed, bathed, read to, cooked for, cleaned-up after, and done whatever else her mother asked her to do.

Besides, Jennie knew the real reason she didn't want to marry now. Pitt didn't want her to work after they were married. Although she loved him, she wanted more in life than being just a housewife.

They rode home in silence. Pitt walked her to her front porch and kissed her good night, but since then, over five months before, the two hadn't seen each other except for an occasional passing after church.

"No, Mrs. Dorsey. I know what you're thinking, but I don't plan on stopping to see Pitt. We're only friends now."

"I'm truly sorry about that, Jennie. You two seemed to be such a nice couple."

"I know, but I think we both came to realize we wanted different things in our lives," Jennie said as she took hold of the reins and stepped up into the seat.

"I'm sorry I brought up the subject. And I know Ida will be sorry she missed you because she had some concerns about all the decorations. My, it's sure going to be a big celebration, isn't it?"

"I don't think our peaceful little town has had a commotion like this in a long time. Important speakers from all over the state. The town businesses have donated so much to spruce up the village. Pa said we could use as much paint as we wanted. Lyons's General Store offered us red, white and blue ribbon. Luther Laughton's giving butcher wrap for the making of signs. Let's see, Boutwell's Hardware said we could have all the nails we need to build the speaker's platform and stencils to write on the paper so they look real professional."

"Sounds like everyone's getting into the act," Mary Dorsey commented. "The last *Clearwater News* said the town's 'all a' buzz' because everyone far and wide will be here."

Jennie added, "That's for sure! I don't remember any event that has caused so much commotion. It should be fun. Friends, family, and lots of new and interesting people will be packing the town. I hope the weather cooperates."

Mrs. Dorsey turned around and recognized the person her husband had asked to help drive Jennie back into the village. "Here he comes."

Jennie saw a dark, handsome man walking her way, leading a beautiful reddish brown horse. With thick, almost black hair, he was about six feet tall and quite lean. Jennie assumed he was about her age, twenty-one or twenty-two.

"Jamie Mooney," Mary Dorsey announced, "this is Jennie Phillips."

"How'd you do, ma'am." Jamie tipped his head toward Jennie.

Jennie noticed his beautiful dark eyes and eyebrows.

"It's nice to meet you, Jamie."

"Now, Jamie, you see to it Jennie makes it home safe and sound," Mary Dorsey instructed.

"Yes'm," Jamie said with a nod before he led his horse to the back of the buggy to tie him.

"I hope to see all you in church tomorrow. If not, tell Ida I stopped. I'll see her sometime next week so we can finalize plans for the celebration."

"Of course, I'll tell her. Now ride safely," Mary Dorsey said as Jamie stepped up into the buggy.

"We will. Thank you, again, for everything." Jennie waved and then handed Jamie the reins.

After his "Click, click," Solly started walking down the Dorsey driveway.

"I'm sorry to put you out, Jamie. I tried telling the Dorseys I'd be fine, but they insisted I need an escort."

"Miz Phillips, I'd be oblig'n to ride along to town with you."

Even though Jamie Mooney hadn't been born in Ireland like his parents, he still had a thick brogue. Jennie loved the way he, like others in the area, rolled words around their tongues. "I appreciate it, and please call me Jennie. By the way, I like your horse. I'm not familiar with many breeds, though. What kind is she?"

"Chessy? She's a Quarter-horse, ma'am. She's an American Quarter-horse. Orrin Dorsey named her Chessy because of her chestnut color, but I like her name. Mr. Dorsey, he's letting me work for him to pay for her."

"She's beautiful and seems quite calm."

"She is most of the time. Sometimes she gets her ire up, though, and can be real disagreeable at times, too, 'specially when I want her to go somewhere she don't want to go."

"I'm happy with Solly. I don't know what breed he is, but he's the calmest of all my father's horses."

"I can't figure Chessy out at times, though. S'pose we need to get more acquainted. I ain't taken her far from the Dorseys. Just rode her around in the fields at times. She still belongs to them so I'm pasturing her there for the time being. This way I can save the cost of feeding her until I have her paid for."

For a few miles, the two continued their exchange of pleasantries, like the unseasonably warm weather after the winter blast last week and how many of the farmers were excited to get started planting soon. They rode between the Murphy and Miller farms. White wooly lambs standing alongside their mothers nibbled on new grass in the pastures.

Ahead, Jennie saw one of the three crossroads that led into Clearwater. The first was north of Larkin's Corner. The one that was coming up cut a mile or two off their route, but it wasn't always safer or drier.

"Which way should we go? I came by way of Colgroves, you know, the St. Augusta road. There were a few ruts but nothing too bad."

"I suppose we'd be on higher ground if we went that way."

"I agree," Jennie nodded.

The buggy rocked and rattled as it crossed the rickety bridge over Plum Creek. Melting snow and healthy spring rains gurgled and bubbled their way to Warner Lake southeast of where they were. She loved this area. They were at the bottom of a little ravine owned by Feldges. Jennie looked to the left over Jamie's shoulders. A few black-and-white Holsteins chewed on tufts of grass around the pond. The air was intoxicating, even with a heady aroma of manure.

So caught up in the nature's beauty, Jennie finally came to when a few unexpected potholes caused the wheels to bounce up and down. Grateful for his company, she realized she had better try to keep the conversation going.

"Speaking of horses, I know very little about them, even though Father has kept a few to get us where we need to go. When I have to hitch up the buggy to go somewhere, I usually take Solly. Like I said, she's usually so calm. I don't know why she got so riled out there by the swamp."

"It can be a scary place at times, Jennie, 'specially late in the day."

"I was picking flowers. When I started back, I heard the strangest sounds."

"Really?" Jamie shook the reins a bit before asking, "What'd ya hear?"

"I know it sounds strange, but first I heard the crunching of leaves. I figured it was a little animal. Before long, though, I could have sworn I heard a child crying. Mr. Dorsey said Sam Stokes believes a bobcat and her cubs are down there, which now makes sense."

"A bobcat? I s'pose that's possible."

Jennie heard the doubt in Jamie's voice. All the times she and her brothers had come out here to deliver medicine to a patient for Dr. Edmunds, she never thought they would encounter danger, especially from wild animals. Now, as she looked around the fields and the wooded areas, she wondered if there were bobcats or even bears roaming around out there.

"No one can remember hearing anything so strange out by the swamp before Alice, well, before Alice Leonard were killed."

"Alice Leonard?" Jennie asked, thinking out loud, "I forgot all about her. I was away teaching when that happened. I read a little about it in the newspapers, and my mother wrote a bit. Otherwise, I didn't get in on all the talk."

"Like I said, it were nearly two years ago now that she were murdered, but some believe she were," Jamie cleared his throat, and added, "violated, too."

Embarrassed, Jennie could only say, "I had never heard about that."

"You may think it sounds like a bunch of balderdash. We Irish know what others think of us with our superstitions and everything, but you ain't the only one to have heard someone moaning or crying out there by the swamp. Ma and some of the neighbor women talk about it sometimes. Hell, s'cuse me, Jennie, most of us have heard it, and no one remembers hearing anything like it before Alice Leonard were done in out there."

For a moment Jennie thought about what Jamie seemed to be hinting at.

"Jamie," Jennie asked nervously. "Are you suggesting that the crying I heard was Alice Leonard's ghost?"

Chapter 2

Spiritus vini tenuis (SVT)

Proof Spirit

WITH THE SUN AT THEIR BACKS, Jennie began to feel cooler as Solly slowly pulled her and Jamie east. They drove beside fields furrowed into rich yet muddy black rows ready for planting. A small herd of white-faced Herefords grazed on green grass while calves nursed or lay beside them.

"I know we could still change our minds and take the Seven Hills Road, Jamie, but let's not, even though it's shorter. I heard the low lying areas are pretty muddy yet."

Jennie hated to admit that she seldom traveled "the hills." The road was steep, and the woods were spooky, even during the daytime. And now after Jamie brought up the subject of ghosts, she knew she would be seeing dark shadows all the way into town.

"You're probably right." Jamie agreed. "Maybe it's a bit out of the way, but let's keep heading toward the Clearwater-St. Augusta Road. It's drier and better maintained, and we've got pretty much a straight shot into the village then."

Most of the farmers around there had enough money to keep the road free of snow and graded from Clearwater north to St. Cloud. As the buggy turned south, Jennie looked over Jamie's shoulder, trying to recollect who lived up this road. Hinkemeyers, Schmidts, and, of course, D.D. Storms, who was a prominent farmer and quite a character. A Civil War vet, he always had an opinion or a funny story to tell.

They would soon cross another bridge that went over Plum Creek as it zigzagged its way to the Mississippi. Whenever she rode out this way, if she had the time, she stopped to get out of the buggy to stretch, relax, and give Solly a break as well. She felt such peace here by the lake that was named after George Warner whose farm nestled nearby.

Usually at this time of the year, she gazed at the serene lake, smelled the sweet apple blossoms, and listened to the gurgling of the brook. Wanting to get her business taken care of delivering medicine and visiting with Ida, she hadn't taken the time to stop when she drove by earlier. Now, as they headed back to town, she couldn't take anymore of Jamie's time than she had to.

While they drove along, Jennie tried to figure out what scared her by the swamp. She didn't believe in ghosts, but something had frightened her. Whether she heard a bobcat or something more sinister, she was curious now to know more about the grisly murder that took such an innocent, young life.

"Like I said, Jamie, I was away teaching at the time they found the girl. Do you remember what happened?"

"Well, me and my brother Frank was up to Uncle Pat's helping him in the fields. So I weren't there when it happened. But, let me tell ya', the whole country went a' buzz. No one felt safe."

Shocked by the man's misuse of the English language, Jennie tried to ignore it while she concentrated on the murdered girl's tragic story.

"How'd it happen?"

"Nobody really knows." Jamie flicked the reins again so Solly would realize he had to work harder to get up the hill. "Oh, a few of us in Irish Town have some hunches, but they say there weren't no clues. Little Alice, that's what almost everyone around here called her, had been over to the school that afternoon to take part in the flag-raising ceremonies."

Jennie knew that many of the public schools had taken part in the events around the state, celebrating both the newly designed Minnesota state flag and the newly written Pledge of Allegiance. As a teacher, she helped organize the celebration for students and parents in Atwater. Many schools, including Clearwater and the one out in Lynden Township, had held flag-raising ceremonies, with special speakers, songs, and recitation of the Pledge.

"My pa made sure we had a flag for the ceremony," Jamie said and then added, "Pa's a teacher, too, you know."

"I knew that, Jamie."

Unfortunately, Jennie also knew that a few of the Clearwater snobs didn't think much of the rural schools, especially out in Irish Town. Some of these same people, even those who made spiritual confessions of faith at her very own Congregational church, displayed a genuine distaste for the Irish. Thank goodness most of the villagers were not so biased.

She could almost hear Livia Paisley. "All they teach them out there is to drink and fight." She'd tip her head, get a shiny glint in her black eyes, and whisper, "And breed too many Catholic brats."

Few people in Clearwater irritated Jennie like Livia, or Livy as her close friends called her, who lived on Main Street and kept an eye on the comings and goings of everyone in town. Jennie wondered if the woman understood that many in and around the community, like the Stewarts and Mitchells, those she called friends, were also Irish. Of course, they were Protestant, but they were as proud of their heritage as the Catholics.

Many people listened to Livy because she was a good friend and neighbor to Ormasinda Peck, daughter of Minneapolis founder John Harrington Stevens and niece of Simon Stevens, one of the founders of Clearwater.

From what Jennie had gathered from the few details her good friend Maude Porter had told her, Livia Augusta Powers Paisley was the daughter of Major Maxwell Powers, a close friend of the John Stevens family. Livia's father and Stevens served together in the Mexican War and helped calm the state during the Sioux Uprising.

Yet, until a few years ago, Jennie hardly knew Livia Paisley. And why would she? The woman had kept to herself on top of the hill that gave them and their close friends a beautiful view of the Mississippi. Here she entertained only her closest friends and family from Clearwater and St. Paul. Jennie rarely saw her out on the streets unless she attended church or a village function that she chaired. She seldom showed herself in any of the village stores because she had a housekeeper who did most of her shopping. Occasionally, though, whether it was cold weather or warm, her husband took out his prized quarter horses, and Livia rode proudly—her head held high—beside her husband for what she called "her Sunday airing."

But then, Livia's husband died unexpectedly. One afternoon, shortly after the noon meal, the bookkeeper for the Roller Mills came back into the office to find his employer, Superintendent Octavious Paisley, slumped over at his desk, apparently dead from a heart attack. Livia mourned for a time, but then she began to change—and not for the better, Jennie believed.

Maybe part of the problem was that her only son, Thaddeus, held the strings to her husband's estate. He told his mother he could not afford to have two large houses, one for his family in St. Paul and one in Clearwater. He gave her a choice. She could move in with them, or he'd buy her something smaller in the village. And she'd have to give up her live-in housekeeper.

Maude told Jennie that Livia had a long drawn-out fight with her son about her financial situation, but it settled nothing. Maude also said that Livia seldom got along with her daughter-in-law whom she believed was behind her son's decision about her future welfare. Livia couldn't abide living with her daughter-in-law any more than her daughter-in-law wanted to live with her. She decided to settle for a smaller house in the village and do some of her own housekeeping so she could have some semblance of independence.

So where did Livia's house get built? Across from the Methodist Church, where from the moment she moved in, she began to keep track of everyone's comings and goings.

None of this was quite so obvious as a couple years before when Jennie decided for once she wasn't coming home from the St. Cloud Normal School for a weekend. She felt as though she had way too much homework to do before the end of her term. She didn't know that Pitt Colgrove had decided to stay at the school too to correct papers. They sent each other notes to tell of their decisions to stay at school but neither received theirs until Monday when the mail resumed after the Sunday holiday.

Apparently, Maude, who usually stood up for her friend, later told Jennie that Livia noticed Jennie and Pitt were both absent from church. Smugly, she started questioning other parishioners about their whereabouts. Because most in town knew the two were a couple, many suspicious imaginations ran wild, leading some do-gooder to bring up the subject with Jennie's parents. Marietta and Stanley told everyone they trusted their daughter, but the damage was done. For a while, Jennie read the scorn in some people's eyes. Although this event was well behind her, she still felt the painful prick of some of the villagers' dirty minds.

Jennie realized she'd been daydreaming again. She told herself she couldn't help it because whenever she thought about Livia Paisley, she wanted to box her ears because of her constant meddling in other people's lives.

As she rode beside Jamie, Jennie glanced at him from the corner of her eye. He was dark and handsome. She could tell this confident and mild-mannered man had been raised well. His strong hands looked as though they had been born with reins in them. Of course, she knew that if he had a bit too much to drink, he could probably turn mean too. Besides, she knew Irish men weren't the only ones to cause problems when they had a few libations. She had heard rumors of other men in town who left Pat Quinn's Saloon down on the river bank to go home and beat up their wives if they didn't give them "certain pleasures."

Jennie grimaced in disgust, but she turned her focus back on their discussion. "Your father helped get the school started in Irish Town, didn't he?"

"Yep! He even taught for a while. Pa's a pretty smart man, Jennie, but with more of us kids sitting up to the supper table, he bought up more land to farm because he couldn't balance teaching and farming."

"I know what you're saying. My family's large, as well. My parents have had to work hard to keep food on the table." Jennie realized they were straying from what she really wanted to know. "Oh, you know, Jamie, I almost forgot. Who said there weren't any clues to the murder?"

"The authorities," Jamie answered. "Doc Edmunds was involved in the case, the coroner from up in St. Joe, and his brother the sheriff."

"Pinault's the Stearns County Coroner. He and Doc Edmunds went out there the next day to investigate the crime. But, Jamie, the girl couldn't have just up and died. Where was she found?"

"Right out there on the road south of Sam Stokes's field where his and Fred Ponsford's fields hook up."

"Oh, sure! I know where that is." Jennie had delivered medicine in that direction earlier in the day. She pictured land dense with trees and brush.

As they neared Warner Lake, the buggy rattled across the Plum Creek bridge. After they crossed, Jennie, who had slid toward Jamie, crawled back to her side of the seat.

"I thought I heard Mike Larkin found her, but then again, I thought her body was found closer to his place, which is quite a bit north of the swamp."

Jamie shook the reins again, nudging Solly to work a bit harder to get up the hill. "No. It were Ed Murphy that found her on the road and—"

"Ed Murphy? I'm confused, Jamie. He lives closer to town. What was he doing out there?"

"Ed's in-laws live out in Lynden, the Morans, just south of where they found little Alice. He and the missus had been out visitin' her folks for the afternoon.'"

"I see. I'm sorry. Please go on."

"No probl'm! Ed said he first thought he seen something ahead of him on the road. He said it were gettin' dark, but it looked like a blanket or pile of clothes. So he and Dennis Connelly jumped out to investigate."

Jennie asked, "Mr. Connelly was with him too?"

"I think they had a buggy full of people out for a Sunday ride, including Dennis."

As Solly pulled them down the sandy hill, Jennie saw that all around from Kellers to the east and Stewarts to the west the sky had turned bright red from the setting sun.

Jamie had to have noticed it too because he said, "Pa always says that a red sunset means we're in for good weather."

"I've heard that too," Jennie said.

Jennie noticed their distorted and shadowy convoy—the gravel road outline of Solly pulling the buggy carrying Jamie and she with Chessy following—like a dark apparition moving slowly ahead of them.

As they approached Fuller Lake, the moon skirted the horizon in the east, taking on the sun's red glow.

"Isn't that odd to see both the sun and the moon at the same time? Usually, we don't see a red moon in the spring. Oh, look! It's like the lake's a pool of fire!"

"Pa calls that a blood moon."

Jennie looked at the man who seemed to take everything his pa said with such nonchalance. As they passed the lake, she looked back over her shoulder. The lake did look like a pool of . . . Jennie bit her lip.

From Fuller Lake, they still had to travel about a mile before they got to Clearwater. She thought of the peaceful little village with its cozy churches and stores that rested on the shores of the Mississippi River. When she thought of death, she thought of people who were old and infirm, not murdered. And yet, for some reason, Jennie felt even more obsessed to know about Alice Leonard.

"After the men jumped out to see what the object were," Jamie went on to say, "Dennis Connelly said he realized it were a person lying on the road. He recognized Alice Leonard due to her long red hair. She laid so still he knew she were dead."

Large trees hid both the sun and the moon as they reached the top of the hill. And although they weren't in complete darkness yet, dusk was settling in. Jennie couldn't see far in front of her, but she tried to imagine coming across a body on the road.

The two rode in silence. Jennie listened to Jamie's breathing, both horses' feet hitting the sand, and the wheels squeaking.

"How old was Alice when she died?"

"Her aunt Bridget said she would've been near sixteen."

Jennie thought about the girl. She died two years ago. So she'd be close to her sister Blanche's age. They both must have been born in 1878 or '79.

She knew how premature death could cause pain for a family. Two of her younger brothers died when they were little. But she couldn't imagine having any of her sisters or brothers murdered. She pictured each of them: Si, Blanche, Pat, baby Ruthie, Carl, Sammy, and little Percy, and wondered, even though they could be a handful at times, what her life would be like without them.

"So how did they finally figure out who she was?"

"I heard they drove over to the old Hayes place, where the girl lived with her grandma, Mrs. Hayes. I guess Dennis Connolly stayed with the body. From there, a bunch of 'em went back with them that found her."

"She lived with her grandmother? Where are her folks?"

"Her pa died a few years ago and her ma remarried, so Alice lived with her grandma most times. But then her ma died a few months before she was murdered."

"Oh, that poor girl!"

"Yeah, well, the story is that when she got home from the flag raisin', she ate supper and then went out looking for the cows to bring them in for the night. According to Mike Larkin, after a while, he got worried because she didn't return."

"Mike Larkin? Why in the world would he be so worried about her?"

"He'd been helping out Grandma Hayes on the farm."

Jennie knew who Mike Larkin was. He'd been in to the drug store many times, picking up special ointments or salves for his livestock. He was short and stocky and had a shock of red hair that showed below his flat cap. Occasionally, he came before Jennie closed up, and she could tell he had had a good time at the saloon because his ruddy cheeks were pinker than normal. But he held his liquor and she never felt threatened. Instead, whether he was talking about the weather or the crops, Jennie felt his happy spirit. Yet, she could faintly recall that he had been a suspect in the Leonard murder. She could never understand how anyone could think Mike Larkin could harm anyone, especially a young person.

"You said he had been helping the family?"

"Since Grandma Hayes's husband died, Mike had been helping around the farm."

"Oh, I see."

"Yeah, well, she got worried and sent Mike out to search for Alice. Apparently, they'd been having some problems with their cows getting into other farmers' fields. Mike searched awhile until it got too dark to see. Then he went over to the Tracy place to see if she'd gone over there. He were about ready to check at the Higgins's farm to see if she were there when Ed Murphy drove in the yard."

Jennie knew the names of the families Jamie was talking about. Danny Higgins, a man about the same age as Jennie, was a drayman for the Clearwater depot agent and often delivered their drug store goods.

"According to all 'counts," Jamie went out to say, "when they brung Mike Larkin back to the scene, he said he were shocked to see her lying on the ground, you know . . . lifeless. He thought maybe she had passed out or something. Then he seen some blood on her head and realized she weren't living no more. They carried her back to her grandma's."

"So when did the sheriff get there?" Jennie asked.

"He'n the others, his brother the coroner. What's his last name? Pen . . . Pen . . ."

"Pinault."

"Yeah, them and Doc Edmunds come out late the next evening sometime."

"I wonder why it took them so long to get out there."

"Larkin didn't send for the sheriff until the next morning," Jamie added.

"Why in heaven's name did he wait so long?"

"I s'pose 'cause it were already late when they brought the girl to her grandma's. At that point, I don't think no one thought she'd been murdered. Mike and Bridget said she'd been having faintin' spells, so they figured she fell, hit her head, and died. He got a lot of finger pointing from the newspapers though."

"I remember that." Jennie remembered that her mother clipped and saved all the articles about the murder so Jennie could read them. Some of the reporters suggested Larkin was hiding something. She even recalled a couple articles that suggested Bridget, Alice's aunt, and Mike were living together without benefit of a marriage license, but another even insinuated a love triangle between Alice, her aunt Bridget, and Larkin.

Of course, some of the rumors were insinuated in the St. Cloud newspapers, and perpetuated by gossips like Livia Paisley, who, like some of the journalists, had little respect for the Irish. Hard to understand people at times, Jennie thought. She was raised to believe people were people no matter if they were Irish, Scotch, English, Indian, or American. Some good, some bad.

She added, "But really, who'd think of murder? It's not something that happens around here all the time."

"As far as I know, no one were saying anything about murder or anything like that. The only thing I remember hearing, though, was . . . well, you're not Irish, so you may not understand this. Grandma Hayes had an omen about a death that was about to take place."

"An omen? What do you mean?" Jennie asked.

"All I heard was a few nights before Alice were found on the side of the road, Grandma Hayes went to visit her neighbor lady, Anna McKey. You know, the woman who you took medicine to?"

"Oh, sure!" Jennie answered, but anxiously waiting to hear more about the omen.

"Anyway, it were dark when Grandma Hayes headed home. Accordin' to those who heard her tell the story, she were coming up to the grove of trees that lines the McKey land when she heard a blood-curdling scream."

"A scream?" Jennie shuddered as she was reminded of what she had heard earlier by the swamp.

"Well, she almost went back to Mrs. McKey's, but she wanted to get home before Alice went to bed. She walked down the center of the road to get away from whatever it was she heard, but then she saw something. Well, I know it may be hard to believe, but she said she saw what she called a banshee."

Jennie thought a moment. She was confused so she asked, "She was afraid of a chicken?"

"No, no, not that kind of banshee. Can't say I've ever heard my folks talking about it neither, but they say a banshee is a spirit woman who appears to someone to warn of an impending death in the family."

"*Really*? I've never heard of such a thing!" Jennie knew even if she had, she probably would have thought it superstitious, but wanting to know more, she asked, "So what did she think she saw?"

"Apparently, at first, Grandma Hayes thought she saw a bit of fog settling in around the bottom of a few trees, but when she heard the screech again, she knew somethin' weren't right. She looked around her because she couldn't quite tell which direction the sound were comin' from. When she looked back at the fog, she saw a white-haired woman dressed in a long white gown swirling in and out of the trees. She knew she were being forewarned that someone in her family were going to die."

Jennie shivered as they neared Acacia Cemetery, or the Masonic Cemetery as some in their village called it. Eerie even during the day, the cemetery's old, overhanging oak trees shrouded the gray tombstones. Now as evening settled in, the graveyard was even more spooky. She had to admit she was glad Jamie was accompanying her home.

"I know how panicked I felt today when I thought I heard that scream," Jennie said quietly. "Like I said, Jamie, I've never heard anyone talk about this before."

"Well, ma'am, none of this were reported to the authorities. Could you imagine what the newspapers would'a reported if Grandma had let this information slip outta her mouth? We Irish get enough criticism as it is."

Jennie knew Jamie was right about the Irish getting criticized. "I know what you're saying. I remember some of the papers pretty much condemned Larkin for what they referred to as "contaminating the evidence.'"

"You're talking about how he poured a bucket of water over the blood that flowed outta Alice's head?"

"Exactly! I never could figure that out. What could he have been thinking when he did that? Seems a bit incriminating."

Jamie pushed his hat back and wiped his forehead. "Incriminating? I'm not sure I know what you're saying."

To clarify, Jennie said, "You know. By dumping water over the blood, he destroyed some of the evidence—and—well—how do I say this? It looked suspicious—like he tried to cover up something?"

"Oh, for sure. Yeah, he got the papers talking over that one, too. There're a couple'a reasons, though. For one thing, blood draws wild animals. Don't need fox or wolves sniffing around and going after our livestock. But I know it were Grandma Hayes who sent him out to do it because she believed, like many of the old-country Irish, that there's life in the blood. Since it's our custom to bury a body shortly after death, and she wanted Alice to rest in peace, she said it had to get cleaned up as soon as possible. Not sure she got what she wanted, though, if it truly be Alice roaming around."

Jennie felt a chill. Something had frightened her out by the swamp, but she had a hard time believing such superstitious nonsense. Yet, she knew the Irish Catholics had different beliefs and customs many non-Irish didn't understand.

She remembered another tragic murder of a young Irish girl that took place a few years ago near Maple Lake. Jennie had read that the girl's father had told the authorities that he had forbidden his daughter from spending time with a certain Protestant boy.

When the man came home from an overnight bender and the girl wasn't there because she had gone for an early morning walk with the boy, he beat up his wife for allowing the girl out of the house. He sat at the kitchen table and continued to drink while he waited for the girl to return home. When she opened the door, the father jumped up and slapped her across the face. She fled to the barn to get away from his blows. He ran after her with a pistol and shot her straight through the heart.

The girl's mother sent the oldest son to notify the sheriff about the incident. After the father was taken away to the Maple Lake jail, the mother and her sisters readied the child for her funeral.

Livia Paisley seemed to have the scoop on this story. Despite the father being behind bars, the family had quite a bash. While lamenters bawled loudly over the loss of the child, others sat around smoking tobacco and imbibing in "evil brew," all provided, as was customary, by the grieving family who could least afford it.

How Livia Paisley could know what went on over thirty miles away was beyond Jennie's imagination, but criticism of the Irish ran rampant in many of the local newspapers.

The Leonard murder was different though. The father in Maple Lake confessed to his crime. Alice's murderer was still at large. "As I said, my folks sent me some clippings about the murder from the St. Cloud newspaper, so I know how critical they were of Larkin."

Jennie remembered how a number of the local news reporters had claimed that not only had Mike Larkin been suspected of beating the girl to death but also of doing other "things" to her. She also remembered how various newspaper reporters jumped to other conclusions. One in particular inferred that because the family lived in an old log cabin with "dirt floors," the young girl was immoral. She could never understand how anyone could make the correlation, but it was often made about young girls of all nationalities who died under certain circumstances.

Jennie didn't want to mention the rumors or the newspaper articles, but she was curious about what others in his community thought about the murder. "Jamie, do you think anyone out in Irish Town did it? The murder, that is?"

Jamie clicked his tongue again as they went past the Colgrove farm. While she waited for him to respond, Jennie wondered if Pitt were home or if he were still in St. Cloud, winding down his term at the teachers' college.

Jamie and Jennie rode in silence for a bit, Jennie thinking about Pitt, and Jamie lost in his thoughts. He startled her when he finally spoke.

"Well, Jennie, I don't know how I feel about it. If ya'r askin' if I think someone I knowed done it, I'd have to say I just ain't sure. I hate to point fingers, but Ma and Pa always held the opinion that maybe a cousin could'a been to blame. He were a bit odd."

Jennie remembered there were other suspects besides the girl's cousin, and another neighbor boy, who were both teenagers.

"What do you mean by odd?"

"Ya' know, not right in the head. I remember him 'cause occasionally, he and I worked together as extra farm help on someone's farm out in Lynden. He'd start laughing over the dumbest things. Like the time he laughed about the way the hay lay out in the field. He said once it looked like a dead body."

"Gracious!"

"Pa said he remembered the boy's ma protected him too much. Shortly after the murder, he took off to Washington state. His folks followed soon afterwards. I s'pose no one'll ever know what really happened. Yet, even the Minneapolis paper said Alice were—well—being harassed, if you know what I mean."

As they made their way down the hill in back of the pulp mill, Jennie wondered if Jamie's meaning of harassed was the same as Jennie's. If what happened to Alice Leonard was what the papers alluded to, she was more than harassed.

"You said there weren't any clues to the girl's death, but how did anyone believe she came to be murdered instead of dying of natural causes?"

Jamie held tight to Solly's reins because the hill was steep and sandy, but he answered in short bursts, "Like I said, that night, no one seemed to know much. But the next day, Bill Forester said—"

"Bill Forester? What was he doing there?" Jennie blurted.

Jennie's heart began pounding like it had earlier in the day. She knew the man. He repelled her like few men had and she would never forget her last encounter with him. One evening a few months before, she'd had a few late prescriptions to mix up. She was closing up the drug store later than usual.

Normally, she and her father did this together, but he and her mother had taken the afternoon train to St. Cloud to do a bit of Christmas shopping. They wouldn't be back until the last train of the day, around ten. Jennie had to lock up on her own.

As she stood in the dark with little more than the street light to see by, she grappled with the door latch. For some reason, she couldn't get the double doors, one that needed to close on top of the other, shut firmly enough so the key would turn. She took off her warm woolen mittens to see if she could get a better grip. She pushed, pulled, and turned, struggling for a few minutes as her fingers grew cold and stiff.

Jennie looked up and down the street to see if any of the other merchants were still open. Unfortunately, everyone in the vicinity had closed up and gone home for the evening. Even Hotel Scott seemed to have little activity. She couldn't leave the building unlocked. She decided that if she couldn't get the door locked soon, she would go back into the store and do some book work. Hopefully, when her father got off the train, he would double check the building before heading home.

As Jennie stood fumbling and fuming, a large, black-gloved hand came out of nowhere and rested on her frozen fingers. Startled, she screeched. When she turned, she came face to face with a man she had seen before, probably in the store. His wide grin exposed tobacco-yellowed teeth, and his breath smelled of booze. She yanked her hand from his.

"Miz Phillips, you havin' some problems?" he asked in a slow, drunken slur.

"Oh, ah, ah, Mr. Mr. . . . ?"

"Forester, ma'am. Bill Forester," he half-lifted his hat and tipped his head as if he were serious about his introduction.

"Well, well, thank you, but I think I have it under control. I think I'll go in and do some work until . . ." Jennie knew she'd better not let on that she was alone in the building. She tried to slide closer to the entryway, but the man shoved his foot against the door so she couldn't get it open.

"Now, why don't you let me help you here? I'm really handy with—certain things."

Repelled by his insinuation, Jennie figured he was handy all right, but she was too frightened to mock him. She knew if she tried to get away, he'd catch her. She'd had a run in or two with other Clearwater drunks before so she told herself to stay calm.

"Where . . . ah, where do you live . . . Mr. Foster, is it?" she asked showing more composure than she felt.

"Bill Forester. Pleased to meet cha'. I live out in the country. Now, let's just try to get this here door, all right?"

Jennie moved away from the door, but she didn't hand him the key. She looked around for someone or something. Then, as she was about ready to make a run for it, she heard someone call her name.

"Jennie! Jennie!" Carl, her younger brother, called from the sidewalk across the street. "Aren't you coming home for supper? We were about to sit down and eat, but we worried about you."

Jennie thought she heard a hushed "dammit" from the stranger, but she didn't care. She blew out a sigh of relief. She'd never felt so happy to see her golden-haired brother.

Jennie's teeth began to chatter. "I guess my brother can lend a hand with the door now. Thank you for taking the time to help, though."

She stepped away from the man and looked straight at her life-saver walking across the street. Tall and blonde, Carl might be only nineteen, but as he walked across the street, he became her hero.

"I'm sorry, Jamie. Again, I was lost in my thoughts. You were talking about Bill . . . Bill Forester."

If Jennie had driven by herself, she'd have made her way into town on the St. Cloud road because the pulp hill was so steep. Even though they had lots of bumps and jolts along the way, Jamie got them safely to the bottom and then circled the bank of the river. She wondered why men usually followed the bumpiest and hardest paths instead of taking smoother routes like women.

No matter how they arrived, Jennie felt safer because she was closer to home. By now, the moon was white and bright in the sky. Its glow shimmered and danced on the gentle waves of the town's peaceful Mill Pond.

"That's okay, ma'am. I were trying ta figure out what I really remembered. Forester said he seen some heel tracks near the fence to the marsh. Then he said he seen a club."

"A club? What kind of club?"

"A tree limb. I remember the image I had in my head when I heard about it. Forester said a limb had been pulled from a branch, leaving the bark still attached to the tree. He said he found the club on the ground close to where they found the body, and it were covered with blood."

"Oh, my goodness!"

"Yeah, he said he seen blood droplets on some of the leaves and heel prints that led into the marshy part of the swamp."

Jennie felt a catch in her throat as she asked, "Are you saying that the person who killed Alice fled to the Tamarack Swamp where I was today?"

Chapter 3

Vesperis

The Evening

As THE PROCESSION CLANKED across the wooden bridge leading into Clearwater. Jamie prompted Solly to turn left, rolling them through the shady and fertile swale behind Tollington's Hill.

They rounded a little curve that brought them to Main Street, passing the imposing yellow-brick structure that housed the Masons and the General Mercantile. Two horses, each hitched to small buggies, were tied to the long hitching post. Since most of the businesses stayed open until nine on Saturday evenings, Jennie figured people were in getting a few supplies they'd need before Monday.

"Well, you're almost home, Jennie."

"I can't say I'm not glad, Jamie. This has been an awful day."

"Sorry," Jamie replied as he glanced at Jennie. "I shouldn't have talked so much about the murder."

"I didn't mean it that way. It was just so hot and humid, and then getting scared out of my wits! But, I'm thankful you accompanied me home. Besides, I was the one who asked all the questions."

They drove past the charred ruins that used to be the post office, Whitney's small office, and Schneider's harness shop. Last week, the village experienced one of the worst fires it had ever had. Although volunteers did a good job controlling the flames, piles of ashes still lay where the buildings used to be. A heavy acrid smell still hung in the air.

Normally, the northern part of town reminded Jennie of the pictures her parents had of their former homes in the forests in Maine and New York. Usually, the dense trees canopying the streets created a protective haven. Now, as she looked at the pyres of black cinders and thought about murder, she felt something ugly had invaded her little community.

"I'd heard 'bout the fire . . . hadn't re'lized it burned so much of the town. It's a miracle Uncle Pat's saloon weren't burned, too."

Jennie didn't want to repeat what the town teetotalers and temperance advocates had said about the saloon and pool hall that like a magnet lured many of the young and older men to throw away their hard earned money.

"We were lucky. Many of the buildings were spared, especially those on the other side of the street and down by the river. My father moved the store closer to home just in time. Otherwise, he might have lost everything."

As Solly trotted them past the Whiting building and through the village's elm-arched Main Street, Jennie said, "Seriously, Jamie, don't feel bad about your telling me about how Alice died. No one around town talks about it anymore. I guess they want to forget it happened, yet I can't believe anyone around here could be a murderer, much less the murderer of an innocent girl."

"I know. Most out where I come from believe it were more than murder."

Astonished, Jennie asked, "What do you mean?"

"Some out in Irish Town, maybe throughout Lynden Township, think someone were out for revenge."

"Revenge?"

Jamie pushed back his cap and scratched his head before responding.

"Of course, it were only rumors, but some say there were . . ."

Obviously embarrassed, Jamie cleared his throat before saying ". . . lechery."

That's what Jamie was referring to as "harassed," Jennie thought.

"You're say she was molested?"

"All I know is there were sort of a well-known secret in Irish Town. After the jury convened the night Alice were found, and the sheriff and doctors left, Grandpa Vallely, Peter's his name, finally spoke up. Pa said it were pretty dark inside the little shack. Grandma Hayes had only a couple candles and lanterns burning, but when Grandpa stood up and spoke, his silver-gray hair glowed in the dark. 'Parently, he said something like: 'We can only blame ourselves,' and 'We must look at home for the murderer.'"

Jennie knew who "Grandpa" Vallely was. He and other Civil War veterans, "Gray Beards" many called them, usually gathered on the front porch of the Hotel Scott, across from the drug store, on Saturday afternoons to smoke and shoot the breeze. Usually quite stoic, the rail-thin, elderly gentleman must have been really upset to get so up in arms.

"What did he mean by 'Look at home?'"

"It seemed there was a few clues something were going on, and that the murder could have been prevented if someone'd stepped in to stop the nonsense."

Jennie had heard that the little Irish community was pretty tight, but she couldn't believe they'd be so negligent as to turn their heads to a perversion or harbor a murderer.

Ahead of them, Jennie saw her friend Maude Porter walk across the street from Livia Paisley's house. She leaned into her carriage parked by the picturesque, white Methodist Church, and lifted a huge lavender bouquet. She was delivering lilacs to the church. *Of course, she'd do this! Her folks' farm is surrounded by lilac bushes.* More than likely, she had enough to decorate the church on the hill as well.

Maude, a few years older than Jennie, was the "Daughter of Clearwater" because she had been the first white child born in the village. Although the early historical records weren't official, it was probably safe to say that Maude Porter was the first white girl born in all of Wright County.

While Clearwater people showed pride in this fact, many in the community didn't understand her. When she spoke up in church to invite everyone to her first temperance meeting, the parishioners declared, "That's Maude for you." When she rode a bike she'd brought back from the 1893 Chicago World's Fair, some women had a fit because "no real woman would ride one of those two-wheeled contraptions." But when Maude rode the bike around town in black pantaloons, many of the men who came into the store declared, "No man will want her now. She'll be thinking she's the one wearing the pants in the family."

If Maude knew what people said about her, she never acknowledged it. In fact, she seemed to take pride in the fact she was stirring up the village pot.

Naturally, no one said anything critical about Maude in front of her folks. They were respected community and state leaders. When her father, Tom Porter, had turned eighteen, he left his home in St. Louis, hopping aboard the first train that went north to St. Paul. Outfitted with two oxen pulling a wagon, he became one of the first to cut a northern trail to the Red River and on into Winnipeg.

Jennie and every other child in Clearwater had been raised on stories of the early settlers. She knew Tom had hauled general supplies—flour, tea, and sugar—from his half-brother's store in St. Louis. He even traded furs with the Indians for a while. Whether he worked around his farm or came into town for a quick supply or two, he wore his raccoon cap, a trademark from his early years.

Quite the story-teller, Tom often told about his experiences in the five years he'd trekked back and forth from Missouri to Minnesota, bypassing many an Indian skirmish and encountering many a native renegade. Because Tom knew the Chippewa and Sioux didn't get along, he stayed clear of their campgrounds.

On one trip north, though, when Tom had traveled little more than a hundred miles from the depot in St. Paul to what eventually became Maine Prairie, he came across a scene he'd never forget. As he reached the top of a little hill and looked down toward a creek, he saw a body lying near the remains of a campfire. He got down from his ox cart, cautiously surveying his surroundings. When he got closer, he saw an Indian lying face down with blood still seeping from where he had been scalped. The cinders from the campfire still felt warm.

He climbed back into his wagon and hightailed it out of there. He decided then and there, he'd work off what he owed his half-brother for this undelivered load, but he wasn't going to continue on toward Winnipeg.

Not really knowing where he was going, he decided to head back to St. Paul. One night, he set up camp by a river that flowed into what he assumed was the Mississippi. The lushness of the green valley intoxicated him. The next morning, he decided to explore the area. He came upon a small settlement. Two men, sitting around a campfire, drank their morning coffee. Horace Webster and Asa White introduced themselves and welcomed him to Eldorado, later to be renamed Clear Water and then Clearwater, after the river that flowed into the Mississippi. After a few encouraging words, Tom Porter decided to stake a claim and settle down to farming.

Maude's mother, Abigail Camp, a young widow from Vermont who had children to support, was an adventurer herself. She had taken a steamboat up the Mississippi shortly after the town had been founded. The woman often told of how she became cook and housekeeper for one of the land speculators who had the first hotel on the banks of the river. The very first evening she arrived, she went to work. She served her first meal on a door the owner had taken off its hinges and set over sawhorses.

Soon after Tom and Abigail met, they married. After that, Maude came into the world. Maybe a bit spoiled, she had an independent spirit. And what else would two independent spirits do but raise a daughter to think for herself?

As they drove by, Jennie waved at her friend. Maude, who had reached the top step and waved, but when Jennie glanced back over her shoulder, she noticed that for a moment, her friend stared after her before going inside the church. She also saw Livia Paisley standing on her front step. *Tonight's little attraction will be tomorrow's news,* Jennie thought.

As they continued riding toward the store, Jennie wasn't surprised to see a few saddled horses, a number of wagons and teams, and a carriage tied to the posts in front of many of the stores at this end of town because they, too, stayed open late. From the northern part of town to the southern, locals shopped for groceries at Lyons, picked up tools or spare parts from Boutwell's Hardware, or purchased a pot roast for Sunday dinner at Laughton's Meat Market.

"Well, we made it," Jamie said as he pulled up alongside the front of the drug store.

Jennie looked at the double windows—eyes that kept watch over the village. "I don't know how I can thank you, Jamie."

"Forget it. I was glad to do it. Give me a second, and I'll help you out."

Jennie appreciated Jamie's thoughtfulness. Her feet pinched inside her stiff shoes. To avoid tripping, she took his arm to get down from the buggy. With the light in the window, she noticed her father had turned around to see who had pulled up in front of the store. As usual, his glasses had slid down to the tip of his nose.

She wished she and her father had the ready cash to install a soda fountain like a couple drug stores in St. Cloud had. She could stir up a soda for Jamie, even though it'd be paltry payment for his kindness in seeing her home. She supposed he would head down to Pat Quinn's Saloon to have some quick refreshment before heading back out to Lynden Township.

"Nonsense, ma'am. I enjoyed getting away from some of the work. I 'specially enjoyed our conversation. No one talks much about Alice anymore. I'm sure there are those who'd like to forget it happened. But there are times, like I said, someone hears something strange out by the Swamp. When the word gets around, many remember the murder and talk about it for a while, but then it's forgot about again."

"I'm sure. It's just sad. But I appreciate you escorting me home."

Jamie walked behind the buggy and untied Chessy.

"Want me ta go in an' talk to your pa? He might wonder what happened."

"No, I'll be fine. Thank you, again."

"I'm heading to my uncle's. I've got a couple free tokens to play pool. If you need anthin', send someone down."

"Thank you, again, Jamie."

Once he mounted his horse, Jamie pulled on the horse's reins and turned him around. As he did, he tipped his hat and nodded a farewell. Jennie watched as he headed back the way they had come. She knew he'd probably have a beer or two, but she hoped he wouldn't stay too long.

Although it wasn't totally dark, and the street lights hadn't yet been lit, night was creeping into town.

Chapter 4
Gratus
Pleasure

THE SCREEN DOOR SWUNG outward. As Jennie stepped over the threshold, Dr. Edmunds, with one hand on the black pipe in his mouth, greeted her.

"Hello again, Jennie."

"Oh, hello, Doc. Father, I'm sorry I'm so late."

"Stanley was just telling me he was getting a bit worried about you. I hope everything went all right out in Lynden Township."

Even in his early fifties, Jennie's father still had a distinguished air about him. A few gray hairs streaked through his dark hair and beard. He was thin, much too thin, because he had little appetite even for his wife's country chicken and dumplings. He stood so straight that many times his clothes bagged all around him. Tonight was no exception. He wore dark-gray pants with a stiff white shirt tucked in and a black tie at his neck. Over the top, he wore a druggist's apron with the white sash wrapped around him.

"Everything went fine. I'm sorry I had you all so worried," Jennie said. "After I delivered the medicine to Mrs. McKey, I ran into a bit of a problem, nothing serious, though. When I stopped at the Dorseys, they insisted Jamie Mooney, one of their farm workers, escort me home."

Again, looking over the top of his wire-rimmed glasses, her father questioned, "What happened? Solly act up?"

"No, no, nothing like that. I'm fine, and we can talk about it later," Jennie assured him as she unpinned her hat. Even though she still felt weak in the knees and dirty, she knew an attempt at work might get her mind off murder and ghosts. As she repositioned her hair clips, she added, "I must say I'm glad to be home. It's been a long, hot afternoon."

"It's been that, all right," Dr. Edmunds agreed as he walked to the bay window and looked out. "I thought that was one of the Mooney boys. There are so many of them. They all have the wholesome handsome looks of their folks, so I don't know who's who out there anymore."

Jennie grabbed her white apron from the hook behind the counter, pulled it over her head, and tied the strings behind her. She looked up at him and responded, "Yes, that's Jamie Mooney. I think he's one of the older ones of—Francis? Francis and Bridget Mooney? I believe his mother's Pat Quinn's sister. Anyway, he said he was stopping in the saloon on his way home," Jennie said rolling her eyes. "Jamie's nice, very polite."

"Good, good, and you're right. Bridget and Pat are brother and sister. I've stopped out at the Mooney place many a time, so I know they've been brought up with lots of plenty of fresh air, hard work, and hearty food."

The doctor turned and grabbed the amber bottle Jennie's father had filled. "Well, I'll let you two finish up here. Thanks, again, Jennie, for running out to the country for me this afternoon. I had two patients to tend to here in town, and your father just filled another order for me. I need to get out to Hasty on Monday morning to check on that little Drew boy who fell from the horse last week. I'm sure his mother will have almost used up what I gave her last week for the boy's pain." The doctor opened the screen door again. "Thanks, Stanley, we can square up with each other next week. Jennie, it was nice seeing you again, and I'm glad you're home safe and sound," he added as he stepped outside.

"Yup, catch up with you next week, Doc." Stanley Phillips hollered as he washed out the mortar bowl.

"Were you awful busy without me?"

"No, no. We were slow today, except for a few locals stopping by to gab about the Decoration Day shindig."

"What should I do tonight before we close up?"

Stanley pushed his glasses up on his nose and slid a pencil over his ear before answering. "Well, let's see. Why don't you start checking some of the compounds and powders on the shelves. See what we're running short on? We'll probably need to place an order or two pretty soon. Look in the backroom as well. Then, we'd better close up here in a bit because your ma'll be holding supper for us."

From a shelf above the counter, Jennie pulled down one of the jars. She loved looking at the white porcelain containers that were gifts from the Eli Lilly Pharmaceutical Company. Lined alphabetically from Aconitum to Zinc with white and gold labels, they made a fine display in the store. Tonight, especially after such a long grueling day, she felt a little relieved to look at something pretty and real.

She dusted off each container with its bell-shaped stopper and wooden finial on top. Peeking inside, she wrote a note on how full or depleted each was. When she was finished, she grabbed a kerosene lantern and walked to the back room, her shoes squeaking and pinching with every step.

"I see we're minus a few cans of paint," she told her father when she returned.

"I forgot to tell you. Sherm and Ida came into town to see you. You must have missed each other coming and going. It was a good thing she was here because some of the boys wanted to get started building and painting the speakers' platform. Ida decided since you weren't here for her to consult with the speaker's platform would look fine with a couple coats of white."

"I'm glad she made some decisions. A white platform will look good with the red, white and blue theme," Jennie agreed.

"Yeah, after Carl, Art Barrett, Evan Sheldon, and young Woodworth, Wayland, I think, constructed the platform, they helped the younger ones, including Sammy and Percy, get some paint on the thing."

"That sounds good. I'm glad something got done today."

"The boys could only give her one coat because it was so humid the paint wouldn't dry. When they stopped here on their way home, the younger boys looked like they got more paint on themselves than on any wood." Her father shook his head and smiled. "They're all home now and probably giving your mother fits, fighting with them to get cleaned up before supper."

Knowing her mother, Jennie figured the whole house got turned upside down to get her little brothers cleaned. She imagined her sisters pouring many teakettles of hot water into the big wash tub to fill it. She could also imagine her mother with a rag dipped in turpentine bending over the tub scrubbing the two boys. Jennie could picture all this going on while supper was getting cooked and clothes were getting ironed and laid out for church tomorrow.

It felt good to be home, she thought, even though in her large family, there was usually no normality, and definitely no quiet. She felt safe.

"Oh, and Ida said she plans on seeing you in church tomorrow. You two can catch up on what else needs doing for Thursday's celebration afterwards," her father added. "She also said Sherm offered to come after her later if Marietta's "there's always room for one or more at the table" invitation was still open for Sunday dinner. I told her, of course, we'd love to have her."

"Good deal! It'll be good to get a few things organized tomorrow."

Jennie didn't mention that she also wanted to talk to Ida about what happened to her out by her folks' place that afternoon.

"I see John Evans's article in the paper about Congressman Towne speaking for Decoration Day festivities," Jennie half read, half shouted to her father who was checking the back door lock. Already fairly dark, Jennie had to stand directly under the overhead lamp to read the front page of the *Clearwater News*.

She felt a rush of excitement about next week's activities. Senators and congressmen often made the state circuit for certain celebrations, especially right before their next campaign, but getting someone as important as the congressman had created quite a stir. Jennie figured everyone could thank Simon Stevens for getting him here. One of the town founders and brother to John Stevens, the Minneapolis founder, Simon Stevens, knew just about every important person in the state and beyond. Of course, Ormasinda Peck, John Stevens's daughter, had to be given some credit as well. She was on the committee to get special speakers for the big event.

"Yes, Evans did a good job on the article. I'm sure the village will be hopping next week."

"I know. It's almost scary how many people will be wandering around this town." Jennie turned the newspaper to the last page where she read "The Local Happenings" columns. Absentmindedly, she said, "I wonder where we'll put them all."

"Hard telling. Suppose some'll be staying with relatives and friends. Others'll be at the hotels." Stanley pulled off his apron and hung it up on the nail by the back door. "Did you read the part about the fire? The three buildings totaled around $1,200 in damages. I can't imagine my loss if I'd have stayed down there."

"Just got to that article. Father, you might have been wiped out there on the south side of the street. You moved in the nick of time." Jennie folded up the newspaper and slid it under her arm to finish reading at home. "So are we about ready? I'm hungry! I wonder what Mother has for supper tonight." Her stomach growled, a reminder she hadn't eaten much since breakfast.

Stanley grabbed the hooked pole from the corner by the front doors and reached up to turn off the two overhanging lights. Jennie stepped out the door and down to the front step, waiting while he returned the pole, took the huge set of keys from the nail at the end of the front counter, and walked to the door. With a quick look over his shoulder to make sure the building looked settled for the night, her father locked the door, and jiggled the handle, making sure everything was secure.

The two of them walked down the steps. Only then did Stanley notice Jennie was hobbling.

"What's wrong with your feet?" he asked as he looked down toward her shoes while helping her step up into the carriage.

They didn't have time to get into a long conversation before reaching home. Jennie decided to tell only what she could explain. "Oh, nothing much. I stepped in mud and ruined my new shoes. They pinch. I'll change when I get home."

Her father seemed satisfied with the answer. He didn't question whether they were the shoes she bought from Webster, nor did he scold her for squandering money on cheap goods.

Stanley Phillips couldn't stand cheap. If he had one sermon, it was this. If a person couldn't buy a quality product, he or she could do without. Nobody needed to spend hard-earned money on goods that fell apart.

The night was getting dark, but there'd be no need for the lamplighter. A couple years ago, the village council decided that, to save money, on moonlit nights they wouldn't light the street lamps in town.

It took Stanley and Jennie less than a minute to travel the block home. Tonight Jennie was glad she didn't have to walk it.

"Tell your ma I'll be in for supper in a few minutes." He would put the carriage away first, and brush and feed Solly.

Gingerly, Jennie stepped down. She felt grit sanding her toes and the sides of her feet. She grabbed the flowers she had picked. As she walked up the sidewalk to the house, she looked forward to her Saturday night bath, but first she had to get out of the shoes. With every step, Jennie winced. As soon as she kicked them off on the back step, she felt instant relief.

She hated going upstairs to put on her slippers because the heat from the afternoon sun always settled up there.

"Jennie's home! Jennie's home! Where's Pa? I'm hungry," Percy shouted as he ran out from the front porch to meet her. *What a towhead*, Jennie thought as she ruffled the eight-year-old's still damp, blonde hair.

"Hey, there. I'm hungry too, Percy. I heard you had a good time painting today. You've had your bath, and you're all cleaned up and ready to eat?" she asked as she walked with him, her arm over his shoulder.

"Yeah! We done a good job, Jennie," he said with pride.

"*Did* a good job, Percy, we *did* a good job," Jennie corrected. She could at least correct her brother's English even if couldn't correct the slaughter of the language by others. "But I'm proud of you. Run and tell Ma that Pa will be up soon. He's down at the stable. I'll be ready to eat in a minute, too."

Jennie had heard about Finnish saunas. When she reached the top of the stairs, she figured her bedroom would be as close to one as she'd ever experience. She could hardly breathe. With only the soft glow from the moon shining in her window, she sat on her side of the bed she shared with her sister Blanche.

Soon she heard "Jenweee! Jenweee!" as her littlest sister climbed the stairs.

"Ruthie, I'm up here."

The little girl clomped up to the top step before turning to sit down. Almost unaffected by the heat, she seemed engrossed in a carpet string that had wrapped around one of the rungs of the railing.

"Supper ready," the little girl prattled.

"Okay, I'm coming," Jennie called, sliding her tender feet into her slippers.

Tipping the dresser-top mirror forward, Jennie loosened her combs to tuck her light brown hair under her bun before pushing the combs back in place. Turning her face first left, then right, she stared at her image. Usually, she had to pinch her cheeks to get some color, but tonight, the heat and humidity had given her face a rosy glow. She looked at her straight nose, which she thought too large for her face.

"Jennie, you have a nice nose; it's almost Grecian," Marietta Phillips said whenever Jennie criticized her own looks. "If you'd fill in a bit, you wouldn't be so self-conscious about it. You're a pretty girl. Remember pretty is as pretty does."

No matter how much she ate, Jennie couldn't gain weight, but that didn't bother her as much as the wire-brimmed glasses, which made her look ogle-eyed. She tried to fluff her bangs. Limp with humidity, they felt like straw. She took one more glance, then gave up, too tired to care how she looked.

As she patted the perspiration from her face with her less than crisp hanky, Jennie met Ruthie at the ledge. Already dressed in her white nightgown with her hair tied up in little bits of pink and white rags to curl overnight, Ruthie smelled fresh and clean.

"I'm ready. Let's go down now," she said as she waited for the plump three-year-old to turn and take slow half steps down the stairs. She slid around her and grabbed for one little hand to help her down the rest of the way.

Sniffing, Jennie called out, "My! Something surely smells good."

She was instantly greeted by her short, plump mother who was scurrying behind Jennie's two sisters. Blanche carried the white ironstone platter heaping with slices of fried ham, and Si had the bowl of applesauce. The room felt hotter than normal, but Jennie didn't care. She was happy to be home.

"You're warm too tonight," her mother said to Jennie. "Supper's ready. I sent Sammy and Carl down to help your father bed down Solly. He's done enough for one day. Besides those boys need to put some of their energy to use."

Normally, calm, her mother sounded tired and exasperated. Like Jennie, Marietta's cheeks were pinker than normal, and her forehead was damp.

"Good thinking, Ma. What can I do to help?"

"Not a thing. Everything's ready. I'm sorry it's so hot in here. The girls and I did the baking in the back porch this morning so it wouldn't get so hot in the rest of the house, but I guess it didn't help much."

Marietta Phillips had always been a pretty woman. But while her husband had little appetite and was nearly bone-thin, she was the opposite. She liked to call herself a bit on the "fleshy side." After the birth of each of her ten children, Marietta kept a few pounds. The extra weight didn't slow her down, though.

"Except for the ham, I made a cool, light supper. Everyone's bathed except for you, your pa, and me. As soon as we're finished eating, we can take our turns. I didn't think anyone needed hot water. I had the boys dump out the tub and fill it up again with clean. Why don't you go right after supper, and then Pa and I'll finish up later?"

"You sure? You look like you're about ready to collapse," Jennie observed as she grabbed a plate of bread and a saucer of butter that had already begun to melt into a yellow pool.

"I can wait . . . besides, I need to rest a few minutes before I do one more thing," her mother said.

Soon, the whole family, all ten of them, took their seats around the dining room table. This room was as warm as the rest of the house, but no one seemed to mind too much. Everyone chattered and laughed as they passed the serving plates and bowls around the table. With only the Rochester light in the middle of the table, the room looked as cozy as it felt. For Jennie, the incident at the Tamarack Swamp and what she learned from Jamie Mooney on the long ride into town seemed a long time ago—a long nightmare away.

Chapter 5
Mane
In the Morning

JENNIE FELT AS IF SHE were on fire. From her face to her feet, she prickled and burned. As she stood in the woods, she saw bright orange flames shooting over the tops of trees. Sharp screeching sobs came toward her louder and louder, closer and closer. Wails whirled around her, blending into a familiar tune. A sweet but sad voice sang words she didn't recognize.

Out of nowhere, something like a sheer white curtain appeared in front of her. The material gyrated into a shapely young woman. Wrapped in a white gown—little more than a toga—the woman was translucent from knees to feet.

The being flew around Jennie before coming to an abrupt stop. Her silver-white hair swirled and covered much of her face except for her red, swollen eyes filled with tears. She stared at Jennie a few moments before she began floating backwards. She bowed her head, covered her face with her hands, and started crying and moaning words Jennie couldn't understand. Hearing the sadness and misery in the woman's voice, Jennie, too, started crying—gut-wrenching, chest-heaving sobs.

As the woman's sobs continued, she puffed out ghost-like vapors that danced toward Jennie, pushing her into a freezing cold room. When she looked around, Jennie realized she was standing in the middle of a freezer like Laughton's meat locker.

Although at first she felt cooler, Jennie soon began to shiver. She ran to the heavy door but found it locked. She pulled and slammed her hands on the door, trying to escape the ghost-like beef carcasses that swayed back and forth toward her. Feeling trapped, she opened her mouth to scream, but no sound came out.

Jennie jolted awake. It took her a moment to make out where she was. Soft light filtered in through the window. A cool breeze puffed at the lace curtains. She pulled up the blankets and snuggled, thankful she had simply had a bad dream.

Wondering what time it was, yet afraid she would wake Blanche if she got up to find out, Jennie tried to appreciate the comfort of the bed and go back to sleep. Unfortunately, the haunting dream reminded her of her trip to the Tamarack Swamp.

Wide awake and fidgety, Jennie figured she might as well get up and get some breakfast started for everyone before leaving to decorate the church. Quietly, so as not to disturb her sister, Jennie pushed the covers back and sat up at the side of the bed.

"Is it time to get up, already?" Blanche asked hoarsely, sitting up halfway.

Blanche, sixteen, six years younger than Jennie, had thick dark hair and long eyelashes. She stood out as one of the town's prettiest girls. She never fell short of boyfriends, but she also never took any of them seriously until she met Roy Ponsford, a rural Clearwater boy. Both Jennie and fourteen-year-old Agnes, or Si as the family called her, could tell almost right away that Blanche and Roy were attracted to each other.

"Shhh!" Jennie whispered back at Blanch as she pulled a slip over her head. "Go back to sleep. I need to go to church early today. I'll see you later."

"Jennie, you all right? You were so restless during the night. I know it was warm, but you appeared to be running in your sleep. You moaned too."

"I'm sorry I kept you awake. I had a bad dream." Jennie didn't want to get into her nightmare right now. She also didn't think she needed to scare her sister about what had happened to her yesterday.

"I was fine. I slept pretty hard because I was tired," Blanche yawned. "Do you know what time it is? I wouldn't mind getting up early, as long as it isn't too early. Yesterday, I didn't get all my Sunday School materials ready."

Jennie tiptoed to her dresser to check her watch. "It's only six-thirty," she whispered. "Go back to sleep."

Blanche fell back on her pillow, lying there with her arm over her eyes. Jennie finished dressing, belting her ivory linen skirt. Once she had tucked in the coordinating ivory blouse, she whispered, "I'm going to finish up downstairs. Talk later."

When she reached the bottom of the stairs, Jennie found her father bent over the *St. Cloud Times* in the dining room and drinking his coffee. "Morning," she whispered to his back in his usual chair, at the head of the table. Although he wore trousers and his good white shirt, his suspenders hung to the floor. Obviously, he was in his "comfortable mode," as he liked to call it. Without waiting for a reply, she went to the back room where he had started a little fire to make his coffee. She poured herself a cup from the black enamel pot her father had pushed to the back of the stove to keep warm.

"You're up early for a Sunday," he commented as Jennie joined him at the table.

"I am. Part of my mission yesterday was to find spring flowers for the altar. I thought I'd better get up there and decorate before church starts," Jennie laughed. "It sure cooled down last night."

"It did. Your ma and I stayed up talking quite late last night. We were so hot, we couldn't sleep."

"I was tired! I fell asleep right away, hot or not," she said, wincing after her first sip from her cup. Her father liked his coffee strong and black—quite the eye-opener.

"Your ma and I were talking about the Eden Valley store. Time's running short. I'll be heading off to open the new business later this fall. You and I've got lots of work ahead of us to get ready for this, but we're worried we're holding you back. You and Pitt Colgrove were so close, and well, lots of your friends are getting married . . ."

"Oh, Pa. For goodness sake, don't worry about me. I'm not ready to get tied down yet. I want to learn the trade. This is important to me." Jennie said as she took another sip of coffee.

Laying down his newspaper, Stanley added, "If you're sure. Unfortunately, our big shindig is getting in the way of my getting you prepared to take over."

"I'm sure the business will be back to normal after this upcoming weekend. If it's any consolation, I know much more about the druggist business than I used to."

"You sure do, and that's good because we'd be in trouble if you weren't so smart," he added as he patted her hand.

"I wish I could have taken the short cut to getting my druggist license like men can."

Even though Jennie had passed all the state chemistry tests, she'd been told by one of the professors at Dr. Drew's School of Pharmacy in Minneapolis that, because she was a woman, she probably wouldn't receive a license until she took the necessary coursework.

"It doesn't seem quite fair, does it? You did well in chemistry in high school and the Normal School. Yet, men can apprentice like you're doing with me, and, if they pass the tests, they can be certified. Someday, Jennie, someday, you women will have more rights. Keep the faith."

Jennie shrugged. "Getting upset about the situation isn't going to help. For now, I'll keep working as your apprentice. Doc promised to help me when you're away. We'll be fine."

"Give me a year or two to see if I can get the business going over there. I don't plan on keeping it. Your ma won't move again, anyway."

"Speaking of Ma, you and she going to church this morning?"

"She's still sleeping. I think the heat took a lot out of her yesterday. I'm not going to wake her."

"You know, Pa, she looked somewhat ragged yesterday. I worry she isn't feeling real well at times, but she keeps going. Matter of fact, I don't think she's been well since Ruthie was born. You think Doc Edwards should take a look at her?"

"Wouldn't hurt," Stanley whispered. He shook his head before saying, "But how are we going to arrange it? She doesn't complain or like talking about her health."

Jennie knew that very well. She was surprised when her mother confessed last night to wanting to rest before taking her Saturday night bath.

"She hates it when we make a fuss over her, but she stews and worries about the rest of us all the time. When we're sick, she hovers over us. Yet she doesn't get much rest, either. We could help her more if she'd just let us."

"I know I'm as guilty as she is when it comes to not wanting to call Doc Edmunds every time my stomach bothers me, but your ma doesn't even talk about what's ailing her. If I mention she looks tired, she goes on a tirade of how she doesn't have time to worry about her health."

Jennie nodded. Marietta Phillips had tried to change her husband's habits. She followed the doctor's advice and tried not to fry too much, which was hard when she needed to get a quick meal on the table. She also made sure her husband had plenty of easily digestible foods like eggs and porridge. When the doctor instructed Stanley to watch how much coffee he drank, she tried getting him to drink weak tea. He hated tea and had no intention of switching. Much to Marietta's chagrin, he drank nearly a pot before she got up each the morning. "You're going to burn your stomach, you are," Marietta scolded in her eastern accent, leaving out r's where r's ought to be and inserting them where they shouldn't be.

Her scolding didn't go any further though because he would nag her as well about how she should rest and allow the children to do more around the house. So, in a way, the two looked after each other. Although neither followed the other's advice, they both made sure their children ate the best, dressed the best, received the best medical attention, and got the best educations.

As Jennie sipped her now cooled coffee, enjoying the peace and quiet of the early morning, she couldn't help but wonder how the murdered Leonard girl out in Lynden felt about her upbringing.

General Sherman, the family's favorite Tabby, meandered into the room, hugging and snuggling between Jennie's legs. She never appreciated the many felines they had in and out of the house until spring and fall when they did their jobs, cleaning up the mouse population.

"You know, seeing the General reminds me we need to take a couple cats down to the store. I haven't seen mice yet, but there are droppings all over."

"I keep forgetting, too. I'll get the boys to take a couple on their way to church this morning. Maybe our four-footed friends can make headway before Monday," he added as he took a big slurp from his cup.

The clock on the mantle above the sideboard chimed seven times, alerting Jennie to the time. She realized she'd better get a move on if she wanted to get to church before the nine o'clock service.

"I'll see what we have for breakfast around here," Jennie said. "The army will be awaking soon and will need to be fed."

"Your mother mentioned we've plenty of homemade bread and leftover ham from last night."

"Sounds good," Jennie said as she carried her cup to the kitchen.

Jennie removed the platter of sliced ham, a dish of butter, and a jar of her mother's famous apple butter from the icebox. She layered a few slices of ham in a cast iron skillet, and carried it to the back room to warm on the wood stove. As she waited for the meat to sizzle, she thought of her crazy dream again. She seldom remembered her dreams, but this was so vivid, from the intense heat, then the freezing cold of Laughton's locker, to the ghostly apparition with the long white hair that shone in the night. She supposed she had so many ideas rattling in her brain—the town fire, the crying she heard at the swamp, the stories Jamie had told her about Alice Leonard's murder. All that must have shuffled together into one crazy nightmare.

She believed in an afterlife but hadn't thought much about the darker side. She knew the Irish had their folktales and mysterious ancient customs, but she really had a hard time believing that she had heard a ghost crying at the swamp.

Jennie went back to the kitchen. After slicing a loaf of bread, she slathered two big chunks with creamy, yellow butter and placed a slice on each of the two plates. She took the curling iron into the backroom with her. She balanced the rod on top of the glass chimney of the kerosene lamp to get warm.

Since she had a couple minutes before the meat heated through, she went back to the wash basin and finished washing her face. After a quick brushing, she wound her long hair around the crown of her head and pinned the pile down with tortoise shell combs.

Finally, Jennie rolled a few stray hairs around the hot rod, holding it firmly for a few seconds before letting go. She repeated this with her bangs as well. She combed and fluffed and patted until she felt her hair looked as good as it was going to get.

She forked a slab of ham for each plate. With a towel, Jennie slid the skillet to the back of the stove.

"Oh, I forgot we needed more coffee," she said as she slid a plate in front of her father.

Once she got back to the table, she saw that he was eating. She was glad. His stomach needed something more nourishing than coffee.

She'd have liked to have asked him what he remembered about the murder, but he seemed intent on reading his paper, not talking. After Jennie finished her breakfast, she excused herself, receiving only a slight nod from her father. After brushing her teeth, she pulled the flowers out of the Mason jars of water she had put them in last night, and gently laid them in a wicker basket.

"Bye, Pa. I'll see you after church," she whispered. Not waiting for a reply, she crept out the front door, slowly closing the screen so it wouldn't slam behind her.

Felix, the Shaw's cocker spaniel, barked as Jennie walked across the grass in front of the family's large green house on the corner of Main and Ash. The sun hid behind the trees as she climbed Blacksmith Hill, named for the Collins and Wilcox blacksmith shops.

The crisp morning air was refreshing after yesterday's heat and humidity. She thought about the spectacle she and Jamie might have caused as they moseyed into town last night. Was gossip flying around the community already? She hoped not, but she planned on talking to Maude Porter before church, hoping between the two of them they could help steer it clear before it got out of hand.

Jennie reached the top of the hill, crossed the road to Bluff Street, and passed banker Whittemore's large white house before continuing on to the Congregational Church, which she attended despite still being a member, along with the rest in her family, at the Methodist Church on Main Street. When she was a teenager, she came up here to be with her friends, to sing in the choir, and to be part of the youth group. Usually, from September to May, the choir sang each Sunday, but now they were on summer break.

She loved the well-known hymns from years ago like "All Hail the Power of Jesus Name." Jennie could sing it from memory, but she didn't know some of the newer ones like "Summer Suns Are Glowing" even though they had wonderful messages too. She tried to remember the words:

> Summer suns are glowing over land and sea;
> Happy light is flowing, bountiful and free . . .

It would have been a good day to sing this, because the morning sun was truly warm and bright.

The brown, two-story school stood right next to the church. Jennie had attended here her first eight years. A remodeling project was soon to begin to expand the building to accommodate a high school so students who wanted to attend wouldn't have to travel to Monticello or St. Cloud.

As a child, Jennie loved climbing the trail below the hill and imagining Indians hiding behind trees. Fortunately, the settlers' Indian problems were long over. In fact, she could hardly imagine her pretty little white church being turned into a fort during the Sioux Uprising, but it had been. She, like everyone who had been raised around Clearwater, knew the church's history.

Jennie remembered one of the first times she had heard Tom Porter tell the story about how the village protected its citizens and area farmers during the uprising. Because he was one of the town founders, he had been asked a few years ago to be the keynote speaker at the Welcome Home Picnic at Cedar Point Park, a half mile out of town and overlooking the Mississippi River.

Tom tarted his speech with, "It all began when some renegade Sioux started killing settlers in the southern part of the state. There were many reasons for the uprising. We can't forget that the Indians had gotten the raw end of the stick on a number of occasions by our own government.

"I'm not saying any of the settlers deserved to be massacred, though. They were innocent victims. But the Indians had been promised payment for the land the country took from them. While this may surprise many of you, and upset others, they weren't always treated fairly.

"It was a fearful time for those of us who lived through this. People in towns and villages all over the state were scared, but those out in the country began to panic. From Redwood Falls to Sauk Centre, rampages, fear of rampages, and rumors of rampages ran rampant. Communities did their best to construct shelters, stockades, and forts to protect those who needed it. Clearwater was no exception."

Jennie knew enough of her Minnesota history to remember that Governor Ramsey sent members of the Minnesota Militia to guard the central parts of the state. Though many young men were already serving their country in the Civil War, he was able to round up enough volunteers to help secure the area.

"Here in town," Porter went on, "a number of us, Horace Webster, Simon Stevens, Asa White, and myself, helped build a stockade around the Congregational Church on the hill overlooking town. In case the town was attacked, we built a tunnel from the east side of the cellar down to the bottom of the hill. This not only gave those holed up in the stockade a place to hide, but it led straight down to the shore of the Mississippi River so they could all escape."

Fortunately, no attack took place, the skirmish was settled, though not to the benefit of the Sioux, and most of the citizens moved back to village homes or rural homesteads.

As Jennie drew closer to the church, she saw the familiar black buggy with the gray fringed top and knew that Maude was inside.

Jennie heard the faint sound of organ music as she neared the front of the church. She couldn't remember whose turn it was to play today. Often in the summer, members, including Pitt Colgrove, took turns playing to give Mrs. Trafton a break. Even Jennie played when she had time.

Was that "Bring Them In" she heard? Although somewhat new, the song had a snappy tune most everyone liked, except for a few older folks who thought it almost sacrilegious to be singing "God's words" so rapidly.

The front doors to the small white building stood wide open. Jennie figured someone decided to air the building after yesterday's heat. Often, in the summer, both churches, the Methodist Episcopal and the Congregational, took on the strong, pungent odor of mildew and bat dung.

When Jennie entered the sanctuary, she saw Maude standing at the altar decorating the white-laced consecration table with bouquets of lilacs. Although she wore her typical attire—white ruffled blouse and black skirt—Maude's hat caught Jennie's attention. Yellow, bright-orange, brown, and white plumes shot up along the sides of the wide-brimmed brown felt glory. Jennie was sure Maude, who had been trained as a milliner, had made this showpiece.

"Hello, Maude," she whispered, trying not to disturb Mrs. Trafton who continued to play and pump the lively chorus to the hymn.

As Maude turned around, Jennie noticed the front of the hat. Trying not to giggle, Jennie pursed her lips when she saw a real robin's nest, replete with tiny blue eggs perched in front.

"Hello to you, Miss Jennie," Maude whispered. "Ma sent me out yesterday to deliver lilacs to the Methodist Church. I decided to wait until this morning to decorate here. Don't they smell lovely? Looks like you have a few we can add."

"My paltry offering? Yesterday, I went all over kingdom come to find these." Embarrassed that she would say such a thing in church, Jennie quickly covered her mouth. "Pardon my expression."

Maude smiled as she pushed another stem in the vase. "Ma said I should pick the best this week because who knows if they'll still be around next." As she moved to the altar, she asked, "Who was that young man driving your rig? I couldn't see him very well, but he looked handsome from afar." She added a wink.

Jennie looked up at Mrs. Trafton, who concentrated on playing. She walked closer to Maude and whispered, "That was one of the Mooney boys from out in the country. I had some problems out at Dorseys in the late afternoon, and he offered to see me home." She hoped the information was enough to stifle Maude's curiosity. She tried to steer their conversation toward church. "I'll tell you more about what happened later, but now, I'd better help get the flowers ready. Where do you think I should put these? The altar looks like it'll be plenty full by the time you're finished."

Grabbing another handful from the basket on the front pew, Maude stuffed a few more stems into the vase before looking around the room. "Oh, how about putting some in that green wicker basket that's been sitting empty at the back of the room since Mrs. Mitchell's funeral last January? We aren't having communion today, so why don't you set it up on the table back there? That way we'll have flowers spread all around."

"That's a good idea." Jennie grabbed the basket by its huge circular handle and carried it to the back table. She took handfuls and made a bouquet of lavender lilacs and phlox. She found another empty urn and filled that up with her remaining flowers. A breeze blew through the opened window, spreading the fresh scent of lilac. By the time the two women finished, parishioners began to fill the pews. Mrs. Trafton continued playing quietly. Jennie and Maude cleaned the pew of the stray buds and greenery. As she followed Maude down the aisle with the empty boxes and baskets, Jennie patted the shoulder of her mother's elderly friend Mrs. Benson and smiled at a few of the locals who always came early for service.

Outside, buggies and carriages of all sizes filled the street in front of the church and school. Jennie saw Dorseys pulling in behind the church. She was anxious to talk to Ida, not only about the last-minute details for Decoration Day, but also about what happened to her out in the country.

When the two reentered the church, Jennie saw that many of the regulars had filled the pews. The Colgroves sat in their places near the front on the left side, and sure enough, Pitt sat on the outside. She felt lonesome for him. He may have been tall and handsome, but something else more important drew her to the man. Jennie admired his intelligence. The two often had spirited debates over politics. He was a staunch Republican, and she a firm Democrat. On long buggy rides or swinging on the Phillips's front porch, the two discussed everything from women's educational opportunities or the lack of, to the need for health reform, especially for women and children. They often didn't agree, but they appreciated each other's viewpoint.

Pitt was a smart man. Jennie knew he would go far. Unfortunately, she doubted she'd be going with him. Right now anyway, she felt as though she couldn't give him what he wanted and needed—a wife and family.

Jennie quietly walked down the aisle to her usual pew, the right side, second row. Maude slid in beside her. At the beat of "Holy, Holy, Holy," Reverend Jones, in his black suit, walked down the middle aisle, leading the congregation in song with his wonderful baritone voice that reverberated throughout the sanctuary.

The pastor led the congregation through the invitation to worship and then invited worshippers to open their Bibles to Daniel 12:2. Jennie read along:

> And many of them that sleep in the dust of the earth shall awake,
> some to everlasting life,
> and some to shame and everlasting contempt.

The stanza made Jennie think about Alice Leonard. She had a hard time believing in the supernatural; she couldn't join in with her friends when they played with the Ouija board because it gave her the creeps. More importantly, she couldn't believe a naïve, young girl who died so tragically could be cast into hell or as the Bible stated in "everlasting contempt." The God Jennie worshipped had more compassion than that.

Reverend Jones then asked the congregation to turn to John 6:47 for the New Testament lesson. He read:

> Verily, verily, I say unto you,
> He that believeth on me hath everlasting life.

As she read along with him, she lost herself in the words. She knew that, like most in Irish Town, the Leonard girl was raised, baptized, and confirmed Catholic. Jennie knew enough about their faith to know they too believed in an everlasting life. Of course, many Irish had a myriad of other beliefs and superstitions that didn't always tie into their religion and even offended some people in the community.

Jennie knew that she had heard something out at Tamarack Swamp. Whether it was a bobcat or a ghost, something or someone was tormented.

After the salvation prayer, the organist began to play the introduction to "When the Weary, Seeking Rest." As Jennie sang along, she couldn't believe how the lyrics, along with the scriptures, laid heavily on her:

> When the troubled, seeking peace,
> On Thy Name shall call. . .

At the end of his sermon, Pastor Jones encouraged everyone to remember the Decoration Day celebrations later in the week, as well as those who served their country and had gone ahead of them to the great beyond.

For the closing hymn, he asked them to sing "Every Morning the Red Sun." Jennie sang half heartedly, paying little attention to the words until she came to the end of the last two lines:

For that Heav'n, so bright and blest,
Is our everlasting rest.

It seemed obvious that if what she had heard wasn't a living creature, it had to be something other-worldly, and it had never received peace in life or the afterlife.

She thought of her dream. The woman in white that flew around Jennie was tormented. When she turned and stared at Jennie, she seemed to be beckoning her for help. But what could she do?

Chapter 6

Vultus

The Countenance

As the congregation started the third stanza to "God Be with You Till We Meet Again," Pastor Jones walked back down the middle aisle to greet his parishioners on the outside stoop.

Mrs. Trafton returned to quietly playing "Every Morning the Red Sun" as everyone took turns exiting his or her pew.

Anxious to get her day underway, Jennie wished she could cut in front of everyone and get outside more quickly, but that wouldn't be polite. The week ahead was going to be hectic. If she, Ida, and Maude, who had also volunteered to help, could get the Decoration Day decorations organized, she could check some items off her list.

When it was her turn to exit, Jennie saw Ida who was closer to the doors waving at her. She looked cool and comfortable in her green lawn and straw hat. Sherm, Ida's husband, wore the same dark-gray coat and gray trousers he got married in a year before. With his black hat in hand, his pink cheeks and forehead proved he was overly warm, but he patiently waited to get out the door. Jennie figured as soon as he got to the buggy, he'd take off his coat and loosen his tie. He, too, gave Jennie an acknowledging smile.

Ida pointed outdoors. Jennie quickly interpreted this as a sign that they would meet somewhere on the grass. She hoped her friend hadn't changed her mind about sticking around for the afternoon to get some work done.

Because she had promised to tell Maude about what happened to her in Irish Town, Jennie decided she might as well invite her for dinner as well. Jennie also wanted to hear what her two friends remembered about the tragic death of the Leonard girl.

Jennie could make sure Maude knew the whole story about why Jamie Mooney drove her home. Maybe she could prevent Livia Pailsey from spreading rumors around town—that is, if Jennie and Jamie had created as big of a spectacle as she surmised.

Jennie realized she hadn't seen Livia during the service. Standing on her tiptoes, she looked over the heads of other church-goers but didn't see the woman anywhere in the sanctuary. She had to be sick or out of town because she hardly ever missed church.

Jennie watched Maude side-step across the pew to talk to Sarah Fisk. An attractive, dainty woman, Mrs. Fisk lived out in Lynden with her family. In the winter she wasn't always able to make it in to church.

Inching her way out the door, Jennie made small talk with another friend, Grace Noyes. "How are you, Grace?"

"Why, hello, Jennie! I'm well."

"Are you finished with your first year of teaching? You had a contract in St. Paul, right?"

"Yes. I filled in for one of the male teachers who took a sabbatical to earn an advanced endorsement. He finished and wanted his job back. At first I was disappointed, but then the superintended told me how happy he was with my work and asked me to come back to teach second graders next year."

Jennie felt a pang of jealousy. For a long time, she had thought she would be a teacher. Until her father approached her last year, she never considered becoming a druggist. She hoped she had made the right choice.

"Well, congratulations, Grace. I know you're a good teacher. We were taught so well at the Normal School in St. Cloud."

"We were, indeed. Of course, if the right fellow comes along, I'll have to quit my position. Speaking of the Normal School, how are you and Pitt doing? Any news on the horizon? "

Knowing Grace knew very little about their relationship since she seldom came back home, Jennie said, "Oh, we are only friends. He and I are so busy we seldom see each other."

After a few moments, Grace said, "I'm sorry, Jennie. I didn't know. You two were so serious, I expected . . . well, we all expected you two to get married."

Here was another person to remind Jennie of what she was giving up by not wanting to get married yet. Grace had no qualms about giving up her career once she found the right fellow. She, too, thought Pitt was the right one. Most women would be satisfied being married to him and having a houseful of children. What was wrong with her? Why couldn't she be content following the traditional path?

"Oh, it's fine, Grace. Anyway, I'm pleased with today's weather. Wasn't it horrid yesterday?"

Jennie barely heard Grace's response. As she scanned the room for a way to make an escape faster, she looked right into Pitt's eyes. The two would be sharing an awkward moment soon as they met up at the back of the church. What would she say? Should she cut through the line to avoid talking to him, or could she act nonchalant and share a few pleasantries?

They were angry with each other when they last parted. One minute they were snuggling in the sleigh, and next, they were fighitng over when they would marry.

"Pitt, you know I can't give up my job right now. We've gone over this," Jennie said, trying to stay calm. "I've made a promise to help my family. Father has taken on the responsibility of starting another drug store in Eden Valley. He needs me to manage the Clearwater store for a while. Can't you understand that I need to help him and the rest of the family? I need to feel useful, to make a contribution to society, to help my family get over—well—a hurdle, a financial hurdle."

Pitt drew Jennie closer to him, circling his arms around her back. He placed his cheek against hers and whispered, "But you'll be useful. You'll be busy enough taking care of the house and, maybe, someday, you'll be contributing to society by raising beautiful and smart children, *our* children."

Jennie felt uncomfortable thinking about the "our children" Pitt was referring to. Yes, someday, she wanted to have a couple children, maybe a boy and a girl, but surely not a houseful like her mother and father. She loved each and every one of her siblings, but she had no desire to slave from morning until bedtime taking care of house and family.

"Like I said, Pitt, if you are proposing, I accept, but not for anytime this year. Maybe next year."

Trying to appeal to her emotions, Pitt became more serious as he coaxed, "Jennie, listen. I hope to be moving on soon to more prestigious positions. I was asked to become principal of the Willmar district. I declined because I feel as though I still have more to do in St. Cloud, but I have no desire to stay around Clearwater forever. There's so much I want to do and I need you beside me."

Feeling as though Pitt wasn't even listening to her, Jennie pulled away and looked into his eyes. She answered quietly but emphatically, "I can't leave my father yet, Pitt. He needs my help. My family needs my help." More calmly, she tried to reason with him. "Besides, I enjoy my new job. I feel, well, I feel as though I am helping people."

"I thought by now you'd gotten that nonsense out of your head!"

"*Nonsense?"* Jennie questioned, raising her voice.

"So are you saying you won't marry me?" Pitt huffed.

"I didn't say that. Can't we wait a couple years? I've passed many of my pharmacy tests, but there's so much I have to learn yet before I feel totally confident as a druggist."

"Dang the drug store! Confound it, Jennie. What about us? What about our future?"

Jennie sat back and looked at him. Used to his temper when he was challenged, she decided she needed to remain calm as she tried to make her point. "It seems as though we are talking about your future, not mine. For someone who argues for women's rights, you sure don't think your future wife, presumably me, has any rights at all."

"That isn't true. But it's time to grow up, Jennie. You can't live in a make believe world forever. Men have their roles and women have theirs."

Even more astonished, Jennie stared at him before challenging him. "Make believe? *Make believe*?" She shook her head. "You know, we've always been able to talk about everything—politics, religion, women's rights, and education. But now you seemed to have changed your views when it comes to what you perceive to be *your* wife's role."

"Jennie! You're being unreasonable."

She turned back and looked at Pitt. "Unreasonable? I'm sorry, Pitt, but I doubt we have much more to say. We may never agree on my role in the marriage. I've told you before . . . for now, I don't think I'm ready for marriage, and probably never a traditional marriage, me staying at home and you out fulfilling yourself. So please, take me home."

They rode in silence except for the soft swish of the sleigh gliding through the packed snow and an occasional snort from the horse. Pitt stopped in front of the Phillips's house, pulled on the brake, jumped down, and walked around to help Jennie. With his hand on her arm, he led her to the front porch. He leaned over to kiss her, but Jennie offered her cheek. He hesitated a moment before giving her a cool and cordial peck.

Jennie watched Pitt turn the sleigh around in the street and ride away, the horse's hooves becoming fainter as he made his way down Main Street. They had often argued, but this time it was different.

Now, four months later, as Jennie awakened from the painful memory, she glanced over at Pitt who was looking at her as he stood against the wall at the opposite side of the church. She smiled. He smiled back but nervously brushed his hair back from his face. He looked toward the door, almost as if he, too, wished for a quick escape. His mother, Mary Louise Colgrove, looked in Jennie's direction, smiled, and waved. Both she and Pitt would have to try to put up a good appearance in front of the remaining parishioners.

Maude leaned over Jennie's shoulder and whispered in her ear, "Do you want to sneak out?"

Ducking out would be easier. Of course, she'd probably create a scene when she knocked over someone in the process. No, she'd be polite and friendly. Besides, she told almost everyone that she and Pitt had parted company but had remained friends. Now she had to prove it.

"I'll be fine. By the way, where's Livia? I thought for sure she'd be in church."

"She left this morning to visit her son and family. She had a couple celebrations to attend. Her niece's getting confirmed today and her sister's boy's graduating from high school. She'll be home tomorrow, bringing a houseful of company back with her for Decoration Day. Uncle John's coming as well," Maude added.

"Oh, of course," Jennie agreed, "John Stevens is introducing Congressman Towne." Jennie knew the elderly gentleman had done nearly as much for Clearwater as his younger brother Simon. The village had both men and Ormasinda Peck to thank for getting such an influential congressman to come help them celebrate the holiday.

Jennie realized she hadn't invited Maude to dinner. Before she could turn around to do so, she realized the awkward moment had arrived.

First, Jennie accepted a hug from Pitt's mother. "Oh, Jennie, it's so good to see you again. We need to have you out for supper sometime soon."

"That would be so nice, Mrs. Colgrove. We'll have to plan that sometime."

Mr. Colgrove reached over his wife and patted Jennie on the shoulder. "Nice seeing you, Jennie."

After returning the welcome, Jennie turned to Pitt, extended her hand in greeting. "Hello! How are you?" she asked cheerfully.

Pitt grasped Jennie's hand and held it longer than a mere friend would.

"Hello to you, Jennie. I'm well, and you?"

Jennie realized they had to live the cliché about putting one's best foot forward so she tried to move through the line to the minister as fast as possible.

"Very well," Jennie replied as she gently pulled her hand out of his grip. "We sure have a beautiful morning," she added.

"We do at that, Jennie," the pastor agreed as he shook her hand. "And thank you for filling our house of worship with the beautiful spring flowers."

"You're welcome," she said. "But Maude Porter donated the bulk of the lilacs. And thank you, too, Reverend, for such a good sermon today," Jennie added as she made her way down the steps.

The pastor's attention quickly turned to Pitt. "Professor Colgrove, I'm glad you could join us this morning." As he gave the young man's hand a firm handshake, he added, "I hope you had a good year at the college?"

As Jennie walked away from the church, she heard Pitt's strong voice answer, "Yes, yes. Thank you for asking. I had an excellent year." Knowing that she didn't have to put up appearances any longer, she exhaled deeply.

Observing the situation, Ida smiled, raised her eyebrows, and watched Jennie as she approached her on the grassy slope. "How did that go?"

Jennie looked up and saw the pastor and Pitt still talking. Maude, who stood behind Pitt, waiting for her turn to greet the pastor, looked between the two men and gave Jennie an eye roll.

Jennie smiled back at her before she answered Ida, "Oh, it was fine!" She held onto Ida's shoulder and turned back toward Maude, crooking her finger to join them as soon as she had greeted the pastor.

Turning back to Ida, she stared into her good friend's green eyes. "You are sticking around for the afternoon aren't you? Joining my family for Sunday dinner too? I thought I'd better invite Maude as well. Hopefully, we can tie up loose ends for our part of the celebration."

Sherm, who had been talking to Sam Whiting, shook the older man's hand and patted him on the shoulder before coming to stand beside his young wife. "Jennie, we heard about your little incident yesterday. You made it home safe and sound I see."

Before Jennie could respond, Mary and Orrin Dorsey joined them on the grassy slope. Both husband and wife looked quite different in their dressed up mode compared to yesterday when Jennie saw them in their country attire.

Mrs. Dorsey wore her black brocade skirt with a white silk blouse and black scarf tied under her collar. A black straw hat with white flowers sat atop her chignon. Mr. Dorsey wore his usual black suit with a gray bowtie. Today, with his black felt hat in his hand, his face was pink and tan, while his forehead showed a winter white, the only telltale sign that he worked outdoors.

"Jennie! How did it go last night?" Orrin Dorsey inquired as he greeted her.

"Oh, fine. Jamie Mooney and I had a nice long talk."

Mary Dorsey put her arm around Jennie, and in her motherly way responded, "I hope he didn't fill your head with any of his foolish talk, Jennie. He, like some of our Irish neighbors, has a different way of—of—well, of seeing things," she said.

"What is it you're saying about the Irish?" Maude whispered as she filled in their circle.

Ida bit her lips to hold back a surprised smile, but Jennie caught the expression of shock in Mary Dorsey's eyes. If she didn't like Maude, she never told Jennie, but her reaction was a clue to how she felt about her. It was obvious she didn't always appreciate Maude's intrusiveness or bluntness.

Of course, Jennie knew her mother liked Maude, but she said her parents spoiled her. Slightly embarrassed for her friend, and yet not trying to be rude, Jennie responded, "Oh, we can talk about it later." She quickly changed the subject. "Sherm, are you going to let your wife stay in town with Maude and me so we can get some work done for Thursday?"

"He sure is," Ida responded without waiting for her husband's input. "He's going home with Mother and Father and leaving me with the buggy so he doesn't even have to come get me."

"Yep, that's what we planned. That is, if you, Mrs. Shattuck, promise to get home before dark so I don't have to come looking for you," her husband reminded her with a big smile of pride and love.

"Well, we will see to it that she gets on home at a decent time. Maude, can you come for Sunday dinner? Mother told me last night she was frying up a couple chickens and baking a beef roast, so we've plenty. Afterwards, we can finish our Decoration Day plans. That is if you have time to come over."

"Oh, splendid! I'll drive home and tell Mother not to set a place for me for dinner."

"Don't rush. I'm sure we won't eat for an hour or more," Jennie hollered as Maude sprinted across the front yard of the church.

After a pat on the arm and a quick goodbye, Mary Dorsey slid her arm through her husband's to walk back to their buggy. Orrin lifted his hat to indicate goodbye. Jennie joined Sherm and Ida as they headed to their buggy. Sherm helped Ida up before coming around to help Jennie as well.

"You know, Jennie," Sherm said quietly, "as I started saying before, Orrin and Mary told us what happened to you yesterday." He looked over at his wife who bowed her head slightly. "Well, I know that her parents don't really believe anything supernatural takes place out by the swamp, but I've been out there duck hunting with Orrin, and he and I have heard similar sounds . . . eerie cries. I know he'd like to believe nothing out of the ordinary's going on, but we can't explain what we've heard, either."

"Thank you for understanding, both of you. Jamie told me what he and others in Lynden believe's going on. I'd love to forget, and, I know this is morbid, I want to know more."

"We can talk about it after dinner today, Jennie," Ida offered. "Maude will be around so who knows what'll fly out of her mouth."

The three laughed.

"Of course, we all love her because she's Maude. Sometimes she says what we are too scared to say but are thinking, nonetheless," Ida added.

Jennie nodded. "You've got that right."

Sherm walked back to his wife's side of the carriage. "Your folks are waiting for me, Ida. Have a nice afternoon." Sherm took Ida's hand and added, "And you, dear wife, try to get home before I begin to worry about you."

Jennie saw the young couple stare into each other's eyes. Knowing they would have liked a moment alone, she turned her head.

Pretty soon they were off with a jolt. Jennie said, "I hate to keep saying this, but today is so beautiful. Yesterday's heat and humidity were too much too early."

"I agree. I couldn't wait to get home to wash up and cool down," Ida commented as she rounded the corner by the Catholic church. "So, what happened yesterday? Mother and Father told us you had quite the scare by the swamp."

"While I was picking phlox, I heard snapping branches and crunching leaves. I didn't think much of it until I heard what I thought was a child wailing. I hightailed it out of there. When I found Solly had run off in a fit, I knew he had heard something weird, too."

Ida was quiet for a moment. "Father wants you to think you heard a bobcat, and Mother refuses to believe there's anything unnatural down there. She especially gets miffed when anyone talks about ghosts or spirits. She, like many English, has a bit of prejudice toward the Irish. She's a good soul, though, and tries to accept our neighbors. Yet, I have to disagree with her. I've seen and heard *things* around the farm I never used to pay attention to before, before, well, you know."

"Are you referring to the Leonard murder?" Jennie asked.

"Yes. Since the girl was murdered, sometimes, in the mornings when I'm out collecting eggs, I've found a few, maybe five or six, on the ground, absolutely crushed—not eaten—crushed. And yet, there's been no sign of a fox or bobcat."

"Surely, that isn't much proof, is it? I mean, couldn't a hen or rooster have done that as well? I've heard stories of hens pecking at or kicking out eggs that instinct tells them won't develop."

"I suppose that's one explanation, but one or two, not a half dozen or so, and always in the spring and summer. The first time this happened, Father said the same thing. But then, like I said, over the last couple years, this and other strange things have happened to make him raise his eyebrows."

"For instance?" Jennie prodded.

"Sometimes the horses go wild in the early evening. They whinny and start running around in the pasture like they're fleeing something. At the same time, the cattle beller hysterically." Ida paused a moment, then added, "Jennie, something's out by the swamp that's startling everyone and everything. There are times I can almost sense, well, I don't how to explain it, but it feels spooky. Sherm says he's felt it too, sort of eerie."

"Hmmmm! I guess I'm glad someone else's experienced what I did."

"I'm surprised Mother told you to look for flowers by the swamp. Of course, she doesn't believe any of this when we talk about it. And Father, to try to please her, keeps his thoughts to himself," Ida admitted.

They pulled into the back of the Phillips's house and hopped out of the buggy. Jennie always thought it strange that women could, if they had to, get in and out of carriages without the helpful arms of men.

She brushed away the wrinkles from her dress while she waited for Ida to wrap the reins around the post by the back shed the family called a barn.

"By the way, Ida, I haven't said a word to my parents about what happened yesterday—mostly because I haven't had an opportunity to talk to either of them alone."

"I won't mention anything," Ida said as she walked in back of the buggy and followed Jennie down the path and up the back steps to the kitchen.

The two entered the back porch where they got their first whiff of Sunday dinner. From fresh-baked bread to the rich smell of onions and celery roasting with beef and chicken, the Phillips's kitchen created an inviting late Sunday morning atmosphere. Ida sniffed. "Yum! It sure smells good in here."

Jennie knew that Ida felt at home here despite the hubbub of the large, noisy Phillips family. Out of the corner of her eye, she saw her friend smile when she heard little girl giggles. Little Ruthie sat in the middle of the parlor floor entertaining her audience—her older brothers.

Deeper voices came from the same direction. Jennie couldn't distinguish which brother's voice she heard, Sam's or Carl's, but sunfish and crappies jumping onto fish lines seemed to be the topic of conversation.

She heard her father's quieter, more soothing voice chip in. "Doc Edwards said the best bites right now are out at Cedar Point." Nothing in this house ever stood still or was ever truly quiet, unlike the Dorsey place where Ida was raised as an only child.

"Hello! We're here." Jennie hollered as they wiped their feet on the rag carpet by the entryway.

"Ruthie, go out into the kitchen and see who's here," Stanley Phillips suggested, trying to entice the child's curiosity.

"Hey, Ruthie," Ida bent down and opened her arms to the toddling child.

"Ida, we're glad to have you come for dinner," Stanley welcomed as he walked into the dining room. Jennie noticed that he had put on a shirt and pulled up his suspenders. "Marietta went to church and Sunday School. I decided to stay home with Ruthie and watch the oven. She should be coming home soon. As you can hear, the boys are already home," he said.

"Hi, Ida," Carl hollered and Sam echoed. Each had already rid themselves of their suit jackets, ties, and shoes and sat on the floor rearranging Ruthie's blocks.

"Hello. You two thinking of going fishing?" she inquired.

"Maybe this afternoon," Carl answered.

Jennie had already grabbed an apron and tied it around her waist. She walked out into the backroom, leaving Ida to play with Ruthie.

"What can I help with?" Ida asked.

"Right now, nothing. I checked on the roast and basted the chickens. When my sisters get home with Mother, I'm sure we'll have lots more to do. I don't know what else she plans to put on the table, but I'm sure she'd appreciate it if I peeled some potatoes. You can keep me company while I do that," Jennie suggested as she came in from the backroom lugging a bucket heaping with dirty brown russets.

"Goodness. You have to peel all those?" Ida asked in shock before turning around to grab a paring knife from the drawer. "I'll help or we'll never be able to eat," she said with a laugh.

Jennie picked up the dish pan from the hook on the wall and filled it with a few dippers of fresh water from the bucket on the porch. After spreading some newspapers on the table, she sat down. Ida grabbed another apron from the peg on the wall and sat across from Jennie. They began to peel. Ruthie sat in the center of the kitchen floor and made quite a racket by pounding a wooden spoon on the bottom of a pot.

"I can't imagine Mother ever cooking up both a pot roast and baked chicken for the same meal. And all these spuds! About the only time we have to peel this many is when we have threshers, and then, we usually have neighbor women come and help."

"I know part of the reason for her cooking both beef and chicken is because we have to feed so many, but the chicken is partly for Father," Jennie said. "His stomach doesn't handle beef very well. Chicken agrees with him better even if he doesn't eat much of it. He'll eat the potatoes, though. She plants many each year because she says she has to fill up her growing boys. We still have a good-sized pile down in the cellar from last summer, but she'll be planting more soon."

Both bent over the newspaper-lined table. Soon circles of dirty peelings lay heaped in brown and white mounds on the table.

"Before Mother gets here with the rest of the family, and before Maude gets here, I want to ask you if you remember much about the girl's murder."

For a moment, Ida stared at Jennie, seemingly confused, almost as if she couldn't transition her thoughts from potatoes to murder. She plopped a finished spud into the tub of water and grabbed another before answering.

"Oh, let's see. I'd just gotten home that weekend from teachers' college. I remember many people were at the schools that afternoon celebrating the raising of the new Minnesota flag. We'd planned on going to the Weyrauch school, but Grandma and Grandpa Ponsford had come for Sunday dinner and hadn't gone home yet, so we never got around to it."

Ida was quiet for a few moments before she said, "We had a light supper before my grandparents left, and Father and Sherm went out to do the chores. Mother and I cleaned up the kitchen. After the men came back into the house, Father went into the kitchen to pop some popcorn. Sherm, Mother, and I were in the parlor. Mother sat knitting, and Sherm and I sat on the divan reading. Everything was quiet except for the light popping of the corn. The house was quite warm because Mother had used the cook stove all day, so we had the doors and windows wide open. Sometime around nine o'clock, Mother, Sherm, and I heard a horse galloping into the yard. Mother went to the door and greeted Sam Stokes. He came inside and told us about the Leonard girl's death. At this point, no one knew the girl had been murdered."

As Jennie started to ask whether Ida had ever met the young girl, Percy ran in the front door, hollering, "Hey, Jennie. Hey, Ida!" The rackety screen slammed behind him. Jennie knew her mother and sisters would be following from their short walk from church. She also knew she and Ida would not have a moment of peace again until later.

"Hey to you, too, Percy," Ida said.

"Did you wipe your feet, young man?" Jennie asked. "Go back and either wipe them or take off your shoes," she ordered with a light swat on his butt to remind him about house rules.

"Okay," he obeyed and walked back to the front door to kick off his shoes.

"Percy, put them on the rug, *beside* the door so Mother doesn't trip over them when she gets home," Jennie reminded him. "Jeesh," she said, shaking her head and looking at Ida.

The eight-year-old ran back into the hallway and threw the shoes on the rug. Jennie decided to ignore their bouncing against the wall.

"I'm hungry. Is dinner ready yet?" Without waiting for an answer, Percy hollered, "Where're Carl and Sam? They're going to take me fishin' with them this afternoon."

"Everyone's in the parlor. Where's Mother?"

"Ah, they're coming. They walk too slow so I ran home."

Jennie and Ida laughed because although the women were probably walking slowly, nothing Percy ever did was in slow motion.

Jennie rinsed the potatoes, then took the pot to the back room and slid it onto the cook stove. After covering it with a lid, she bent over and opened the oven door. She pulled out the cast iron roaster with the beef roast and slid it to the back of the stove. She also pulled out the chicken to check it for doneness. The thigh seemed to bend up and down easily so she also lugged that out. Not sure what kind of gravy to make, she decided she'd wait for her mother to come. Besides, no one beat Marietta Phillips's gravy.

When she got back into the kitchen, Jennie untied Ida's apron and said, "Now go. You're company. Sit down with the rest of them in the parlor. Soon there'll be more than enough cooks in the kitchen," she laughed. "Besides, Maude will arrive early so you can keep her company, too."

"Can't I set the table for you?" Ida begged.

No sooner had she opened her mouth than Marietta Phillips and the two girls came in the house.

"Ida, how nice to see you. How're the folks?" Marietta asked as she wiped her feet at the door.

"They're great, Mrs. Phillips. Thank you for inviting me for dinner. Now what can I do to help?" Ida asked after she gave each of Jennie's sisters, Blanche and Si, a big hug.

As if on cue, each of the Phillips girls began doing what they probably had been told to do on the way home. Si opened up two quarts of corn and poured them into a pot to heat up. Blanche grabbed some plates from the shelf and carried them into the dining room. Taking her lead, Ida plucked forks, spoons, and knives from the table drawer and carried them to the dining room.

"Hello, I made it," Maude hollered from the front door. She walked in without anyone answering her.

Ida peeked around the dining room door, "Most of us are in here, Maude."

Jennie hollered from the backroom, "Go on into the parlor, Maude. Dinner isn't quite ready."

"Mother sent you some lilacs for your table. What should I do with these, Si?" Maude asked.

"Vases are on the shelf in the back porch. You'll find a bucket of water out there too," Si answered as she opened a quart of pickled crab apples and arranged them in a pickle dish.

Maude soon returned with a vase of fragrant lilacs. "Hello, everyone!"

"Hello, Maude," Stanley Phillips hollered over the voices of the boys, who hollered their greetings one by one.

Within a short time, the potatoes were cooked and mashed, the gravy was made, the meat sliced. Jennie called for everyone to come to the table. The parade of women carried bowls, platters, and pitchers of milk to the table. Without being invited twice, Maude plopped down and waited eagerly to eat.

With all the food placed down the middle of the large, oblong table, the large family and guests squeezed in to get their places. Stanley Phillips took the lead and bowed his head in prayer. He thanked the Lord for the gift of good friends and a good family. Then the rest of the group joined him in their traditional mealtime blessing:

God is great, God is good.
Let us thank him for our food.
Amen.

After grace, platters of meat and bowls of steaming potatoes and vegetables started circling the table as everyone took his or her serving. Soon the room buzzed with compliments for the good food and a mix of chatter over a myriad of topics. Jennie looked around the table and felt a tingle of pride for belonging to such a happy family and having such good friends.

After the delicious dinner, Marietta encouraged Jennie to take Ida and Maude to the back porch where it was cooler and where they could get some work done. She said she and the girls would clean up. The men took this cue to grab their fishing poles and head for the river. Stanley decided he'd follow as well. Soon the house was quiet except for the occasional clatter of dishes being scraped and porcelain and silver being plopped into the enamel dishpan.

Maude, Ida, and Jennie carried their coffee cups to the porch and sat around the small wooden table. Maude pulled pencil and paper from her bag and laid it on the table. She started taking notes as each told what they had already accomplished to get the town decked out for the celebration.

Jennie started. "Thanks to Ida, my brothers and some of their friends got the platform painted yesterday."

"It was hot and humid, but the boys wanted to get started," Ida responded.

Soon the young women had a list of places that needed decorating—the depot, the river landing, the speakers' platform, store fronts, and the buggies that would carry special guests. Unfortunately, a few of the buildings in the northern part of town no longer needed decorations because they'd burned to the ground. Jennie reminded Maude to talk to her father, who said he would make sure the rest of the ash and rubble got cleaned up before the big event

"He's on it," Maude said. "Tomorrow, Pa'll have a crew of men and some of the boys already out of school meeting him up there. He said he'd bring his hay wagon to haul it all away." She looked at her notes and suggested, "Let's tally our donations. I know Mother and Father donated some cash for us to use however we please." Even though she didn't really say exactly how much cash the Porters had given, Maude added, "The Stevens family, including the Pecks, gave cash too. With that I have a total of about thirty dollars."

"Even though I haven't seen it yet, my Sunday school class has been building and decorating a float," Ida said.

Maude stated that she knew of two other floats being built by some of the youth in town. They all agreed the committee could give them some money for decorations.

Ida said, "Mother's sewing circle donated nearly fifty yards of red, white, and blue ribbon."

"I know Father gave the paint for the platform, and he donated a few flags as well," Jennie added. "I almost forgot. Father said the band will be decked out in their best suits and wearing straw hats. So I was thinking that maybe we could use some of the ribbon for their rims."

"Good idea!" Maude exclaimed, making note of it on her pad.

Jennie reported that when she talked to some local business owners they said they would indeed have their colors flying that day. The Hotel Scott and Whiting building would be hanging bunting below their windows.

"We need to make a couple welcome banners," Jennie said. "Carl already volunteered, even though he said he'd probably use stencils."

"Oilcloth would be great for some of the signs," Maude said. "Maybe we can buy some at the hardware store."

"I'll see if Boutwell will give us a bargain, and we need some arrows that'll direct our visitors to the Whiting building. Has Mr. Laughton offered any butcher wrap or string from the meat market?" Ida questioned.

When Ida mentioned Laughton's Meat Market, Jennie remembered the odd dream she'd had the night before. She blinked hard to get the images of carcasses dancing toward her in the cold building out of her head. "Yes, he did."

Maude said, "I'll go down and talk to him again tomorrow. We've got to get Carl on this right away." Maude suggested she and Jennie should go around the village on Wednesday evening and put out a few decorations. "And Ida, you don't need to make a special trip into town for this," Maude said. "We can make the rounds to finish the job Thursday morning."

"Thanks! It would be hard for me to get back home before dark."

The three agreed on all their details and that the backroom of the drug store would be the handiest place to keep everything.

"Have you heard anything else about the parade, Jennie? I know your father was on the planning committee. Has he said what else is going to happen Thursday?" Ida asked.

"Father said they were trying to talk some of the clowns into coming down from St. Cloud. The Clearwater coronet and drum corps will play and lead the parade to and from the Whiting building out to Acacia Cemetery. I think after that everyone will gather out at Cedar Point for a potluck and then return to town for the ice cream and pie social at the Methodist church in the afternoon. We'll have horseshoe and bean bag games until about four when the baseball game will start up. When it gets dark, fireworks start."

"Oh, my, we're all going to be busy," Maude chimed in.

"I know Mother soaked Carl's league jersey in bluing yesterday. The shirt and pants didn't look good last year, but she said she wanted him to shine from the waist up as he pitched the first ball of the season!"

As Ida and Maude started packing up their handbags, Jennie stood, went to the door that opened to the kitchen, and called, "Mother, would you put on more coffee?"

Maude looked at Jennie with an expression of surprise.

Jennie looked at her friends and asked, "Neither of you are in a hurry, are you? Could I entice you to stay and chat a bit?" With both hands, she held a beautifully brown-glazed, three-layered chocolate cake.

Jennie knew few people ever turned down a cake made by Marietta Phillips.

Chapter 7

Cyatho thea

In a Cup of Tea

MAUDE BENT HER HEAD, focusing on the thick, dark chocolate frosting. Ida relaxed, her feet plopped on the ottoman in front of her, her head against the back of the brown wicker rocker. She slowly savored every rich bite of Marietta Phillips's delicious, chocolate cake. Jennie tipped the black enamel coffee pot and filled her friends' cups. The smell of rich, steamy coffee was what she needed to get the conversation going.

Jennie took a sip of her mother's brew, dabbed her white napkin on her mouth, and then laid it down neatly beside her dessert plate. She was ready to get some answers to what happened to her yesterday.

Even though Maude and Ida seemed preoccupied, they came to attention as she began to talk.

"I wanted to talk to both of you about what happened to me yesterday. Maude, I haven't had an opportunity to tell you everything that took place before you saw Jamie Mooney and me riding down the middle of Main Street. I told Ida a shortened version this morning after church. Of course, her folks know what happened. I ran into some problems while out by Tamarack Swamp—between Dorseys and Mooneys. You know where I'm talking about?"

Maude dabbed her lips. "I've been out there a couple times. Isn't that where that little girl, Arlene, Anna, Audrey, whatever her name was, died?"

Jennie stared in surprise at her friend. "You're close. Her name was Alice."

"Oh, sure. So what happened?" Maude asked, laying her napkin by her plate.

"Ida's mother told me about some purple phlox she'd seen on the Tamarack Swamp Road. So I took Solly and rode over as close as I could get. I walked down the path, going deeper into the wooded area because I saw some of it lining the road.

"After a while, I heard a strange noise. The further I went, the louder it was. It sounded like a child crying. I ran back to the buggy. But whatever scared me spooked Solly. He took off, the buggy behind him. When I caught up with him, he was hopping and snorting and had a wild look in his eyes."

"That's odd," Maude said.

"I led him back to Dorseys. Both Ida's folks believe I heard a bobcat. Ida's father insisted Jamie Mooney take me home. He told me folks out in Irish Town believe the spirit of Alice Leonard, that murdered young girl, roams around the swamp."

The little porch turned quiet. Jennie couldn't help but wonder if she had imagined everything. *No*, she told herself, Ida had said she had experienced something out there as well.

Maude broke through the awkward quiet by clearing her throat. "I can only tell you what I have heard others say," she began, playing with a few chocolate crumbs on her plate with her fork.

"Fanny Biggerstaff, Pitt Colgrove's sister, told me some of those who live out there say they've often heard a child crying, usually toward dusk, mostly in the springtime and early summer. She said a few of the neighbors have even thought they'd seen the girl's spirit walking in the woods. Some say when they've been riding at night, they've come upon a ghost-like person wearing a white sheet walking right down the middle of the road. Others say they've seen a young girl with long white hair wrapped around her body wandering the hills and pastures around the swamp."

Jennie's hand covered her mouth as she recalled her nightmare—the white sheet, the long, grayish white hair that nearly wrapped around the woman whose eyes seemed to bleed with tears. She'd heard people talking about seeing ghosts walking around graveyards, but she never believed any of that nonsense. Until yesterday, she thought people had let their imaginations run wild.

"That sounds like the dream I had last night, Maude. I figured it was my vivid imagination" Jennie exclaimed.

"I know the Irish have some strange beliefs, but some think the poor girl has no rest since her murderer is still out there," Maude proclaimed.

"I wouldn't bring this up in mixed company. I know there has to be a logical explanation for what I heard."

"I told you, Jennie, I'd heard something out there as well," Ida interjected. "Earlier this spring, I was in the pasture riding Sam, my Appaloosa, around the circle. It was getting close to supper time. I knew Mother could use my help in the kitchen, but I was having such a good time. Sam and I were rounding the western part of the circle, closer to the swamp, when I heard a scream, what I thought was a cry of pain. Sam stopped fast, whinnied and backed up, then started fighting the air with his front legs. He almost threw me, but I held on as he galloped back to the barn. When I told Father what I heard and about Sam getting frightened, he said the same thing. I must have heard a bobcat."

"Our cats yowl at times, but what I heard sounded like someone was screaming in pain," Jennie added.

"That's what I think! So after Father went back to the barn, some of the hired help—I don't remember Jamie Mooney being there—started talking about what they had seen and heard and telling what they others had said as well. At first, I thought the stories were fed by wild imaginations. But some of those men seemed so sincere, and told the same stories Maude had just told. They all seem to believe a girl is roaming the swamp, and she can't or won't rest until someone solves her murder."

Maude nodded. She added, "Maybe you should talk to Doc Edmund's housekeeper. She's from Ireland, you know. She hangs out with some of others out in Irish Town but seems sensible. Now what's her name?"

"I'm not sure what you mean by sensible, Maude, but I think her first name's Claire," Jennie added.

"Sorry. Wrong choice of words. Let's just say she seems quite respectable."

Jennie went on to say, "She's come into the drug store for Doc a couple times to pick up some medication for him. He's been real busy lately out in the Silver Creek area."

"I've heard that Silver Creek and Hasty are really being plagued with diphtheria," Ida said.

Jennie picked up her cup and took her last sip. "That area's been hit hard. I know Doc's grateful his brother-in-law, Gil Tollington, finished his medical training down in Minneapolis and has been willing to help him. Between the two doctors, they're running wild taking care of everyone."

"Doc's a good man. Everyone's grateful we have him, and we're happy to have Gil here to take over when he has to," Maude said, also sipping her coffee.

"Anyway," Jennie continued, "I met the housekeeper this past winter. I thought she was really nice. I'm not sure how old she is, but I think she's older than she looks. According to Doc, she seems to have had a hard lot. I guess she came over from Ireland a few years ago, lost her mother when she was a teenager. Her father slaved to pay her passage to America so she could have a fresh start."

"I heard that and that she's a cousin to the Murphys," Ida added.

"I think that's how Doc became familiar with her, "Jennie continued. "He told me she'd stayed with an aunt in New York while she worked there for a couple years. He also said his wife was looking for a housekeeper, so when he went out to Irish Town on a house call, he heard she planned on moving to Clearwater soon and would be looking for a job. He hired her sight unseen!"

"For goodness sake! Sounds like she's a brave woman to travel half way around the world on her own," Maude commented.

"She's come into the store a few times and seems quite friendly. I love listening to her. She has the most melodic voice, but that hair! Have you ever seen anything as beautiful as that thick red hair?"

"Well, she's a beauty, for sure." Maude paused before she added, "And, please forgive me. I didn't mean to imply that all Irish are foolish or anything like that. But you have to admit some of them have a few odd customs. Remember that other girl who was murdered out by Maple Lake? Anyway, that Eunice girl, can't remember her last name, but I remember her father shot her for disobeying him or something . . . and . . ."

"I remember that," Ida interrupted. "So sad. Apparently, he told her she couldn't see a young Protestant boy."

"Yes, that's right," Maude added. "Of course, he was liquored up, which just fueled his anger. A misdirected type of religion if you ask me. The paper quoted him as saying his daughter was better off dead than disgraced by going with a Protestant boy. I know the Irish have their customs, sort of mixed in with their religious beliefs, but that family was left nearly destitute after that father was hauled off to the Wright County jail. And yet, after a collection was taken up all around the county to bury the child, the family spent a lot of it on booze and tobacco for the wake and funeral."

Although she had been sitting quietly for some time listening to Jennie's and Maude's conversation, Ida lifted her shoulders, shook her head, and sighed. "I suppose it isn't our place to judge," Ida began. "The Irish have come here to make a new way of life. Yes, they have different customs, different beliefs, and habits. But like Mother and Father say, we aren't going to change them, so we might as well learn to accept them."

Jennie nodded in agreement.

Ida went on. "Father also says it takes two generations for the family of an immigrant to become totally Americanized. Mother usually frowns at him when he says this since she was born in England. But he always adds, whether it is to appease her or get himself off the hook, she and Grandma and Grandpa are English. Except for the fact they have accents, they blend in with everyone. They have the same religion and the same basic core values as the rest of us."

"Probably because most of us have English heritage," Maude added. "But back to Irish customs. They want everyone to understand them, but it's hard to gain sympathy for a destitute family, no matter who they are, when they throw away good money on such trivial things as smokes and drink. Where in the Bible does it say that it's okay to drink and smoke, especially at funerals?"

Jennie could hear her friend's temperance beliefs coming through loud and clear. "I know what you're saying, Maude," Jennie said, hoping she could keep Maude from sermonizing like Carrie Nation. "But really, except for a couple who cause trouble, we've found the Irish hard working and happy. Mike Larkin, for instance, is such a happy man, always full of cheer and Irish blessings, and . . ."

"Mike Larkin!" Maude blurted. "For heaven's sake, Jennie, some think he's the one who probably murdered that girl in Irish Town. That's what the newspapers suggested, anyway. How could you possibly like him? If I see him walking down one side of the street as he comes from Quinn's liquor joint, I cross to the other side. I don't trust him. Besides, he and that woman weren't even married and yet they were living—"

"Oh, Maude, you aren't serious?" Ida interrupted. "How can you believe Mike had anything to do with the murder? It sounds like something Livia Paisley would say."

As soon as the words slipped out of Ida's mouth, Jennie could see she regretted what she had said. But it was too late. Maude looked back and forth at Jennie and Ida. Her eyes became red.

"I'm sorry, Maude. I never meant to say that about your friend." Ida looked at Jennie before lowering her head.

Maude and Ida had never been real close, and Jennie knew Maude often blurted out her feelings on any subject before she thought it through, but not Ida. Jennie knew she had to reconcile the two before they left her house.

Jennie folded and unfolded her napkin. "I'm sorry. I shouldn't have brought up the conversation. I just wanted to know more about the murder and what others said. I never realized . . ."

"It's okay. Anyway, I'd better be going home before Sherm starts looking for me," Ida conceded, starting to gather her belongings.

Jennie felt even worse.

Maude cleared her voice. "Ida, it's okay. Please don't feel like you have to leave on my account. I know Livia's a know-it-all and a gossip. To tell you the truth, I need to sift through what she says before retelling it. I think it was she who told me Larkin was living out of wedlock with that woman. I suppose one issue shouldn't be confused with the other."

Silently, Jennie blew out a sigh of relief. "No, they shouldn't, but we all make judgments at times, Maude. She stood up. "Can't I get you two more coffee?

"What time is it?" Ida asked. "I need to be going here in a few minutes. But I wouldn't mind a dash before I head out."

"Maude?" Jennie asked.

The oldest of the three looked up at Jennie and nodded. As Jennie stepped over the threshold that led to the kitchen, she knew that somehow the heat of the moment had been doused by forgiveness and understanding. Unfortunately, she still hadn't gotten down to the heart of the subject about Alice Leonard.

As she reached for the coffee pot, she saw the cake. She judged that there would still be enough left for the rest of the family even if she brought her friends small second slices. Her father always said Marietta Phillips's cakes were the balm that calmed rifts at church and united enemies at town council meetings. Maybe, cake could get these two friends of hers talking again.

Chapter 8
Manu calefacta
With a Warm Hand

THE SUN CAST A LONG, triangle of yellow dust through the front door of the drug store. Jennie had cleaned late last week, but horses, wind, and even train engine smoke had quickly blanketed the floors and shelves again. Jennie coughed as she pulled down a white jar labeled FOXGLOVE. With a dry rag, she wiped off as much as she could before removing the cover to see if she needed to write it on the order form that needed to be mailed to Eli Lilly by two o'clock that day.

"The dust is thick around here. Having the doors open during our hot spell created quite a mess," she said from the bottom rung of the ladder.

Stanley didn't answer. Jennie looked over at the prescription counter where her father stood with his head bowed as he concentrated on measuring accurately. She made a mental note to ask her sisters if they wanted to earn a bit of spending money by cleaning up the place.

She continued wiping the canisters, jars, and tins, and then checking their contents.

As soon as her father wasn't so engrossed with his prescriptions, she might broach the subject of Alice Leonard's murder. She hadn't had a moment alone with either of her folks to talk to them about what happened to her in Lynden. Yesterday afternoon, after Ida and Maude had made up and Jennie could get them back to their discussion, they really didn't come to any conclusion because neither of her friends knew any more than she did about the girl's murder.

"Sorry. Trying to read Doc Edmunds prescription." Stanley Phillips walked toward the front window and held a small sheet of paper up toward the light. He pushed his glasses up further on his nose. "I can't read his handwriting."

"Let me take a look and see if I can figure it out." Jennie stepped down from the ladder. "Let's see," Jennie said, staring at the script. "Oh, I know. He's ordering serum."

"Well, of course. Thanks. I should've figured that one. Yet, sometimes his S's look like R's." Stanley walked back to his work table. "He told me the other day he's having a devil of a time dealing with the diphtheria out in the country. Silver Creek and Hasty got hit the hardest, so I think he wants to take a few extra doses with him when he goes tomorrow."

"I know. We had to make up a few extra bottles for Doc Tollington to take with him last week when he went out there. I remember he said, 'for good measure' because he said he didn't know exactly what he'd be dealing with." Back on the ladder, Jennie stood on her toes to reach the jar on the next shelf. "Don't forget, I can help you fill those orders."

"I know you can, Jennie, but it seems like when you and I get started working together, we get interrupted by a customer. Making up the orders for the serum isn't difficult, but the measurements are so exact, I'd hate to make a mistake."

"I know! It's a delicate process." Jennie said as she reached for another jar above her head.

"Be careful there! You want me to lift those jars down for you?"

"No, I'm fine. But you know, if we have time, I'd really like to talk to you and Mother about what happened to me out in Lynden on Saturday."

Before her father answered her, the bell over the front door jingled, and Jennie almost dropped the jar. Startled, she caught it in time but thought for sure she would be turning around to see Doc Edmonds. Instead, before her stood Louisa Lyons, wife to the owner of the mercantile store kitty-corner to the drug store. A small, thin woman, Mrs. Lyons had been married to Robert Lyons, the owner of Lyons's General Store, for a number of years and had children from twenty-one years on down. Not only had the couple lost a three-year-old daughter to small pox a couple years ago, but Louisa also had a miscarriage recently.

"Good morning, Mrs. Lyons. How are you today?" Jennie asked as she set the jar on the counter and placed the rag over the top.

Louisa Lyons seldom had much expression, but today she looked blank and fidgety, almost agitated. Often somewhat timid, she hardly spoke above a whisper. Today, though, she spoke clearly if not too loudly and somewhat shrill. "Yes, Jennie, do you have any of that pastor's remedy? Is it called Nervine or something? Whatever it is, you folks advertised it in the paper last week. It's supposed to calm nerves. I'm beside myself lately."

Jennie and Stanley exchanged knowing glances. Every time they advertised an over-the-counter concoction, they knew Mrs. Lyons would be in to buy it. Last week, she bought Digesto Malt Extract because she was "so tired."

Jennie grabbed a green box of Pastor Koenig's Nervine from behind the counter. "Is this what you're looking for?"

"Oh, that must be it. How much do I owe you?" Louisa Lyons set her black handbag on the counter and opened it. She rifled through its contents.

"Why don't I put that on your husband's account?" Jennie offered as she pulled out the charge log. "I'll add ninety-five cents to your bill."

"Oh, would you be so kind to do that? I don't think I have the correct change anyway," she added as she squeezed the small box into her black bag.

"I could wrap that for you," Jennie called after Mrs. Lyons as she walked out the door.

Stanley walked to the window and watched the woman cut across the street to go back to her store. Jennie joined him at the window, shaking her head.

"Isn't there anything else we can do for her?"

"Just keep a log like you've been doing. Robert doesn't give her much money because she'd buy more. Charging is the best way to keep track of what she's buying. He and Doc Edmunds are keeping an eye on her. It's hard to see her like this, but she has lots of people looking out for her."

"I hate seeing her suffer so. Isn't there something Doc Edmunds can give her? Most of the things she buys are full of alcohol."

"I thought so too, but Doc said he told Robert to dump out some from each new bottle as soon as he sees it and fill it with water or juice."

"She's not stupid. She's bound to figure it out sooner or later."

"In the meantime, it's all we can do for her. That and keep an eye on her."

"I've heard others say they hate going into the store if she's there. I know since the Clearwater Mercantile opened uptown, a lot of them go up there. That can't be good for Mr. Lyons's business."

"I don't think Robert's hurting too much though. Mostly, Louisa stays in the back room unless she's having a good day. Doc said she experienced some of this absent-mindedness a few years ago, and then it cleared up again. If she doesn't get better soon, he could give her an opiate like laudanum—"

"An opiate?" Jennie asked. "Oh, I hope it doesn't come to that again. Opiates are so addictive."

"That's why they're trying to wait out this episode. Doc and Robert are hoping her mind clears on its own. Every time she gets with child, she goes through this. If she hadn't lost the last one a few months ago, she'd have something else besides herself to think about."

Jennie wanted to say it might be better for her if she wouldn't "get with child" all the time, but she decided to keep her mouth shut. She still wasn't ready to have this discussion with her father.

"I hope she gets better before Minnie's wedding this fall," Jennie said. "If not, what will happen? Minnie's still at home to help. With little Charlie so crippled, she needs to help her mother as much as possible."

Jennie pictured Charlie. Only seven years old, the child limped lopsidedly due to his dislocated hip. Late last winter, Gilbert Tollington, who had taken leave from working on his advanced degree at the Minneapolis College of Physicians and Surgeons, filled in for Doc Edmunds while he went to Chicago for a medical conference. Robert and Louisa brought Charlie to him one evening. Once he saw the festering sore, Doc Tollington knew he had to drain some of the pus near the dislocation, hoping the process would relieve some of the boy's pain.

After surgery, the doctor kept a watchful eye on Charlie for nearly a week before he let the family take him home. In fact, he had even hoped that opening up the hip like he had would help the boy walk straight.

Unfortunately, within a few weeks, after Dr. Tollington went back to finish his training, Robert and Louisa brought the boy back into town, this time to see Doc Edwards. Charlie went under the heavy cloud of ether again. Jennie knew that Doc was researching the case, hoping he could find experts in the field of this type of disability that he could recommend to the boy's parents.

"According to Robert," Stanley began to say, interrupting Jennie's thoughts, "Louisa's been wandering off the farm place lately. Their son and daughter, you know, Frank and Minnie, have enough farm work to keep them busy while he's in town handling the store. With all their chores and keeping their eyes on Charlie, they don't have time to be running after her, too."

"Oh, that poor family!" Jennie knew Charlie was a handful, and admittedly too much for his mother to handle.

"We need to count our blessings. Robert told me he brings Louisa into town with him every day to keep an eye on her. He admitted he and Doc talked about sending her up to Fergus Falls, but Robert said he can't do that yet. Apparently, he fears if he puts her in the hospital there, she'll never come out again."

"Fergus Falls? Father, she's not that bad!" Jennie proclaimed. She felt sorry for many women—those who had too many children, hard farm chores, and unending housekeeping duties to tend to. Despite their hardships, most still had their mental faculties. Jennie wished there were something she could do for Louisa Lyons so they wouldn't have to send her to the state hospital.

Jennie couldn't imagine all those years of childbirth ahead of her, like her mother and other women had endured after they were married. She knew of the pain they experienced during the birthing process. In fact, she'd never forget the night her mother gave birth to Ruthie. Her long-suffering mother, a woman who never complained of pain or hard work screamed out in misery for over half the night. So frightful were her mother's screams Stanley had Jennie take the youngest children to his parents, who lived in back of them.

Jennie wasn't sure she was cut out for the pain a woman had to go through to be married. Matter of fact, as she stood there at the counter staring past Lyons's store, Jennie couldn't help but think that she and Pitt's break up was for the best. She knew she loved him and missed him so much, but she didn't have that sacrificial love, a love that made her forget herself for the sake of someone else.

When her father finally answered, "I agree." Jennie, who had been so lost in her own thoughts struggled to recall what they were talking about. It clicked when he continued, "Even though, right now, Louisa can't be much of a helpmate to Robert, she'll probably pull through like she has in the past.

"Speaking of helpmates, your mother's coming down to clean on Wednesday. Stanley wiped down the scales and slid them to the back of the table.

Jennie shook her head in acknowledgement before adding, "I need to get a few things done before Thursday's shindig. It'll be good having Mother down here as well. She doesn't have to be told what to do, and she's helpful on the cash register. I forgot to ask if either of the creameries will be serving ice cream."

"Yep. Crescent Creamery will be there to dish it up at the pie social. As soon as the train rolls in Thursday morning, the band'll lead the parade to the platform for the speeches. Luther Laughton told me former Lieutenant Governor Barto is going to be coming down from St. Cloud tomorrow night. Congressman Towne and our master of ceremonies, John Stevens, will come up from the Cities on Thursday's morning train."

"The village council really made excellent plans for this year's celebration." Jennie added, "From now on, if we don't meet or exceed expectations for these festivities, everyone will be disappointed."

"I'm not sure we'd have gotten Towne without the Stevens's influence. The brothers have some pretty good connections since they're known all over the state." Stanley sat down by the work table, pulled off his glasses, and rubbed his eyes.

"Well, our day is going to be exciting for everyone," Jennie said as she wiped off the last jar, pulled off the cover, and peeked inside before returning it to the shelf behind her. Bending over the counter, she finished tallying her order so she could get it in the mail. "I've heard so many people tell me they're coming, and I know others who used to live here say they wouldn't miss this celebration for the world. The town'll be packed, but it'll be a good time."

"I agree," Stanley said. "And Wednesday and Thursday morning should be quite profitable as well."

"I was thinking about Ruthie. Won't she love the clowns?" Jennie asked, shaking her head and smiling.

"I wish I could see her when they appear. She's at the right age to appreciate all of it this year," Stanley said as he stood up and browsed his medical book collection above the table. "Unfortunately, I'll be near the front of the parade, and they'll be closer to the middle."

"Hello to the Phillipses!" Doc Edmunds announced as the bell over the door chimed. "You two seem to be keeping yourselves busy. I wish I didn't have to ask you to fill those orders for me, but I'd rather be safe than sorry when I head out this morning."

"That's what we're here for! We're glad to help out, Doc," Stanley answered. "Give me a second, and I'll be finished."

"Jennie, how're you today?" Doc Edmunds asked as he leaned into the counter. "I must say, you seem more relaxed than you were the other day."

Jennie chuckled. "You've got that right. That was quite the day. And can you believe how nice the weather turned? Saturday was too hot too soon. Today, it's about sixty and beautiful."

"Yes, yes, it's fine spring weather, all right. It's a good day for a ride, even if I have a hard day of work ahead of me trying to contain some of the diphtheria out in the country."

"Father and I were talking about that. Are you making headway?"

"It's hard to say. I see some hope with a few of the children closer to Hasty."

"By the way, Doc, Louisa Lyons was just in."

Doc Edmunds shook his head, as he walked to the front bay window and stared across the street towards Lyons's store. "What'd she buy this time?"

"Koenig's Nervine," Jennie said, handing him a green-and-beige package.

"She said she was nervous and 'beside herself,'" Stanley offered as he finished labeling the last of Doc's orders.

The doctor read the back of the box Jennie had handed to him. He looked across the street again and then announced, "I'll be right back. I've got to check on her so I don't worry all the way out to Hasty and Silver Creek and back."

The bell chimed as the screen door slammed behind him. Jennie watched as he walked across the street.

Jennie could only imagine what he was saying to Robert, but she was sure the two spoke about Louisa as quietly as possible, especially if she was in earshot.

After a few minutes, Doc walked to the drug store. Jennie could almost feel the large sigh he released before he stepped into the building.

"There she was, sitting in a corner behind a pickle barrel. Her head hung down as though she were asleep. I said, 'Good morning, Louisa.' Her head popped up immediately, but she didn't seem to know who I was. She stared right through me. Robert came out from the backroom where he'd been sweeping.I wanted him to know that she had bought another over the counter, yet I didn't want her to hear what I was saying. I asked her if she had any coffee made. She got up right away and went behind the curtain.

When she was out of sight, I told Robert our suspicions. That is all the time we had to talk because she came back with my coffee."

"I hope Mr. Lyons can dump it before she takes any more. One of these days, Doc, she may catch on. Like I've said before, she isn't stupid."

"When I saw her sitting there, I figured she was sleeping off what she took. I know, when he can, Robert's dumping and diluting them. So far, she isn't on to it, but I agree, she may figure this out soon. On the other hand, while none of the ingredients are helping, I don't think they're hurting her either. She may get more drunk than anything if she takes too much of it."

"So, Doc, I'm sure Father has this written down," Jennie acknowledged as she looked over at Stanley and pulled out a scrap of paper to write on, "but I want to know the medical term."

"Well, the medical term is puerperal mania. Although many women experience a mild state of depression after childbirth, Louisa has experienced a severe case after each birth."

"What will help her?" Jennie asked.

"Could be time or she might have to be institutionalized."

Jennie shook her head before climbing up the ladder to return a jar and finish dusting the top shelf.

"Well, I'm finished here, Doc." Stanley loaded all the bottles into a box and pushed it onto the counter.

"Thanks, I'll check in with you as soon as I get back to town. We'll see what I find when I get out there. I'll be gone for the day. If anyone needs me, tell 'em I'll be back on the late afternoon train."

"Will do," Stanley said.

"Good luck!" Jennie hollered after the doctor as he walked out the door.

The morning went quickly, yet Jennie didn't feel she accomplished much. Although she tried to help her father with some of their drug orders, they kept getting interrupted by customers. Some were killing time before the train came in to look for paint or ribbons. Others needed shaving soap or hair tonic.

After all the morning's hubbub, Jennie admitted to her father she couldn't wait for all the fuss and bother to come to an end so they could get back to their real jobs.

Jennie had no sooner asked her father, "Do you want to try to escape for lunch while I hold down the place?" when she noticed her mother walking across the street. With one hand she carried a wicker basket and with the other, she held onto Ruthie. "Oh, leave it to Mother to solve it for us so we don't have to worry about who was going home to eat first."

"Papa, Papa, lunch," the little girl hollered as she stumbled up the steps and into the drug store. After tripping a little, she steadied herself and looked around for her father who came out from behind the counter.

"Ruthie, what're you and Momma doing down here?" he asked as he scooped up the child and set her on the counter.

"Momma bringing you an' Jennie picnic."

Both Jennie and Marietta Phillips giggled. Soon the four of them stood around the counter while Marietta opened up the basket and put out the sandwiches, cake, and lemonade.

"Should we take our picnic and sit out on the stoop, Ruthie? Momma and Papa can sit on the chairs in here and eat. I'll carry your sandwich and lemonade, okay?"

The little girl tottered behind her older sister. Soon they were sitting on the front step eating ham sandwiches made from Marietta Phillips's wonderfully light white bread. Jennie pointed to the carts and wagons that drove up and down the street.

"That's Mr. Collins, Ruthie," Jennie said as she waved to the elderly man who pulled up to the sidewalk. As he stepped down to tie the team to the post, she added, "He owns the blacksmith shop down the street."

The little girl who was eating the center out of her sandwich stood up, put her hand on her sister's shoulder for balance, and looked down the street. Jennie looked north toward uptown and recognized Frank Hoffman's wagon coming toward them with a load of milk cans for the Crescent Creamery.

"Remember Mr. Hoffman, Ruthie? He gave you that cinnamon stick a couple days ago when you and I went to the creamery? Here he comes from up the street. Oh, look! You remember how he delivers milk to us? See the milk cans he has in the back of his wagon?"

Ruthie looked in the direction Jennie pointed. Soon two men rounded the corner in a horse-drawn wagon. They seemed to be coming from the direction of the depot. They pulled over to the side of Hotel Scott.

Jennie didn't recognize the strangers, who looked like they had not been around civilized society for quite a while. Both wore scraggily beards and dirty brown hats. The driver looked up and down Main Street before he spit on the hotel sidewalk.

Coarse! The men were coarse, Jennie thought. The steamboats on the Mississippi and the trains that went north to St. Cloud and south to Minneapolis and St. Paul brought all kinds of people, some genteel, some riffraff.

Before long, her mother opened the screen door behind them. "Are you ready to go home, Ruthie?"

By now the little girl's sandwich had tiny half-circle bites out of the middle and lay on the step. She had lost interest in eating and sat on her haunches focusing on the ants in the cracks in the sidewalk. Looking up at her mother and pointing, she said, "Bugs, Momma, bugs!"

Both Jennie and Marietta smiled. Marietta answered, "Oh, yes, they are sure working, aren't they?" She then turned her attention to her older daughter. "Jennie, I told your father I'd come down Wednesday afternoon and help around the store so you can have a break to get whatever you need done for our festivities."

"Thanks, Ma. I can't seem to keep up with the cleaning with the doors and windows open all the time. I know Maude and I thought we'd start putting out decorations Wednesday night. We could use help. I was telling Pa I can't wait until all this is over so I can focus on my job more."

"I know, dear. But we need to be grateful to the Lord for every day we're healthy. We don't want to bother today with tomorrow's worries."

"Yes, Ma, I know. But I'm glad you'll help out. What time's the pie social? Father said Crescent Creamery is dishing up ice cream."

"We're starting the social after the noon picnickers get back from Cedar Point. We ordered twenty gallons."

"Twenty gallons of ice cream? My! Do you think we'll have that many people in town?"

"By what I've heard, we'll be needing more before the afternoon is over, but if we don't use what we've ordered, we may have to have a big party afterward." Marietta laughed as she gathered Jennie's glass and tucked it under the towels in the basket.

Jennie stood up and stretched. "I'd better get back in and get something done. Thanks for bringing us lunch, Ma."

"We needed an outing. Now I should head home and start baking pies. I'm bringing five rhubarb. And don't worry. I'll make a couple extra for supper."

Just as Jennie waved at her little sister and mother as they headed home, a man on horseback galloped down the middle of the street. Jennie thought he looked familiar but didn't know his name. He pulled on his reins to steady his horse beside the strangers who had moved up the block closer to park their wagon near Luther Laughton's Meat Market. Jennie noticed the man pointing to Lyons's store and then back at the drug store. Odd, she thought as she stepped inside the door, but she didn't have time to think about anything. She had to get back to work.

Chapter 9
Partitis vicibus (Part. Vic)
In Divided Doses

TUESDAY STARTED OUT about the same as Monday at the Phillips's Drug Store, but it didn't take long for Main Street and the businesses that lined it to come alive with activity.

Shortly after eight, when Jennie and her father opened up, Doc Edmunds rounded the corner of the building.

Both Jennie and her father returned his "Morning," but then Jennie caught a good glimpse of him. If she hadn't known better, she would have thought he had been on an all-night binge because of his drooping, blood-shot eyes.

"You look tired today, Doc," Jennie declared. "How'd everything go in Silver Creek and Hasty?"

"I'm dog tired, Jennie. I didn't get home 'til past midnight," he groaned as he rolled his eyes. "I hate to be too optimistic, but I think I'm seeing progress out there except for the Locke boy. I can't get him to snap to. You know, I saw the tike about six months ago for tonsillitis. He never got over that bout—now diphtheria. I told the family I'd be back out sometime today."

"Too bad you have to head out there again," Jennie said.

"Well," he said as he yawned and reached into his chest pocket, "I've also a few more orders for you to fill. I made a list." Finding nothing, he dug deeper, patting both pants pockets. Soon he scratched the back of his head in bewilderment and admitted, "I must have left the list at home."

"That's okay, Doc. Someone can come up to your house to pick it up," Jennie offered.

"I was so tired when I got up this morning, I must have left it in my bag," he admitted as he continued to fumble around in his pockets.

"I know I need some spirits of juniper for sure. I don't know what else I can do for Mrs. Frank out in Lynden. Her gout is acting up again. I wrapped her right foot and told her to keep off it, but I know she won't, and truth be told, she probably can't because of all the farm work she still has to do. You'd think a woman of seventy could relax. I keep telling her she needs to lose some weight and quit eating so much sausage and sauerkraut, or at least not eat it at every meal. She just waves her hand at me and says, 'Ach!'"

Jennie smiled, mostly because of Doc's disheveled look. No matter how tired he was, he always thought of his patients first.

"Maybe the juniper will give her some relief. Ah, let's see. What else did I need? I'm so tired, I can't even think straight. I need more serum, but I know there is something else . . ."

"Why don't you just come back later, Doc? We can get the serum made up. How much do you need this time?"

"I think four bottles ought to do it. I think you're right, Jennie. I'm no good to anyone in this condition. I'm heading home to get some sleep."

As Dr. Edmunds turned to leave, he stopped and stared out the door. "Have you heard anything from her since yesterday?"

At first, Jennie couldn't follow the doctor's nod, which aimed across the street toward Lyons's.

"Louisa? No, we haven't seen her since she came in yesterday. Actually, we don't see much of her until after the paper comes out on Saturdays. The ads seem to bring her over in search of a miracle on Mondays."

"Let me know if you see anything out of the ordinary. Say, when I find my list, I'll send my housekeeper, Claire, down with it."

As busy as she had been, Jennie had forgotten she wanted to talk to Claire O'Casey. Maude had suggested that she do this since the doctor's housekeeper had Irish ties to friends and relatives in Lynden Township. Maybe today, Jennie could set up a time to visit with her.

Jennie waited on a few, early morning customers. Elizabeth Collins, the blacksmith's wife, came in and introduced her niece, Susanna Crosby, who she said had arrived the day before from Chicago.

Feeling as though she were a good judge of character, Jennie summed up the woman pretty fast. About Jennie's age, Susanna, who was a petite and pretty blonde haired-woman, had a distant manner about her. Looking as though she just stepped out from a page in *Harper's Bazaar*, she wore a fashionable white and black striped suit and a wide, black hat with pink plumes. Susanna smiled pleasantly after the introduction, but as Maude often said about snobs, the woman "had her nose up in the air."

Jennie welcomed her to Clearwater, "It's nice to meet you, Miss Crosby. I enjoyed Chicago when I was there for the World's Fair two summers ago."

Mrs. Collins, with a smile on her face and a ring of pride in her voice, stated, "You know, Jennie, Susanna was born in Springfield, Vermont, but she just graduated from Columbia School of Oratory."

"Really? How wonderful!" Jennie answered, realizing her voice sounded artificially excited. "Oh, that's your hometown, too, Mrs. Collins," Jennie said, remembering her mother and Mrs. Collins discussing the hometowns they left behind to come west.

"How do you like Minnesota, Miss Crosby?"

"Your state seems to be nice. Of course, the purpose for my trip is to visit my favorite aunt before going home to Vermont, but I have enjoyed seeing a bit of Minneapolis so far and hope I can return to do some shopping."

Jennie noticed how perfectly Susanna Crosby spoke slowly, enunciating every syllable, using perfect grammar without the use of contractions. In addition, she had developed a perfect tone—no hint of an Easterner's slurring of vowels or silencing the R or placing it where it wasn't supposed to be. Elocution, of course, was Miss Crosby's trade, and she had apparently learned it well in Chicago. Even though Jennie was impressed, and hated to hear the English language slaughtered around the village like she often did, she had to admit to herself, she appreciated the language of her fellow villagers, which was easier on her ears.

"That sounds exciting, Miss Crosby. I am sure you will find many places to shop in downtown Minneapolis," Jennie tried to speak as properly as her customer. "Donaldson's is my favorite. Of course, Schuneman's in St. Paul is wonderful, too." Jennie suggested. "I hope you enjoy your stay here in our village as well. We are small, but this week we will be busy." Noticing how disinterested Susanna Crosby was in her opinions, Jennie shifted her attention to Mrs. Collins. "Is there something I can help you with, Mrs. Collins?"

"Goodness, Jennie, I nearly forgot why I came. I need facial cream. I want your special blend."

Jennie had developed a formula that many women in the area loved because of its smoothness and sweet smell. As she grabbed a white porcelain jar, she realized she had only two left. She made a mental note to stir up some more.

"That'll be seventy-five cents, unless there was something else you needed."

Mrs. Collins reached into her blue-and-silver brocade handbag. "I know I have some change in the bottom somewhere."

Jennie patiently waited, then said, "I hadn't realized I was getting warm until I felt that breeze come through the door. Wasn't Saturday just awful?"

"It sure was," Mrs. Collins answered. "Oh, here it is. Anyway, yes, the heat—the humidity—and all after a short ice storm the week before! Strange weather, strange weather!"

"I'm sure Mother told me you had family back East close to her hometown in Maine. I read that many states—New York, Massachusetts, Maine, Vermont, and New Hampshire—are experiencing the beginning of their third year of record heat and drought."

"My sister, Susanna's mother," Mrs. Collins added as she turned half way around to look at her niece to try to pull her into the conversation, "has written me often how bad it is out there. I heard in New York City, people have dropped dead on the street because of the heat."

"I read that as well. The paper said the temperature in one tenement reached one-hundred twenty-five degrees. Imagine that!"

Jennie watched Susanna strolling around the store. Stopping at the racks of hand-painted scenic Mississippi River postcards, she daintily fingered through them. Jennie was mortified when she realized Susanna had looked down and was trying to rub loose the soil on her once clean white gloves. *Mother can't get here soon enough to help clean the place!*

Before nine, Jenny Belle Barrett and her daughter Mae came in. The senior, known to most in Clearwater as Bea, seemed a bit dolled up for an ordinary shopping trip around their humble village. Dressed in a royal-blue skirt with double-breasted black buttons down the front and a light-blue blouse tucked in at the waist, Bea prettied up the store.

"You look like spring, Bea, bright and fresh."

"Why, thank you."

"And I love your hat. Is it new?" Jennie commented, admiring the simple style of the blue bow and small delicate yellow flowers atop the wider brimmed-white straw hat.

"I bought it at Ida Friend's Millinery. Have you been down there lately?" Jennie recalled that Ida Friend was thinking of going out of business, and Maude had told her she wanted to either buy it or get set up in her own. "She has so many fashionable pre-made hats and custom-designs as well. I'm not into having birds and their nests perched on my head. I don't mind the feathers for some of my winter outings, but I like simpler styles. I saw this one down at Ida's a couple weeks ago, but it had way too many doo-dads on it so I told her I'd buy it if she'd clean it up a bit."

"It's sure smart looking, Bea. I don't want all that nonsense on my head either. Why a woman would want to wear wildlife or a bowl of fruit on her head beats me."

A bit older than Jennie, maybe in her early thirties, Bea already had had two children, nine-year-old Mae and seven-year-old Harry. Jennie knew Bea had been born in Detroit, Michigan, and had relatives all over the area, from Minneapolis to South Haven to St. Cloud. She loved to entertain so it wasn't unusual for her to have a house full of guests.

Jennie looked over at Bea's daughter, who focused on the many jars of root beer barrels, lemon drops, and red and white peppermint sticks lining the front sill. Mae, like her mother, seemed a bit done up for Clearwater. The young girl's blond ringlets were tied up in small, white bows. She wore a blue-and-white striped pleated dress with ruffled collar and muffin-leg sleeves.

Jennie remembered that, when she was younger and went uptown to do some shopping, she begged to wear her church clothes. Her mother said no. She had a system she and her daughters followed. They wore their best dresses, skirts, blouses, and shoes for church. Those clothes and footwear that were in fairly good shape—with no stains or tears—were worn to school. When a daughter outgrew an outfit, she passed it down to the next sister. If it was still wearable but looked a bit tattered, she could still wear it around the house while doing her chores. When an article had "seen better days," it was thrown in the rag heap to be made into rugs because her mother's moto was: "Waste not. Want not."

Wondering if the girl had ever wiped supper dishes, Jennie asked, "How are you today, Mae?"

"Good. My cousins are coming up from Silver Creek on the train this afternoon. Papa gave me a dollar so I could buy them something."

Bea had married Edgar Barrett, a successful road grader and Lynden farmer, but they didn't live out on the farm. Bea, not raised in the country, insisted on a house in town so "I can be close to civilization."

A lot of gossipy women said it was a good thing Edgar was an independent and ambitious young man who kept busy with road construction. He could well afford to hire out some of the farm work and even have an older couple living in the house to lighten his wife's load. Others laughed when someone said that Bea didn't know the difference between a broom handle and a butter churn plunger. Even though Jennie didn't know Bea well, she felt she was pleasant and personable, even though she was a bit out of place in their slow-moving village.

Edgar kept busy year-round with either road grading or snow removal all over Wright and Stearns counties. With Clearwater as his hub, he cleared the pathways as far north as St. Augusta, back down to Lynden Township, through Irish Town, skirted North Clearwater Lake and then crossed over to the Wright County side, heading back to Clearwater. In fact, if people needed roads cleared, all they had to do was ask Edgar Barrett. He and his team would get the work done.

Old and young alike knew and liked the man. Word got around that if he came upon youngsters struggling through the heaps of snow to or from school, he would give them a hitch. Oftentimes in the spring and summer, he handed out penny candy to anyone he saw walking on the roads or working in the fields. Jennie remembered something about the Stearns County sheriff interviewing Edgar after the Leonard murder, hoping he had seen something suspicious since he had been out that way just the day before the flag raising.

Two weeks before, Editor Evans reported in the *Clearwater News*, "Edgar Barrett has begun his spring rounds, cleaning, clearing, and smoothing out roads. From sun up to sun down, our friendly road grader is on the job." For some reason, even those who spoke judgmentally about people working on Sundays turned their heads when it came to Edgar Barrett.

Jennie remembered the other evening at the supper table her father had made the comment that Edgar had gotten the contract to clean up the streets again because he was trustworthy, and his prices were reasonable.

"He must be doing okay," Stanley said after he swallowed a sip of coffee, "because he just bought another team of Percherons up in St. Cloud."

Jennie remembered how despite a few bumps, the ride was smooth when she and Jamie drove by Warner Lake, past Acacia Cemetery, and on into town.

"Let's see, Mae. A dollar will buy a lot," Jennie answered, wondering how many children in town were able to spend hard-earned cash on mere trivialities. "Do you have some ideas about what you'd like to purchase?"

"I'm not sure. Maybe I could get them some candy and some postcards?"

"Edgar's cousin and family are coming for part of the week," Bea said as she browsed the glass display cases while Mae continued to search for something special for her cousins. "They didn't want to miss out on the celebrations. Do you know the Ridleys, Alvah and Mary? Mary was a Day."

"Effie was a bit older than I, but Billie and I were the same age and graduated from Monticello together. Are they all going to be around? I'd like to see them."

"The younger ones are coming, but I don't think the older ones are. Effie's twins keep her busy. They're three now and into everything. I know Bill's studies keep him busy. You know, he's going to medical school in Minneapolis?"

"Your house will be jumping," Jennie said.

"I told Edgar, if he thinks I'm going to feed his family for nearly a week, he needs to butcher a cow and a hog," she added with a chuckle. "Why some of his cousins chose to have so many children beats me, but as long as I don't have to be responsible for them on a daily basis, I can handle the hubbub for a while."

Jennie joined in Bea Barrett's joviality but wondered what woman ever had that much control over how many children she had. She also wondered how much she cooked since she had a housekeeper.

Just then Maude walked in.

"Morning everyone!" she said, nodding at Stanley, Jennie, and Bea. She noticed Mae admiring the candy counter.

"Hello, Mae. Are you trying to satisfy a sweet tooth?"

"Oh, no, Miss Porter," Mae answered as she turned around to see who had walked through the doors. "I'm looking for some treats for my cousins. They're coming up on the one o'clock train."

"So with your company coming are you still able to come to our youth group tonight? I made cupcakes and lemonade."

"I don't think so, Maude," Bea answered for Mae. "She needs to be a proper hostess and keep our company entertained."

Jennie, who had been listening to the conversation, suddenly realized that Bea was looking up at the blue-and-white jar labeled, "Talcum Powder." She must have come for something besides buying treats for the relatives.

"May I help you find something, Bea?"

"The weather has turned so warm. I thought I'd buy some fresh talc."

"I don't mean to interrupt again," Maude cut in, "but Jennie, part of the reason I came here was to see if we are still on for tomorrow evening to set up signs and decorations."

"Oh, sure, Maude, but Carl's taking care of the signs so we don't have to worry about them. How about we meet after supper tomorrow night and take care of the rest? Should we say about seven here at the store?"

"Sounds good." Maude patted Bea's shoulder as she walked out the door.

"Well, let's see now, Bea. We were talking about talc. I can bag some of our bulk, or I can show you some pretty smelling bath sets I just received," she suggested as she reached under the counter for her sample bottle. "This lilac bath water comes with powder."

Jennie pulled off the copper-looking topper from the bronze bottle. She took the corner of a handkerchief, covered the top of the bottle, and tipped it over fast.

"Just push up your sleeve a bit, and I'll wipe this on your wrist." Jennie suggested.

Bea followed her suggestion, and Jennie dabbed the handkerchief on her customer's wrist.

"How pretty!" Bea exclaimed as she sniffed her wrist. "It's very delicate."

Jennie reached for another bottle from below the counter. "And this is called Lily of the Valley. It's also sold with a matching powder." She tipped the bottle onto another corner of the handkerchief.

"I'll dab this on your other wrist so you can compare the two."

Jennie realized Mae seemed to have forgotten the candy and had come closer to the counter to watch her mother.

"Would you like to smell this, Mae?" Jennie gave the handkerchief to the little girl. "Sniff both sides now. Maybe you can help your mother make up her mind."

Both mother and daughter breathed in deeply.

"Oh, Mae, isn't this lovely? And you say both of these come with dusting powder of the same scent? I can imagine it's expensive."

Jennie pulled up a green-and-white striped box and looked on the bottom for the price. "The set of Lily of the Valley is a dollar and a quarter, and let's see, Maria's Lilacs set is ninety-five cents. Right now, I can't sell the talcum powder separately. A sachet bag of the bulk is a quarter but doesn't smell as wonderful as this," she added, knowing that for the Barretts, money wasn't much of a problem.

"You know, I'd like to smell pretty this week. I just can't decide which I like better. What do you think, Mae?"

"Oh, Momma," Mae said as she inhaled the corners of the hanky again. "I really like the lilac. It smells just like Porters' bushes. Let's buy those. Do you think I could wear some too?"

"I think you can have a bit of the talc, Mae, but you are a bit young for toilette water. Jennie, I'll buy Maria's Lilacs," she said as she started counting out her change.

After Bea and Mae left, Jennie realized she had gotten little accomplished except to wait on customers. She yearned to get busy mixing up the medicines Doc Edmunds ordered.

"Father, what can I do to help you?"

"Right, right," Stanley acknowledged as he carefully spooned a tiny pile of white powder onto one end of the brass scale. His glasses had slipped to the end of his nose again, his attention devoted to the task of measuring and weighing.

He took a small, razor-like scraper, and pushed some of the powder back into the clear bottle.

About ten o'clock, Danny Higgins and his dray pulled up. Jennie watched as he jumped down and lifted a huge pine crate from the back of the wagon. She ran and opened the door for him.

Danny, one of the draymen who worked as a regular day laborer for Great Northern Railroad, was a son of another Lynden family. He was a medium-height and medium-weight man of Irish descent, maybe twenty-five years old. Jennie thought she remembered something about him and a romance with Claire O'Casey.

"Morning, Danny," Jennie welcomed as she stepped aside so he could heft his cargo into the building.

"Morning to you, too, Jennie, Mr. Phillips. You've quite a few supplies here off the morning train. Where da'ya want me to put 'em all?"

"Why don't you set this one over on the floor by that counter?" she instructed, pointing toward the south side of the interior of building.

"Okay, I've a couple more crates just like this. Should I put 'em there as well?"

"That's fine. I'll get the door again," Jennie volunteered as she walked behind him.

As she stood on the outside step, she looked up and down Main Street. She recognized John Kaufman riding up from the south. She remembered reading in the *Clearwater News* he had recently been appointed commander of the Collins' Post of the GAR, the Grand Army of the Republic, an organization made up of those who fought in the Civil War on the Union side.

After Danny had unloaded all the crates, he pulled out his leather logbook for Jennie to sign. As he stuffed the book in his back pocket, he cleared his throat and looked back at Stanley, who was working quietly behind the counter. "I heard a bit a news over by the depot dock this mornin', Mr. Phillips. George Newell said he got a telegram this mornin' from the Elk River sheriff."

This information caught Stanley Phillips's attention. He laid down his pencil and looked up over his glasses.

"'Parently, there've been a couple a break-ins over there. Clear Lake's seen some trouble too. I guess the meat market's back door got jimmied open last weekend.

They ain't caught no one yet, but George Newell figured he oughta let us know so we can be on the lookout in case someone sees something outta order."

"Good grief!" Jennie answered. "How does Mr. Newell expect anyone to know 'out of order' with all the hubbub going on around here this week? I hope, since he's the agent for the Great Northern, he informs others about this, like the Wright County sheriff or other authorities."

"I'm sure he's doing that, Jennie. George is on the ball," Stanley said. "Danny, they know who's responsible? More than one guy, a gang maybe?"

"Newell didn't say. And I don't think he knows much else. He just told me I need to keep a sharp look out for suspicious characters and tell others to do the same. Well, I gotta keep moving. I have a whole load here for Leme and Wolff's Mercantile."

After Danny left, Jennie took a small claw hammer, grabbed hold of the first nail in the crate, and pulled. In a few minutes, she had yanked open the first box. She removed the top layer of straw packing, found the order form, and read McDonalds's Drug Company."

"I can't believe it. This has to be the fastest order we've ever received. I think all these boxes must have come from McDonalds. Aren't they located out in Pennsylvania? How'd we get all these supplies in less than two weeks?"

Stanley looked up from his work and then out the window toward the railroad tracks. "We can thank Jim Hill for that! Having the Great Northern railroad come to Clearwater on a regular basis sure helps to speed things up. To give McDonalds credit, I think the moment they get an order, they fill it."

Jennie filled her arms with bags, boxes, and tin cans. As she carried the stock to the backroom, she thought about her latest trip to Minneapolis aboard Hill's Great Northern. She had no idea how fast the massive steel machine ran, but she felt as though she had just snuggled down in her seat when the whistle blew the train's arrival at the depot near Minnehaha Falls.

Before she had everything shelved in the storeroom, Jennie heard the bell over the door signaling yet another customer. She sighed. As she stepped back into the store, she was happy to see her brother Carl.

"Morning, Jennie. I just told Pa I saw a few of the Civil War vets marching in the vacant lot over by the depot. They must be going to start the parade from there," Carl announced.

Happy to see him, she looked at her father and asked, "I thought the parade was starting after the master of ceremonies and Congressman Towne finished speaking, and then they'd lead everyone out to the cemetery."

"Not sure." Stanley answered. "Maybe Kaufman and D.D. Storms decided to give everyone more of a show this time."

D.D. Storms was a successful farmer and well-known teacher from Lynden Township. He was also fun to listen to, whether he was standing at their counter telling stories about his early youth in New York or about the skirmishes he was involved in during the Civil War.

Jennie knew he had received a good education, had an extensive knowledge on many subjects, and intelligent opinions about almost everything. Because he supported new agricultural ideas, he had made a name for himself in the surrounding communities. He helped many beginning farmers by keeping them up to date on what to plant and when.

"What are you up to this morning?" Jennie asked Carl. "I thought you told me last week you were working out at the Rice farm."

"Actually, Rices got home from their funeral in Wisconsin earlier than expected. I have to help with the early morning chores tomorrow and Thursday. But I have the rest of the week to help you with getting these signs made up." Carl unrolled a long sheet of white paper. "You knew Luther Laughton donated some of his white butcher paper, didn't you?"

"Yes, and that was generous of him." She was even surprised when Mr. Coleman, the new owner of the lumberyard who hadn't made many friends in the community because he had raised the price of wood, said they could take anything they wanted from the scrap heap to mount their signs.

"Give me your opinion of what I've done so far." He held up the sign that read, "Festivities" and an arrow pointing to the left showed off Carl's neat penmanship.

"Nice job!" Jennie unfolded the paper and stretched it out on the counter. "Where's this one going?"

"Right over there on the corner of Main and Maple," Carl declared, pointing across the street. "Bob Lyons said we could pound it into the ground by his store so visitors see it if they come from the south or west. The arrow will aim north to where the opening ceremonies will be taking place. We have enough paper for all we planned, Jennie, and even some left over to pound on the back of the hotel or hang out a couple of the top windows for those to see who step off the train. It'll be over four feet long. It's going to say, "WELCOME TO CLEARWATER'S 1895 DECORATION DAY CELEBRATION," if that's okay?"

"Of course. Sounds like you have it all planned out."

Carl told Jennie about one sign that would read, "PIE AND ICE CREAM SOCIAL." He would hammer that on the oak tree in front of the Methodist church. Another would read, "FREE LEMONADE" and would be nailed to the booth that the Congregational church had planned on building.

After Carl left, Jennie tried to get her mind back on business, but activity on the street became busier and noisier. She walked to the window and looked out.

"What in the world?" Jennie asked out loud. "It looks like the Civil War vets are marching down Maple and heading this way. I wonder why they aren't up by the Whiting building where all the activity is supposed to be."

Some of the aging vets were so deaf Kaufmann had to shout, "Attention!" so everyone could hear. Then, in step, the soldiers of the Civil War, became a choir, shouting back, "Hut, two, three, four; hut, two, three, four."

"Why Kaufmann chose to practice here on Main Street, beats me!" Stanley looked up from the counter where he was writing in his ledger. Jennie could tell the racket was distracting him.

Jennie recognized many of the men. One of the early movers and shakers of Clearwater, William Webster, tried to march, but at times, he hopped and limped off beat. The elderly farmer had painful bouts of rheumatism. As she looked at the man with his long, white beard, she wondered if the Murfreesboro hero's hip was bothering him today. If it was, the pain wasn't stopping him.

Jennie also recognized George Warner, Curt Shattuck, and Warner Smith as they kept in step with Kaufman's commands. Before she closed the door, she saw Mike Larkin. Just a momentary glance at Larkin brought back the memories of her experience out by Dorseys' near the Tamarack Swamp. Could he have murdered the Leonard girl? She had a hard time believing it.

Nor did she have time to think about it. Twenty-five-year-old Donald John Wolff, most people except his family referred to him simply as Donald, the new village constable, sauntered in to tell Stanley he thought now was the time to get in some band practice. Jennie thought her normally composed father was going to lambaste Wolff.

"It's fine we're all excited around here about Thursday's event," Stanley said through clenched teeth, "but some of us have to work. If you have all the time in the world to practice now, you have the time to organize the band members for practice tonight when most of us are finished working."

"But everyone knows we gotta look sharp, Mr. Phillips. We gotta impress those big wigs from Minneapolis and around the state. We can't let them think we're a rinky-dink outfit."

"That's fine, Donald," Stanley replied more calmly. "But I'm trying to run a business here. I don't have time right now to be practicing. If you can rally the band to meet tonight, say around seven, I'll be there."

To Jennie's trained ears, she could feel her father's patience being stretched. Normally, Stanley Phillips was a calm man and held no ill feeling toward anyone.

She knew her father was sympathetic toward Donald, who had lost his father and had been raised by his doting mother and sisters. Yet, she knew he also got on her father's nerves. He was a couple years older than Jennie, cocky and, in her opinion, not as intelligent as others thought him to be. Seeing beyond the young man's good looks, she had no clue what Lucy Smith, his fiancée, saw in him.

Jennie wondered if her father knew Donald went after anything in skirts. In fact, she could almost hear Maude's wisecrack, "Donald likes his women, and like rhubarb, the younger the better!"

Truth be told, the men in town liked him because he was one of them. He fished with the Shaw boys, often coming back with twenty- or thirty-pound fish tales that Editor Evans wrote about in the Clearwater paper. He became the talk of the town when he and the Shattuck boys went to Montana and came back with a train load of moose, elk, and deer.

Although he had many of the men in his hip pocket, Jennie thought he was way too young to be elected village constable and spent too much time down at Quinn's Saloon. Nevertheless, for now, neither she nor any other woman had the right to vote their say-so.

As the young village constable replaced his wide-brimmed hat, Donald Wolff bowed slightly at the waist, an act Jennie construed as restrained and condescending, and replied, "Well, of course, sir. I'll get the word out. Tonight, then, about seven?"

As Donald stepped backwards toward the door, he nearly knocked over Claire O'Casey. Jennie read the looks they passed each other, but the interpretation was left to her imagination.

Chapter 10

Directione propriâ (DP)

With a Proper Direction

CLAIRE'S EYES NARROWED, dark and threatening as Donald backed out the door, hopped on his horse and galloped away. If Jennie hadn't seen their confrontation, she wouldn't have believed it. Stanley, who also witnessed the scene, looked at his daughter with a quizzical expression before shrugging his shoulders and lowering his head to return to his task.

Jennie had been waiting to see Claire again, hoping she could learn more about the Leonard murder out in Irish Town. As Claire stared down at the display case, she seemed to be searching for something, and Jennie knew this wasn't the time to get to know her either. Jennie looked at the woman, admiring her beautiful red hair. Even though she had much of it covered with a green hat while the rest was pulled into a bun, a few wisps had strayed from behind her ears. On the collar of her gray plaid dress, she wore a round gold pendant with a tree in the center and green emeralds outlining the branches.

"Miss O'Casey? May I help you?"

For a moment, Jennie wasn't sure the woman had heard her, but then, as if awakening from a dream, Claire raised her head and blinked her eyes. Her near flawless white skin showed blotches of red on her cheeks. Jennie didn't know how to respond to the loud quiet when she realized Claire had been trying to overcome an uncomfortable, maybe even embarrassing, moment.

"Please, call me Claire," she said in her melodious Irish voice.

Jennie noticed how her eyes matched the stones in her pin—clear, green, and stunning. "Were you looking for anything special?"

"Oh, I don't think so. I was just admiring your pretty combs."

"Any of them would look wonderful in your hair. Would you like to try one? I have a mirror here," Jennie offered.

"Thank you, but not now." Claire looked down, smoothed out her skirt, rearranged her hat, and started to leave.

As she pulled open the door, the bell tinkled above. Jennie thought she heard Claire say something like, "Ah! Gorney Mac!"

She turned back. "Oh, you must think me very rude. I'm thick as a brick today, I am. The good doctor asked me to deliver this note to you or your father." Claire opened her black bag and pulled out a folded paper. She handed it to Jennie. "He said he'll be down later to pick up what he needs before he heads out of town."

Taking the note, Jennie unfolded it before laying it down on the counter. "Tell Doc it'll be ready for him whenever he comes to pick it up."

"Thank you, Miss Phillips."

"Please, call me Jennie."

"Jennie, then. Thank you again. I don't mean to be rude again, but I need to rush to pick up some cream for the doctor and the missus' coffee before I finish preparing the noon meal."

With that, Jennie watched the beautiful redhead step out the door. She regretted she hadn't had the opportunity to talk with her about her Lynden associations. Yet, she rationalized the time wasn't right, especially after Claire's and Donald's obvious embarrassing encounter. The store, with her father overhearing everything, probably wasn't a good place to discuss such matters anyway.

"Jennie. Do you have a moment? I'd like to show you how to fill these scripts."

Jennie walked over to her father, looking intently over his shoulder. "First, you're well aware that your hands have to be clean. I wash mine with soap and rinse with the hottest water I can stand. I dip a clean rag in camphor, alcohol, or bi-chloride solution, and wipe them with that as well. Only then do I touch a sterile vial."

Watching her father delicately and steadily pour the cloudy yellow serum into a small, clear bottle, Jennie thought about Doc Edmunds, who was first in the area, maybe even the state, her father had said, to use this experimental treatment for diphtheria. She knew that great strides had been made in developing this antitoxin from horses, but she also knew many experts, druggists, scientists, and doctors disagreed on its efficacy. In fact, many experts had discouraged its use since it was still in the experimental stage.

Their village doctor, who worked hard to keep up in the medical field, had gotten his hands on a supply earlier that spring. Jennie knew children and adults died every year from the dreaded disease that attacked both the throat and nasal passages. This spring Doc Edmunds had heard of cases developing further south in the state. He decided it was only a matter of time before it reached his patients.

As soon as the first case was diagnosed, he decided to see if the serum would help. Doc asserted, "One success story is better than none!" She was proud that Clearwater's village doctor was willing to give the new treatment a try.

Before Stanley had finished his demonstration, the bell over the door interrupted them. It was Doc Edmunds. Stanley finished filling up the prescriptions for him, took off his apron, and hung it up.

"Everything's ready for you, Doc. I think I'll go home, Jennie, to eat some dinner. I'll be back soon."

"Thanks, Stanley. I'll try to check in with you before you close. Don't wait for me though. I don't know what I'll find out in Silver Creek today. Gilbert is home this week so if anyone has an urgent need, send them up to him. I wish I could stand here and chat, but I want to get home before nightfall."

Doc Edmunds and her father walked out together. She thought the doctor looked more refreshed. As her father crossed the street, Doc hopped on Rusty, a beautiful horse with a shiny black tail, and galloped south on Main Street. Jennie knew that driving a buggy would take too long, even if it provided more comfort. Since it was late, he needed to make miles today, and the morning train had already come and gone.

The streets quieted down over the dinner hour. Alone with her thoughts, Jennie began to hum and sing a song she had been teaching herself to play on the piano, "Oh, promise me that someday you and I, will take our love together to some sky."

With a damp rag in one hand, Jennie half-heartedly swiped the glass counters. She remembered two falls ago when both she and Pitt heard Sarah Whiting sing the lovely tune at Frank Bentley and Alice Stewart's wedding in the Methodist church. On the way home, Pitt squeezed her fingers and repeated some of the words, "Oh, promise me that you will take my hand, the most unworthy in this lonely land." Whether it was the combination of the hypnotic scent of the white and pink peonies and the beautiful words, Jennie was thrilled to be wanted by such a respected and up-and-coming man.

Pitt had pulled over to the side of the road and grabbed Jennie close to him. He kissed her with such intensity, she felt weak afterwards.

"Marry me, Jennie," he'd pleaded. "We're so good together."

Jennie was a bit taken back when he added, "I want to take care of you—to protect you." She wasn't quite sure why she needed protection. She was so caught up in romance, she agreed to think about his proposal.

She didn't tell her folks right away, but when she arrived home for a weekend furlough from the St. Cloud Normal School, she informed them of her decision to give up her schooling.

She tried to sound persuasive as she parroted Pitt, who had said his career was more important than hers. He was going to be a great educator someday, maybe even enter into politics. He needed her by his side.

"Well, if that will make you happy, Jennie, we won't stand in your way," her mother said glancing sideways at her husband.

"Maybe, you should finish your schooling first, Jennie," her father added, picking up on his wife's cue. "You always wanted a good education. Even if you marry next year after you graduate, your education will never spoil."

So united were they on this issue, Jennie promised she would hold off setting a date until she thought about it a little longer.

That Sunday afternoon, she and Pitt met at the depot an hour before the train arrived to take her back to school.

"Pitt, my folks want me to finish my schooling before we set a date. I think they're right. I have always wanted an education. Once I finish school and teach a year or so, we can make plans. Okay?"

While Pitt seemed disappointed, he remained calm and optimistic. He carried her valise to the train and helped her up the stool and then the high steps. He squeezed her hand as they said their goodbyes. As the train pulled away from the depot, Jennie watched out of the side window as Pitt disappeared.

They would not see each other for nearly two months. Pitt had taken the afternoon train to Minneapolis where he was to finish his administrative courses at the University of Minnesota to become a principal.

Even though they were both busy with their studies, they found time to write back and forth. At first, their letters oozed with promises of love and devotion. Jennie always asked about Pitt's studies. She wrote that she loved her classes, but she added that they were difficult. She shared her worries about passing her exams. Pitt, on the other hand, only asked about her health, warning her to cover her head or wear her galoshes to avoid a cold. He seldom responded to her concerns about a chemistry test or essay on elocution.

At first, Jennie didn't grasp the significance of Pitt's lack of interest in her education. His messages became more fervent with love and loneliness, insisting that they set a date to get married. At first, she thought he was overly lonesome.

One day a letter arrived that changed the direction of their relationship. Pitt wrote that he had confidence in her finishing her courses with all A's. But he added that he knew that once they were married, her love would be "dedicated to him, their home, and their children," Jennie knew she wasn't ready to commit.

Awakened from a romantic dream, Jennie realized Pitt had no interest in her ambitions or her love for learning. Even though she loved him, she replied that she had no desire to give up her life so he could live his.

As month after month went by and neither made contact with the other, Jennie knew time was no longer on their side. They often bickered, but this time everything seemed different—more serious. Were they in an arm-wrestling match to see who loved the other more? And this was the first time they broke up, nearly two years ago.

Despite their differences, Jennie missed Pitt's friendship. She missed their lively conversations about the future of education and women's suffrage. Pitt taught both men and women to think for themselves, teach with their hearts, and think critically about the issues of their day. He joined in Jennie's vision of women becoming more independent and getting the vote. He even agreed with her when she voiced her opinions about women having the same professional opportunities as men, such as becoming doctors, lawyers, and pharmacists.

Although Pitt seemed to sympathize with her concerns about women's rights, at times, he teased her if she got too serious. "Jennie, you want to wear bloomers just like that Stanton woman?"

She tried to explain that one misunderstood action shouldn't be seen as a red herring for the rest of what she, Matilda Gage, Susan B. Anthony, and other women stood for.

The beautiful lyrics, "Oh, promise me that someday you and I, will take our love together to some sky," burned deep within her. Jennie knew there was little hope for Pitt and her. They agreed on politics, health issues, and women's rights, but he didn't understand *her need* to work for herself and her father. Why hadn't they broken it off completely back then instead of going another round? He would be totally out of her system now.

"Enough!" Jennie said out loud. "I've had too much quiet and too much thinking."

Pulling a hanky from her sleeve, Jennie blew her nose and wiped her eyes. After taking a deep breath, she patted her hair, opened the door and went outside to sit on the stoop and wait for her father to return from dinner.

The streets had turned quiet, so quiet she heard robins talking to each other. Across the street and through the hotel window, Jennie saw Mr. Scott standing at the front desk. With his head bowed, she imagined he was probably sorting mail and getting the ledger and ink pen ready for guests stepping off the soon-to-arrive train.

Kitty-corner, Robert Lyons swept his sidewalk. He glanced over at Jennie and waved. She waved back and wondered how Louisa was doing today.

Looking north, she could hardly make out any activity because the tree branches hung with healthy green leaves. As she turned her head toward the south, Jennie knew she would soon be seeing her father leave the front door and begin his short walk up the sidewalk. Even though she figured she should get back to work, she loved the light breeze, the soft heat of the sun filtering through the trees, and the streets waking from their noon-hour slumber.

She heard the one o'clock train whistling—coming up from the "Cities," as everyone called Minneapolis and St. Paul. Jennie loved taking the Great Northern to downtown Minneapolis, hopping on a street car, and shopping the many floors of goods displayed at Donaldson's and Powers.

Despite both stores offering top-of-the-line women's clothing, hats, and shoes, Jennie seldom purchased anything. Everything was so expensive. Instead, she nearly always came home with a bag of salted cashews, a new pair of hose, or maybe a few dainty white hankies she could share with her mother and sisters.

Although Jennie couldn't afford to live in Minneapolis, she loved what the city offered—a wide variety of shopping, many types of museums, and a potluck of places to eat. Still, when she reboarded the Great Northern and headed north to Clearwater, she felt a sense of relief to be going home to her quaint, safe little village on the Mississippi River.

The train whistle blew a warning to clear the tracks. The din of wheels and the screech of the brakes announced that the huge machine was attempting to stop and alerting the draymen to get back to work. Art Merrill, wearing a wide-brimmed, brown hat Maude called a slouch hat because it shielded the eyes from sun and rain, pulled out from Barretts' Livery next door. Danny Higgins drove down the street from the north where he had been eating lunch at Quinn's Saloon. As the two drays met, the clatter of chains, wood rattling, and the hooves galloping on packed dirt was deafening.

Since the train hauled goods and people, Jennie wondered who'd be stepping off the Great Northern. She expected visitors would start filling up the town, whether they were visiting family or just coming from local towns to take part in the Decoration Day events.

Driving down the middle of the street from the south, a two-seater carried Bea and Mae Barrett. The little girl waved as Bea directed the horse to turn right. Jennie remembered that both mother and daughter had mentioned their relatives were taking the train up from Hasty.

Behind them, two horses pulled up beside the Hotel Scott. Two rough men hopped down. They climbed the steps to the hotel and walked in. They did not appear to be part of the usual crowd that paid homage to the hotel. Sometimes, though, travelers were pretty rugged after a few days' ride. Jennie thought the two might have been camping out. Their saddlebags bulged.

She was hungry, yet Jennie saw no sign of her father. Maybe he was waiting for her mother to pack a lunch for her. All she needed was a sandwich and coffee. So engrossed in thoughts of lunch, she hadn't realized a customer had come around the corner.

"Miss Phillips? Jennie?"

Jennie jolted before she looked up toward the musical voice. She raised her hand to shade her eyes from the sun.

"Oh, you startled me, Claire! There's so much noise out on the streets now, I didn't hear you coming."

Jennie stood up, grabbed the handle of the door for support, and came face to face with Doc's housekeeper.

"I'm sorry. I didn't mean to give you a fright."

"I'll be fine," Jennie said as she clutched the handle of the screen door and pulled it open, allowing Claire to go ahead of her. Just as she started to enter the store, she heard someone holler her name. She looked up the street toward her house and saw her teenage sister, Blanche, walking fast and swinging a white, cloth-covered basket. Jennie looked into the store where Claire stood searching the shelves stocked with patent medicines. "I'll be right with you," Jennie said as she stood holding the screen door open with her back.

"Jennie," Blanche said, trying to catch her breath. "Ma thought I'd better bring you some dinner. Pa's not feeling so well. He ate some soup at lunch, but shortly afterwards, his stomach started hurting. Ma got some medicine in him right away, but he's lying down right now. Even though he tried to get up, he just couldn't make it. He said he'd be down later when he felt better. Ma said if you need me, I should come help you until she can get down to help."

"Blanche, tell Father I'm sorry that he isn't feeling well. We're slow right now so I don't need any help. Just tell him to rest and not worry about anything. I can make up the orders Doc Edmunds needs. Maybe someone should check on me later, though."

Blanche handed Jennie the basket and looked both ways before hiking her skirt and crossing the street. Jennie entered the store, slipped behind the counter, and set the basket on the shelf behind her.

"Sorry about that, Claire. Now, what can I help you with?"

Claire O'Casey looked toward the door and then cleared her throat, "I need to look over a few of your over-the-counter products. A friend of mine is having a problem with, well, she's having female troubles," Claire admitted, again glancing out the door and through the windows.

"What sort of problems?" Jennie turned her back to the woman and started searching through the shelves of boxes; occasionally, pulling a box to inspect the list of ingredients. "We have some patent medicines, which some women swear by. Supposedly, Cardui is helpful. Some women have trying times every month. Unfortunately, most contain a lot of alcohol. I suppose if nothing else helps, they'll sleep."

Again, Claire looked out the door before responding, "Do you have anything with . . . with pennyroyal in it? Maybe even tansy or black cohosh?"

Jennie thought a moment. "Anything with those ingredients should be taken with caution, Claire."

Stepping up on the small stool, Jennie scanned the shelf before grabbing two boxes—McElree's Cardui and Lydia Pinkham's Vegetable Compound—and placed them on the counter.

Claire quietly read their ingredients.

"Surely, if your friend is having problems with her monthlies, she could talk to Dr. Edmunds."

Claire continued to read the back of the boxes, ignoring Jennie's suggestions.

Just as Jennie stepped back on the stool to pull down Orange Blossom suppositories, Claire said, "I'll take this one," and reached in her bag for money.

Jennie stepped down, picked up the green box of Lydia Pinkham and read the price.

"Let's see. That'll be a dollar."

Claire opened her purse and plucked out coins, clicking them one at a time onto the glass counter.

"Thank you," Jennie responded as she swept the change from one hand into another. As she pressed down on the keys of the till to ring up the sale, she asked, "Anything else I can help you with today?"

Claire looked at Jennie before she put the box in her purse. "No, that'll be all. Thank you," Claire added. "Good day!"

Jennie watched Claire O'Casey walk out the door and pass by the front window. The vision of her gray plaid dress and the back of her red head under the green hat were the last she saw of her.

As she re-shelved the products, Jennie wondered why Claire wanted any of those premixed concoctions when the best medicine could be prescribed by Doctor Edmunds. Why did she want these specific and potent compounds? Maybe Claire knew these products worked in Ireland and was too embarrassed to talk to Doc about her monthlies.

The words black "cohosh," "tansy," "pennyroyal" rolled around in Jennie's head. She decided to do a bit of research. Grabbing a box of Pinkham's product, Jennie slipped behind the prescription counter. She reached over the worktable to grab *The Pharmacopoeia,* a heavy reference manual full of information her father and she used on a daily, almost hourly, basis.

She turned page after page, scanning fast, looking for the ingredients from the back of the box. She turned back to the table of contents to search for chapters on women's health issues, specifically the menses. She knew some women would be more comfortable talking to her about women's problems than her father. Yet, she wondered if her father had ever given advice on such personal matters. She couldn't imagine it, and he had never said anything to her about it. In fact, most women seemed to know what they wanted when they came in. Trying to act nonchalant, they asked for Cardui or Chichester's Pennyroyal Pills. Because Jennie could tell they were embarrassed, she wrapped up the packages in white butcher paper as fast as she could, and tied them with strings before the customers slipped the products into their purses.

Jennie reread the ingredient label from Chichester's. The herbs and their components had the ability to get a woman's "uterus contracting" again. As she paged through the text, she came upon pennyroyal and read the indications. She felt her mouth drop and heat rise from her shoulders to her forehead as her stomach somersaulted. The product's claims had not mentioned the obvious.

Could it be possible that Claire intended to use Pinkham's medicine to abort a baby—her own baby?

She had heard about women using certain products to cease pregnancies long before she came to work with her father. She knew that in some parts of the country, mostly the larger cities like New York and Boston, midwives made up potions to help women get rid of unwanted pregnancies.

Of course, none of these boxes stated that this was an added "benefit," because that would be against the law. All the same, Jennie didn't know what she was supposed to do in this situation. She had never talked to her father about drugs like these, nor had she brought up questions concerning women's complaints. Jennie felt she had to find out whether the over-the-counter medicines were potent products or quack formulas.

The bell above the door shocked Jennie back to the present.

"Afternoon, Jennie!" Editor John Evans stood in the door frame, dressed in his traditional khaki-brown pants and shirt with a notebook in his top pocket. His matching brown felt hat had slid to the crown of his head, showing a pencil lying over his ear. "I'm putting out an extra edition of the *Clearwater News* tomorrow to update everyone on the Decoration Day events. I have some room for a few advertisements or short news items. You got anything you want me to include?"

News? Jennie might have had something to say, but, ironically, she had nothing she could share with the village. She was glad for the interruption, though, because at least for a while, she could forget about her suspicions.

Chapter 11
Gradatim
By Degrees

"LET ME THINK A MOMENT, Mr. Evans," Jennie said. "Father didn't come back from lunch because he's feeling a bit under the weather." Jennie stood up from behind the counter, trying to gather her thoughts as she scanned the drug store.

"Sorry to hear that. Anything serious?"

"Hard to say. My sister came down to tell me his stomach started acting up again right after he ate lunch."

"He has a few health concerns, doesn't he?"

"Yes, at times, but, please don't mention that in the paper.

"I wouldn't think of it, Jennie."

"I know he wouldn't want it spread around town, and besides, he usually rebounds. I'm sure he'll be back this afternoon or tomorrow morning."

"No problem!" The newspaper editor removed the pencil from behind his ear and pulled the note pad from his front shirt pocket.

"Thank you," she said as she stepped on her tiptoes to see some of the top shelves. "Hmmm! Let'see." With hands on her hips, she scanned the glass counters. "How about some picture postcards of Clearwater?"

"That might go over nicely, Jennie. Seems like we might get lots of newcomers and maybe even former residents."

"Well, instead of a penny a piece, we could advertise, something like, 'Buy ten, and get one free.'

"That's a good deal," Evans said as he wrote on his notepad.

"And, I need to make up a batch of cold cream anyway. Why don't I price each jar for sixty cents instead of the usual seventy-sive cents? You could say something about Jennie Phillips's 'special formula' for smoother complexions."

"Sounds good! How about I give you a spot in the 'Local News' section, Jennie?" the editor suggested. "I'm limited for space, just putting out a one pager, so if you think that's all for now, you can get more in the weekend paper. This edition will be out Wednesday afternoon sometime."

"That'll be fine, and I'll make up a special display of postcards and get the cream ready as soon as possible, too. When Father gets back, he and I will decide on the specials to advertise for the weekend edition," Jennie offered, knowing that any type of over-the-counter product advertised on Saturday would bring Louisa Lyons on Monday. "Anyone tell you about the break-ins over in Elk River and Clear Lake?"

"Newell filled me in on the incidents when I went to the depot. I wrote up a short article for the bottom of the front page. Of course, this edition's focus is our celebration on Thursday so I've got an article on Congressman Townsend, another on John Stevens, and one short one on Simon, as well."

"The town's sure filling up," Jennie added as she walked toward the window and looked out. "Bea Barrett and Mae came in today and told me she and Edgar are having lots of company."

"Well, I'm including a schedule for all the day's events. The back page is mostly what's going on around town—who's visiting who, et cetera. I need to write a short article about those who helped clean up the northern part of the town. I heard Edgar hauled in some clean dirt and then graded it. Well, I gotta keep on a movin', Jennie."

By two o'clock, Stanley hadn't returned to work, nor had anyone from the family come to tell Jennie how he was feeling.

In the past, every time her father had an episode, and that was usually from nibbling on the foods he loved like his wife's fried potatoes or crispy chicken, Marietta reminded him to see Doc Edmunds for a checkup. She reminded him that a few passing remarks to the doctor about his "slight stomach upset," didn't provide enough information to make a valid diagnosis.

Her nagging usually brought eye-rolls from Jennie's siblings. They knew their father turned a stubborn deaf ear to her concerns about his health. In the past, his bouts hadn't kept him down for too long, though. Now, Jennie thought her mother might have been right about her father needing to seek medical advice. She might have to have a few words with him herself.

Although her visit with Claire O'Casey during the noon hour gave Jennie plenty to ponder, she wondered what she should be doing around the store. She could dust and sweep to get ready for the celebration, but her mother said she'd do that. Jennie fiddled with some of the postcards in the carousel.

Each print had a different view of Clearwater and the surrounding areas. A couple from the top of the hill by the Peck home showed the Mississippi snaking its way south. A handful of the cards depicted various views of the Mill Pond, the villagers' beloved swimming, canoeing, and fishing hole. Jennie couldn't wait for warmer weather so she and her sisters could wade or sit on the sandy beach and watch the sunfish jump. She knew her brothers often went down after dark to skinny dip with other young boys. Her parents would have reprimanded them if they knew about their escapades.

Jennie was lost in thought as she puttered around the store until the far off whistle of the mid-afternoon north-bound train announced its arrival. Main Street became alive again. The dray from Barrett's and Rice's livery next door rattled down the street, off to pick up goods that might have come up from the Cities. The manager from Scott's untied the horse that pulled his black, two-seater surrey, and hopped aboard to collect potential hotel customers.

Jennie prepared for customers too by pressing the NO-Sale on the cash register. She started to count her cash when she heard heavy footsteps and a light jingling sound on the walk in front of the store. Looking toward the door, she saw a man she thought she'd recognized. His wide-brimmed hat shadowed his face, yet she could see he had dark eyes, and a scruffy, gray beard.

Jennie thought he had intentions of coming into the store. When he pulled the screen door open, she said, "Hello!"

After a small pause and with a gravelly voice, he replied, "Howdy!"

He made a sucking noise as he moved a toothpick from one side of his mouth to another. Without saying another word, he gave the inside of the store a good looking over before removing his hand from the handle and continuing on his way down the steps toward the northern part of town.

"I wonder what that was all about," Jennie whispered, admitting to herself that at times she hated being alone when rough characters hung around town.

She continued counting the cash and change in the till. She had a few ones and fives to handle some small sales. She needed to get some change from the safe in the back, but she didn't feel comfortable leaving for even a moment.

Muffled, quick steps on the sidewalk had her look up to see her mother walking in front of the store.

"Mother! "What are you doing here? Father's no better?"

"No, he isn't. I brought some instructions for orders you need to do up for Doc Edmunds. He said you probably know how to fill them anyway. Now he's sleeping. He had a bad spell after eating dinner. He was hungry, and I think he ate too much. I decided with the train coming into town, you might need some help. If you don't, I'll start cleaning up."

Jennie took the note and read it. "I'm relieved you came. I wanted to go into the storage room and get some cash out of the safe, but I had a rough character walk by. I didn't feel like I wanted to leave."

Marietta looked at her daughter and then looked out the door and up and down the street.

"I was on my way down here when Deke Collins saw me and came out of his blacksmith shop to talk. Mostly, he wanted to know if I knew about the schedule for Thursday. While we were standing there shooting the breeze, a couple of tough-looking characters rode down from Blacksmith's Hill and tied their horses in front of his shop. They talked a bit and then separated, each meandering down a different side of the street, stopping, and snooping in the windows and doors." She walked closer to the large, bay window and added, "The one with the wide-brimmed hat looked familiar, but I can't place him."

"That was one of the fellows," Jennie replied as she concentrated on her father's note.

"There's another reason your pa needs to get back on his feet and get down here. I remember when the steamboats used to bring all sorts of characters to town. Many were up here to help with logging and make a few bucks to support their families. That was all fine and good, but some of them came only to make enough to go to Quinn's Saloon and drink it up. It seems like every town celebration brings crud from the cornfields." A teetotaler, except for an occasional sip of her homemade wine, Marietta Phillips often used the same maxim to refer to anyone, man or woman, who spent too much time at the saloons.

"Hmm! Did Father tell you about the robberies over in Sherburne County?"

Jennie read the shock and worry in her mother's eyes before she answered, "Jennie! You don't think they have something to do with all that?"

Trying to remain as calm as possible, Jennie answered, "Oh, no! We're worrying ourselves about nothing." She laid the note on the prescription counter. "Besides, we've never had much trouble here in Clearwater. Even Quinn makes sure his customers hold it down when they enter his saloon. He sure doesn't put up with much riff raff."

While Marietta tied a white apron around her plump middle, she walked to the door. She searched the streets, looking north and south, for some telltale sign of trouble.

Jennie knew her mother worried about her unnecessarily when she was managing the store by herself. Jennie had to reassure her Clearwater was a safe village and that she and her father were safer since he had moved the business from the northern, wilder, part of the village.

"As long as you're here, I need to get some change."

Marietta had already begun cleaning with a damp rag when Jennie returned. She pulled out everything from under the display counter— pink celluloid dresser sets, cameo broaches, hair picks, and jade rings—and laid them on top.

"I think you'll be getting a couple customers," Marietta announced as she looked up from her task.

Looking out the window, Jennie saw two women approaching the store. Dressed in what Jennie could make out to be something green and ruffled with leg-of-mutton sleeves, one woman crossing the street carried a parasol and wore a large brimmed hat with white plumes. She looked all dolled up for Clearwater. The other young woman, a bit more dressed down, wore a feathered, wide-brimmed hat that matched her blue dress. She could almost hear her father calling the women lady-dandies.

Jennie tried not to stare as they climbed the sidewalk, opened the screen door, and walked in.

"Is there something I can help you with?" Jennie asked.

"Oh, no, thank you," the young woman in the green ruffled dress answered. "We were told to wait here at your drug store if our ride didn't meet us at the depot when the train pulled in."

Jennie noticed the other woman seemed somewhat put off that she had to wait for anyone much less in the drug store. "May I ask who was supposed to come get you? Maybe I know them."

"My uncle is Professor Rankin. He teaches at the teachers' college in St. Cloud. He's riding up from Clearwater Lake, and . . ."

Marietta, who concentrated on sweeping the floor, looked up and over at the girl.

"My gracious, you aren't little Mary, Mary Chase, right?"

"Yes, I am. This is my friend Alice Jacobs."

"Well, I'm pleased to meet you," Marietta nodded toward the other young girl.

"Likewise," Alice answered as she turned and walked toward the display counter.

Jennie felt satisfied in her judgment of Alice Jacobs. Indeed, she was a bit standoffish. Either Marietta didn't notice or she wasn't going to be put off because of the girl's snobbishness.

"Jennie, do you remember Mary? Her aunt and uncle are Jean and Albert Rankin, and Albert is Simon and John Stevens's nephew."

"I'm not quite sure I remember you, Mary, sorry, but I know Professor Rankin quite well." Jennie didn't share how many times she had been to his office or his summer cottage on Clearwater Lake when she accompanied Pitt, who was a colleague and good friend of the professor.

"Oh, of course you know Mary. Her folks live next door to the Hardins. Remember, Spenser and Lucy Hardin, my old friends from Maine?" Marietta reminded her.

"Oh, of course, Mary. I'm sorry. When I saw you coming across the street, I thought you looked familiar, but I couldn't recall where we'd met."

Marietta added. "Gracious, Mary! Let me take a look at you."

With such an enthusiastic invitation, the young woman twirled around the store, the bottom of her dress scooping and swaying as she moved.

"What a pretty dress! My, you've grown up. How old are you now?" Marietta asked.

"I turned twenty. Both Alice and I graduated in May from the St. Cloud Normal School. I haven't found a position yet, but Alice has."

Trying to pull the other young lady into the conversation, Jennie asked, "Where will you be teaching, Alice?"

Alice gave Jennie a look that meant it wasn't her business, but after a moment's pause, she answered, "I've accepted a position with the Annandale School District." Alice looked at Mary, who was all smiles and friendliness. "Professor Rankin and his wife graciously invited me to come with Mary to look over the town. Apparently, we're also coming back for Thursday's events."

There was no mistaking it. Jennie could tell the woman was bored with the town and bored being in the store having to share small talk.

Mary added, "He and Aunt Jean rent the same cottage every summer. That's where Uncle Albert is coming from today. He teaches at the Normal School, you know."

"Yes, I know," Jennie answered. "He's friends with Pitt Colgrove, my . . . ah . . . friend."

"Oh, we both know Professor Colgrove," Mary remarked. "He was one of our instructors last year. He's an excellent teacher, and oh, so handsome," Mary added, turning to look at her friend.

Did Jennie see Mary wink at Alice? She couldn't help but wonder what that less-than-lady-like gesture meant. Unfortunately, she had little time to ponder this. She heard the rattling of chains, clopping of hooves, and a "Whoa!"

"This must be your ride," Marietta announced as she walked to the door and opened it.

The professor, a short man with a mustache, removed his hat before stepping into the store. Marietta greeted him. "Welcome. Are you looking for a couple of strays?"

Jennie glanced at Alice and saw the shocked expression on her face. After the professor straightened a few mussed gray hairs from his balding head, he nearly fell backwards when Mary ran to him and hugged him.

"Uncle Albert, it's so good to see you. I'm glad you found us."

"And it is good to see you as well. I hope you haven't waited too long. I didn't know how long the ride would take from the cabin. I'm glad you had a nice place to wait." He turned to Marietta and nodded. "Jennie, it's good to see you again." As he untangled himself from his niece's embrace, he welcomed his company. "And hello, Alice. I'm glad you came with Mary."

"Thank you for inviting me," Alice said, offering him her hand.

After taking both her hands in an affectionate shake, the professor looked back at Jennie and then toward Marietta.

"Pitt Colgrove assured me this was a safe place for the ladies to stay until I arrived. Thank you."

"Of course. We've been having a good conversation, too," Marietta leaned on the broom, taking a rest from sweeping.

"Jennie, Pitt also told me you have lots of important responsibilities for the big event on Thursday."

"I'm not sure that my responsibilities are any more or less important than others, but my committee's responsible for putting up signs and decorations. I can't take sole credit for the job. I've had some good helpers."

"Good, good. Well, ladies, should we be going?"

"Yes, Uncle Albert. Thank you, Jennie, and Mrs. . . . Mrs. . . ."

"Phillips," Marietta offered. "You're very welcome."

The girls followed the professor to the door. As he grabbed the door to open it, he turned back and looked at Jennie.

"I just remembered, Jennie. I'm sure Pitt already invited you, but he and many others are coming out to the cabin Sunday afternoon for dinner. I think he's bringing another colleague from the Normal School, Rex Holms. Maybe you remember him."

"Of course. I remember Mr. Holms. He was my English instructor."

"Well, good. We thought we'd entertain each other by reading a few of our favorite passages from Twain's *The Adventures of Huckleberry Finn*. I also have a new short story by Kate Chopin I'd like to share with everyone. Please think of joining us."

Jennie didn't know how to answer. Obviously, the professor didn't know that she and Pitt were no longer a couple. Jennie glanced at the young women who stood behind the professor and noticed a look of surprise on their faces. She knew she had to respond quickly, yet she stuttered, "I'd . . . I'd love to come." After a helpless look from her mother who knew the situation between Jennie and Pitt, Jennie added, "I really enjoy Twain and his descriptive passages about the Mississippi, but I'm not sure I can make it. I have church in the morning. And then we always have a big family dinner afterwards. This is about the only time all week we can sit down together."

"I understand, but if you can make it, we'd love to have you. We should have a good time."

"Thank you. I'll see what I can do."

The three walked out the door. The drug store seemed empty without chatty conversation and colorful dresses. Jennie watched as Albert Rankin offered his arm to each of the girls as they climbed into the buggy.

Chapter 12
Continuantur remedia
Let the Remedies Be Continued

AFTER THE PROFESSOR AND YOUNG WOMEN left, the screen door squeaked open and slammed shut for a little over an hour. Customer after customer kept Jennie and her mother busy, buying penny postcards, hat pins, and even the decorative cuckoo clock her father acquired ten years before.

Although a couple town regulars came in looking for bath soaps and candies, many were strangers looking for gifts for their hosts. The biggest seller was talcum powder. Women seemed to worry that the weather would be warm and humid over the next few days.

When the steady stream slowed and Jennie had a moment to look around, she noticed her mother with her dusting rag as she glided around the store once again, wiping everything she came upon. She went from one display counter to another, removing perfume bottles, powder boxes, and men's porcelain shaving mugs and razors, cleaning as she went.

As Marietta made the store shine, Jennie reread her father's note:

"Jennie, I'm sorry, but I am not feeling well this afternoon. I'll try to come down before closing. If you have some time, you might make up a few orders for Gil Tollington. I left the list on the work table. I know you can handle this, but if something else comes up, either you or Mother come get me, and somehow, I'll try to make it down there."

After grabbing the clear jar marked "Sp. Junip. C.," Jennie took one of the amber bottles she had sterilized and set it on a towel to dry. She knew Doc Edmunds usually prescribed spirits of juniper for patients whose conditions required a diuretic. Placing a white label in the typewriter, she tapped out the script for Mrs. Frank, who lived out in Lynden Township:

"Take one teaspoon in the morning before breakfast and one teaspoon before bed to treat gout."

For a while, Jennie busied herself filling bottles with pills and tinctures while her mother went from one project to another. Jennie paid little attention until she smelled the familiar lemon-scented sawdust her mother sprinkled on the floor. Jennie loved that smell, especially in the winter when they couldn't open the windows. Marietta pushed boxes and swept behind them, something Jennie never had time to do.

The train whistled again. The locomotive chugged. Jennie figured her rush was over as the train pulled out of town and headed north to St. Cloud.

"I'm about done here," Marietta announced.

"Thank you, Mother." Jennie looked around the room. "The place shines." She inhaled and added, "And it smells good too." The store always had its own particular aroma—a mixture of chemicals, herbs, and various perfumes, but whatever her mother added to her bucket of scrub water made everything smell clean and lemony. "Are you heading home now, or do you have errands to run?"

"I need to go to Laughton's to pick up a couple fryers. Last weekend, your father butchered our last."

"No wonder, I haven't heard any squawking lately."

"The town's getting too big for poultry roaming the streets. I don't think I'm raising any more. Your pa said I should buy what we need from the locker."

Jennie flashed back to the dream she had early Sunday morning, the coldness of the locker area and the beef carcasses coming at her.

Marietta returned from the storeroom where she had taken the broom and dust pan. "Bob Shaw hollered at your pa when our chickens got into his rhubarb last year. I know it wasn't funny," she added with a smile that she tried to cover with her hand, "but we've had to listen to his dogs barking. Seldom have our animals bothered anyone."

Jennie shook her head in agreement. She knew her mother seldom got upset about anything so trivial, but sometimes a couple people in town got their ire up for little reason. "At least Mrs. Shaw is easy to get along with."

Marietta added, "Anyway, I need to head out and buy a couple hens for supper tonight. I think I'll throw together some potato salad."

"Mmmmm. That sounds so good." Jennie didn't know anyone in the area that made a better potato salad than her mother. One of her secret ingredients was dill weed. Along with finely chopped onion, her potato salad had a unique flavor.

As Marietta gathered her sweater, she said, "We'll be busy, won't we? Everyone I waited on today is going to a relative's or expecting company."

"I wish I had time to help you in the kitchen, Ma, but I have to be here, and then help set up everything tomorrow."

"Oh, I've plenty of help at home. Your sisters can straighten up the house and peel potatoes. I think we have enough canned rhubarb down in the cellar to fill the pies I promised for the social." She went back to the storeroom and hung up her apron. When she returned, she announced, "For goodness sake, if it isn't George Newell. Our paths haven't crossed for quite a while, George. What brings you in?"

The middle-age man removed his hat and tipped his head to each woman. "Mrs. Phillips, Jennie. Town sure's pickin' up speed, wouldn't ya say? I heard lots of excitement about the upcoming holiday. I hope we've a good turnout." He looked over around the store and asked, "Jennie, is your pa around? I forgot to bring over a message."

Both women started to answer at once, but Jennie let her mother talk.

"Stanley's under the weather this afternoon. He's home resting. Is there something urgent you need?"

"I'm not sure. The note's from Doc Edmunds. I meant to get over here earlier or send young Higgins with it, but he's out on delivery. We've been so busy. I forgot to bring it." The depot agent handed Jennie the note.

Because Jennie knew her mother wondered whether she needed to get Stanley, Jennie summed up what she read. "Doc needs to stay out in Hasty and Silver Creek for the night. He says here that Mary Broat came down with diphtheria when she was helping nurse her grandchildren. He's asking for Father or me to go out to southern Lynden Township to administer the medicine to Mrs. Frank. He suggests we pick up Claire O'Casey because she knows where the Franks live. He also needs us to make up more of the diphtheria serum and send it on the morning train."

"Sounds like it's bad out there with the 'theria," Newell said.

"What a shame! I hope Mary doesn't have it too bad. She lost her husband last year." Marietta walked toward the door. "Jennie, before I run, I'll go home and ask your pa what he wants us to do. I doubt if he'll handle all that jostling in the buggy. It's getting late in the afternoon so if you go with Doc's housekeeper, you need to get out there and back before it gets too dark Maybe your pa will feel well enough to get that order for Doc." Marietta seemed to be thinking out loud. Without a goodbye, she was out the door.

"I'm sorry, Jennie. I should have brought the message earlier."

"Don't worry, Mr. Newell. We'll work it out."

Just as he started to leave, Jennie remembered to ask him about the burglaries in Sherburne County.

"All I know is that a couple of safes got cracked open and lots of money taken. The sheriff wanted to make sure we were on the lookout for trouble. With all the hubbub about to happen here, we might not notice much. Seems to me Donald Wolff'll have enough to do to keep the crowds controlled." With his hand on the door knob, Newell paused a moment, then said, almost reluctantly, "I don't have much faith in that boy. But, I won't worry you with my 'pinions. Anyway, I'd better get back to the yards."

"Thanks, again, Mr. Newell," Jennie said as the agent headed out the door. *Interesting*, she thought, *many people seem to see through Donald Wolff.*

Jennie wondered how she was to get out to the country and back before dark. She needed to go home, get her hat, sweater, and get the carriage ready. Before leaving town, she'd have to go up to the Edmund place at the top of the hill and pick up Claire. She hated imposing, but she really didn't know her way around Lynden Township, and the Franks lived way past Irish Town.

Behind the counter at the work table, continuing with the labels for the serums, Jennie looked up at the clock. Three-fifteen. She might make it by eight if she hurried. She worried her father wouldn't be well enough to last the rest of the day. They could lock up store, but Stanley Phillips didn't believe in closing early. She knew he'd crawl out of his sick bed to get down here. She wouldn't even put it past her father to bring a bed down here to keep the store open.

Lost in her thoughts and work, Jennie didn't see her brother pull up to the front of the store with Solly and the carriage.

"Jennie? Where are you?" her brother hollered through the screen.

"Carl?" Jennie stood up for him to see her. "Are you coming to deliver the prescription or are you minding the store?"

"Pa's getting ready to come down here. He wants you to go out to the country, but if that housekeeper of Doc's can't go with you, I'll go with you. I'm going to run up and ask her now while you wait for Pa."

"All right. I'll be ready when you get back."

Jennie got a small basket from the back room. She wrapped the spirits in some packing paper and tucked the package safely in the basket.

There'd be no time to get her riding hat, so Jennie looked into the mirror on the storage room door, patted down her hair and placed her everyday hat, a soft yellow felt cap with yellow satin ribbons, on her head.

The bell announced a visitor. Jennie peeked behind the door and over the counter. "Father, how are you feeling?" she asked, pulling the pearl pin from her mouth and snuggly securing the hat on top of her head.

"I'm not going to lie. I still feel tough. If Carl can get Doc's housekeeper to go with you, I'll have him watch the store so I can go back home for a while."

Jennie noticed how he gripped his middle.

"What do you think brought this on?"

"I'm not sure. I was pretty hungry when I got home, and everything tasted wonderful. Then the pain started," Stanley added. "Oh, here they are, Jennie. It looks like Doc's housekeeper will join you on this trip."

"Father, take care now. Maybe you can concoct something to make yourself feel better," Jennie advised. "The spirits of juniper might help you."

"Yeah, I could try that," he said.

Jennie heard the insincerity in her father's voice. She thought it ironic that he made up medicines and helped customers so they'd feel better, but he wouldn't do the same for himself.

"Go home and rest. Let Carl mind the store. Doc asked us to send out more serum on the morning train. I can fix that when I get back tonight. Please, don't worry about anything."

"I'll have Carl watch the store for a while. If I feel better, I'll come down again and make up the orders."

Jennie met her brother at the door. She nodded to Claire, but turned back to Carl, "Make sure he goes home."

Carl walked her to the buggy, giving her his arm so she could climb aboard. He handed Jennie the reins. She adjusted herself on the seat before clicking for Solly to back up.

"Jennie!" Stanley hollered as he came out the door.

Carl handed the basket his father held out to Jennie.

"I almost forgot. Your mother made up a lunch for the two of you."

That was like her mother Jennie thought as she grabbed the basket, thanked her father, and waved goodbye.

"Hello, again, Claire." Jennie noticed that Claire was still wearing the beautiful round pendant with green emeralds filling in the branches of a tree. "Thank you so much for accompanying me."

Claire O'Casey returned Jennie's greeting with her own. The musical lilt of her voice made Jennie smile.

As the two traveled north out of Clearwater, Jennie recalled their earlier encounter that morning. She hardly knew the woman and wondered if they'd have enough to talk about on this long trip.

Chapter 13

Aggrediente febre (Aggre. feb.)

While the Fever Is Coming On

FOR A FEW MOMENTS, Jennie and Claire O'Casey traveled in silence, crossing over the Clearwater River bridge, riding in back of the pulp mill, and heading north. Steam puffed from the mill's chimney, covering them like a cloudy roof as Solly pulled them away from the Mill Pond.

Recalling her recent trip to Lynden a few days before, Jennie noticed that the buds on the maples and oaks had swollen over the last few days. A cool, damp breeze stirred the branches. She was thankful when she saw that her mother had thrown her thick gray shawl in the back of the carriage.

"Claire, which road would you prefer that we take out to Lynden Township? Last weekend when I went out there, I took the main road by Warner Lake because it's pretty reliable."

"Well," Claire replied in her melodic voice, "I'd have to take your word for it. I've not been out this way since Easter when Danny Higgins took me out to visit his folks. I can find my way to the Frank farm because it's a wee bit from Higgins's place."

"I know at least two other ways to get out there, and both are probably shorter, but they're more hilly. Ida's father said much of Lynden Township is still too wet for planting and many of the low-lying roads are under water or quite muddy."

"You be the judge, Jennie."

Relieved that Claire hadn't suggested taking the Seven Hills Road, where the trees, cast deep, black shadows, Jennie nudged Solly up the small incline that wound its way toward St. Cloud. "I guess I'd rather be safe than sorry."

"That's fine! Once we're near the Higgins's place, I know my way 'round pretty good," Claire added. "I went with Danny's mum to buy up some of Mrs. Frank's homemade sauerkraut. The family loves it with bangers and mashed potatoes. Mrs. Higgins says no one in the area makes kraut like Mrs. Frank. Her kids tease her 'bout eating German food, but she laughs and says it's their duty to become part of the melting pot."

Jennie laughed. Soon they reached the top of the hill, a crossroads before continuing down the St. Augusta road. Straight ahead, Jennie recognized James Colgrove riding behind his team. She knew the elder Colgrove well because of her friendship with his son Pitt. He was too far away to wave a greeting.

"That's Mr. Colgrove out there, Claire. Have you ever met him?"

"No, but Danny's mentioned him on occasion. Apparently, he's quite a respected man in the community."

"Yes, he is." Jennie told Claire about both Colgrove's and D.D. Storms's improved farming techniques and the help they gave other farmers in the area. "Mr. Colgrove recently applied for a patent on a corn binder he invented," Jennie said as she tried to slow Solly.

"My, it's a nice afternoon for a ride, Jennie. We've a saying in Irish, '*Giorraíonn beirt bother,*' which means two people shorten a journey."

"Oh, I like that," Jennie said as she grabbed the shawl from back of the buggy.

Soon they passed the Acacia Cemetery and started down the hill by Fuller Lake. Jennie gave a little shudder, remembering how the moon looked on the water the weekend before.

"Chilled? I brought a cover," Claire suggested as she turned to grab the green plaid blanket.

"No, no, I'm fine. I was remembering the other night when Jamie Mooney accompanied me home. As we drove by this lake, the sun was setting. The horizon was absolutely beautiful, almost like someone had painted long strokes of burgundies and pinks. The moon had started to rise above the lake. The sun reflected on the moon, and in turn, the moon reflected onto the water, making it look like a large pool of blood."

"I've heard of that, but I thought that only happened in the fall. Mum usually called a May moon the Flower Moon to honor Mother Earth's awakening after a long, dark sleep."

"That's beautiful! I love how different cultures celebrate similar beliefs. My father came from upper state New York. He often talks about how the Iroquois celebrate the fifth month as the moon of flowers."

"Interesting!" Claire said as she looked all around the area.

"We had a late, wet spring, but I think we're going to see the countryside in complete bloom soon." After riding for a couple minutes, Jennie asked, "Claire, I've meant to talk to you about what happened a couple days ago."

"D' you know, Jennie, I meant to apologize for my behavior. I didn't mean to be so evasive when I came into your store."

Jennie could read the sincerity in Claire's lilting voice.

"Well, you seemed to have an awkward moment with Donald Wolff. I didn't wish to embarrass you even more."

"I meant to explain. Wolff, well, we've come to a wee understanding."

Jennie wasn't quite sure what Claire had alluded to, but she waited for her to finish her story.

"My friend has found herself in trouble and needs help. Her friends and family would be extremely embarrassed, no shamed, if they were to find out about her condition." Claire looked to her right and quietly said, "She's with child, Jennie."

"Surely, she and the father could marry. They wouldn't be the first to find themselves in this predicament," Jennie said, not understanding what this had to do with Donald Wolff.

"She don't want to marry the man. She says she can't carry this babe."

Still a bit naïve about the real problem Claire was presenting to her, Jennie asked, "But, really, Claire, what can she do about it?"

Claire didn't answer right away. Jennie thought maybe she hadn't heard her.

They rode along again for a few hundred feet before she finally answered, "I can help her make it go away."

"What can you make go away?" Jennie asked. A light came on in her head. "You didn't buy that product at my store the other day to try to—"

Very calmly and slowly, Claire said, "Yes, Jennie. Yes, I did, but—"

"Isn't this sort of drastic? If anyone were to find out you were involved in such a . . . a terrible deed, I don't know what would happen." Jennie was shocked that Claire had actually used one of the over-the-counter products she bought at her drug store to try to terminate a woman's pregnancy. She could hear the bite in her own words as she asked, "Why couldn't your friend and her love interest get married? Many women have to hurry their marriages because of 'accidents.'"

Claire enunciated each word slowly and carefully. "This weren't no accident, Jennie!" Claire cleared her throat before continuing quietly as if someone might overhear her, "My friend had an unfriendly encounter with a strong young bloke a bit more than a month ago when she came into town."

"What? Where? Not in Clearwater!" Jennie exclaimed.

"Yes, Jennie, in Clearwater," Claire answered emphatically. "Seems like wherever we Irish women go, men assume we're loose and willing to hand out whatever they need." The two rode quietly for a few moments before Claire continued. "Maybe you don't understand what some women have had to put up with, Jennie. Whether I'm in Ireland, New York, or Clearwater, I've had to help many a friend who found herself in trouble." Claire looked down at her hands and paused before adding, "I've stood at both ends of the birthing bed. I've watched many a woman have babies they couldn't afford to feed. And I've been called to nurse a few back to life after they were carved up by quacks who rid their bodies of unwanted babies. Unfortunately, in the process, some of the poor women nearly hemorrhaged to death."

Jennie cringed. She couldn't watch when her mother or father cleaned the scrapes and cuts of her younger siblings. She couldn't stand the thought or sight of blood. Pharmacology was cleaner.

Approaching a hill on the backside of Warner Lake, Jennie hardly noticed the new vegetation that had popped up over the week. The world had a fresh green smell, but all she could think about was how Claire was using over-the-counter medicines to help a woman abort a child. Jennie had read about situations some unfortunate women had been caught in. They were always somewhere else, not in her safe village.

Again the women rode in silence except for the creaking wheels and an occasional snort from Solly. When they rolled down the sandy hill, Jennie held tight to the reins until they leveled out and drove across Plum Creek. The wooden wheels rumbled loudly as they rolled across the bridge.

The air between Claire and Jennie felt as if she was breaking through a sheet of ice when Jennie finally spoke. "But, Claire, who . . . who could do such a terrible thing to your friend?"

"Like I said, I'm not free to tell you. My friend's beside herself with guilt, blaming herself for what happened."

"Why would she feel guilty? If she were taken . . . taken advantage of, she has nothing to be ashamed of. Surely, she could notify the authorities who . . ."

"The authorities! Oh, Jennie!" Claire's laughed sarcastically. "You can't believe any man'd take her claims seriously, least of all your Clearwater constable!"

Jennie recalled Claire's anger when she encountered Donald in the drug store. He seemed so nervous after he saw her that he literally backed out of the door. "What do you mean, Claire? And what does all this to have to do with Donald Wolff?"

"D'nt you know, Jennie, how some men treat women? Clearwater's no different than bigger cities or other parts of the world. Like I said before, some people assume that since many Irish are poor, their women are loose. Since most men believe women are truly the weaker sex, they try to intimidate them. My friend got caught by one of these blaggards, and now she's punishing herself with guilt because she couldn't run fast enough to get away from him!"

Jennie tried to keep her eyes on the road, yet she noticeed that under the woman's green hat her red hair looked like the Biblical fiery bush. "Blaggard?"

Claire must have read the surprised look on Jennie's face for she soon regained her composure and relaxed against the back of the seat. "How can I explain this? It means he's always up to something no good!" Then, very gently, and almost sympathetically, she answered, "Maybe you're not too familiar with these kinds of dealings."

Jennie didn't want to admit she really wasn't. "Of course, I know men can be raw at times." She remembered her one encounter with Bill Forester, but she couldn't imagine her brothers, much less her father, behaving so badly.

A few times, she had been surprised by Pitt's passion when they had gone beyond holding hands. She had heard of men's "needs," but when he leaned down and kissed her, she lost her breath because she, too, felt a stirring inside.

"The cold, hard truth is I've trusted only a few men in my life besides my brothers, my father, and now Danny Higgins," Claire confessed. "A lot of them are bullies in how they treat women. In fact, I've had an occasional battle or two of my own. The blokes were strong, but my brothers taught me a few tricks so I could take care of myself. In fact, Jennie, I had a run-in with the same young man who attacked my friend. But I can tell you, he won't be tangling with me again anytime soon. I got his attention off me and back onto himself."

It took Jennie a minute to comprehend what Claire was inferring. Once it registered, she winced. Jennie recognized her brothers' moans and groans when they had horsed around too much, misdirecting one of their blows into a delicate part of their anatomies.

Again, Jennie had a memory flash of Claire's meeting with the village constable. Could it be? Could she be insinuating that it was Donald Wolff who had taken advantage of her friend and tried do the same with her?

For a moment, Jennie remembered a few innuendoes she had heard between Livy Paisely and Maude Porter. Maude had said something sarcastic about the upcoming marriage between Lucy Smith and Donald. The two had remarked that he would have had to pick someone self-absorbed to ignore his "comings and goings."

Claire continued, "I'd never get caught in the predicament my friend has found herself in. You can be sure of that. " She added, "But if I had, I'd never want to bring that child into the world. I'd hate the poor thing, and that wouldn't be fair."

Shocked, Jennie replied, "Claire, you can't mean that."

"Jennie, I'm sorry. I'm sure you know few women who don't want their babies, but there are some who are in awful bad straits and have no means of financial support."

"Still—" Jennie started to argue.

Claire interrupted her, "In Ireland and America there are those who can't afford doctors. My mother was a mid-wife and provided other types of health care for women and children near our home in County Cork. At least once a week, during warmer summer weather, she and I went on long walks together. She taught me how to identify many plants and roots, and how to make herbal teas, poultices, plasters, and other potions she used in her practice. She were no quack, Jennie, and she were well respected." "

"Claire, I wasn't inferring you or she were quacks. Our religions can't be that different. Don't we all believe in the sanctity of life?"

"Of course, Jennie" Claire said calmly. "I believe in God, but I believe Christian charity also means that we sometimes have to help others less fortunate than ourselves."

Jennie argued. "Yet, taking a life, Claire? Isn't this contrary to what the Bible teaches."

"It's an age-old debate, to be sure, Jennie. But, I ask you, is it also God's will that woman fall victim to evil men?"

"No, of course not, but it seems as if there should be another answer."

"First, I won't help any girl or woman who is too far along. She *cannot* be showing. That's totally against my beliefs. The mother and I are ending a mistake, almost as if the woman had an early miscarriage."

Jennie tried to understand Claire's moral rationality. She, who had so little worldly experience, didn't want to act ignorant or judge unfairly, but Jennie asked, "Are you not acting like God, though, Claire?"

"Or am I helping Him when I show mercy to the poor and misfortunate?" Claire looked down at her hands again. "I suppose you think what I say is blasphemous? I don't want you to think I'm without spiritual convictions, Jennie. But when I can help, I will."

Jennie didn't know what to say or think. She had never thought about her duty to God in the same way as Claire.

"I were only thirteen when Mum died, but she taught me a lot. Years later, when I came to America, I stayed with some of her family in New York. They were poor, so I had to help them when I could. I worked as a servant for a rich family in Upper East Side, across from Central Park. On my days off, I visited my relatives in the Lower East Side. I saw many of the neighboring women. They seemed to be either nursing or with child all the time and always sickly because of their poor diets. Many of the babies hardly lived beyond a month or two." As if the deaths were too painful for her to think about, Claire paused a moment before she continued. "In a way, those innocent babes might have been the lucky ones because they wouldn't have to live through near starvation, filth, and even beatings by their drunken fathers."

"It sounds hopeless. Can't some overcome their lots in life?"

"No doubt some can, but they're the lucky ones," Claire said. "Others can't fight their way out. When I first got to New York, I was shocked at the masses of people. As I tried to make my way down the streets, I felt as if I had to struggle through a swarm of flies coming at me from all directions. My regular visits to Dublin never prepared me for such crowds."

"I heard Maude Porter say the same thing. She said it took her a few days to get used to all the comings and goings of people. She held tight to her handbag and buried her cash elsewhere on her body."

"Of course, the wharf's no place for a woman anyway. But I have to be honest with you, Jennie. If a lone woman can survive the immigrant inspections to make her way out of that part of the city, she can make it anywhere."

"I have little to compare that to," Jennie said. "Minneapolis and St. Paul have their poor, too, but apparently nothing like the larger cities. When I went with a few of my friends and their families to the Exposition in Chicago a couple summers ago, we had to make our way through a few shady neighborhoods. Even though the city claimed to have cleaned up some of the dangerous areas, what I saw was deplorable. I can't imagine having to live like that. Maude said Chicago was nothing like parts of New York."

"I'm glad I'm independent enough so I didn't have to call New York my home," Claire said. "When my dad's cousin, Cathy Murphy, wrote me last year that Doc Edmonds and his wife were looking for a housekeeper, I jumped at the chance to get away. I hated leaving my aunt and her children, but I hope I never go back. I can understand why people give up there. If you have no money and nowhere else to go, you're lost."

"Sad. Very sad."

"Anyway, back to what I were saying before. Once I arrived at my aunt Katy's, before I got placed into service, I had to earn my keep. She asked me to help some of her friends and their families. Most couldn't afford doctors. From bruised knees to broken bones, I tried to patch them up the best I could. I got paid a few cents to a few dollars. When a woman needed help to, well, let's just say, restore her monthlies, I created teas from the herbs my aunt and her friends grew. I mixed them into the patent medicines I purchased at the drug stores."

"But, Claire, what you were doing, what you *are* doing, is illegal! If you were to get caught, I couldn't begin to tell you how much trouble you'd be in!"

"I know about your country's Comstock laws, Jennie. The help I give isn't illegal because I don't pass along any written information. All I do is help a few who can't help themselves. So far, there are no laws on what a woman grows in her garden, and, truth be told, some of those medicines specifically formulated for female problems on your shelves have provided women answers for their problems for years."

"I didn't think any of the over-the-counter products were strong enough, except in alcohol, to help anyone except to get some sleep." Jennie struggled a moment before asking, "So which of the products are the culprits?" As soon as she asked, she said, "No, don't tell me. What if something were to happen to your friend because of what you bought from our store? I'd feel responsible."

"I'm sorry to cause you so much concern, Jennie, but for one thing, you aren't responsible. Women aren't as ignorant as the men who created the laws think we are. We've been helping each other since the beginning of time."

"But, Claire, you aren't a doctor. You shouldn't be playing around with potentially dangerous products. What if something bad happens to the girl or woman you help?"

"If you're concerned about me using or misusing this product, you can be assured I know what I'm doing. This isn't a new science, Jennie. Some women have always known ways to prevent pregnancies or take care of what they didn't want or couldn't handle. When some like my friend find themselves in trouble and don't have the skills to take matters into their own hands, they need a little extra help."

"But Claire, to end an innocent life! They didn't ask to be born, but they don't deserve to die, either."

"I agree, but think about it. What kind of life will these children have if they're unwanted and have to struggle every day to get enough to eat?"

Struggling with her convictions, Jennie pondered what to say. She had never known anyone who willfully aborted a child, nor did she know of any woman to come in and buy any of the women's products for that specific purpose. She knew some of the medicines claimed to help women with their monthly pain and discomfort, but she and her father gave little credence in their claims and knew Doc felt most of the patented products were nothing more than quackery.

Even though she felt ignorant about these issues, the past thirty minutes had opened her eyes a bit to the problems some women around Clearwater were experiencing. This knowledge should help her become a more alert druggist. Still Jennie worried about the possibility of getting in trouble if she were accused of helping Claire commit a crime.

Jennie promised herself, and God, she would talk to her father as soon as she could about this. She didn't want to cause problems for him or their business.

In the meantime, Jennie felt she needed to talk to someone besides Claire O'Casey, someone who could give her some advice about these issues people didn't discuss in polite company. But who?

Maude! Jennie thought. *Maude might be the only one she could talk to right now.*

Chapter 14
Adhibendus (Adhib.)
To Be Administered

WHILE THEY CONTINUED THEIR RIDE into the country, Jennie lost in her own thoughts and Claire in hers, the gentle rocking of the buggy had a calming effect. The damp air smelled like slimy worms crawling around the hard-packed earth behind the Phillips's house after a warm, summer rain. Jennie felt invigorated by the beauty of the spring afternoon. She took a deep breath, exhaled slowly, and then leaned back against the seat.

"Look, Jennie, a hawk! What a grand thing to see this fine afternoon!"

Jennie looked toward the sky, admiring the wide wingspan of the bird, dipping and swaying with an intermittent and gentle flap of wings.

"It must be spotting its dinner."

Although Jennie appreciated the beauty of all vegetation, she paid little attention to birds of the air and creatures of the ground except for family pets like the housecats and her favorite horse, Solly. If a bald eagle swooped down onto her head, she'd hardly notice.

When she and Maude sat on the riverbank of the Mississippi during one of their walks and talks, Maude often teased Jennie about her lack of "nature" observation. "You can't learn everything from books, Jennie."

Nevertheless, Jennie admired the hawk as it soared in the sky. She scanned the country side. "It seems like the whole country has awakened since I was out here a few days ago."

Gold and green spikes of grasses swished back and forth by the sides of the road. Meadowlarks warbled a fluted trilogy. Warmed by the late afternoon sun, Jennie shrugged off her shawl.

As they rounded a small curve, fluttering blackbirds came out of nowhere. Skittish, Solly whinnied as he pulled toward the middle of the path.

"Whoa, whoa!" Jennie commanded as she pulled up on the reins. As the flock scattered, she calmly coaxed the horse to keep moving. "It's okay, Solly."

"It's a beautiful afternoon, Jennie. The swamp's alive, isn't it? Look off over there by the reeds. Don't the marsh ducks move gracefully?"

"They do! This whole area is full of sloughs and lakes. Every puddle has its share of wildlife."

"Jennie, can you see way over there to my right? There's a whole grove of lilacs."

"Oh, I see! I'm trying to think of who lives out there." Jennie pondered a moment before she continued. "I guess I can't remember right now, but lilacs line most of the farmers' properties. I'm sure you've seen them all along the railroad tracks in town, as well."

The rebirth of the earth intoxicated Jennie.

Before long, Claire began humming a lively tune.

"I recognize that melody, but I'm not sure I know the words," Jennie said.

"Oh, let's see. 'Green grow the lilacs, all sparkling with dew. . . .'"

"Of course!" Jennie said before joining in. "'I'm lonely, my darling, since parting with you . . .'"

They both laughed.

"I love those old songs, but I'm surprised you know that one, Claire."

"Why? It be an Irish tune!"

"I didn't know that!" I thought it was created during the Civil War."

"It goes back further than that, but it became popular here when our Irish men sang it during their marches."

Solly towed them down wagon tracks beside a fence line. Jennie wasn't sure whose farmland they were crossing, maybe the Mitchells. They owned and farmed much in this area. Whomever it belonged to, she knew it connected with the main road up ahead.

"Have you heard this, Jennie?"

> Sleep, my child, and peace attend thee
> All through the night
> Guardian angels God will send thee
> All through the night
> Soft the drowsy hours are creeping
> Hill and dale in slumber sleeping
> I my loving vigil keeping
> All through the night.

Jennie admired Claire's sweet voice. "That's lovely!"

"When I were but a wee one, Mum'd rock me to sleep, singing the lyrics, but she sang it in Welsh."

"The melody's familiar," Jennie said, coaxing Solly to turn onto the road that would take them further into Lynden Township.

"Where there's a gathering, someone starts singing it, and others start harmonizing the chorus. It's a beautiful thing to hear."

The carriage rattled as it crossed another Plum Creek bridge, this time by the Feldges's farm. Since Jennie had been out last, the brook had risen considerably. Even though it gurgled louder than before, the quick-moving stream stayed contained in its banks.

Jennie shook the reins, guiding Solly up a slight slope. Once they reached the top, they landed on a flat plain that led in different directions, each to a different part of Irish Town.

"I love this time of year. The maple, oak, and cottonwood look like they're ready to burst," Jennie announced, taking in a deep breath. "Oh, the pine and cedar have a wonderful scent!"

"The earth's alive, it is!" Claire declared as she looked around. "We've got to be getting closer. Can't be more than a couple miles before we come to a crossroads and turn west."

"A couple miles?" Jennie thought a moment before thinking out loud. "Hmm! I wonder if I know where the Franks live after all. They're not out there behind Cassidys' place on the south side of the Tamarack Swamp are they?"

"Indeed! D'you know where I mean then, Jennie? Herr Frank and his frau live on the old Tracy farm."

"I'm pretty sure I know where I'm going then. I've been out here a few times. My friends, the Dorseys, live north of the swamp. We should turn down the road by Lyons Lake, which is coming up here soon. It's a fairly good road, too. Mother and I come out here occasionally to visit her good friends, Jim and Mary Lyons. You know Bob Lyons who owns Lyons's General Store?"

"Oh, to be sure," Claire replied.

"Well, Jim's his brother." The sun had lowered behind the tops of the trees. Jennie thought about the lateness of the day and said, "I think we should at least try this way. It's a bit shorter, and we need to make up some time."

"You know, Jennie, I've been meaning to ask about Mrs. Lyons. She's an odd one, she is. At times she's gabby, and other times, she disappears into a corner of the store."

"I know. Louisa used to be such a lively woman. Over the years, she's sunk lower and lower into her dark moods. Doc told me the medical term for her condition. It's a type of melancholia. He said it's common for some women to be affected by it after giving birth. Louisa had problems like this before, but she always bounced back. She miscarried a number of months ago, but she hasn't returned to her old self."

"How sad!"

"I remember a few years ago, before I went off to college, Maude Porter insisted I read a short story about a woman's bout with what some doctors call hysteria after the birth of her son. Her husband, a doctor, doesn't want her to tire herself out working around the house, caring for the baby, or thinking about anything, much less writing and keeping a journal like she had made habit of. He wants her to rest her brain."

"Imagine that! Trying not to think!" Claire shook her head and added, "Sorry, to say this, Jennie, but it sounds like something a man'd dream up."

"It's impossible," Jennie said, remembering how many times she had lost her concentration when she listened to lectures in school or sermons in church. "The husband rents a house in the country and puts her in a run-down nursery with dirty, half-torn yellow wallpaper on the walls. The woman concentrates on the paper for so long she begins to imagine a woman locked behind bars in the background. In fact, by the end of the story, the main character appears to go completely insane trying to free the woman."

"Lord!" Claire proclaimed. "I can't believe how vulnerable some women can be, especially in the hands of their husbands, well-meaning or not!"

Jennie cringed when she heard Claire take the Lord's name in vain, but she swallowed hard before admitting, "I have to agree with you. There seem to be a few rascals out there."

Apparently too warm, Claire shoved her shawl to the back of her shoulders before saying, "I wouldn't mind reading that story, Jennie."

"I'll see if I can find it for you. I probably gave it back to Maude. She doesn't throw much away," Jennie said with a laugh.

"I don't know Maude real well, but she sounds like a remarkable woman."

"Oh, she is. She may be criticized by a few people in town at times because she is a feminist, but her heart's right."

Jennie remembered how Maude used to foist news articles at her when she went off to college. At first, Jennie's homework load wasn't heavy, so she dutifully read each story. She read depressing account after depressing account of women losing their homes when their husbands died. Some had to serve time at county poor farms working off debts their husbands ran up when they drank up their wages. Others took in boarders and washing because they had no other way to take care of themselves or their children. Some were more desperate and turned to prostitution.

For a while, Jennie didn't make a fuss about what she was reading. These were women from different places. She didn't believe anyone she knew had it as hard as the women in the articles or stories. When her homework load got too heavy, she didn't have the time for much outside reading and had to tell her so.

Then when Jennie started work, teaching out near Atwater, she came to recognize the haggard farm wives who frequented many of the small village's businesses. While she could tell most of the women weren't that old, she could see how broken down they were as they shuffled along despairingly, shoulders hunched from their many labors bearing child after child and keeping up with their homes and farms. They often wore their best dresses, but their best were old and tattered. While Jennie didn't always understand Maude's suffragette or temperance beliefs, she came to agree with her friend's concerns for powerless women whose fates fell in the hands of uncaring men.

Claire interrupted Jennie's thoughts when she said, "I understand where Maude's coming from, Jennie. Most men think they need to run the world. We women can rely only on each other."

"I guess I'll have to think on that, but, at least to a certain extent, you're right. I've been fortunate, though. My father's an open-minded man. He and Mother have encouraged all of us to get good educations and to think for ourselves."

"I doubt most women have been as lucky as we, Jennie."

"I know," Jennie admitted quietly. She couldn't imagine not being able to talk with her parents, yet, she didn't bring up certain topics, even with them.

"I had a pretty permissive father, too. While Mum were alive, he supported her in her attempt to help women who weren't as fortunate as she."

"Sounds like you and I *are* the lucky ones, Claire. We come from good homes with protective and supportive parents."

"Indeed!" Claire added emphatically. "We're the lucky ones!"

Lucky, Jennie thought, yes, luck might be part of it, but she also knew how hard her parents worked at being a family, a family that loved each other, although they hardly ever mentioned the word. They showed it mostly by helping and encouraging each other.

"Back to Louisa Lyons," Jennie said, remembering she hadn't finished making a point about the grocer and his wife. "Robert's a good husband. And Doc does all that he can do. He tries to make sure Louisa's kept safe during her bad spells. He's told Father and me he can't do much for her. Recently, he suggested Robert send her to Fergus Falls, but I know Robert isn't ready to give up yet."

"I've heard of Fergus Falls, but I don't know anything about it."

"It's one of Minnesota's state asylums."

"In Ireland, we'd refer to women like her as knackered, meaning broken down. She isn't that bad, is she?"

"I don't know what to say. She can go days being coherent and helping Robert in the store, but then she folds into herself. Often she comes into our drug store to buy some of these over-the-counter products we advertise. Doc and Father refer to the products as quack medicine. Louisa knows something's wrong with her."

"What does she usually buy?"

"Mostly, elixirs that claim to do everything but make a person rich," Jennie laughed wryly. "I'm sorry. Yet, it's getting so that every Monday morning she shows up at the counter after she reads an advertisement for one of these products in the *Clearwater News* on Saturday. I've asked Father why we even sell these products, but he reminds me they keep our business afloat. Last week she bought something that promised to clear the blood, but mostly, she buys what claim to help cure the blues."

"Sounds to me like she's searching for her own answers."

"I think so too. Unfortunately, many of the medicines are high in alcohol, higher than liquor sold at Quinn's. Lately, Doc's asked us to warn Robert when she buys something. After she takes the first dose, she falls asleep so he searches her handbag for her latest purchase. He either throws it out or dumps some of it and fills the bottle with juice. Doc's a progressive man, but he doesn't believe in alcohol therapy or the rest cure the woman's husband in that story prescribed."

"I haven't worked for the good doctor long, but I've come to realize he's an intelligent man who's got a good reputation."

"He is and he wants Louisa watched carefully for her own protection, but when she has good spells, he wants her to be as active as possible." Jennie flicked the reins to steer Solly down the middle of the road. "She has good moments, too. Unfortunately, the bad have caused needless problems."

"Like what?"

"Let's see. One time she couldn't figure out how to make change for a customer. When Robert walked into the store from the backroom, he saw the customer helping himself to the cash register. Robert told Doc that, when he looked at Louisa, he could see she was not herself again because she had that familiar far-off look in her eyes. He told my father and me he was thankful the customer was an honest man. It could have been a financial disaster for him."

"Oh, my! She *is* in a bad way, isn't she?"

"At times she's in her own world," Jennie answered.

Claire paused before answering. "From what I've heard, there's a lot more to melancholia than anyone would believe."

"I've heard that too. My mother said she didn't have a problem after birthing me, but she experienced something for a week or so after delivering each of my younger brothers and sisters. When she got that way, she'd tell my father to mix up some chamomile tea. He also helped her as much as possible around the house for a couple weeks until she felt better. My grandmother and aunt came up from Monticello to help out. After a while, their lively conversations seemed to jolly her up."

"Your mother were lucky. Unfortunately, I know a woman back home in Ireland who killed each of her babies shortly after they were born."

"What?" Jennie gasped.

"Each child lived no more than a month. The woman always seemed to have the same story. When she tried to wake the babe to feed it, she found it dead. She never let anyone see their tiny bodies, not the priest nor her husband. After each death, the husband would build a coffin. She'd swaddle the babe in satin and lay it down inside. When the husband nailed down the cover, she went into hysterics, screaming, ringing her hands, and throwing herself on the caskets during the wake and funeral. She put on quite a show, she did."

"How terrible!"

"Indeed! Neighbors finally got suspicious when the last one died. Someone summoned the constable. He came and opened the casket. When he unwrapped the child, he found the baby's neck had been wrung. The woman finally admitted that something'd come over her a few weeks after each birth. She'd take the baby out of its cradle and kill it."

"Gracious! Yet the husband never became suspicious?" Jennie asked.

"He blamed himself, he did. He said his own mum lost a few babies so he figured it were something in him that caused them to die so early."

Jennie pulled on Solly to slow him down before they turned west. "Personally, I've never known anyone as bad off as Louisa."

"It's sad, to be sure." Claire said as she looked off to the right.

"We don't have much further to go." Jennie nodded her head forward. "Lyons Lake is right around the curve. I'm pretty sure I know where the Tracy place is from here. Did you ever know the family?"

"Only from what I heard about them. Apparently, they took off shortly after the Leonard girl were done in. It were that youngest boy who some suspected knew about the murder of the girl."

"I've been meaning to ask if you knew anything about the case."

"Little, little. I only know what Danny Higgins and others told me. According to them, the girl were only sixteen but looked much younger. Someone, a real Jack the Ripper, he was, seemed it have it in for her."

"A Jack the Ripper? Around here?" Jennie asked skeptically.

"Some say the poor girl were with child, even though she were only a wee bit more than a child herself."

"I hadn't heard that. Who could have had it in for her, though?" Jennie remembered receiving letters from her mother who told her how many in town waited half in disgust, half in anticipation, for each Saturday edition of the *Clearwater News* that reported updates on the sordid murder.

Claire shook her head and whispered, "No one really knows, except the murderer, I suppose. Some say the person who killed her were the same person who got her in the family way."

"So, you're saying there are those out Lynden that believe the Tracy boy got her in trouble and killed her?" Jennie asked.

"Some believe that, but he weren't the only one suspected."

"I heard about a few others, like her cousin Tom and Mike and Bridget Larken. Who else did the authorities point to?"

"I think they've eliminated Mike and Bridget. Bridget was like a mum to Alice, and Mike was good to her, watching out when the cousin and Tracy boy came around with their horseplay. They teased and pushed her around, but Mike'd have enough and go after 'em with his belt. I think the only other name I heard mentioned was a Forester or something like that."

"Not Bill Forester?"

"Indeed! That *were* his name. I guess he said he found the club used to bludgeon the poor girl."

"I had a run in with him myself once," Jennie admitted. She gave Claire a shortened version of how he came out of nowhere when she was trying to lock up the store, placed his hand on hers, and offered to help her lock up the store.

"Jesus, Joseph, and Mary!"

Again, Jennie was taken off guard by Claire's obvious nonchalance about taking the Lord's name in vain, but she went on to say, "It was scary, let me tell you. I know God was watching out for me because Carl, my brother, came looking for me in the nick of time," Jennie shuddered, remembering Forester's breath reeking of stale booze and cigarettes. "Anyway, I wouldn't put it past him to have had something to do with the murder. I can't imagine what that poor girl had to endure in her short years."

"To be sure! Yet, I heard about a couple colleens in New York who were barely thirteen when they got themselves in the family way. I were asked by a mother to . . . well . . . help her daughter . . ." Claire paused.

"What did she want you to do?" Jennie asked.

"The girl's mother said she knew her daughter had had at least two of her monthlies, so she knew she weren't dormant. Yet, the girl started gaining a lot of weight. I checked her over, and there were no doubt about it. She *were* in the family way even though she hadn't turned fourteen yet."

"But how? Who?"

"The girl claimed it were her stepfather—"

"Her stepfather? You can't be—"

"It's shocking, to be sure. The mother didn't believe it neither and nearly beat the girl to death for telling such a lie. When the woman confronted her husband, though, he 'fessed up."

"I hope the wife booted him out!"

"The family'd soon be living on the streets! No, that weren't the answer—"

"But, surely—"

"The man weren't a bad man," Claire interrupted, "or so the wife claimed, but she were in the family way herself for so many years and were too tired too often for . . . well—"

"What some women have to put up with!" Jennie exclaimed.

"And, of course, he'd been drinking . . ."

"Maude's an active member of the Clearwater Temperance Society. She rants about the evils of alcohol."

"They're a bit radical, though I've known other women in New York and Ireland who've suffered because their men indulged too often."

"So what finally happened to this girl in New York?" Jennie asked.

"I helped her. I had to," Claire said almost apologetically yet emphatically. "She were too young and too small to carry that child, much less try to support it."

"How . . . how did you do it?" Jennie felt a sickness in her stomach. "No, I don't want to know." Yet Jennie did know Claire had to have stirred up one of her concoctions. "It's isn't the baby's fault he got started."

"I know, Jennie," Claire spoke calmly and quietly. "But there's a stigma attached to such a child. If it had lived, it'd be condemned the rest of its life and called nasty names."

"I can't believe this was the only alternative. Why couldn't the girl have given the baby to someone else to raise?"

Claire sighed as she looked across the prairie. She didn't answer right away. "Maybe you don't know how it is with us. There'd be no long line of people waiting to take such a child, much less one of ours."

Jennie didn't know how to answer. She knew many in the community were prejudiced against the Irish, but they were the same ones who didn't have anything good to say about Indians, Negroes, and anyone who wasn't Protestant. And yet, Jennie also knew Clearwater citizens weren't alone in their biases. All anyone had to do was read some of the articles in the *St. Cloud Times* and *The Minneapolis Tribune* to understand that many people were prejudiced. "I suppose," Jennie whispered.

"If it helps any, the girl felt only a few pains, and then she released. Nothing had formed yet. It were like she were having her monthly again, only a bit more painful."

"So what happened to the stepfather?"

"When the word got out, he weren't treated real kindly. He were nearly kicked to death by a few men in the neighborhood because they, like everyone in the world considers what he did a big . . . how do you say it? Taboo?"

"Most cultures would consider it taboo."

"It's a horrid thing to think about, to be sure. Last I heard the girl were doing fine. She went to work for a family in upstate New York. She's probably married by now."

"What about the stepfather?" Jennie asked.

"Like many Irish matters, some things have to be swept under the rug. The man is again taking care of his family."

"You can't tell me the family's all living under the same roof yet?"

"Survival can make people do what they never thought they could do."

Jennie wondered how the man dared show his face in public, but she didn't say that. Instead, she commented, "How awful for . . . for everyone!" The carriage juggled back and forth. Jennie tried to guide Solly, but the horse's excellent instinct had him side-step the muddy ruts. Unfortunately, the buggy and those inside didn't benefit from his horse-wisdom. "This road's terrible! I don't think we should come back home this way. It's going to be late, and I don't want to deal with this mess at dusk."

Once they reached flatter land, Claire said, "Oh, and another thing. Even though some don't deserve their lots in life, some of the younger colleens in New York might've been asking for it."

"What do you mean?"

"Some of them, especially those from a rougher crowd, dallied around in herds on street corners when they had some time to themselves. Maybe they didn't know no better, but they seemed to love drawing attention on themselves, especially from men."

Jennie tried to visualize one of her younger sisters hanging around anywhere, much less a street corner. Of course, nothing much happened in Clearwater except an occasional skirmish between drunks down by the saloon.

"Life's hard in New York if you're poor. Women turn old early. Their daughters see their own fate when they look at their mothers who are tired all the time. Their hair turns prematurely gray, and their teeth fall out. Young girls are put out to work to help their folks. And even though they get to keep only a few coins every payday, they want to have a bit of fun before they turn into their mothers. Unfortunately, boys are looking for the same thing. And as soon as they've had their 'fun,' they're gone, leaving the girls to carry on."

As the carriage jostled and juggled them, Jennie tried to imagine one of her sisters or her sisters' friends getting in trouble like the girls Claire talked about. They were guided at home on how to sit at the table, talk to their elders, and behave when the parents weren't around.

Jennie and her siblings knew their parents were strict out of love. "It's hard to believe how some have to live."

About a week ago, her little brother Percy got into trouble again. The boy loved baseball and couldn't get out of the habit of throwing the ball in the wrong direction. He broke a window down by the coal sheds. Her father paid the bill, but Percy was confined to the house to help their mother with chores until she felt he had paid for his mistake. Her parents hardly ever used the rod. Once in a while, though, someone got a swat, but that was usually for out-and-out disobeying or using rough language.

"Ah, it is, it is." Claire shifted forward on the bench and pointed straight ahead. "That fence line looks familiar, Jennie."

"Isn't that Quinns' place over there?"

"It is, for sure!"

"Good, then we've only a couple more miles." Jennie slowed Solly to make the turn at the Y in the road. As the sun lowered in the west, Jennie felt anxious because of the lateness of the day. The talk of rape and abortion didn't help to calm her nerves. Jennie knew Maude would be interested in her afternoon discussion with Claire. Much more a woman of the world, Jennie's older friend didn't shy away from embarrassing or publically censured topics.

Jennie concentrated on keeping Solly on the path so the carriage didn't toss them around more than necessary.

"Well, God be praised! Jennie, look to your right and see that beautiful may tree."

Looking over to a boundary line of pine trees, Jennie saw a burst of white amongst the green. "May tree? You mean the flowering hedge over there?"

"It be a type of hawthorn."

"Really? I guess I never knew that, and yet, they cover the whole area out here. That one is particularly beautiful."

"When I were a child in Ireland, I learned their thorns were used in Christ's crown. Supposedly, it's bad luck to cut down any part of the tree, including its twigs and flowers, and bring it into the house. Some believe a person could die if that were to happen."

"I've never heard of that before," Jennie said, believing it superstition.

"On the other hand, some people put twigs and flowers about their doors to ward off evil spirits. So I'm not sure if that is good luck or bad." Claire laughed. "I've dried the leaves to seep into a tea. A cup calms a body so the person can sleep."

Jennie gazed off toward the west and noticed a plow and horses in the field. She had no idea who the plowman was, but she figured she and Claire were getting closer to the Frank farm. They were surrounded by more small lakes and swamps, which covered this part of the township.

"You seem to know a lot about herbs and roots, Claire. Often in the summer, Mother and I take walks to find chamomile plants. She dries the flowers and then crushes them into powder to make tea. This used to help my father with his stomach, until it got so bad he had to see Doc Edmunds. I remember when my siblings were babies, she'd mix a small amount with sugar and warm water and feed it to them when they were colicky. She always has a few aloe vera plants growing, too. Whenever one of us gets a burn or a cut, she cuts a leaf and smears the jelly all over it."

"Some people drink aloe for their stomach, too." Claire acknowledged.

"I've had to mix a couple aloe 'cocktails' for Doc when he thought that would help a patient's indigestion."

"Indeed! The plant's remarkable!"

"Father's been teaching me a lot about herbs and roots, how much to use for tinctures and tonics and how to use them in the teas and cocktails that Doc prescribes. My biggest concern's been the over-the-counter medicines we sell, though. Some of them are awfully high in alcohol or laudanum. Others have a combination of herbs and other ingredients I think could hurt more than help."

"You have to know what you're doing when you start concocting, to be sure. I'd prefer fresh herbs, instead of those over-the-counter. In Clearwater, we have little to pick from. I wish I could plant what I need. Unfortunately, I'm sure my employer wouldn't approve."

"No," Jennie laughed. "He's open-minded, but I'm pretty sure Doc wouldn't approve of you planting a garden of herbs if he knew what you were going to use them for." She maneuvered Solly toward the right of the tree-lined road. "It won't be long before we get to the Frank house."

"That'll be good! I hate to bring this up again, Jennie, but being out here so close to where the Leonard girl were murdered makes me think about her final moments. She were found over east, about three-fourths mile from the Higgins's farm. I can take you by there on our way home, if you wish."

Jennie shuddered. "Well, let's see. I didn't realize we were that close. But after what happened to me last weekend, I'm not so sure I want to get any closer to the Swamp."

"Why? What happened?"

"I doubt I can get into the whole story before we reach the Franks, but I was out picking flowers in the north end of the Tamarack Swamp by Dorseys' farm. I thought I heard crying. It became louder and louder. It was so loud, Solly ran off." Jennie cringed. "Just talking about it makes the hair of my arm stand up," Jennie added as she looked down and rubbed her left forearm.

"That's interesting!" Claire responded with a bit more enthusiasm than Jennie wished. "I don't want to alarm you, Jennie, but Sarah, Danny Higgins's mum, mentioned she's heard lots of wailing and sobbing this spring. Others have heard it too."

"Really?"

"You know, Sarah Higgins were one of the first women to arrive at the girl's home after Alice were brought back. She helped Mrs. Hayes, the girl's grandmother, wash her body and get her ready to be buried. Sarah doubts she'll ever have a good night's sleep again. The child's neck, shoulder, and skull were crushed. You probably read about it in the papers. I heard after the coroner and Doc Edmunds examined her, they whispered she'd been taken advantage of."

"I'm not surprised. There was speculation in the papers, and of course, lots of gossip around town."

"I know. The grandmother lives over there by Danny's folks. D'you want to talk to Sarah about what you heard? We can stop on our way back. They don't live too far from Franks."

"Let's see if we have time. The sun's already lowering in the sky. As it is, I think we're going to have to light the lanterns when we head home. I wouldn't mind talking to her sometime though. Orrin Dorsey thinks I heard a cougar, but I saw the look in his wife, Mary's, eyes when I told them what happened."

"You're probably right. We'll have no time to stop today. It's too bad. Sarah probably baked today. And I know she'd never let us go without a bite to eat."

"Mother packed us a lunch. As soon as we're finished with our errand, we should dig in. I'm starving." The carriage bounced and jostled them up and down as they made their way through the ruts. "Is this the wagon road into the Frank's?" Before she received an answer, Jennie pulled up on the reins, directing Solly to take a wide right turn.

"This's it. Not much of a roadway, though." Claire grabbed hold of the side of the seat for balance. "There's their house over there by the trees, Jennie."

Jennie held tight to the reins so she could keep both her and Claire on their seats. "I can't imagine anyone living out here." She could see the front of the house as well as the barn and some of the out buildings. They all needed a good paint job. Weathered gray made them look forlorn, not happy like the painted farmsteads in the area. "All I can say is it was eerie. If Solly hadn't run off, I'd have thought it was all in my head, but he was stirred up too."

"Truth be told, you aren't the first to have thought you'd experienced something out by the swamps, Jennie."

"I know. Jamie Mooney said the same thing. I wonder why the Dorseys were so evasive then."

"They're probably in denial." Claire said as she repositioned her green hat, which had slipped backwards. "Some don't want to admit the presence of the supernatural."

"I'm still not totally convinced, Claire. Yet, I know something scared me—*dead or alive*."

"I've never experienced anything and have been out this way many-a-time, so I'm telling you what I've heard, Jennie."

"Makes me wonder why the authorities never solved the case, and I still don't understand why Mr. Larkin went back to destroy the evidence; you know, he supposedly dumped a bucket of water over the Alice's blood. Very suspicious, if you ask me."

"Well, like we said, there seem to be a number of suspects, but as far as I can tell, the sheriff dropped the case. But when it comes to Mike destroying the evidence, as you claim, many people don't understand that the Irish believe that if a person comes to a horrid end and blood is left to dry on its own, the soul will not rest. The person who did the sinister deed to that poor child left her on the side of the road where her blood spilled out of her body. Mike only did what our customs told him to do."

"That's what Jamie Mooney said too, as well as trying to clean it up before it drew animals to the scene to sniff and paw around."

"Just common sense, Jennie."

"As I said before, unless Mr. Larkin has a dark side to him, I don't believe he could kill anyone."

"No, no! And yet there sure were gossip about him and Bridget living in sin. The newspapers did a lot of finger-pointing about it, but what they neglected to mention was he were helping Mrs. Hayes with spring planting. He often worked so late at night, it were hard for him to get home so he slept on a cot in the kitchen."

"I remember the article you're referring to. I know there are those who believed the rubbish and spread it around town," Jennie admitted.

"Mike and Mrs. Hayes's husband were good friends. When he died, she couldn't take care of the place by herself. He weren't the only one to help her. Many of the neighbors pitched in with the everyday chores as well as with the planting and harvesting. Mrs. Hayes had a lot to contend with. First, Bridget's husband died, maybe a year ago. She went to live with her mother with her little girl, Nell. Then Alice's mum died last winter and Alice came to live with her grandma as well—all of them lived in the tiny house."

"Sounds like a lot of tragedy hit that family."

"To be sure, Jennie. Then the murder and all the implications in the papers and the community. Mike and Bridget got married to end the gossip."

"Some people want to believe the worst in others." Jennie remembered three years before when she came home from Atwater for a short visit. On Saturday, she, like everyone else in the village, eagerly waited for the *Clearwater News* to get an update about the crime. This particular edition had an article alluding to Alice's aunt Bridget and Mike Larkin living together without benefit of a marriage license. That bit of information gave many in the town something to smack their lips on. Jennie remembered the village's high and mighty, Sarah Kingsley and Livia Paisley, whispering in the pew in front of her the next morning before church started. She overheard them mention "that Smith woman and Larkin right under Mrs Hayes's nose."

"Danny and the folks around here are still upset by what the newspapers suggested about Alice being a bad girl."

"Like I said, the papers jumped to lots of conclusions. Whoa, Solly, whoa!"

While the carriage came to a stop by the Frank house, white, red, and black chickens scattered in all directions. Jennie set the brake, jumped down, and grabbed the black medicine bag from the floor. She, like Claire, hefted her skirt to keep it from dragging in the furrows and potholes of mud.

As the two women approached the house, a brown-and-yellow kitten stepped off the stoop and rubbed up against Jennie's black skirt. Claire knocked on the door. After a minute or two, she knocked again. Jennie began to wonder if the elderly woman was in the back of the house. A few seconds later, the door opened. A short, heavy woman, her silver hair wrapped in a bun, greeted them with "*Willkommen*!"

"Mrs. Frank? I'm Jennie Phillips from the Phillips Drug Store in Clearwater." Jennie spoke through gray screen door. "This is Claire O'Casey. Dr. Edmunds asked me to bring out medicine for your gout."

"Oh, *danke, danke*! Claire, it's *gut* to see you again."

"Frau Frank, it's good to see you again, too. *Wie geht's*?"

"*Nicht gut, nicht gut.*"

"I'm sorry to hear that. May we come in? Miss Phillips needs to show you what to do with your medicine."

"*Bitte, bitte.*" The short woman waved an invitation to follow as she hobbled down the hallway, leaning on a knobby, brown cane.

Claire and Jennie moved through the entryway that led to the kitchen. Jennie noticed strange smells like roasted pork, onions, and something that smelled like black licorice. Warmed from the oven, the room had little in it besides a stove, a dry sink with a gray enamel dish pan hanging above it, and a wooden table and four chairs. *Sparse but clean,* Jennie thought.

"Now, Mrs. Frank," Jennie spoke as she read the indications for the prescription, "Dr. Edmunds wants you to take a tablespoon of this liquid in the morning and another at night, and he wants you to stay off that foot as much as possible."

"Yah, yah, is not so easy. I got to feed the chickens and slop the pigs. I got to finish planting the garden or we no eat this winter."

Jennie had to listen hard to understand every word the older woman said as she slurred her w's into v's and her t's into z's. "I know it's hard, but you should try to stay off your foot." Swollen, near-gray flesh puffed out of the bandage near her ankle. She looked at Claire, who looked concerned, too. "The medicine will work better if you do that."

"I will try. But lots of work to do on farm, and this no *gut* farm. It wear my *alten mann* out. He work in fields all day 'til dark. I try to help him some, but I am alt too. But where we go? It's no *gut* to get alt."

"I'm sorry, but don't forget, Frau Frank," Claire interrupted, "Sarah Higgins said she would be willin' to send the boys to help your husband. And she said she'll send over one of her daughters to help cook and work in the garden."

"*Das ist wunderbar,* but *mein mann* no ask for help. He's proud. How you say, ah, *störrisch*?

"Stubborn? Ornery?" Claire asked in jest as Jennie laughed.

"*Ja,*" Mrs. Frank joined the younger women in their laughter. "He ist stubborn, as you say. But if *mein Tocher* were still here, she'd help. Selma in Virginia *mit* her *mann*. She'd make her vater listen to her und end his foolishness."

Seeing a darkening shadow outside the window, Jennie felt a pang of anxiety. The day was coming to an end, and she and Claire were far from town.

"Mrs. Frank, I know the doctor wants you to take it easy for a few days anyway, at least until he can check on you again. Do the best you can." She wished she could do more—like talk to the Higgins family to make sure they checked in on her, but like her father often reminded her there is a fine line reputable druggists walk. They aren't counselors; they are simply agents between doctors and patients.

Claire stood up, patted Mrs. Frank's shoulder, and walked back toward the entryway.

"Please, don't see us to the door. Keep your foot up and rest, Mrs. Frank." Jennie grabbed her shawl and black bag and followed behind Claire.

"*Danke, danke*! *Und guten tag*!"

Jennie turned and closed the door. The sun had settled behind the trees in the west. She knew it had to be near six o'clock. If she and Claire left now, they could make it to town, possibly, without lighting the lanterns. They would have to hurry.

Chapter 15
Spiritus vini rectificatus (SVR)
Rectified Spirit

JENNIE CLIMBED UP into the carriage and sat next to Claire.

"So, which way do you think we should go? We can possibly get home before it gets too dark if we head east a bit and then southeast."

"Jennie," Claire interrupted, "I realize it's getting late, and I hate to ask this, but could we please stop over at the Higgins place? I'd like someone to look in on Mrs. Frank. We aren't going much out of our way." Pointing across the field, Claire said, "You can see the farm from here."

"Of course. Mrs. Frank needs someone to look in on her," Jennie agreed. Trying not to worry, she asked, "How do we get there from here?"

"I think we'd better get back out on the road."

Jennie shook the reins, "Let's go, Solly."

"Sorry, Jennie. We're racing against time here, but that woman can't take care of herself. She's in her late sixties or early seventies. He's older, but as you heard, they've no family here. She's needing help, but his foolish pride probably won't let her ask for it."

"Of course, you're right. I'm glad you thought of it, and I'm sure it won't take us that much longer," Jennie said, looking at the sun in the lower sky.

"We have to turn left here," Claire directed as they reached the end of the rugged pathway. "See where the road turns south up ahead? We have to go a short ways down there, past a small swamp, and then turn down Higgins's long driveway. It's no more than a half mile from here."

Jennie pulled on the rein so Solly would turn. The wind had picked up a bit, blowing the horse's black mane to the side. He looked back at Jennie and blinked as if he, too, were a bit concerned about the lateness of the day.

When they neared a slight incline, Claire said, "This here's Grandma Hayes's place, Alice Leonard's grandmother."

Jennie saw a tiny building, little more than a gray, two-story log shack, with its roof caved in over its tiny porch. "Oh, it *is* small, isn't it?"

"Did ya know, Jenne, Alice were brought back here after she were found dead on the side of the road. It's in shambles now, for sure. Grandma Hayes's daughter Mary owns the place and kicked the whole family out after the girl were murdered."

"Why?"

"All that blather in the newspapers about Mike Larkin living with Bridget Smith without benefit of a marriage license. Some say Grandma Hayes never got along much with her daughter Mary, so she moved in with Bridget and Mike Larkin after they got married. His place's north of here. "

Near the road, a small swamp was full of life. A hen mallard glided across the water with eight downy ducklings following her. As if on stilts, a tall, blue heron stepped out of the tall reeds and grasses and waded into the water. Red-winged blackbirds hopped from cattail to cattail. A meadowlark warbled his flute song claim to the territory. Jennie thought the beauty of the landscape clashed ironically with the tragic murder that transpired nearby a couple years before.

"I know where Larkins lives, but what kind of woman would kick out her family, including her very own mother, after all they'd been through?"

"She was something, to be sure! According to Danny, her son were a strange one, he were. Danny said he was a bit off, and the neighbor boy were no better. Apparently, the two were often up to no good. They tortured dogs by burning them with cigarette butts and stuck pins in chickens. Shortly after the girl were killed, the neighbor kid took off for Canada, and Tom moved to Oregon. Never a word why."

"That sounds suspicious—probably the reason why the crime has never been solved."

Claire nodded agreement. "Sarah Higgins told me Mary were shocked and embarrassed when the newspaper article implied Mike Larkin and her sister were together. I tell you, I've little tolerance for self-righteousness. How she could be so blind to her own son's behavior, and yet treat her mother and sister the way she did. We turn down this roadway, Jennie."

Jennie steered Solly into the turn, down the long driveway to the bottom of a little hill, and past the swamp, marsh grass, and wheat fields. The Higgins's farm had a welcoming feel. A black and white collie headed toward them barking loudly, but his tail wagged happily. Jennie held tight to the reins. "It's okay, Solly, the dog looks friendly."

"Well, here we are. Laddie, you remember me, don't you?" Claire hollered down as the collie came closer to their buggy. "Did'ya want to come in, Jennie?"

"No, no, that's fine. I'll stay here with Solly."

"Then I'll hop down and ask Sarah to look in on the Franks." Wagging his tail, the dog came up to Claire and sniffed her hand. "Good boy!" she said as she patted him lightly on the head before he sprinted off to watch over the corralled sheep.

Jennie watched Claire sprint to the side door and go inside. Left alone, she talked to Solly, trying to fill the void of space and time. "We won't be here long. We'll get you home, brushed, and fed soon. I'm getting hungry, too." Jennie looked in the back of the carriage and spotted the lunch basket her mother sent along. She was tempted to grab a sandwich but figured she'd better wait until Claire returned.

Resting her back against the seat, Jennie enjoyed the solitude of the farm. The large shadowing trees made the place cozy, but they let in little sunlight at this time of day. The barn sat a few hundred feet from the driveway that circled close to the house. The large building with its attached gray rock silo looked like it had recently received a fresh coat of red paint. The porch at the front of the white, two-story house jutted out like a smile. Jennie imagined the home to be a happy one.

Claire soon opened the screen door. A dark-haired, slightly plump woman clutching a dark basket followed her. Both of them lifted their skirts before stepping down from the porch. They chatted on their way to the buggy.

"Jennie, this is Sarah Higgins."

"Mrs. Higgins, of course. You've been in our store in Clearwater," Jennie said as she grabbed the reins in her left hand and reached with her right to shake her hand.

"Please, call me Sarah. It's nice to see you, Jennie. Many a time, you've waited on me behind your counter," Sarah Higgins answered in her Irish accent, which wasn't as strong as Claire's, but still soft and lyrical. "Claire says you don't have time to stay for supper so I packed you a few dried apple scones with jam and butter to go with your sandwiches. I wrapped up a jar of hot tea to go with everything. Maybe you can pull over and take a bit of refreshment."

"How thoughtful! Thank you."

Claire lifted her skirt and stepped up into the buggy.

Once she settled on the seat, Claire said, "We've got food galore, but now we best be heading back. Thank you for everything, Sarah."

"John and the boys won't be in for supper until later. I'll take Katie with me, and we'll head over to see what we can do for Frau Frank. Katie can stick around to make supper for her and clean up her kitchen afterwards."

Feeling reassured Mrs. Frank was in good hands, Jennie nudged Solly to move on. They circled the driveway and headed toward the road. Jennie's stomach growled. She also felt a chill. Pulling up her shawl, she realized nighttime wasn't far off.

"I guess there's no way we can avoid it, Claire," Jennie said. "We'll have to light the lanterns soon. Maybe when we do, we can grab a bite. I'm hungry!"

"Let's see. If we go back the way we came, we might be going out of our way."

"So what do you suggest?"

"It's getting darker by the minute. When Danny and I leave his folks' place, we turn right instead of left. I think that's the quickest way."

"I can still see, and Solly has great vision so we won't go off the side of the road," Jennie said.

"Would you like me to pour you a spot of tea? We should drink it while it's still warm. We don't have sugar or anything, but it'll still warm us up a bit."

"If you can handle it while we bump around, that would be wonderful. Tea would warm our stomachs. I wouldn't mind if you gave me a few crumbs of a scone as well. Maybe that'll hold me for a bit. I didn't eat much before we started on our trip today."

"Oh, I can do that. Sarah gave us a couple of her old cups." Claire unwrapped the kitchen towel from the basket, but quickly grabbed hold of the seat because they were bouncing around. When Solly maneuvered them from the end of the driveway onto the road, their ride became smoother. Claire draped a towel over Jennie's lap. She handed her a scone. She then poured a half cup of tea and handed that over to her as well.

"Can you manage?" Claire asked.

"It's harder than I thought," Jennie said. She put the scone on her lap and tried to sip her tea. "I can handle the reins with one hand until we turn off this road. Could you hold the cup for me while I take a few bites of the scone? If I can tame my hunger a bit, I'll feel better."

Claire took the cup, which gave Jennie the opportunity to bite into the scone. The butter and jam squeezed out into her mouth. *Ambrosia*, Jennie thought. She looked down to make sure the juicy and delicious butter and jam hadn't squeezed out and down the front of her blouse.

As dusk settled all over the countryside, the night came alive with sounds. Crickets chirped, frogs croaked, and birds warbled their many different songs. A light breeze swished and shushed as it blew through the grasses.

They soon reached the top of the incline where Claire had said Mrs. Hayes's cabin stood. In the darkening hour, the small house looked even more decrepit peeking eerily from behind the trees and brush.

"That was delicious," Jennie proclaimed after she picked up the towel and dabbed the crumbs from her mouth. "I had always wondered what a scone tasted like. I can take my tea now. Thank you."

"Danny's mum's a good cook for sure. I think our road's up here. We'll need to be turning right."

"Isn't it a beautiful evening? It's a bit chilly," Jennie said after she took a sip of warm tea.

"It is lovely tonight. I prefer cooler weather anyway. Ireland's like this most of the time. Summers can be warm, but they're rarely hot. We need shawls or jackets almost every night and in the wee hours of the morning."

"We have lots of heat and humidity between July and September. Farmers love it. With rain and lots of heat, the cornfields grow fast and turn bright green."

"When I think of my homeland, I think of green because we get lots of moisture. Sometimes, we go days without seeing the sun. Fog and mist hang in the air." Claire took a sip of her tea and was silent for a bit. Jennie assumed she was thinking of her home so far away. "I think we're close to our turn. D'you remember, Jennie, we came from the left when we left the Frank farm?"

Jennie looked to where Claire pointed. "Oh, sure," she acknowledged as she guided the horse into the turn. The road became smoother. *Obviously, Edgar Barrett's road grading signature,* Jennie thought.

"The Mooney school's up here on the left. We'll drive right by it. It's quite small. Francis Mooney started the school. He taught for a bit, but now he's president of the school board."

"His son Jamie told me that last week."

Dusk settled in, but Jennie could see a small, square building, no bigger than a shed. She couldn't imagine attending such a tiny school. She'd been used to the two-story Clearwater school and then the larger Monticello High School. Not even the Atwater school she taught in out in the country was this small.

"Which direction are we?"

"We're in the southern part of Lynden. From here, we've about another half-mile or so before we hook up to the Lynden Township road."

Instantly, Jennie remembered that the Leonard girl had gone over to this very school with her family to take part in the flag raising the afternoon before her murder.

"Claire," Jennie said, hearing the alarm in her own voice. "We're not near the southern part of the Tamarack Swamp, are we?"

"I suppose we are. If you want, we could head back the way we came, but in the dark, I'm not sure we won't get lost."

Suddenly, an ear-piercing scream came out of nowhere. Solly whinnied loudly and reared. Jennie nearly lost hold of the cup before Claire grabbed it.

"Calm down, Solly," Jennie hollered, pulling as hard as possible on the reins so the buggy would come to a safe stop.

"Holy Mary, Mother of God!" Claire answered, nearly standing so she could see into the bushes toward her left.

"What was that?" Jennie whispered.

Soon another loud cry, almost a sob, came from the swamp grass. Solly stood up on his hind legs and whinnied again. Claire fell back against the back of the seat. Again, Jennie pulled on the leather to get the horse under control. She knew he was smart enough to get them home in the dark, but as anxious as he was, if she let up on the reins he might run away with the carriage.

Somehow, after a minute or two, Jennie was able to get the horse moving forward at a slow trot. Occasionally, he let out a loud nervous snort and shook his head.

They entered a thick copse, with large trees and heavy shrubbery that enveloped them in blackness. All the while they moved forward, Jennie kept thinking she saw white dots. Were they small bugs or spots before her eyes?

As Solly trudged along, Jennie realized she no longer heard night sounds. The birds had quit singing. Crickets had stopped chirping. Frogs had quit croaking. It was like every living creature had taken a deep breath and hadn't exhaled.

She kept her eyes focused in front of her in case a cougar jumped out at them. Jennie whispered into the darkness, "Do you see anything?"

"I'm not sure," Claire whispered. Focusing her attention on the swamp to the left of the buggy, Claire was so close, her warm breath nearly kissed Jennie's cheek.

Before long, another loud cry came out from the vegetation. Claire stood up at the same time Solly whinnied and pulled to the right. A low lying ground fog reached across the road into the ditch near the swamp. Solly saw something as well because he whinnied and reared again. Then crying began again, this time more like whimpering. The pitiful cries sounded similar to what she heard last weekend.

"Jennie, can you pull your horse to a stop and hold him still? I need to get down and see what's happening out there."

"You can't be serious, Claire!" Jennie cried softly in alarm. "If that's a cougar, it could kill you."

"It's okay, Jennie." Claire's voice sounded like liquid satin, smooth and comforting.

Reluctantly, Jennie pulled Solly to a stop. As Claire stepped down, the wailing increased. Swirls of ground fog moved back and forth across the road.

Jennie was so afraid she began to shiver. An odor of something dead overpowered her. It smelled like the time when a mouse died and decayed in the family loveseat.

As Jennie kept tight hold on Solly, she couldn't believe how out of control she felt. How had she gotten herself into this situation? Would Claire come back? She wanted to let Solly run, run for home!

"I'm still right behind the carriage, Jennie. Try not to be afraid."

Claire's voice sounded almost ethereal, yet soothing. Even Solly seemed to settle down.

Jennie listened to the crunching of steps in the sand, tall grasses swishing, and a few soft shushes. Then she heard more sobbing. Soon Jennie heard a melodic chant.

Not sure how long she sat there in total darkness and quiet, Jennie seemed to awaken to the familiar sound of a fingernail scraping across a comb, which she recognized as the call of the leopard frog. It wasn't long before she heard heavy movement in the grasses and the crunching of sand on the road. Jennie knew she was no longer alone. Something was out there and coming toward her. Solly snorted a sneeze and shook his head, as if to ask why they were still resting by the side of the road.

"I'm back, Jennie," Claire announced softly as she walked behind the buggy. "We can be going home now."

Chapter 16
Addantur
Let Be Added

AFTER CLAIRE CLIMBED INTO the carriage, she said little as Solly led them home. After they were away from the swamp, Jennie felt calm enough to stop and light the buggy lanterns.

She hadn't asked questions; Claire hadn't offered explanations. And, although Claire replied quietly and in monosyllables when Jennie said something, the two didn't converse as they rode along. Jennie felt as though the woman's energy had drained from her. In fact, for a while, Claire seemed to have slumped over and slept.

When Solly finally pulled them into town and arrived at Doc's place at the top of the hill, Claire quietly gathered her belongings, including the basket that Sarah Higgins had given them. She had little Irish melody in her voice as she said, "Good night, Jennie," and stepped away from the light of the buggy into the darkness of the night.

In fact, even though the street lamps had been lit outside and the Rochester and other lamps had been lit inside, evening hadn't settled in on the Phillips's household. When Jennie walked in the back door after combing Solly and getting him some grain and water, four of her siblings were sitting around the dining room table playing cards.

Carl hollered, "Hey, Jennie," and immediately started hollering at Sammy, "What *were* you thinking? What *were* you thinking?"

Carl couldn't handle losing any type of game to a girl, much less a game of cards. Si laughed at her brothers as she pulled the trick from the center of the table. Blanche covered her smiling mouth with splayed cards.

Sammy, who at eleven hadn't reached the age of competition between the sexes, responded, "I'm sorry, Carl, but it's *only* a game. Hi, ya, Jennie. We're playing Whist."

Si and Blanche, dressed in their white nightgowns, greeted her as well. Her folks sat in the living room. Eight-year-old Percy lay in the middle of the floor reading *The Adventures of Tom Sawyer,* which he'd been working on for a couple of weeks already. The only one in the family missing was Ruthie, who, obviously, already had been put to bed.

"Jennie," Marietta exclaimed, "I'm glad you made it home. We were beginning to get worried about you."

Her father sat with a blanket over his legs, reading the newspaper. She felt encouraged to see he was sitting upright and had some pink in his cheeks. "Carl," Stanley hollered into the dining room, "you and Sammy go feed and put up Solly for the night."

Carl laid down his cards and stood up. Sammy, who was too young to hide his disappointment, rolled his eyes in exasperation and sighed deeply.

Jennie waved at her brothers. "I bedded him down already."

She sat down on the only available seat in the living room—the piano stool—and twirled around so she could look at both parents.

"How did everything go? How is the Frank woman?" Stanley asked, as he laid the newspaper on his lap.

"I don't think she is doing so well, but she doesn't complain," she admitted. With her left hand on the keys, Jennie rolled her fingers up the octave. "I hope Doc can go out to see her soon. Claire O'Casey and I stopped at the Higgins's farm because they are neighbors to the Franks. I don't understand gout enough to explain her condition, but her leg was swollen and gray. She's been on that foot too much. I wish I could have done more for her."

"Well, you did all you could. You'll understand that someday. We aren't doctors, Jennie," her father reminded her.

"Did you eat? Do you want me to fix you something?" her mother asked as she laid aside her darning.

"I'll eat a bite or two once I wash up. I'm tired and want to go to bed."

In truth, Jennie wished she had the house to herself. She'd loved to unwind by sitting and playing the piano. In this household that seldom happened.

Marietta stood up and stretched before hobbling a couple steps. "Been sitting too long. I needed to get up and move about," she commented as she walked behind Jennie through the dining room again where the others were still noisily playing cards. "Jennie," her mother started once they reached kitchen, "are you all right? You look really tired."

Looking at her mother's face, Jennie noticed the furrows above her brows and the puffiness under her eyes. She remembered how, as she walked, her question came out in huffs like she was having trouble breathing. Marietta had had quite a day herself, worrying about her husband and her eldest daughter. She wished she could tell her what happened when she and Claire went by the southern end of Irish Town in Lynden Township, but right now, she didn't feel like talking.

"I'm fine," Jennie tried to reassure her mother as she patted her arm. "It's been a long day," she added as she trudged up the stairs to her bedroom.

* * *

JENNIE'S PILLOW FELT HARD and lumpy. She plumped it and tossed and turned, trying to get comfortable. She wished she had a room to herself so she wouldn't disturb Blanche.

She mulled over everything that transpired on her trip back and forth to Lynden Township. Jennie marveled over Claire's intelligence. Her mother raised her to know about plants, roots, and herbs, something Jennie was now learning. While she admired Claire's selfless ambition to help others, she struggled with her self-imposed responsibility to help unfortunate women who found themselves in sticky situations. While Jennie had a lot to work through with all of this, she knew she had lots to think through about Claire's ability to calm strange noises in the night.

Despite a fairly tolerant religious upbringing, as a Christian, Jennie believed she had no business playing around with ghosts or spirits of the netherworld. In fact, she had often refused to listen to a few of her friends who talked about what they learned from their morning tea leaves, card readings, or Ouija board communications. As far as she was concerned playing with spirits was one of the *Thou shalt nots*. Despite her strong belief, Jennie couldn't deny or pretend she hadn't experienced something—she had heard it, felt it, and last night, she had seen it. Something or someone was restlessly roaming around Tamarack Swamp.

Jennie had no idea when she finally fell asleep. Even then, she felt her conscience weighing all the issues of the day. Sometime, though, she had to have conked out hard because she woke with a start and realized the other side of the bed was empty. Alarmed that she'd be late for work, Jennie popped up out of bed. She ran to the top of the steps and whispered loudly as to avoid waking the house, "Mother?"

A couple moments went by before she heard a shuffle of steps and a soft answer. "Jennie." Blanche whispered loudly. "Mother and Pa wanted you to sleep in. They went to open the store. Mother wants to get a few shelves ready for the pies. She told me to tell you to take your time this morning."

"I'll be down to wash up and eat a bite of breakfast."

Jennie tiptoed back to her room. She figured Ruthie was still sleeping because she hadn't heard the little one's chatter. The rest of the clan had to be off to school at the top of the hill. Jennie remembered this was their last day. At lunchtime, after all the children ate and cleaned out their desks, they'd hike over to Upper Park and have a potluck picnic. After all the games, the students would be dismissed for the summer. She could almost hear Sammy and Percy shouting for joy as they ran down the Blacksmith's Hill and headed home.

Sitting at end of the bed, Jennie leaned her forehead against the footboard. She had so much to make sense of in her tired head. Tempted to lie back, Jennie mustered every ounce of energy she had to get up and get ready for her day. She gathered her black skirt and white blouse, under garments, and shoes and headed downstairs.

After eating a tasty breakfast of fried eggs and fresh bread and butter, Jennie felt more revived. She brushed her teeth, looked into the mirror, and patted down her bangs. Stepping out the back door, she noticed four pairs of brown trousers, ranging in size from long to short, and many pair of socks and underwear on the line blowing like white flags. Because of her large family, Marietta usually did laundry a couple times a week. What was the old saying?

Wash on Monday, Iron on Tuesday, Sew on Wednesday, Shop on Thursday, Clean on Friday, Bake on Saturday, Rest on Sunday.

As she headed down the sidewalk, Jennie admired the family garden. The long block of black dirt had been turned over, pulled and raked free of weeds. Jennie enjoyed working in the soil. Unfortunately, she had little time for getting her hands down into the rich earth. She loved watching the onions growing, especially the salad type. She could hardly wait to pluck a tender one, wipe off the dirt, and munch on the spicy white bulb and sweet green top. But that wouldn't happen for a couple weeks yet. For now, she was satisfied with the beauty of the little sprigs of green lettuce that sprouted through the long lines of mounded dirt and the smell of the fresh, clean earth.

Jennie cut across the street and walked in front of the green, two-story Shaw house. As she got close to Collins's blacksmith shop, she heard the familiar clucking of horse's hooves coming up behind her. She turned to see Donald Wolff, the town constable. He saw Jennie at the same time, smiled wide, tipped his hat as he bowed from his waist. As he and his horse continued north, Jennie realized she would never look at him again without thinking about Claire's friend's delicate condition.

Just as she reached the edge of the store, Jennie noticed a long, white sign strung across Main Street from the top of the large oak tree in front of Whittemore's Bank across to the other oak near Lyons's store. It read:

WELCOME TO CLEARWATER'S
1895 DECORATION DAY CELEBRATION

She admired the professional looking sign and was proud her brother had been the one to create it. While some others in town would do a slip-shod job and say it was good enough, Carl had decided if he were to do the job right, he would use stencils.

"Here she is," Stanley said as she opened the store's screen door.

"Child, I was hoping you'd get more sleep. You looked totally exhausted last night," her mother added.

"I feel much better this morning. Besides, I know Maude is going to need me to help sometime soon."

"Oh, she's been here already. Ida's in town, too. They're putting up decorations," Marietta said. "My! Everything's going to look patriotic with red, white, and blue all over town. Didn't Carl do a nice job on the welcome sign?"

"He did!" Jennie exclaimed, taking another look out the window to admire her brother's work.

Marietta said, "I think they started down at the Whiting building. I know Carl said the stage is up. Go check it out, if you wish."

Jennie asked, "Are you sure you don't need me here?"

Marietta and Stanley said, "Go!" in unison.

"Besides," Marietta added, "some of the women are coming in later this afternoon to drop off their pies and to start setting up so they're ready for the social tomorrow. I'll be here if your father gets a rush."

"Okay. I'll see what they are up to. But I won't be long."

The door slammed behind Jennie when she stepped down onto the sidewalk. The streets had suddenly turned noisy and dusty from horses kicking up the hardened earth.

The village's din nearly swallowed the sound of the train's far-off whistle. She promised herself she'd get back before her father had a rush of customers. Chances were the day's trains from both north and south would bring in more visitors for the Decoration Day events.

Even though the streets had been mucky last week, they had gone from mud to a fine brown powder in a short time. Now that the weather had warmed up, the doors had to be open. She doubted her mother's dusting and sweeping, which was a never-ending task, would do much good for any length of time.

Two drays, each pulled by a team of plodding, light-colored, work horses, clanked and squeaked their way toward the river landing. She saw Danny Higgins steering one but couldn't make out who was in the seat on the other. She assumed both were trying to make time hauling goods from the steamboat before the train's cargo got into town.

A single-horse buggy sat in front of the Laughton's Meat Market. A gray-speckled horse stood in front of Lyons's. From what she could see toward the northern part of town, it, too, looked busy. Teams of horses, wagons, and black buggies stood in front of the General Mercantile store below the Masonic Hall and Boutwell's Hardware.

When she walked in front of the Methodist Church, Jennie noticed Carl had nailed up the "PIE AND ICE CREAM SOCIAL AT 2:00" sign on the large oak tree. Across the street, Jennie could see Maude and Ida, each carrying a corner of the red, white, and blue bunting, walking it to the railing in front of the stage. Carl stood with hammer in hand, waiting to nail it down. More bunting decorated the three first floor windows of the Whiting building.

As Jennie came closer, she smelled the freshly cut pine boards and paint. Although her brother and his friends did a good job building the platform, the structure looked almost too white as it stood out between the two gray buildings, two-story Whiting building and Jim Lyons's house, and all the trees that surrounded the properties. Nevertheless, Jennie knew by the time it all was decorated, it would look quite festive. She was also pleased that this part of town looked and smelled better after the townspeople chipped in to haul and clean away the black char from the fire two weeks before.

"Good morning, everyone! You're going to get all this work done before I get a chance to help," Jennie said.

"Hello, Sunshine! I heard you were sleeping in this morning," Maude said as she looked down to where Carl was hammering.

"Hi, Jennie! I got into town earlier than I expected," Ida said as she waved with her free hand. "Father and Sherm are out checking fence line. They needed a few supplies picked up at the hardware store, so since Mother's busy baking pies for the social and I wanted to come in to help decorate the town, I told them I'd do the running today."

Carl, dressed in a pair of well-worn brown pants and shirt with sleeves rolled up to his elbows, nodded to his sister. He had a nail in his mouth so he couldn't greet her. He then moved over to where Ida stood holding the flag and began nailing down her side.

"You did a wonderful job building the stage, Carl."

With a nail in his mouth, he mumbled, "Thanks!"

"So what can I do?" Jennie added. "I told Mother and Father I'd be back before the train starts unloading."

"You can tie some of the ribbons around the speaker's stand," Maude said, nodding backward toward the dark wood podium they had borrowed from the Methodist church. "As soon as Carl's finished here, I'm going next door. Sam Whiting offered chairs for the speakers to sit on. How many do you think we need?"

Jennie started counting, "We have Commander Kaufman, maybe D.D. Storms, John Stevens, the former Lieutenant Governor Barto, Congressman Towne, Simon Stevens. Your father's going to say something, Maude, so another for Tom Porter, and Rev. Barkaloo is going to open the ceremony with a prayer. That's what? Eight?"

"Sounds right! "Maude said. "I could use your muscles to help carry the chairs, Carl."

Carl didn't say anything. Jennie noticed his neck and face had turned red, which was his usual reaction when he was angry. For a few cold seconds, she wondered if her brother might not walk off and refuse to help them anymore. Carl was nearly always agreeable, and, normally, he liked Maude, but sometimes she was bossy, and that caused a lot of men, and some women, to get a bit frustrated with her.

Ida must have sensed the tension as well. She said, "Why don't I go and help Carl?" Without waiting for approval from Maude, she followed behind the young man.

Jennie looked over the stage. "I don't think eight chairs will fit up here, Maude. Maybe we should place only four here and the rest down by the foot of the steps." Hating to add more tension, Jennie hollered at the two as they climbed the steps of the Whiting building. "Why don't you see if you can get a few more. I bet the older folks, especially a few of the town founders, would appreciate a place to sit."

"Fine!" Carl shouted back. Jennie could hear the agitation in his voice.

Once Carl and Ida were out of site, Maude followed behind Jennie and said, "You look tired. Why were you sleeping in so late this morning. Are you sick?"

Pausing to answer, Jennie looked out onto the street and then toward Whitings. She took a deep breath before answering. "We don't have time to talk about it here, Maude. And I don't want to say anything in front of Carl because I don't want the folks to know yet."

"Hmm! Sounds mysterious." Maude teased.

"I was out in Lynden, down in Irish Town, with Claire O'Casey yesterday."

Even though her head was bowed as she tied ribbons into a large bow, Maude's expression was easy to read even before she answered "Really?"

"We were running an errand for Doc Edmunds. Do you know the German woman, Mrs. Frank?"

"I'm not sure."

"Well, Doc was too busy to deliver her medicine. So he asked if I'd do it. He sent Claire with me because she knew where the Franks lived, which I eventually figured out I knew as well." Jennie glanced next door again. "We didn't get home until after dark," she added, biting her lip.

"So what happened?"

"Claire and I experienced something or someone by the Tamarack Swamp."

"Are you referring to what you, Ida, and I were talking about last Sunday—about where that young girl was murdered?"

"Claire and I encountered something weird out there." Jennie saw Ida carrying one chair while Carl carried three toward the platform. "We can talk about this later."

"You two have been gabbing too much. We need work, work, work," Ida teased as she shoved her chair across the floor of the platform.

"I was telling Maude I'd better get back to the store," Jennie said as she finished tying her bow. "I'm sorry I couldn't have been more help. I'll try to make up for it later, though."

"Don't worry about it. You did all the planning. We're doing the legwork," Carl said in a much more agreeable tone. Maybe Ida had had a bit of a talk about Maude with him. She was good at jollying anyone out of a bad mood.

"So right, Madame Organizer!" Ida said, bowing from her waist.

When everyone quit chuckling, Jennie asked her brother, "Do you have to head back to Rices' this afternoon?"

"Yeah, I thought I'd stop in at the house for a bite to eat, then head out."

"Okay, well, Ida and Maude, why don't you two stop down and see me at the store when you're through? We can discuss what else needs to be done today."

"Sounds good," Maude said.

The train's whistle alerted Jennie to its impending arrival. "I'd better get going."

Jennie headed back on the boardwalk toward downtown and the drug store. From a block away, she saw a few travelers carrying baggage. One man walked to the steps of the hotel. Two women, each dressed in dark suits and wearing straw hats, walked toward the drug store.

Jennie picked up her skirt and began sprinting. She knew her mother could help her father, but sometimes she got a bit flustered if it became too busy.

When she got closer to Lyons's store, she made a quick decision to cut across the street. With her attention on the ground to avert plopping down in horse muck, Jennie stepped down between two horse rigs. In doing so, she collided with a man coming up from the rear end of the buggy.

"I'm sorry. Did I hurt you?" he asked, reaching out and grabbing Jennie by the shoulders before she went flying backwards.

"No, no, I'm fine. I should have been watching where I was going." As she regained her balance, Jennie looked up into a handsome face. A bit taken aback by his looks, she felt self-conscious when the stranger stared down at her.

"No, it was my fault. I was in such a hurry I never thought I'd be running into such a lovely woman."

Now even more self-conscious, Jennie felt her cheeks turn red. She had no idea who this man was. He was immaculately dressed in black coat, striped gray-and-black trousers, and white shirt with a black tie. He was of medium height, had large brown eyes, dark-brown hair, and a dark-brown mustache that crowned his smiling lips and white teeth.

"Well, excuse me, but I need to—" Jennie tried to walk around the man, but her foot caught on an object on the ground. As she started to trip, she heard what sounded like the rattling of chains. The stranger grabbed her and lifted her up before she landed face down in the dirt.

At first, Jennie felt a bit rattled. She tried to fix the wisp of her hair that came loose from her braided bun.

"I must apologize again. When we first bumped, I dropped my bag. Now you nearly fell over it because of my carelessness," he said.

"I . . . I'll be fine," Jennie said as she began nervously brushing wrinkles and dirt from the front and back of her dress."

The handsome stranger lifted the satchel. Jennie noticed the quality of the brown leather bag with its leather handle, double lanyards, a shiny, brass lock, and more clinking noises as he set it on the front seat of the rig.

"A gentleman should accompany said lady across the street," he said in his silky voice.

"No, no, I'll be fine," Jennie said, before adding, "but thank you."

Wanting to get away from the man as fast as possible, Jennie had to wait for two men on horses who were heading south from the northern part of town. She also saw a man holding the door open for a woman at the drug store. Her mother would be totally lost. She had to hurry.

Chapter 17
Cordis
Of the Heart

JENNIE KEPT BUSY THE REST of the morning with a steady parade of customers. Men, women, and children wandered into the drug store. She had so many patrons she hardly saw faces. Most of the customers were strangers and dressed in their finest. She had glimpses of flashy styles—dresses of blue or green plaids, tight collars buttoned at the neck, and big blousy sleeves that tightened at the elbow and traveled to the wrists. Some women carried flouncy parasols that matched their dresses.

She had only a few moments to think about the newer styles. She wasn't sure she liked all that material and wasn't sure how practical any of the dresses would be here at work in the store. She imagined getting her arms caught on the nails of the walls or on the rough edges of the counters.

At times, through all the hubbub, Jennie heard people talking about their Decoration Day accommodations. Some said they were staying at the Scott or Whitney hotels. Others mentioned they were staying with relatives like the Lemes, the Collins, or the Ranneys, all local names.

She glanced over once or twice and saw her mother and father standing near the dispensing counter talking to an elderly couple dressed in travel gray. They looked familiar, but she had little time to figure out who they were.

Like players' pieces strategically scattered on a chessboard, jeweled tortoise hair combs, lilac and lemon powders and puffs, pink and blue bottles of perfume lined the glass counter for some of the customers to examine.

Jennie scooped and packaged small bags of chewy gum drops and spicy root beer barrels. The cash register's *ka-ching* resonated in her brain.

Sometime before dinnertime, Marietta slipped out. Jennie heard her mother encouraging her father to come home and rest when he could. But before long, when the store had been nearly cleaned of customers, Jennie felt a pang and heard a large gurgle in her stomach. She looked at the clock on the wall and realized she hadn't even heard the noon whistle nor the clock chime. It was nearing one o'clock.

"Father, do you see the time? You want to go home while I watch the store? You probably could use some rest."

"I feel pretty good right now. Besides, your ma's sending dinner down with someone. I have a few things to do around here yet. Donald Wolff came in while you were gone and said the band's practicing at four this afternoon. So whether I'm up to it or not, I have to keep upright and movin'."

Her father's bout was hitting him at a bad time. "Still, take it easy today."

His mention of Donald Wolff reminded Jennie of Claire's accusations. He was an excitable character and quite self concerned, but Jennie could hardly believe he'd ever really harm anyone.

"After we eat something," Jennie added, "I'll see if I can help Maude, Ida, or Carl. I'll be back before you need to go. "

"Pa, Jennie," Carl announced as the door swung open and the bell jingled.

"How's it going, Carl?" Jennie asked. "I thought you told me you were going home to get something to eat before heading out to the farm." Jennie read the furrows of wrinkles on her brother's forehead. "Oh, oh! Now what has Maude done?" Jennie said with a laugh.

"She's so bossy!" He said grunting and shrugging his shoulders. "After you left, she told me she wanted another sign made up and a coat of paint on all the tables for the pie social."

Jennie shook her head and laughed sympathetically. That was Maude.

"I have to get back out to Rices' now to finish chores. I'll try to start the project when I get back, but it might not be until late tonight."

Jennie read Carl's frustration. "Why does she think we need another sign and a coat of paint on the tables?"

"I don't know. We have one for Lyons's corner," he said as he jutted his thumb backward toward the general merchandise store. "Most will see the welcome sign on the depot as they get off the train. But now she thinks we need one down by the ferry landing. I know some may be coming over from Clear Lake and getting on the river ferry, but how could anyone miss the platform since almost everything is located down by the landing anyway? "

Stanley shook his head. Although he was always congenial when Maude came around, Jennie knew he had a problem with her too. Maude, definitely, had a strong personality.

"Have you eaten lunch yet?" *Where did that come from? I'm beginning to sound like Mother who seems to think all bad moods need nourishment.*

"No, I'll stop in at home and get a bite before I head out to finish up my chores."

"Yeah, make the best of it all. We'll get through this mess before you know it," Stanley promised.

Carl nodded a farewell to his father and Jennie, and walked out the door.

"Poor Carl!" Jennie said as she stared at her brother crossing the street and heading south towards home. Even though Maude was a good friend, she could be quite intimidating when she wanted to be. Marietta always said the biggest problem with Maude was her parents never told her no. She acted a bit bullish at times. Most men didn't like such strong-willed women.

"Maude'll never get herself a husband if she doesn't tone it down a bit," Stanley said.

Jennie had to agree. Maude was a force to be reckoned with at times.

"Father, with all this hubbub, I never got to ask if you'd heard from Doc Edmunds today."

"I knew there was something I was going to tell you. Doc was waiting for me to open this morning. I told him what you observed about the Frank woman. He said he hopes to get out there later this week."

"Good and the sooner the better. I don't think she's going to follow my suggestions. She has so much work to do. She shouldn't have such a hard life at her age."

"Well, I'm sure she's miserable, but I don't think she has anything life-threatening. Her husband, Fred, has been in here a couple times. He's no spring chicken himself. They don't seem to have much of a family here to help them."

"That seems to be the consensus. I can't believe at their ages they're trying to start all over."

"Doc said they have a married daughter living down in Virginia where they came from."

"Claire told me that yesterday."

"Doc said their place is little more than a rock farm. They bought it sight unseen. Apparently, they've got some relatives up in St. Cloud who heard about this farm, but they have no one young and strong enough to give them a hand out there."

"Danny Higgins said the farm's never made much profit. Tracys didn't stay there long either." For a moment, Jennie thought about the Tracy boy who Claire said might have had a hand in the Alice Leonard murder. "It's a shame

. . . just a shame! I wonder why they didn't go further west into the Dakotas to homestead."

Jennie knew before her father answered. An elderly couple like the Franks didn't have enough time nor energy to make a go of it out west. Homesteading was a hard enough task for younger people, but for older people, it would have been impossible. Unless they bought an established farm, they'd have to build some temporary home, a shack or a dugout. The Tracy place offered them an established place with at least a roof over their heads even if it had little else.

"They'd be too old to try that on their own," Stanley said as he turned back to his mortar and pestle.

"Father, I see Blanche coming. Looks like she's carrying our dinner basket."

* * *

AFTER A QUICK DINNER, Jennie waited on the afternoon train crowd. Although smaller, this group was more familiar. Jeanette Sanborn, Ella Kirk, and Gert Sheldon came strolling in to bid Jennie a big hello. All three young women had caught the train at St. Cloud after finishing their teaching terms in and around the area north of Clearwater.

Barely a year older than Jennie, Jeanette and she had always been good friends. A few weeks ago, she had come down from Benson where, for the last three years, she had been in charge of the third-grade class. On her last visit, she swore Jennie to secrecy. She had heard there was an opening in Clearwater for an elementary school teacher and decided to interview for the job. If she could get it, she would be closer to her family.

Tall and fine boned, Jeanette had a delicate beauty. She and Jimmy Baxter, a distant cousin of Jennie's, had been somewhat engaged before Jeanette headed off to get her teaching degree at the St. Cloud Normal School. Unfortunately, Jimmy wasn't willing to wait for her to get her education and teach awhile. Shortly after Jeanette left, he met Delores Munce and the two fell in love, so he told Jennie. This seemingly impromptu action nearly broke Jeanette's heart, even though she put up a good front. Because of this, she seldom came home because she was afraid she'd bump into the two. Over winter, Jimmy and his wife left Clearwater and returned to upper New York state where he was going to take over his father's farm. Now, Jeanette felt like she could come home. Seeing the glow in her good friend's face, Jennie hoped she had good news about getting the position at the Clearwater school.

Ella Kirk was already in her thirties and had been teaching for over twelve years in St. Cloud. She took the necessary coursework to be able to teach at the Normal School and had had many opportunities to teach with Pitt Colgrove.

A short, plump woman, Ella piled her thick brown hair on top of her head. Her blazing blue eyes were her best feature. Equally independent, she and Maude Porter were close in age and friendship, sharing a concern for women's rights. Ella took pride in the fact she taught in the same area where the famous newspaper woman Jane Grey Swisshelm had stood her ground against Sylvanus Lowry and others in favor of slavery. She fought to continue writing and publishing her newspaper that advocated women be able to hold onto their own property, to vote, and to have access to information to help them govern their own bodies.

Happy-go-lucky Gert loved her students in St. Stephen, a little community thirteen or fourteen miles from St. Cloud. She often talked about this Slovenian and German community with its old country ways. Most of the children had to be taught English because at home they spoke only their parents' native tongues. Although she could often figure out what the German children were trying to tell her, she said the Slovenians had such a strange language that she had to be more strict with them: "Speak English; speak English."

Seeing her good friends and hearing about their endeavors to teach well despite obstacles made Jennie a bit jealous. She missed the feel of chalk, the smell of sawdust and lemon oil she used to mop the floor planks, and the pride of accomplishment after a hard day calculating sums, memorizing presidents, and conjugating verbs.

"It's so good to see you three. The town has been quiet since you've been away. Won't we have fun this summer, gabbing and taking our little shopping trips to St. Cloud and Minneapolis?"

"Jennie," they all greeted in unison. All of them said hello to Stanley as well, but it was Jennie they'd come to see. "We can start tonight and continue all summer. What can we do to help you get this shindig off the ground?"

Of course, Jennie realized, the three would be great assets in getting some of the work done. "I may be tied up here most of the day, but I know Maude needs some help setting things up. I never got up to help her with the youth float, and I bet our mothers would be grateful if they had some help with the lemonade stands and pie social."

"We can do that," Ella added. "By the time I get home, unpack a bit, and visit with the folks, I'll be ready to turn around and get back in town." The Kirks lived a short half mile out of town on a farm. "Would we be able to meet up about seven or seven-thirty tonight? Maude sent me a letter last week and gave me orders on what I needed to do to help." Everyone in their circle laughed, knowing how Maude always took charge. "She kindly offered me a bed for tonight if I'd help her tonight and tomorrow."

"The time's good for me," Jennie agreed.

"Jeanette and I wrote back and forth, as well," Gert said as she patted her friend's arm. "She and I are bunking together at her place tonight. I'll go home with the folks tomorrow after the celebration is over. I sent them a letter last week so they didn't waste a trip into town to pick me up from the train."

"Speaking of trains, Jennie, guess who sat with us on our way home." Jeanette said. "Pitt! He said to tell you he'd be over to see you before he heads home."

Pitt coming here? Jennie wondered why he told her friends that unless he was being cordial. She knew she hadn't said much to anyone about their relationship. Ida and Maude were about the only ones who knew that they had not seen each other lately. She realized she had a lot to tell these three to get them caught up on what was going on in her life.

Each of the women purchased gifts to take home. Ella bought a bag of lemon drops. Gert bought a half pound of licorice for her brothers and sisters. And Jeanette bought a white shaving cup for her father.

"As I was riding up the street, I saw you three walk past the Scott," Maude said as she walked in the door. "I swear I could hear you giggling blocks away, and I got jealous because I wanted in on the joke."

After all the hugs and welcome backs, the four women paired off, visiting and gabbing until the clock chimed three times. Alerted to the time of day, and everyone's need to get something done, the women all agreed they'd meet up later at the store to put some of the day's finishing touches on the decorations.

"I've got room for all of you and your bags," Maude said. "I can give everyone a ride, and we can drop off luggage, wherever it needs to go."

As the women stood on the sidewalk, Maude started piling bag after bag on the floor of her two-seater. The women hiked their skirts, stepped down from the sidewalk, and climbed aboard.

As Jennie looked out the window to watch Maude ride away with all her friends, she noticed the handsome man she had bumped into earlier in the morning. He had walked out of the hotel and stood looking across the street at the drug store. Jennie wondered if he had seen her come in here. He turned around, apparently being summoned by two men walking over from the livery stable behind Lyons's store. Although she couldn't really tell who the men were, they looked familiar, rugged, but familiar.

"Jennie, if you want to get out of here for a bit, you can. I'm going to have to go home to pick up my drums in thirty or forty-five minutes."

"Honestly, I wouldn't mind going out for a stretch. I might wander down to see what else needs to be done at the speakers' platform."

"Go for a bit, and I'll mind the store," Stanley said as he took off his apron and hooked it on the nail behind him.

"Okay, Father. I won't be long," she added as she patted her hair, and tucked in her blouse.

Self-consciously, Jennie looked across to where the stranger and she had met. His buggy and horse were no longer parked by Lyons's store, nor did she see him standing around anywhere. Danny Higgins waved at her as he and his team came lumbering down the street and heading for the depot. Usually, the morning train from Minneapolis brought the most visitors to their village, but today, both trains brought lots of people to the community. The sidewalks had a number of men and women strolling up and down. She nodded to a few, even though they were unfamiliar.

A light breeze had picked up. Jennie wished she had brought her shawl, but she hadn't planned on being gone long enough to get cold. She walked by the Methodist Church, admiring the beauty of this white building. Marietta said it looked like one of the quaint churches back in Maine.

Under the trees on the south side of the building, Carl had put the unpainted table for the pies and had placed four small tables with chairs around them. Jennie counted the chairs. In all, they'd have about sixteen places for people to eat at one sitting. Of course, if it became busy at any given time, many would have to stand or sit on the church steps after they filled their plates. If it became really busy, she figured they would have to eat in shifts, but it couldn't be helped.

She looked over the scene and knew her mother said there'd be white cloths on each table. Maybe that is why Maude figured the serving table should be white. She wasn't sure any painting had to be done, especially if they covered it with a cloth. Perhaps, if she bumped into Maude before she saw Carl again, she'd ask her, delicately, why she thought it had to be painted. As she pushed in one of the chairs closer to the table, she thought she heard her name being called. The street noise had picked up with more horses' hooves clopping, wheels turning, and chains clanking against wood as the wagons moved up and down the street.

"Jennie?" She definitely heard her name this time. When she turned to see who was calling her, her stomach flip-flopped when she saw Pitt walking toward her.

"Why, hello there!" she said.

"I'm glad I could finally catch up with you. I got off the train and saddled up at the Barretts. Pa always leaves a horse for me when he knows I'm coming home. I stopped in the store. Your pa told me you'd gone for a short walk down here to check on things. You have much left to do?" Pitt asked as he looked around.

"I've done little, haven't had time. Maude, Ida, and Carl have done the most. I was looking everything over," she said while following his gaze.

"I really need to talk to you, Jennie."

Realizing he was staring at her, she slowly looked up into his eyes.

"Pitt, what's wrong? Are your parents ill?" Jennie asked anxiously. All of a sudden, she felt she had to sit down. She pulled out the chair that she had taken such care to push under the table.

"I'm sorry, didn't mean to frighten you. We're all fine," Pitt answered softly as he, too, pulled out a chair and pulled it closer to her. "Jennie, I need to talk about . . . well, I want to talk about us."

Jennie looked down into her lap and fumbled with her skirt.

"All week, I've regretted that we didn't take the time to talk after church on Sunday. I felt closed out when you were talking with Maude, Ida, and Sherm. All week long, I've regretted that I didn't hang it all and drag you away from everyone. Yet, I had to get back to St. Cloud to close out my term." He reached over and pulled up her chin. "Jennie, maybe this isn't the right place, maybe not the perfect time, but I love you, and I want you to marry me." Pitt begged as he grabbed hold of her hands and squeezed hard.

Shocked beyond speech, Jennie felt his strong hands trembling. She stared into his handsome and gentle face. His forehead had creases, sort of like Carl's when he was so frustrated with Maude. Always strong, Jennie felt Pitt's eyes penetrating into hers.

"I don't know what to say. We can't seem to agree on this journey of life we're supposed to share together. Isn't that what's caused our problems before? I wanted to be a teacher. You encouraged me to get the education, but you hardly tolerated my year away when I was teaching in Atwater."

"Oh, can't we forget all that and move on?"

Jennie looked at him and wanted to say *yes, yes yes*, but she knew they had never come to a conclusion about how she fit in with his life. "Pitt, all we've done is argue since I've come home to help Father in the drug store. I feel duty as well you do. I need to help him. He has no one else he can trust. Besides," she added, "I like what I am doing and think I'm learning the trade."

"But we belong together. Can't we marry and worry about the details later?" Pitt pulled her up and put his arms around her, holding her so close she could hardly breathe. "I love you and need you."

They kissed long and with so much passion Jennie felt all the tension they had had between each other melt away. At this moment, she didn't care if anyone walked by and saw them. She had no shame. Nothing mattered to her except being with Pitt.

"I love you, too, Pitt," she whispered. She felt lightheaded and nearly selfless. They had always been a couple. At this moment, Jennie understood how her parents had meshed. They were partners in their marriage. At the same time, she knew she wanted to marry Pitt, and yes, have his children. This is what life was all about.

"Are you serious, Jennie, you *will* marry me? When? Can we get married this weekend? If Reverend Jones or Barkuloo can't marry us, we could go to St. Cloud or Minneapolis and find someone."

"Oh, Pitt, wait, wait! Let me think. This is all too fast. Give me some air." Jennie saw worry come back into his face. "Surely, we can wait a few weeks," she said, searching his face.

"Why? We love each other. We deserve to be together." As Pitt argued, his cheeks turned red.

At that moment, a tuba blasted a few deep resonating notes. A horn blared out higher; both instruments woke Jennie back to reality. "I forgot. What time is it?" she asked in panic. "I promised Father I'd get back to the store so he could practice with the band."

"Damn the store, Jennie! This is our time!" he shouted. Then he softened his tone, "We have to make plans."

All of a sudden, Jennie had a clear understanding of how life would be married to Pitt. Although they had argued about her desire to continue working after they had married, she knew now he would never show any interest in her interests, nor would he accept her feeling of responsibility toward her family. She pulled away from him and stared into his face. After a moment, she started for the sidewalk.

"Jennie? Jennie!" Pitt took long strides and caught her by the arm. "I'm sorry. We can work this out."

Now feeling as though the world were watching them, Jennie looked around to see if anyone was observing their scene. The sidewalks had nearly emptied. No horses clopped down the streets. Livia hadn't come outdoors to snoop on their conversation. Kitty-corner from the church yard, Laughtons' Meat Market had a buggy and horse tethered to the post, but no one seemed to be staring at them.

Having no intention of causing commotion out here for anyone to see or give fodder for rumors, she said in a hushed yet emphatic tone, "I thought, maybe, for a moment, nothing mattered except us, but it will never be *us*, Pitt. It will always be you and what's best for you." Jennie felt like crying. *Not here and not now. I have to be strong*!

"Jennie, please, I know we can work this out."

"No!" Something deep inside calmed her. "No, we can't, Pitt," Jennie said, realizing, finally, that their relationship would never work. She'd be lost in his life. "Oh, I don't blame you for being self-centered because you're a man."

"Maybe I have been selfish. I'll try to change."

Jennie read the insincerity in his voice. Maybe he thought he could change, or sooner or later, she'd forget her needs and focus on him.

Jennie continued, feeling power in her voice even if she quivered as she spoke. "Yes, you're proud you educate men and women to go out to teach the world, but while I believe you want the men to make it a career, and maybe a few women, for the most part, I really don't think you're as liberal as you make out to be. I always thought you wanted me to be your equal—educationally and intellectually—but you want me to stay home and have my world be you and only you. And for a brief, passionate moment, I thought I could do that. But we're fooling ourselves if we think passion will last forever, Pitt."

"What're you talking about, Jennie? I'm interested in you and what you know. I've always respected your theories and beliefs. But maybe, Jennie, it's time for us to grow up and face our future."

"Future? You said it in the plural form, but you mean your future. You'll continue with your career, and I will be left, with what? Oh, I know, children, home, and social engagements. Possibly for some women that'd be more than enough. If that's really what you want, I have to be honest with you, I wouldn't be happy or content, and I'd blame you for not letting me continue in a career. Maybe, sometime in the future, maybe in a year or two, I'll be ready, but not now, not in two weeks."

"Maybe, Jennie! That is the best you can offer?" His voice had turned harsh and almost cold, without the sweet fervor he displayed a short time before.

"Yes, I'm sorry, but for now, I can't do any better," Jennie said.

Pitt slowly let go of Jennie's arm. She looked at him, and for a few moments, she could have abandoned everything and flown into his arms again. Nonetheless, as she stood there staring at his irresolute facial expression, Pitt couldn't fool her anymore. He would never change. Her desires and needs would always come second to his.

What Jennie had longed for with Pitt came to an end right there on the sidewalk and in front of God and anyone else observing their scene. As she turned and walked toward the drug store and her job, Jennie vowed no matter how painful it would be, she would never look back.

Chapter 18
Frustillatim (Frust.)

In Little Pieces

SHE AND PITT WERE FINISHED. That was that. Before she stepped over the store's threshold, Jennie had to get control of her emotions. She took two deep breaths and opened the door.

"I'm sorry it took me so long," she said with as much cheer as she could muster. "I hope you weren't worried I wouldn't get back in time."

"I wasn't even watching the time," Stanley replied as he laid a note on the counter for her. "You sick? You don't look so well," he said as he walked toward her. "I don't need to go to band practice if you don't feel well."

Jennie noticed her father's alarm. "I'm fine," she said, managing a smile.

"Your ma and I are a little worried about you. You don't have your usual get up and go. Last night when you got home, you were as white as a ghost."

What an ironic choice of words!

Jennie took a breath before saying, "I know. Mother said the same thing last night, but I'll be fine."

"Did you see Pitt? He came looking for you."

"Yes, we saw each other. He and I are through." Feeling as I she could start bawling, Jennie breathed in deeply and then exhaled slowly

"I'm sorry, Jennie. Why don't you go home for a while? I can handle the store this afternoon, or I can put up the closed sign. I don't think we're going to be that busy anyway."

"I'll be fine. Why don't you go to band practice like we planned? Work is what I need right now." She loved her father, but she didn't want to talk to him about this right now. Jennie could hear her mother say, "When tough times come, bear and forebear." It never seemed truer to her than that moment.

"Okay, then. There isn't much more to get caught up on except a couple tinctures so we don't run low. Doc needs quite a bit now. We don't want to run short. They're pretty easy," He tapped his finger on the note. "He ordered a couple other things, too. I wrote them all down here," he said, pointing to note on the counter. "He'll be in later to pick them up before he heads back out to Silver Creek and Hasty again."

As Stanley turned to leave, he spun around and had a puzzled look on his face. "There's something I need to tell you, but darned if I remember."

Jennie attempted a smile.

"Well, I suppose it wasn't important," Stanley said as he aimed for the door.

At the door, he turned so quickly, he startled Jennie, who again had returned to her own thoughts. "I remember now. I think we'll close earlier tonight. Both Bob Lyons and Luther Laughton dropped over to tell me they thought they would. Luther said he sold so much beef, chicken, and ice this morning that he doesn't have much left until he receives supplies on Saturday."

"The business is good for the town."

With his hand on the doorknob, Stanley seemed to be talking out loud. "Yep! Lots of people have company. I doubt we'd be missing out on much business anyway."

"I have lots to do tonight. So what time do you think? Five . . . six?"

"How about five, five-thirty. I shouldn't be gone too long. We won't sound any better after practice," he added. "Let's see when Doc comes before we make a decision."

After her father left, the store seemed so quiet, so empty. Jennie looked around. Everything—the shelves of clear and cobalt medicinal bottles, the rows of pink and blue stationery, the metal showcases of postcards, and the jars of hard candies—had always seemed so exciting to look at. This afternoon, they looked foreign.

She grabbed her white apron, pulled it over her head, and tied the strings around her waist.

No matter how rattled she felt, she needed to be alone. She needed time to think, to put everything in perspective. Maybe, after they shut down this afternoon, she'd go to the river and sit on the bank. For now, she would buckle down and try to get her mind off her confusion.

Jennie walked to the prescription counter and read her father's notes. The tinctures would be easy to mix up. After turning on the gas burner, she grabbed a large, deep pot and scooped water into it. Watching it, hoping it would reach a boil quickly, she remembered the old saying, "A watched pot never boils!" Yet, how easy it was to stare numbly into the water.

Focus! Jennie looked at her father's note and started writing a list of everything she had to get done.

Soon, she heard the water's rolling boil. With tongs, she carefully placed a clear, glass jar in the pot to sterilize it for a few minutes. Jennie pulled the towel off the scales where it rested on the back table. She placed the scales on the counter so she could see them better. Even though they looked clean, Jennie wiped them down in case they had some dust. Selecting two clean white towels from the cupboard, she laid one flat and dipped part of the other into the boiling water. Being careful not to burn herself, she wiped each brass dish clean. These were good quality scales. Her father seldom bought anything that wasn't.

For a few seconds, Jennie stared absentmindedly, almost hypnotically, as the shiny bowls swung back and forth. Her mind blurred. She saw a side to Pitt she could never accept and realized, once and for all, they could never have a relationship. Their future would always be about him. She would make it through this; she had to.

Shaking her head and blinking, she told herself to concentrate. She grabbed the pocket formulary from the shelf and turned each page until she found the tincture recipe Doc Edmunds wanted mixed up for a patient's toothache.

What size weights do I need? The recipe called for four drams of bruised pellitory, three drams of camphor, and one dram each of oil of cloves and ginger. Jennie picked up the weights from the box and the measuring spoons from the drawer. Dipping the cloth into the boiling water again, she wiped them down and laid them on a clean cloth to dry.

Bending over the book, she tried to read, but her mind again retreated to her trip out to Lynden, especially around Irish Town, with Claire O'Casey. Black words on white paper blurred into one another as she mulled over everything she had learned and experienced over the last few days—ghosts, babies aborted in and around her safe little community, her break up with Pitt.

Pay attention! She needed two scruples of opium for this batch. Other recipes called for more opium, but Doc Edmunds did not believe in overusing such a potent and addictive drug. He prescribed more only when he felt it absolutely necessary. After Jennie wiped down the smaller weight, she picked up the tongs, lifted the vessel from the boiling water, and set it on the clean towel to dry.

Pulling all the ingredients from the shelves, Jennie began measuring and weighing carefully before dumping all the ingredients into the container. She poured in eight ounces of rectified spirits last. Since this was a large batch, Jennie knew Doc wasn't too concerned about the amount of alcohol that went into it.

She covered her mouth with her apron and gave the whole concoction a quick stir. She quickly set the glass stopper in place and put it on the shelf above the prescription table. The recipe said it had to "digest" for eight days, stirring once each day, so, she wrote the note, "Doc's Toothache Remedy," along with the date it would be ready "June 6, 1895," and slid the note under the jar.

Stepping back to the counter, Jennie looked down at her father's list. He wrote that they needed to prepare a double portion of the camphorated tincture of opium. Doc treated his diphtheria patients with blood serum, but they suffered from such painful sore throats, he also prescribed something like this tincture to give them some relief so they could rest.

Pulling a larger bottle from the box, Jennie carefully dipped it into the hot water. Reading the recipe again, she saw she needed opium, camphor, oil of anise, and rectified spirits. She pulled the bottle from the boiling water and set it on the towel before turning off the burner.

While she waited for the bottle to dry, Jennie wandered to the front window and stared outside. For now, the streets were quiet. Absentmindedly, she looked left and right, her mind trying to make some sense of the confusion she felt. A painful sting squeezed her stomach. She commanded herself to stop thinking about Pitt.

Holding her head high, Jennie walked back to the dispensing table and began to prepare the ingredients for the cough medicine. After weighing two drams of powered opium into the bowl of the scale, she took a little brush and carefully swept every bit of it into the container.

Now she needed a scruple of camphor. Taking tweezers, she pulled a tiny chunk from the jar and dropped it into the mortar. With the pestle, she crushed it into a fine powder that smelled clean and cool like menthol.

As she worked, Jennie wondered how she could have been so blind when women came in to buy over-the-counter products that could potentially cause such harm like aborting a child. *This can't be happening in Clearwater! Not in my Clearwater! Maybe in dirty corners of the world, but not here where everyone seems happy and content!*

How could she ever look another woman in the eye when she purchased one of the products?

For a moment, Jennie wondered if it might be easier to marry Pitt. She wouldn't have to deal with any of this. She could go to all the faculty dinners and sit and smile. She could raise her children to be strong and responsible.

Carefully, she measured a scruple of camphor on the scales. Using another clean brush, she swept the powder into the bottle. She hefted the jug of alcohol onto the table and measured sixteen ounces before pouring it into the container. Pulling up her apron again, she covered her mouth as she slowly stirred the concoction, watching the white powders stir around like the apparitions in her dream. She felt goose bumps. She had never believed in ghosts, but she couldn't deny that something weird took place out there over the weekend and last night.

She sealed the container and placed it to the shelf. She wrote on another label, "Doc's Cough Remedy," and the date it would be ready for the town physician to use, four days later than the other tincture, "June 10, 1895." When he was ready to treat a child or an adult with it, he'd have either her or her father mix in a little cherry syrup to make it more palatable.

The rest of the afternoon went fairly quickly. Jennie finished getting Doc's orders ready for him to take to Silver Creek. One was a small order for packets of sodium salicylate and sodium carbonate. This combination was rheumatism treatment for Jake Keller, a farmer who lived a few miles from the village. She also mixed up a batch of her face cream that she had promised John Evans she'd run a special on in the newspaper.

Lost in her thoughts, Jennie looked up suddenly when Maggie Marvin, Sam Marvin's wife, who was carrying a pie, nearly tripped as she entered the store because she was coughing so hard. A pretty woman with graying hair, Maggie was a devoted Methodist in town and a very good friend of Jennie's mother. Sam, or S.H. as his friends called him, kept busy as one of the village's best carpenters.

One of the very few older women she called by her first name, Jennie asked, "Maggie, are you all right?" Jennie hurried from behind the counter to grab the towel-draped pie she assumed was for the pie social.

"Jennie, do you have anything to sooth my throat from all this coughing? I caught a cold last week. I'm feeling better, but I've been hacking so much I can't sleep. I'm keeping Sam awake too. I've tried nearly everything, including a bit of hot water, whiskey, lemon, and honey. Nothing seems to work."

"Let's see," Jennie said as she turned her back to the woman to reach for a box of Ranson's Hive Syrup Compound. "I'm not sure this is really what you need though. How about some horehound candy or, maybe, Ballard's Horehound Syrup. It's pretty safe. Honestly, though, Maggie, some of what we sell fringes on quackery. Father and I agree we wouldn't advise taking many of our own products unless either Doc Edmunds or Gil Tollington gave the okay. They're loaded with alcohol, drugs, or both, and can be so addicting."

"Well, you pick out something safe for me. I'd like to get a good night's sleep for once."

Pulling one box after another from the shelf, Jennie scanned the ingredients. "This might help the dry hack," she suggested, handing her the box of Ballard's. "I think it's milder than the rest, but please, if you don't get better in a couple days, get in to see Doc Edmunds. He can have us mix up something that might be more effective," Jennie said as she reached for a bag to wrap up the medicine.

Maggie Marvin laid two quarters on the counter. "Don't bother wrapping it. I might take a swig on my way home. See ya' tomorrow. A little cough isn't going to keep me from this celebration."

The door had no sooner slammed when a well-dressed older man stepped in. He removed his rounded, black felt hat, displaying a halo of white hair stretching from one ear to another. "Afternoon!"

"Good afternoon," Jennie greeted, admiring his black herringbone jacket, white shirt, and black bow tie.

"You carry cherry pipe tobacco?"

"We do," she responded. She took down the green ceramic jar with the black Labrador face on the front.

"That's it," the stranger said.

Jennie lifted the lid and inhaled a sweet, earthy aroma. "How much do you need?"

"Why don't you give me two bits worth? I forgot mine when I left home this morning. That ought to hold me for the next couple days."

Spooning the brown and red flakes into the pouch, Jennie hoped the man would light up in the store. After putting the cover back on the jar and replacing it on the shelf, she said, "That'll be twenty-five cents."

Sure enough, before he left, he struck a match and puffed in short breaths until the pipe started smoking. The sweet fog of warm cherries filled the room and broke through some of Jennie's gloom.

For a moment or two, Jennie watched him as he walked across the street and stood on the sidewalk outside the door of the Hotel Scott. Seemingly enjoying his pipe, he looked up and down the street before looking back over at the store. When he made eye contact with Jennie, he smiled and tipped his hat to her.

Embarrassed that he had caught her staring, she started to turn away from the window when she saw the good-looking man she had bumped into earlier. The two men nodded and tipped their hats to each other. The man she had bumped into walked across the street toward Lyons's General Store. Jennie watched as he untied his horses and climbed into the buggy. He turned the whole rig in a semi-circle and headed down the street. For a moment the older of the two, still holding onto his pipe, watched as the other man headed south. Then he dashed across the street toward the hotel livery stable behind Lyons's, hopped on a horse, and galloped after the other man.

Jennie thought the whole incident odd, but she lost focus when the streets turned busy again, a whole lot busier than usual for a mid-week afternoon. She decided she had better get back to work before she was interrupted again.

She scratched off every item on her father's list, then packed up everything Doc needed to take with him when he came in.

No matter how she tried to keep her mind on her work, she felt wave after wave of homesickness for the Pitt she thought she knew. When they first started seeing each other, they took long walks by the Mississippi River and talked about everything. Jennie knew she fell in love with Pitt's mind first. He was an intelligent man. They could talk about politics, education, women's rights, their parents. While they loved and respected their mothers because they were the cornerstones in the families, they admired their fathers for what they had done with their lives—Jennie's father became a druggist and store owner, and Pitt's father taught, farmed, and invented the potato digger.

Bitterness bubbled up in Jennie. She knew she could not live with Pitt's inflexibility, nor could she forget her responsibilities and sacrifice her own dreams.

Jennie wished her father would come back. She longed to sit on the grassy landing below their house where she could watch the Mississippi roll gently south toward New Orleans and dream she were somewhere, anywhere, but here.

The loud clap of the screen door startled her. Painfully, she pulled herself up and focused on Maude. In that moment, Jennie convulsed into deep sobs. Her older and wiser friend grabbed hold of her and held her against her shoulders, patting her on the back and trying to calm her.

"Shhh, Jennie, shhhhh. It's going to be okay. I was down working on the platform when I saw your father heading to practice with the band. He said he had talked to Pitt about the two of you. He asked if I'd come down and check in on you because he's worried."

Jennie choked out, "I know he is."

"Then as I made my way down here I saw Pitt sitting on a chair by the church. If it's any comfort, he's miserable too."

"Good!" Jennie burst and then sobbed a bit more before, adding, "I really don't mean that. It isn't his fault. I have made my decision. I can't be Mrs. Pitt Colgrove the way he wants me to be. But it still hurts."

"Of course it hurts, and it will for a spell."

Sobbing tears she didn't know she had, Jennie began to feel relieved that her friend, the stronger, more self-assured Maude, had arrived to talk her through this. "I'm sorry, Maude. I'm so sorry you have to hear this."

"That's what friends are for, Jennie. You've had quite a week."

"It's been awful!"

"I would've been here sooner, but after I left Pitt, I saw you had a couple customers so I raced home and packed a lunch for us. I told Ma we were going on a picnic. She had made up some of her famous lemonade for tomorrow and told me to take some." Maude picked up a towel from the back counter and handed it to Jennie so she could wipe her eyes. "Your father hoped he wouldn't be long. Then we can get out of here."

With Maude's hand on her back, Jennie didn't feel so alone. She put her glasses on the counter, used the towel Maude had handed her and wiped her eyes and blew her nose.

The door swung open again and both women looked up. Stanley stared at his oldest daughter. Never one to really become aggressively physical with his children, he, too, patted her on the shoulder and said, "Now, now." After a few moments, he cleared his throat before saying, "You and Maude go on now. I'm closing here soon anyway."

Jennie didn't argue. "Okay, Pa. Doc hasn't come for his orders, but I stirred up the tinctures we needed."

"That's fine. I'll wait for him before I close. You two go and forget this place."

Knowing now that Pitt and her father had had words, Jennie gathered her shawl and followed behind Maude as she left the store.

They both stepped up into the buggy, but before Maude directed her horse, she asked, "Where should we go, Jennie?"

With confidence, she responded, "Can we go down by the river?" Not wanting to see Pitt Colgrove again for a while, Jennie added, "But, please, let's head south," and forced a small smile.

Chapter 19

Aqua fluviatilis (Aq. fluv.)

River Water

MAUDE STEERED THE HORSE SOUTH. "Let's head down below our farm. I go there sometimes when I feel out of sorts."

Jennie never thought of Maude getting low. She always seemed on top of the world. If there were a wind, she faced it head on.

As the horse trotted under the arch of budding trees, passing the blacksmith shop, the large, two-story Shaw house, and the smaller Phillips home, Jennie felt a cool breeze sweep over her. Maude's light-brown hair untangled from her bun, but she didn't seem to notice. She did little fixing up, and in fact, she could walk around in a gunny sack and still look fine. A bit taller than Jennie, and in Jennie's eyes more graceful, Maude seldom primped even if she came in from wind and rain.

Even though her mother told her she was pretty, Jennie knew fate hadn't been so generous with her looks. Her nose was too large, she had to wear spectacles, and she had to work with her hair because it was so straight.

Maude turned off into a narrow path that trailed toward the river. "We can't go any farther with the buggy," she said as she pulled up to the fence line. "We'll have to hike the rest of the way." She hopped down and tied the horse to a small oak tree. "Why don't you grab the blanket? I'll take the basket."

Maude led the way to a black wire and post gate, unlatched it, and pushed it through the grasses so they could walk through. "I don't think Pa's been down here since last fall. The cattle are in the west pasture because it's still so muddy, but I'd still better latch the gate behind us."

The hay stack, a giant golden beehive, stood in the middle of the meadow that had begun to show signs of new life. Sprouts of green grass shot up all over the area. Jennie didn't want to argue with Maude, but it looked like someone, either Maude's father or one of his hired men, had been out there recently. She noticed fresh footprints and sprigs of hay strewn all around.

Maude and Jennie walked side by side for a few hundred feet. Her friend took the lead when the path tapered to little more than a two-foot swath of flattened grass. The two of them, simultaneously, pulled up on their skirts, taking gentle steps as they walked down the slopping hill.

"Let's go over there a ways," Maude suggested as she walked toward a flat landing. Her father owned much of this rich farmland above the bend in the river. "It doesn't look so damp."

As Jennie began to unfold the blanket, Maude grabbed hold of one end to help spread it flat. "I love picnics," Maude said enthusiastically. "I brought some fresh bread and a little butter. Pa told me to unhook a sausage from the smoke house. With Ma's lemonade, we should have a feast." She handed Jennie a towel before she poured the fruit jar of sunny lemonade into one mug and then another.

"I'm not very hungry, but I'd love something to drink."

They both focused on the river as they sipped their drinks. A few abandoned logs, deadheads, had been caught up all winter in frozen water. Now they were rolling haplessly toward the south.

"I heard that up north at the beginnings of the river around Bemidji the water is clear and blue as it bubbles toward us. Once it arrives here, it is brownish green. Further south toward Hannibal and St. Louis, it becomes like my father's coffee and cream, murky and a bit uninviting. When it arrives in the Gulf, it spits out everything it's picked up along the way.

"It's almost human," Jennie said.

"It starts as a trickle, babbling and tottering along like an infant. Around here, it's wild like a teenager, especially in the springtime. By the time it rolls further south, it's turning and tossing, tearing up that part of the world like some people want to when they are making their way out in the world. Then, at its end, south of New Orleans, some books say it becomes as placid as an elderly person as it flows gently into a bigger sphere, becoming part of the ocean."

Jennie relaxed, stretching out her legs and sipping her lemonade. "I feel as though I'm one with the Mississippi when I sit and watch it flow south. I suppose most of us who live near its shores feel the same."

For a moment, the two friends relaxed and watched the tranquil scene. "Have you ever seen the view from Peck's hill?" Maude asked.

"Many times." Jennie thought of Ormasinda Peck who often hosted fancy teas and dinners in her large home on the hill. Born and raised in Minneapolis, she had seen so much of the state's growth and advancement on her father John Stevens's front lawn. When she and her husband William Peck moved to

Clearwater, William made a name for himself as he moved up the chain from baggage man to conductor and now general manager of the Great Northern. At any time, they could have moved back to Minneapolis, but they loved Clearwater's peace and quiet. They bought a house on a hill overlooking the river. "I love it, but up there, the bend in the river seems so foreign and far way, almost as if I'm looking at a picture postcard. Down here I recognize its moods. Some days, it's black and wild. Other days it's playful, lapping lazily against its shores.

"Like you said, the Mississippi's alive." Maude paused and then said, "I forgot to tell you. Today, Pa and I signed the lease for one of the spaces in the Whiting building."

"Oh, Maude! I'm so happy for you! You're going to open the hat store. You've been talking about that for a long time."

"I wanted to travel first, sow some seeds, and get all my 'I wishes' out of my system. I've discovered a lot out there—San Francisco, New York, Chicago, and of course, last year, England with Ma. Now, it's time to settle down."

"Once you open your doors, I'll be your first customer," Jennie promised.

"I know you will, Jennie. I always thought I'd be good milliner."

"You will. You've designed some lovely hats," Jennie said, then began giggling.

"I know why you're laughing," Maude said. "No one liked my Easter hat this year."

Jennie wanted to say it looked ridiculous, but she couldn't be so mean. "Some of the new styles are a bit much. I don't think I'll ever get used to bowls of fruit or birds and nests on someone's head."

"I have to tone it down, you're saying?" Maude asked, joining in Jennie's fun.

"For Clearwater, anyway."

"I'll take that into consideration," Maude said. "Let me tell you, though, I had a problem when I looked over the remaining rentals in the Whiting building."

"Why? What happened?" Jennie asked.

"Sam agreed to rent me a space, but he wouldn't let me sign my own lease. He said either a husband, which I don't have, or Pa had to sign for me."

"That doesn't surprise me, Maude. Women have no rights—here or anywhere," Jennie said. "Maybe someday, if we ever get the vote."

"I was angry. I went home and hollered about it for a while. I vowed I was going to give up and try to do something in St. Cloud or Minneapolis. The folks hated that since I'd be so far away. They talked me into staying here. In fact, Pa talked me into letting him go with me to sign the lease." Maude looked down at her mug, twirling it in her lap. "I suppose it's for the best. I probably wouldn't fare any better anywhere else, but it was humiliating. For once, I felt powerless, but Pa pulled a fast one on Sam. He had me sign my name right under his and then I handed over the rent of $200 for the next two years."

"What did Sam say?"

"What could he say? He had cash in his hand!" Maude said and then laughed.

Jennie smiled. "It's like your father to try his hand at something new." One of the first to claim Clearwater, he believed women should have more rights than they were given.

Maude's own mother also had a strong, independent spirit. "Ma's had two husbands. Her first one died out East, leaving her with little. Not much for a woman to do when her husband up and dies. But she's pretty self-reliant, as you well know. I'm proud to say I inherited her spunk."

Indeed, Jennie knew the legend about Abigail Camp Porter, the first woman in the village, who worked for the land company as housekeeper for the first hotel, the Webster-Stevens, down by the river landing. As soon as she stepped foot off the boat, she went to work. Everyone who knew Maude had to agree that she came by her independence and determination quite naturally.

"You're probably disappointed you couldn't do this transaction totally on your own, but you have your store. You've wanted to start one for so long."

"I know. A bittersweet victory. Ma and Pa will leave me with everything they own, the house, the farm, all their land, but how ironic is it I couldn't sign my own lease? I'm nearly thirty-three years old and have money of my own, and yet, *my daddy* had to sign the papers because I have no husband."

"Sam Whiting's an open-minded man, Maude. Goodness, he's an educated man who studied law with Harriet Beecher Stowe's brother-in-law in Hartford, Connecticut. Everyone knows about the Beecher family's suffrage and abolitionist activities. On top of that, I believe Sam's been influenced by all three of his daughters, Grace, Helen and Sarah, and their thoughts about women's rights. Unfortunately, the law is the law, at least for now," Jennie said.

"So much more reason to keep hounding our congressmen to get something passed."

"You're right there!" Jennie said. "Yet, I understand what you're saying about this husband thing. Pitt's been a friend and confidante over the years. I thought we were on the same path, but now he wants me to turn into something I don't feel ready to do . . . to just be a wife."

"All I can say is if you and Pitt are meant to be, it'll all work out. If not, you wouldn't have been happy in such a restrictive relationship," Maude said as she sliced a thin slice of sausage and bit into it. Lost in thought, she finished chewing before she continued speaking. "I've had my loves, Jennie, but I've never found one yet that made me want him so much I'd give him the authority to pilot my ship."

Thinking back to everything she had experienced lately, Jennie said, "I suppose you're right, but I also wonder if it wouldn't be easier to marry and let the man do the thinking in the family."

"You don't mean that, Jennie."

Looking off in the distance, Jennie thought she could see a boat coming up from the south. She set her mug in the grass. Grabbing a chunk of bread, she spread some butter across the top and took a bite absentmindedly.

"I'm not so sure it wouldn't be easier, Maude. Some things over the last few days have opened my mind a bit."

"And what's wrong with having your mind opened?" Maude asked. "Sometimes it hurts to learn new things, but in the long run, knowledge is power."

"I'm not so sure I want to be that powerful!"

"I've heard you say many times how you've never felt so alive as when you've helped someone from behind the counter at your store."

"I know. I feel whole once I enter the store. I never completely felt that as a teacher. I enjoyed working with my students, don't get me wrong, I felt I was good at it, but it's not the same."

"Maybe this is your calling after all, at least for now. I guess only you know what you really want."

"For sure, I can't give Pitt what he thinks he wants and needs, nor what he thinks *I need!* If he'd only be patient and wait, but he wanted us to run off and get married this weekend or next. While I was thrilled to find out he still loves me—Lord, the last few weeks I thought that was over—his urgency scared me. Then we fought because of my commitment to my father, to my family."

"I think you and I are alike in so many ways," Maude said. "Maybe we'll change someday, but for now, we don't want any man bossing us around."

Jennie sipped her lemonade. It was tart, yet sweet and refreshing, the way she liked it. She had to agree with Maude. She knew she could bend like the river, but she knew if she bent too much, she'd be unhappy and break, hurting everyone around her. Yes, she loved Pitt, but not enough to give him her soul.

"It might be easier, though," Jennie admitted. "A lot of women have figured out how to get their way in their marriages, but they have to play stupid games."

"*Both* husbands and wives play games to get what they want. They usually end up the same way, in *la boudoir*."

Jennie, embarrassed by such bawdy talk covered her mouth with her towel and giggled. She had to admit it felt good to smile and have fun. "Eh-hum! I have to admit Pitt's needs seemed urgent."

Maude laughed with Jennie, then set her mug down on the blanket and looked back at the river. "They all seem to be such needy creatures, wanting and using everything women have. Ma calls it their urges. I've seen many women abandon all common sense to give their husbands what they need—even after a doctor orders them not to have relations. They have child after pitiful child. In many cases, the children aren't to be pitied; it's the women. Each child takes more life from them. Some don't live through childbirth, and for what? Men's urges!"

Becoming more serious, Jennie said, "Pitt gave me an ultimatum, be married now or never. I have to confess, Maude, for a few moments, it was tempting. When we kissed . . . well, I totally forgot everything around me."

"I know the feeling, Jennie."

"Then I heard the band warm up. Like Cinderella, I realized what time it was. I had promised Pa that I'd get back to the store so he could go practice with the band. I told him I had to leave. Oh, was he mad! It felt like he threw a bucket of ice water in my face. Then we started the same old argument about my feeling responsible for my family right now."

"Yet, I have to say, Jennie, we can't always be beholden to our folks. Sometimes we have to fly out on our own. I'm not saying you should go back to Pitt, but your folks would understand and be excited for you if you said you two were marrying."

"Of course they'd be excited. They'd figure a way to get some help in the store and help me make it all happen, but I'm not ready yet. Father's not getting any younger or healthier, and while Ma isn't old, she's worn down, too. I promised Pa I'd look out for the family and manage the store while he tries to start up the new drug store in Eden Valley. He wants to get the family ahead financially. I can't keep my promises if I run off and get married. I owe this to him and to the whole family."

"I know. I wonder why Pitt behaved the way he did. If he loves you as much as he says, you'd think he could wait and give you some time."

"I have no idea why he is so urgent."

"Oh, come on now, Jennie, "Maude said. "You aren't that naïve."

Staring off, Jennie said nothing for a while. "Well, I have to keep my head about me. I didn't need this today on top of everything else that's been going on. So much is weighing on me right now, Maude. I can't even begin to tell you the pressure I feel."

"Are you talking about your trip to Lynden and your learning about the little girl who was murdered out there?"

"Yes, and more. Claire O'Casey and I talked about the murder, but she doesn't know much more than we do." Jennie blew out a sigh. "She did tell me about a woman friend of hers who's in trouble . . ."

"What kind of trouble?"

Jennie cleared her throat. "Let's say that if it were possible, she needs to get married as soon as possible."

"Oh, I see. So you're saying she's with child?"

"Yes. Maude, until I rode out to Lynden with Claire, I thought I knew so much about what goes on in Clearwater. I've come to realize I've lived a pretty sheltered life. Of course, I haven't had the same type of encounters she and others have had. Maybe I came close when Forester came out of nowhere when I was locking up the store that evening last winter. "

"I remember that. We've been sheltered like a lot of young people around here who come from stable environments. So what happened to the woman?"

"Claire said the woman was . . . well, taken by force."

"Goodness! Who's the woman?"

"She wouldn't tell me," Jennie said.

"What does she think you can do about this?"

"Nothing," Jennie added sarcastically, "She seems to be able to handle this on her own."

"What do you mean?"

"Maude, Claire came into the store. She seems to know how to mix up herbs and those over-the-counter medicines to get rid of such problems."

"I see. So you're saying she is trying to help this woman abort?"

"Exactly! Maude, seriously, can you imagine this going on in Clearwater?"

"You don't think anyone from Clearwater has come in to purchase any of these products before?"

"Of course not! I'm surprised you'd even ask such a question."

"That's interesting!" Maude said quietly.

"How could I turn my head to this if I had known the patents were used this way? Besides, as I told Claire, I doubt any of them have anything strong enough in them that could help anyone except allow them to nap for a while."

"I don't mean to disagree with you, Jennie, but I know a number of women who've come into your store to get some help to end a pregnancy."

"What are you talking about, Maude?" Jennie asked angrily.

"I suppose you're going to find out anyway, Jennie, but I've learned a few of the over-the-counter products do more than they claim. When a woman has asked me what she could do when she found herself, well, caught, I've suggested a product or two to get them through their ordeal."

Jennie jerked so fast she felt a twinge in her back. "Maude, you?" She stood and rubbed her back. How could anyone, a person she called friend, use her and her store this way?

Maude brushed back the blanket to straighten it and nodded toward Jennie to sit down. "What would you have a woman do? I know of one who nearly died during her first two births. Doc Edmunds warned her not to have any more children, but apparently, her husband wasn't listening. He wasn't much for the little ones, told her when they got older they could help around the farm, but for now, they were nothing but a bother. She knew there'd be no one for them if she died by carrying the child to the end."

"Still . . ." Jennie started to say.

"Jennie, maybe you have to wake up. You come from folks who gave you a good upbringing, but they protected you, as well. My folks did the same, but early on, my ma told me our little village wasn't as rosy or idyllic as it seemed at times."

Jennie sat awhile without saying anything. "Are you saying I should wake up or grow up?"

"Does it matter? Maybe you needed to see what you were meant to do with your life. You have brains, Jennie. You were always the smartest girl in town. Now, maybe you need to be a smart woman."

"Smart! All the while this is going on behind my back? It shows me how stupid I really am."

"You're too hard on yourself. You'll learn. And some things? You might have to turn your head until you can figure out a way to help. The products you're worried about are being sold legally anyway. You're doing nothing wrong. Sometimes women have to be smarter than the men who write their stupid laws. Men can't always have it their way. If it's illegal for us to have information on how not to get in the family way, then some of us have to go around the law to get educated and help others."

"But, I can't believe people in and around Clearwater are using these products this way and doing it right under my nose. I wonder if Father and Doc realize what is happening."

Maude turned and looked directly at Jennie. "I'm not sure, but I hope you don't say anything to either of them. I know you, Jennie. You have a hard time not telling the truth especially when you think something is unethical or immoral, but if you think women are only now using products or concocting herbs to rid themselves of their babies, you're mistaken. Women have had to help their friends and sisters since the beginning of time. Not every baby born has been a blessing."

Jennie remembered Claire O'Casey saying nearly the same thing. "I suppose," she whispered, half believing what she was saying.

Yet, for Jennie, the issue ran deeper than all this. Surely, Maude couldn't expect her to keep this secret from her father or Doc. She could be the cause of lots of trouble if anyone were to find out. And now, as her father busied himself getting ready for his move, he depended on her to be responsible and make wise decisions.

Maude must have read the frustration on Jennie's face. "Like I said, you and your father have done nothing illegal. If women can't buy the products easily, they'll find someone who grows them. For that matter, I've heard Indian women grow pennyroyal and seep it into a tea to drink to prevent pregnancy."

Maude took a sip of her lemonade. Jennie pulled her knees up to hug them. She watched the river and pondered what Maude said. She had heard that women of all nationalities grew herbs and dug up roots to concoct teas, rubs, and inhalants to help the sick. But that was an old-fashioned world, without the benefit of today's medical wisdom.

Returning her mug to the blanket, Maude continued. "The medicines women are buying are on the market legally. There's already talk about clamping down on some of the products. Didn't you read that article in last week's paper? Maybe on the second page? A doctor's pressuring the AMA to hone in on the patent medicine trade because of all the false advertising. He claims abortion's on the rise. I haven't any idea where he got his information. But he believes women are aborting after they feel the quickening."

"I barely skimmed the article. I didn't think I needed to know any of that."

"Well, I can't abide that, and won't point fingers either because I don't know all the circumstances. It's beyond me why they didn't do something sooner, but while having babies is expensive, doing something about it isn't cheap either. How much does one of your tins of pennyroyal something cost? Nearly two dollars, I believe."

"Chichester's Pennyroyal Pills? Actually, they're a bit over a dollar. I've sold plenty of them since I started working at the drug store. I assumed the women who bought them believe they're going to help with their monthlies. Some have even said they're picking them up for their daughters."

"For their daughters. That's a good one!" Maude mocked. "Well, I suppose women aren't going to come into the store advertising what they want and why they want it, Jennie. But haven't you heard it called the morning after pill?"

Jennie thought about the advertisement she placed in the *Clearwater News* about Chichesters. She recalled something about it being "safe and reliable" for women's "difficult days." *Now isn't that ironic?* "I doubt there's much pennyroyal in it, though," Jennie said, trying to understand the situation.

"If used correctly, there's enough to abort a baby."

"I can't believe it, Maude. As I tried to tell Claire, I don't think Clearwater women would stoop so . . . so . . ."

"Low? Jennie, some women have to take it upon themselves to survive. And those who can't help themselves have to rely on other women to see them through. It sounds like Claire O'Casey's one of those women. I think she realizes we can't always depend on men to do what's best for us. Besides, I don't believe a morning after pill is abortion. It's certainly more logical to take care of a situation before something more drastic is needed."

"I don't know what to think anymore," Jennie said. "To tell you the truth, I thought the stories I had heard about such women happened in New York, Chicago, London, maybe Minneapolis, but not in Clearwater."

"There are more problems in the bigger cities because there are more people. Big pools or little, women are women, Jennie. Unfortunately, some men are just thoughtless men."

Jennie watched a small steamboat slowly moving northward up the river with its paddles flapping foaming waters. The small boat glided like a swan.

From a distance, Jennie thought she could read the black letters of *J.B. Bassett* on the front of the wheelhouse.

What was it about this stream of water that had such a hold on her? Usually, as she sat in solitude on its banks, Jennie could stare long enough to come to some conclusion or gain some peace, but not today. Today her mind was all a-jumble, bouncing all over the place.

"Right now, I feel as though Clearwater, the whole world, for that matter, isn't a very nice place to live. I don't believe aborting a child is right. I'm sorry, Maude, but I have an ethical responsibility to the field I'm devoting myself to. I'm not unsympathetic, though. I understand some women have been caught and think they have no other way out."

"I know." Maude touched Jennie's shoulder. "You won't get used to it, either. It's more prevalent than you think. Women all over are being held hostage by men. They need our help, understanding, and knowledge."

"I can't be the one to give them that information, Maude. I could get into big trouble. Father and I could lose the business or maybe even go to jail."

"Of course! No one's asking for you to help them that way, Jennie."

"What can I do?"

"Maybe you have to continue to be kind and caring in all health matters, and maybe, right now, you have to try to ignore certain things Claire and I have talked about. Let those of us help—at least until you can justify that some women need help and have no one else to turn to."

Jennie thought on this for a moment. "I suppose, but I'll never be able to look any woman in the eye again who buys one of our products—like Lydia Pinkham's Vegetable Compound or Chichesters. We have a number of these items on the shelf that I always thought were quack medicines. I'm going to do a bit of researching, but for now, I won't say anything."

"Thank, you, Jennie. We have nothing else, no information on how to prevent pregnancy or understand any other health issue for that matter."

Maude sliced another piece of sausage, speared it, and offered it to Jennie who took it without argument. As she sat nibbling, Jennie began to feel more relaxed. Good friends could do that—the river and Maude.

After a few moments, Jennie asked, "Have you heard anything suspicious about Donald Wolff?

"What do you mean?"

"When Claire and Donald met up in the store this week, he backed out of the store. I thought it was strange. You know how Donald is. Father doesn't have much to say about our village constable. On top of that, Claire's led me to believe he's the one who's been up to no good with her friend."

"Sounds like Donald. It wouldn't be the first time I heard that. I don't understand what Lucy sees in him, but I suppose he can be dashing if he wants to be. He's the baby in the family and the only boy. He was spoiled by his folks and sisters and probably never learned right from wrong." Maude sat a moment before adding, "Now that you ask, it seems like I heard the name of the woman who's in trouble, too."

"Really? Why am I always the last to find out about everything?"

"You work all the time, Jennie. Besides, it's not drug store talk."

"So who told you?" Jennie asked. "I'm sure it was Livy."

"She's a gossip, yes, but apparently, Francis Vallely told her. She's from out in Lynden and has been cooking and cleaning for all the company Livy's expecting over the long weekend. No one mentioned Donald Wolff, but like I said, I wouldn't be surprised."

"I don't think Claire's friend wants her business known, though, if there is business left to know," Jennie said with a smirk. "If what Claire says is true, how can we allow him to get away with it?"

"Because he's one of the village's golden boys. Few in town would believe it if the news came out anyway. On top of that, in some circles, there's so much antagonism toward the Irish, the girl he took advantage of would have a hard time proving rape in a court of law. She's better off letting Claire help her or going away for a while and then giving up the child."

"You are certainly seem relaxed about this!"

"Not really, Jennie, but I think there are battles to fight, and this isn't one of them. I'm not saying the girl had any of this coming to her. I'd never say that, even if the girl were brave enough to press charges and go to court, Donald Wolff would never be convicted. Her only other alternative would be for her father to force him to marry her. If the family finds out, this may happen. Can you imagine what kind of marriage they'd have?"

"But Donald and others like him shouldn't be allowed to get away with this," Jennie said.

"True. Yet, you know as well as I do, there isn't much recourse for a woman caught in these situations. Bad boys are bad boys. The world will never rid itself of all of them."

"It's not right, though."

Maude made them a sandwich. Handing half to Jennie, she added, "Lots in the world isn't fair. Some have tried to pass laws to protect women of all ages from abusive or domineering males, but I believe we need to educate women on how to defend themselves. The Temperance Society's stance on this is pretty clear. They even consider unwanted attentions within the home as domestic violence, not as a husband claiming his natural and legal rights. Men have gotten away with it for too long. Liquor often plays a big part in the crime, and everyone knows the Society's stance on that. Yet, it goes deeper than that. All booze does is intensify the problem. Husbands consider wives their property. And women have permitted this because of the whole 'submissiveness' spiel handed down from church pulpits. Like I said, women need to get more educated and take responsibility for their lives."

Maude had often gone off on tangents before, but this time, Jennie had to agree with her. Yet, she knew being silent about Donald's behavior wasn't right. "I have no idea what I'm going to do exactly, but for starters, I'm going to talk to my father."

"I may say something to my father as well, but Jennie, please don't say anything about your patent products or what Claire's up to with her herbs. As I said before, women have to help women."

"For now, I won't say anything. I'm not happy about this, but I understand where you and Claire are coming from. What was it Susan B. Anthony said about abortion? She opposed it and said women would be found guilty of committing the crime, but men should be found 'thrice' guilty for committing the act that drove the women to the crime—or something like that."

"She's right. This shouldn't be our only option, but the knowledge we need is being withheld by men." Maude took a last bite of her sandwich, chewed it slowly, and then finished her lemonade. "I hate jumping from one topic to another, but we're going to have to head out soon and you were going to tell me what happened out in Irish Town."

Jennie watched the riverboat round the bend. Now she could read *J.B. Bassett* much clearer. As it drew closer, she could see two men dressed in black suits standing on the deck and the pilot inside the wheelhouse. She knew it was pulling into Clearwater. She figured one of the men had to be John Stevens, but who was the other?

For a moment, she remembered how she and her friends used to go down to the ferry landing to watch the boats dock. Her folks would have been upset if they'd known. They considered loggers and steamboat crewmen to be ruffians, who, as soon as they hit the shore, took off for Quinn's to drink up their wages.

She knew her brothers and sisters and almost all the Clearwater youth were fascinated by the river and had the same excitement about the steamboats that helped move floating logs.

Sometimes the *Bassett* pulled a wanigan, a little boat house with food supplies and a cook shack, behind it. If they pulled in close enough to the Clearwater side, the cook handed out freshly baked sugar cookies. Today, the boat was traveling up the river alone, and Jennie's childhood seemed a long time ago.

Inhaling deeply, Jennie said, "I don't know where to begin. It seems like a dream now that I'm back in the peacefulness of my village." From the visit she and Claire made to Mrs. Frank to the quick stop at the Higgins's farm, Jennie told Maude everything she could remember. "Then as we neared Tamarack Swamp, we both heard a wild scream, then crying. It sounded like what I heard last weekend when I was over in the north end by Dorseys' farm. Deep, shrieking sobs seemed to be coming from all around us. Solly reared and whined, then jolted to a stop, nearly tossing us out of the rig."

"Oh, for goodness sake!" Maude asked.

"Even though it seemed so real when it was happening, I'm now questioning what I saw." Jennie bit on her lip. "You're not going to believe this. I find it hard to believe. It looked like a very sheer sheet or curtain, swirling in a fog across the road. I begged Claire not to leave the buggy, but she hopped out and followed it into the prairie grasses near the swamp. At first, I was frightened to be left alone, but I began to feel calm. Solly settled down as well. Everything became quiet. I heard Claire shush whatever it was out there."

"Oh, Jennie! No wonder you were shaken. What did Claire say was out there?"

"That's just it. Once we she got back in the buggy, we took off. She hardly said anything the rest of the way home. I don't know if she was lost in her thoughts or asleep, and I haven't seen her since to rehash what took place."

"You *have* had lots to chew on, lately, Jennie."

"That's for sure. This isn't a subject that can be talked about in polite company, especially with our church friends. Oh, I'll talk with Ida, of course, when I have time. Like she told us the other day, she believes something's out there by the swamp. This isn't as innocent as reading tea leaves or playing with our little spirit board. Nevertheless, was it the spirit of a little girl brutally murdered and still wandering the swamp? I don't know. Both incidents are taboo as far as the church goes."

"Whew! All I can tell you is that, of course, I believe in God. The Bible gives us a model for life, but I can't support all its demands. Like I said before, I won't be submissive, like scripture requires, to any man, but when it comes to the supernatural, I don't take much of that seriously, not even the Ouija board."

Both women stared at the river. The steamboat paddles busily propelled the water to move the boat.

"I played once. But it knew things about me it shouldn't so I've never tried it again. No way! Now thinking of that poor murdered girl, I get the chills," Jennie said, pulling up her shawl. "What's more remarkable is that the murder hasn't been solved. The killer's still out and about."

"There was quite a stir after the murder. Now you hardly hear anything, except for what you've told me lately. The murderer has probably gone into the woodwork somewhere, so I bet there's nothing to worry about anymore."

"I suppose you're right, but I feel so bad for the girl. I know this sounds stupid, but I wish I could have known her when she was alive." Jennie nibbled on her sandwich. The taste of spicy sausage, fresh butter, and yeasty bread stirred her hunger. One bite led to another, and soon the sandwich was gone. She washed it down with the rest of her lemonade. "I wonder why the *Bassett* isn't hauling a wanigan behind it," she wondered aloud.

"Hard to say," Maude answered as she pulled up the chain of her watch fob and glanced at the time. "Do you feel better? We told Jeanette, Ella, and Gert we'd meet up with them tonight so they could help us finish setting up."

"I do. I feel much better. Thank you. The lunch was delicious too."

The two friends took the corners of the blanket and folded it up. Jennie clutched it under her arm while Maude grabbed the basket. As they walked back to the buggy, the *J.B. Bassett* whistled twice, announcing its stop.

Chapter 20
Somnus
Sleep

THE MATTRESS SANK in the middle when she wasn't sharing it with Blanche, enveloping Jennie like a cocoon. She pulled up the sheet and light blanket and snuggled her pillow. *This has been a long, hard day.*

By the time she and Maude returned to the drug store, Jennie had only a minute or two to help her father cash out the register and close up. Their busyness had paid off. The cash register was full.

Since the banks had already closed, Stanley tossed the cash and handfuls of change from the register money into the deposit bag. He put it in the small, black safe in the backroom, swirling the combination lock before he left.

Stanely closed the door behind them and secured the padlock. "It's not much of a safe, but we have to do something. I don't know who's going to be moseying around this week."

As they walked back to the front of the store, Jennie told her father about sitting on the hill above the river by Porters. She said, "I forgot to tell you. I saw the *Bassett* pull into town. What's that all about?"

"When I was uptown practicing with the band, I heard the whistle and someone said John Stevens was on board. I don't know why he didn't take the train, unless he is trying to avoid the crowds. He probably wanted to get here early to spend some time with Ormasinda and Simon."

"I'm sure Orma's opening her doors to many this weekend. I wonder if the *Bassett*'s co-owner came with him. I know I saw a couple men standing on its deck as it neared Clearwater. One could have been Joel Bassett."

"It's hard to say. I heard once Congressman Towne was coming up on hte train with him. Now I heard he is speaking in St. Cloud today, so I doubt it was him. I suppose Stevens could have brought almost anyone with him since he knows nearly every important person in the state."

While Jennie and her father finished checking the store, Maude returned from picking up Gert, Ella, and Jeanette. Jennie walked out the front doors ahead of Stanley as Maude tied her horse to the post.

"We decided we needed some exercise. We're going to park here and walk around town to make sure everything looks spiffy," Jeanette said as she hopped down from the carriage.

All the women admired Main Street's lamplights. From the drug store north, eight lined the streets, four on each side all the way up to the Masonic Hall. On the left side of the street, the sign read: "WELCOME TO CLEARWATER." On the right, the sign read: "DECORATION DAY 1895."

Tomorrow morning, following the proper rules of etiquette, Carl and his friends would hang the flags on the opposite side of the signs.

"I wonder who hung them up," Jennie asked out loud, knowing they weren't up when she and Maude had taken off to picnic by the river.

"I suppose one of Carl's friends," Maude answered. "Everything looks grand, no matter who did the job!"

"Let's check the depot first," Jennie suggested. "I want to see if the large sign is posted yet, but by the looks of everything, Carl's gang might have gotten that done already too."

The group walked behind Hotel Scott. The last train had come in a couple hours before, so the depot was quiet. As they approached the front steps, they saw a large welcome sign hanging under the white building's eaves for passengers to see as they disembarked from the train in the morning.

Returning to Main Street, they walked past Lyons's store and Laughton's Meat Market, admiring the bunting under their front windows.

Sitting in a tiny grove of oak and evergreen, the new pine platform smelled woodsy. The chairs sat as if waiting for something big to happen.

Maude murmured, "Please, Lord, protect this spot from young pranksters or old drunks stumbling out of Quinn's."

Jeanette said, "Amen to that!"

Jennie walked to the end of the porch of the Whiting building. Maude followed, both admiring the front of the building, which had also been festively decked out in red, white, and blue under the two windows.

From where she stood, Jennie could hear piano music and loud laughter coming from Quinn's Saloon behind Boutwell's Hardware Store, even though Pat Quinn himself advertised the place as quiet and respectable.

Looking down toward the river landing, Jennie saw her brother Carl half-kneeling as he hammered a white sign into the ground.

She turned to Maude, who was walking up behind her. "I've been wondering how the street signs got up while you and I were gone, Maude." Jennie nodded toward the landing. "There's our suspicious character. I bet he's the same person who's responsible for getting the street light signs up, too."

"Oh, that Carl!" Maude exclaimed loudly enough for him to hear and turn toward them. He waved a hammer and then pounded the white sign one more time before standing up to shake it to see if it were sturdy enough to stay put. Seemingly satisfied with his work, he grabbed his tool box and took long, man-like strides toward them.

Jennie climbed down the steps and walked a ways down the path toward her brother before trying to talk to him. "I thought you were out working at Rices' this afternoon."

"I finished up early."

"I can tell! You accomplished a lot while Maude and I were gone."

"Actually, I didn't do it all. Art and Wayland told me they'd get started if I weren't around later in the afternoon."

"Oh, that's right. Father told me the Barrett and Woodworth boys were helping you with some of the building and painting," Jennie said.

"I couldn't have done all this without them," Carl said. "Pa said they took his ladder and got to work this afternoon. Didn't he tell you?"

"He was closing up when I finally got back and the ladies were waiting for me so we didn't have much time for conversation."

Carl hefted his tool box to the other hand. "Mr. Rice said he figured I had enough to do in town today. He ain't usually in such a generous mood, but even he's getting into the spirit of things."

"I forgot to ask. Did you see anyone get off the *Bassett* while you were down here?"

"John Stevens and someone I didn't recognize jumped off at the boat landing. It dropped anchor on the Clear Lake side and they took the ferry across."

"Who's running the ferry this afternoon?"

"Billy Kirk," Carl said.

Jennie knew that Billy, the eighteen-year-old son of James and Marva Kirk, had aspirations to become a riverboat pilot. As a youngster, he, like many of his friends, loved the adventures of Tom Sawyer and Huck Finn, especially when they embarked on a raft and explored. Later, when he became a teenager, Billy felt a real calling to the river after he read *Life on the Mississippi*. Although content to help his father with the ferrying business, Billy made it clear to his folks and nearly everyone else in Clearwater that he had plans to "light out for a new territory to learn to captain my own boat as soon as I graduate from high school," which was in a couple days.

"Stevens said hello, but the other was a bit pompous and didn't even look in my direction. I tipped my hat and returned Stevens's greeting as they walked by. I know Stevens isn't the uppity type, but the other guy struck me as a real dandy."

Jennie laughed because she could hear her father say about the same thing. Brother and sister met up with the four women as they walked toward the Masonic Hall. Darkness was settling in. They all agreed the large yellow building looked imposing as it kept an eye on the southern part of town. The General Mercantile housed on the bottom floor also had bunting below its front windows.

Jeanette and Maude led the way as they headed to the Methodist Church. Gert and Ella walked behind them, and Carl and Jennie took up the rear. Jennie wished she wouldn't have to revisit the scene where she and Pitt had had it out, but she knew she couldn't avoid it forever. When the group arrived at the open area in back of the church, Maude walked about, straightening the chairs around the tables.

"Mother told her friends to leave white tablecloths on the back pew of the church. We should make sure they're there," Jennie said.

Because the church was never locked, Gert offered to go in and check. Ella followed her up the steps and in through the white double doors.

Soon they emerged, "We think we counted eight, but there's a nice-sized pile there."

A wave of relief and pride washed over Jennie that every promise her family and friends made to her about helping with the preparations had been accomplished. "Good, good! I figured we could count on Mother and her friends. They'll come after the speeches and set up everything. We can all rest assured this part is in capable hands."

"You know, Carl," Maude said. "I forgot we were putting a cloth over the big table. Let's forget about painting it. Besides, if we get the crowds they're predicting, no one's going to be paying any attention to such little details," she concluded.

Jennie looked at Carl who looked relieved and exhausted at the same time. *And why shouldn't he be? He's probably been up before dawn racing all day—out to Rices' to do the early morning chores, back to help set up in town, back out to help with evening chores, and then back to town to put some of the finishing touches on everything here. I bet he'll be glad when all this is over.*

Carl nodded and said slowly, "If you don't mind, I think I'll say goodnight to you all."

Jennie noticed a far-off look in her brother's eyes and said, "Oh, of course, Carl, for goodness sake. I'm sure you have more important things than listening to us women chatter about tablecloths."

"Thank you for all your hard work," Maude said.

The rest of the women thanked Carl for everything he and his friends had done. Jennie watched her younger brother walk toward home. She could tell he didn't have his normal zip. Besides that, Jennie knew he was uncomfortably shy around women. Jennie hoped her brother would find that perfect woman someday who could bring him out of his shell.

Jennie's friends giggled and gabbed. Amazed no one had asked her about Pitt, Jennie wondered if Maude had said something to the women about the couple's breakup.

"So why are they storing some of the pies at the drug store, Jennie, instead of the church?" Gert asked.

"Ma decided that at the store, we could keep a closer eye on mice and bugs. The church has had an infestation of bats lately. Even if the pies are covered, she didn't like the idea of storing them there."

"That makes sense," Gert said. "I don't know which I hate worse, bats or mice."

After a backward glance, Maude led the women back toward the center of town. "Yuck! Such talk! I know they're a fact of life, but I prefer neither," Changing the subject, she said, "Anyway, the town looks downright patriotic with the gas lamps lit."

A few people were out walking. A couple of men came out of Lyons's, a carriage pulled away from Laughton's, and two well-suited men stood outside of Scott's smoking their pipes. Jennie thought she recognized the one man who came into the store to purchase the cherry tobacco.

As the women crossed the street, Jennie looked behind her and saw a few men standing with their backs against the hotel livery stable. In the twilight, she didn't recognize any of the faces, and she was glad she was in the company of others.

"In the morning before I go in to help Father in the drug store, I'll take a quick walk around town to make sure everything's where we left it tonight," Jennie offered.

"Sounds good! What else are we going to do now?" Gert asked. "It's too early to settle in for the night. I feel like kicking up my heels."

The five of them laughed because unless one was a drinker and hung out at Quinn's Saloon, Clearwater had little to do other than walk down to the grain elevator and watch a couple of old timers in a heated game of checkers, join in literary meetings if one was going on, or spoon with a boyfriend.

"Well, I, for one, am exhausted," Jennie declared. "I know I'm a party pooper, but I'm heading home."

By the time they all got close enough to see the drug store, Jennie could see someone riding horseback and rounding the corner.

"Doc, is that you?" Jennie called out.

"Jennie! You folks closed up already."

"We did! What do you need?"

"I was going to see if I could get something for my housekeeper."

"For Claire? What's wrong?"

Maude, Jeanette, Gert, and Ella walked over to Maude's buggy to give Jennie and the doctor some privacy.

"She's a bit under the weather, not feverish or anything, just sleeping a lot. After she came downstairs this morning, she said she felt very sleepy so she went back to bed. At dinner time, the missus tried to get a bit of chicken soup down her, but Claire said she wasn't hungry, wanted to sleep. It's too early to diagnose anything, but I thought maybe I could get her a tonic or something."

Doubting Claire had said anything to her employers about what had transpired out in Irish Town last evening, Jennie said, "She slept all the way home." For only a second, she thought about telling Doc about their experience near the swamp, but Jennie knew if she had a hard time understanding, he would too. So she changed the subject. "Father and I closed up early tonight like most of the businesses," she said, looking around Main Street. "He took the key with him, but if you want, I can run home and get it."

The doctor thought a moment, and then said, "Jennie, maybe you should. I'd rather be safe than sorry."

"Okay, I won't be but a few minutes."

"While you're gone, I'll step across the street and check in on Louisa Lyons."

Jennie told her friends not to wait for her; she'd finish up with Doc Edmunds and then go home for the night. She hiked her skirt and sprinted the block home.

"Do you need me to come down with you?" Stanley asked, pushing his chair out from the dining room table.

"Heavens, no! Doc and I can handle it," Jennie said as she grabbed the key from the nail on the wall in the kitchen.

"Mmmmm! Mother, that fried chicken smells delicious. Save me a plate." Jennie hollered as she ran back to the front door. "Add a couple of your onions and carrots as well, please. I shouldn't be long."

Jennie hadn't realized how hungry she was. She had eaten the bread and sausage earlier when she and Maude had gone on the picnic, but that had been a few hours before.

She cut across the street. The lamplights sparkled festively, even more than at Christmas.

She unlocked the front doors, lit the lantern on the counter and brought another one from her prescription table.

"Hopefully, this won't take long, Jennie," the doctor announced as he walked in.

"No problem. How's Louisa tonight?"

"Actually, she seems better, almost giddy."

"Giddy? That *is* a change. I haven't seen her smile in months."

"I know, but she was chatty and excited about tomorrow's celebration. She said the children are all coming into town, too."

"My goodness! Was Bob there, too?"

"Yes, as she and I talked, he actually winked at me once, seemingly pleased Louisa was acting so normal. Maybe she's finally on the rebound!"

Doc Edmunds wrapped his wire-rimmed reading glasses around each ear before joining Jennie behind the counter.

"Well, let's see. What do we have here? I don't think Claire needs much. She's probably fighting a bug."

A bug! Well, I suppose she could have a case of swamp fever. "What do you think we should look for?" Jennie asked.

Holding up a lantern to see better, Doc Edmunds grabbed a box of Lydia Pinkham's Vegetable Compound and began reading the ingredients.

"As far as I know, she isn't having menstrual problems. I know some women swear by Pinkham's, maybe because of the alcohol. What else do you have here?"

He continued to look at a number of bottles and boxes, each time announcing, "quackery."

Jennie wondered if Claire's encounter with *whatever* by the swamp had taken everything out of her. If so, nothing on the shelves would revive her. "Maybe . . . maybe Claire should sleep it off."

"Maybe you're right. There isn't much here I'd give her. You, your father, and I've talked about this before. Many of these products don't do what they claim to do. In most cases, they won't hurt either unless they're misused. Unfortunately, some are downright dangerous because they have either opium or alcohol in them." Doc looked at the ingredients on the back of a small round tin before returning it to the shelf. "Maybe she needs a good dose of whiskey, unless that was her problem to begin with."

"I can tell you she wasn't drinking, at least while I was with her," Jennie said.

"She doesn't seem like the type, does she? Look at this." Doc said as he showed Jennie a bottle of Dr. Kilmer's Female Remedy. "So much of these products do nothing for a woman. I've read articles that some of them even contain ingredients that could stop pregnancies. As far as I'm concerned, they need to be taken off the market."

Astounded Doc Edmunds had brought up the subject of abortifacients, Jennie's conscience prickled. Here was her opportunity to discuss what she knew and how some women were using a few of the patent medicines.

"Doc?"

Jennie raised the lantern higher so he could see as he climbed up another step on the ladder. He searched a moment or two before he answered, "Hmmm?"

Where would I begin? If she started talking right now, Jennie knew she wouldn't be able to quit until she had spilled her guts. Doc stepped down and set two more bottles on the counter. Jennie lowered the lantern for him to examine what they professed to cure.

Maude's voice came through loud and clear. "*You might have to turn your head until you know how you can help. The products you're worried about are being sold legally anyway.*"

"Claire . . . uh . . ."

How do I explain who Claire is and what she does? Jennie felt a moment of anger that she should be caught in this situation. She thought of the beautiful red-haired Irish woman who had opened her eyes to some of the town's problems. How much easier her life had been a few days ago.

Despite her uneasiness, Jennie couldn't help but feel sorry for the unknown woman who found herself pregnant after a sordid encounter with someone she probably knew. If the woman carried the child to term, she'd be vulnerable to the community's shame. On the other hand, Jennie felt that ending the life of a baby was morally wrong.

Again, Jennie heard Maude echo Claire's opinions. "*Not every baby born has been a blessing.*"

Jennie knew her father depended on her so much now. She needed to act responsibly, of course, but she also needed to chew on all of this a while longer.

"Oh . . . maybe . . . Claire needs some cod liver oil. Ma always makes us have a teaspoon in the spring. She calls it our spring housecleaning," Forcing a small laugh, Jennie added, "Then we take a sip of her dandelion wine."

The doctor paused a moment and added a chuckle of his own. "You know, your mother's wisdom is not too far off. I think a lot of folk remedies are what's kept people alive for generations. My mother gave me soda crackers after my dose. I've no idea if it kept us healthy, but it didn't hurt us either."

Doc read the ingredients on the back of the bottle of Dr. Kilmer's Female Remedy. "Jennie, I think you're right. If it's sleep she needs, she's getting it. I don't think it'd hurt for me to give her a few sips of the wife's wine, though. It'll probably be the better tonic than any of this stuff."

Jennie thought it ironic that if Claire were alert enough, she could probably concoct her own tonic. He started to replace the boxes he had pulled from the shelves.

"Don't worry about that, Doc. I can straighten this in the morning, but I've been meaning to ask how everything is out in Hasty and Silver Creek."

"Everyone seems to be coming around. No one else has gotten sick, anyway. I'm hopeful I can take a day off tomorrow to join in on the celebration."

"Then you think the diphtheria has been contained out there?"

"For now. We need something stronger to fight this disease, though. The serum has helped, so it's better than nothing. Jennie, I think I'd better move on. I'm going to help you close up here though. There are way too many strangers in town right now."

"Oh, that's not necessary. I'll be fine."

"No, I insist, and I'm walking you home, as well."

Jennie was glad Doc Edmunds hung around to help lock up. After she slid the key into the door, she struggled with the lock again. Doc helped by jiggling the door and key until he was able to secure it. Jennie made a mental note to remind her father it had to get fixed again as soon as possible. She couldn't be sure the next time she'd be able to lock the door on her own.

The spring night was mild as they walked the block to the Phillips's home. With Doc leading his horse, the two chatted about Louisa Lyons. "I'm hoping she's turned a corner," Doc said.

Doc seemed relaxed. When they reached the sidewalk in front of the Phillips's house, he saddled up.

"Thanks for accompanying me, Doc. Hope to see you tomorrow."

Jennie waved as he turned his horse north. She noticed the village had an intoxicating radiance. For now, she felt at peace.

Chapter 21
Opus
Occasion

THE DEEP, RESONATING BLARE of the tuba, the rhythmic pounding of the drum, and the mellow and melodic blasts from the cornets signaled the start of Clearwater's 1895 Decoration Day events.

Less than fifteen minutes earlier, the train whistle had announced the Great Northern's approach a mile or two out of town. Stanley Phillips grabbed his drums, and followed Jennie, locking the drug store's front doors behind them.

"We're going to have to keep the side door unlocked so your ma and the other churchwomen can get their pies set up while many of us make our way out to Acacia Cemetery. Unfortunately, I don't see another way because the front door is too difficult to handle. "

"Right after the speakers are finished, I'll come down and check to make sure everything's safe," Jennie said.

"Sounds good! With the shades pulled down, I think we look locked up. I'm not too worried." Stanley jiggled the lock one more time.

"I'm sure we'll be fine," Jennie said. "Everyone will be heading out to the cemetery right after the speakers are finished."

"That's how it's been done in the past," Stanley answered as he slid his arms through the drum straps. "I wish I could fill you in on the itinerary for the day's events, but I don't know much more than you. The band will play "The Battle Cry of Freedom" as the parade heads to the platform by the Whiting building."

"Good luck! I'll see you later," Jennie hollered as her father headed to the depot to join the band in welcoming the day's speakers.

In the last half hour, Clearwater had turned very busy. Crowds had already gathered on the Main Street corners. Obviously waiting for the parade to begin, men, women and children all wearing their finest clothes meandered up both sides of the sidewalks toward the northern part of town. Some women were decked out in frilly dresses and wore wide-brimmed hats of all colors and shapes. Many men sported black suits and top hats.

Maude and Ella stepped down from the buggy where they were comfortably waiting for Jennie. Dressed in a long black dress and wide-brimmed black lace hat, Maude had out-dressed everyone there. Jennie had decided to wear her white lawn. She tossed her straw hat on top of her head. Ella wore a traditional teacher's outfit, a tan skirt and cream blouse pinned at the top with a pink cameo.

One and two-seated black carriages lined the road and side streets. Between the chatter of conversations, the shouts of greetings, and the clatter of buggies heading up and down the street, Jennie could barely think.

"Here come Jeanette and Gert," Jennie said, nodding toward them as they walked across the street.

"Glad they made it!" Maude shouted back. "By the way, Jennie, many of us have been invited out to Clearwater Lake for the Sunday get-together at Rankin's. Do you want to come along? I know Pitt is going to be out there. I saw him earlier this morning. He wanted to make sure you knew about the gathering. He figured you'd appreciate the literary banter and games."

Jennie had forgotten about the literary get together. Just hearing Pitt's name made her stomach jump. A literary meeting with games and intellectual discussion was something she craved. While she knew she couldn't avoid him forever, she also doubted she'd feel comfortable enough to join in on the fun.

Wishing she could go but knowing she couldn't if Pitt were there, and he would be because he and Professor Rankin were good friends and colleagues, she said, "Professor Rankin invited me too, Maude. Let me think about it, okay?"

"Hello, everyone. Are we ready to go?"

"Maude! You look wonderful!" Jeanette said.

Never one to take too many compliments, Maude smiled and nodded. "The train's in, and the parade's getting into formation."

"I took a quick look this morning before I went to work," Jennie said. "Everything's where we left it last night."

Maude looked toward the sky and said, "Thank you, Lord!"

The air felt warm. A few clouds drifted across the sky. Earlier in the morning, Carl and his friends had gotten the flags mounted on the lamp posts. A slight breeze caused reds, whites, and blues to sway back and forth all the way up the street. The whole scene was merry and alive. It was going to be a fine day, Jennie told herself.

The town's racket was almost deafening. D.D. Storms and Sam Marvin came from the depot and led the parade on horseback, each holding an

American flag. John Kaufman, the newly elected commander, shouted orders rhythmically to the marching soldiers of the Grand Army of the Republic.

The band turned the corner and marched up Main Street. Referred to as the coronet band, despite the fact her father played the drums and Donald Wolff blew the tuba, the band was made up of all ages of Clearwater men, including her brother Carl who played the coronet but occasionally filled in for her father on the drums.

Two colorful floats, each pulled by a team of black horses, followed the band. Decorated in the same patriotic colors as the rest of the town from the goods donated by the community, each float carried boys and girls dressed in their Sunday best standing on the flatbeds, smiling and waving. Jennie thought the youngsters creative in the way they used their ribbons. Most of the youth wore white shirts or blouses and dark pants or skirts. The boys had tied red streamers into their neck ties. The girls wrapped blue streamers around their waists and tied them into bows in the back. Along the skirt of one float, a sign read "MYF" for the Methodist Youth Fellowship, and on the skirt of the other, "CONGREGATIONAL YOUTH" was neatly spelled out.

Walking beside the last float and on the opposite side of the street, a clown dressed as a police officer bobbed up and down. Wearing a larger-than-normal gray cap and a white shirt with a crooked black tie, he had bright red dots on his cheeks and a huge red nose. Jennie hoped Ruthie could see him.

Two carriages, also decorated with red, white and blue ribbons and bows, pulled up the rear, each taking its turn to move out onto Main Street from the corner of Lyons's. Simon Stevens drove the carriage in front, and a younger man sat beside him. Jennie wondered if this was Congressman Towne.

The second carriage pulled behind the first. Reverend Barkaloo sat up front driving the two-seated carriage. Jennie recognized John Stevens sitting in back and confirmed for herself that indeed, he was one of the men she saw standing on the *Bassett* yesterday when it paddled up the river. Although she believed the man who now sat beside Stevens was the same man standing by him on deck of the small steamboat, she still didn't recognize him. Up close, she saw he was a bit stout and had a short gray beard.

Wanting to get their places before the crowd huddled around the platform, the women walked fast, weaving in and out of small crowds. Jennie realized the whole town had turned out for this grand celebration. She waved to a few of her friends. As soon as they started to cross the street, she literally bumped into Ida, Sherm, and Mary and Orrin Dorsey as they, too, tried making their way to the platform.

"I see your father's pounding his drum, but where's that busy mother of yours, Jennie?" Mary Dorsey hollered.

"Good question," Jennie said, nearly shouting to be heard. "I didn't have time to talk to her this morning before Father and I headed to the store. I know Ma has to help set up for the pie social, but she's not doing that until all of this is over and everyone heads out to the cemetery. I bet she's hanging on to Ruthie right now, though," Jennie said.

"Can you believe this turn out? It's like the whole state of Minnesota showed up," Ida shouted within Jennie's hearing distance.

As the crowds of people huddled close to the stage, Jennie surmised that maybe three hundred people had arrived for the event. John Kaufman commanded his men to halt. He shouted a few more orders. Then D.D. Storms and Sam Marvin, each carrying a flag, marched forward, parting the crowd down the middle. Once they reached the steps, Kaufman ordered the men to place the flags in their stands.

After more commands, the men stepped backwards and faced each other. John Kaufman led a couple of the older veterans to their chairs in front. Each man stood at attention while Donald Wolff led the speakers and the guest of honor to the steps.

"Fellow citizens of Clearwater," Donald Wolff began in his deep voice. Under the budding oaks and within this small grove of pine, the town constable stood respectfully before the crowd. He seemed confident, strong, and leader-like as he announced the morning's events. If Jennie hadn't learned what she had about him, she would have been proud of him. After welcoming friends, relatives, and first-time visitors to the village, Wolff asked Reverend Barkaloo to lead their assembly in prayer.

Heavy set and tall, the pastor walked to the podium. Dressed in a white collar and black suit coat and pants, the pastor bowed his head. A wave of "*shushs*" floated from the front to the back of the crowd while the minister waited for wisdom on high. Once he had the audience's attention, he began thanking God for the goodness of the land and the soldiers who fought so bravely to protect the unity of the country. He went on to ask for the Lord's continued guidance for the nation's leaders, as well as His protection from evil.

As the pastor returned to his seat, Wolff returned to the podium to announce the order of speakers, starting with "the influential, humble, and kind gentleman who was one of the important founders of Clearwater, Simon Stevens."

Everyone clapped. Maude was one of the loudest. Uncle Simon, as she called him, and her father Tom Porter were best friends, coming to Clearwater about the same time in the 1850s. Those who knew Stevens agreed there was no one in the area quite like him. He was an extremely soft-spoken and humble man, yet he was always generous with praise toward others, giving them more credit than himself for the settlement of the village.

The short, thin man, whose gray hair and beard showed his age, limped to the podium. He laid a piece of paper on the stand, and turned back and thanked the master of ceremonies, "Young Wolff," for the kind introduction.

He quickly looked down at his notes before starting. "Those of you who live in Clearwater are familiar with how our village got its start, but, for those of you who are first-time visitors, I'm going to give you a brief history of how this beautiful community began.

"I was out looking for a change of scenery when I paddled up from Lake Minnetonka where I helped build a dam and a mill. From the moment I saw this beautiful spot on the Mississippi, I knew where I wanted to spend the rest of my life. The timber and bluffs that surround the river contributed to the area's charm. It made me feel homesick for the farm in the Canadian east I left behind so long ago.

"When I got here, though, I found I wasn't alone. The names of White, Boyington, Webster, and Markham will also be remembered for their contributions to the development of our scenic village on this short bend in the Mississippi. Yet, no proper recognition stops here. No one can say enough about Tom Porter, who was also one of the early settlers, coming in 1855 to settle on what would eventually become one of the finest farms in the area. He so appreciated this state and community, he not only agreed to be county commissioner, he also accepted the call to become a representative for the state legislature."

The crowd clapped and cheered until Tom Porter stood and gave a slight bow.

Once everyone quieted down, Stevens continued. "He and other humble men like him, so many I have time to mention only a few, like Stan Phillips, owner of our respected drug store, Bob Lyons and Will Webster, who keep a good stock of groceries and anything else a person needs at their general merchandise stores, Luther Laughton, who has some of the freshest meat in the area, and G.P. Boutwell, who with his unlimited cache of wires, tin, hammers, and nails has supplied the goods to those who worked hard to build up this community."

Simon Steven's right pointer finger went up in the air as he became more solemn. "Mostly, though, our village, state, and country wouldn't have become what it is today, a place of prosperity and peace, without those men who fought to protect us during its time of civil unrest. You can look around and see the real heroes. Those who are leading our celebration today, such as D.D. Storms, John Kaufman, Mike Larkin, and all you others," he said, nodding his head to those sitting up front. "They are the ones who left comfortable homes and families to defend the country from its evil split."

The sun peeked overhead as Stevens continued to talk about the brave and upright men like Major Will Webster, who fought in the battle of Murfreesboro. Later, he was taken captive and sent to Andersonville. "For over ninety days, he was tortured and nearly starved to death before he was released and sent home to Clearwater with a broken body but not a broken soul.

"We don't want to forget those who paid the premium like the Ponsford boys. Bill fought and was injured at Murfreesboro. James was part of the Mounted Rangers' First Minnesota Volunteers who fought the Indians on his way home with the Sibley Expedition, died of typhoid and is buried out in Dakota Territory, and John, who died in combat in Louisville, Kentucky.

"Join me in a moment of silence as we remember those who paid the ultimate sacrifice, and thank our Maker for those who fought for all of us, and with His guidance, made it back home to their loving families."

As more "*shushs*" echoed backwards, the elderly gentleman lowered his head.

After a minute or so, Simon Stevens looked up. A smile slowly appeared on his face, as he said, "I do not need to tell you much about our next speaker."

Jennie felt prickly with anticipation. The audience seemed to be of the same mind, in rapt attention as it waited for bigger fish to speak.

"He became captain in the U.S. Army, served in the Mexican War. When he first arrived in what was to become Minneapolis in the grand state of Minnesota, he settled on the west bank of the Mississippi. Here he built a small house that became the heart of many important matters like the formation of Hennepin County, the inception of the first district court, and the creation of the first Agricultural Society. In addition, right out on the lawn, he oversaw many Indian council meetings.

"This man helped organize the state militia, and eventually, during our nation's time of trouble back in 1862, he was appointed as Minnesota's Brigadier General to help with the Sioux outbreak. A member of the first Minnesota House and Senate, he became Hennepin County Register of Deeds and Clerk of the Board of Commissioners. While all of these are notable deeds, history will remember him as the founder of Minneapolis.

"Ladies, and gentleman, let's welcome my brother, Colonel John Stevens."

As the crowd gave the elder Stevens a huge welcome of whistles and claps, Jennie reflected on how often Simon's famous brother came to their little village. When he was younger, he occasionally came up on the steamboat that he and Joel Bassett co-owned. She knew he visited many other town founders and often brought other associates with him. Of course, he had come to visit his brother and to oversee his land across the river. Yet early on, he also had a vested interest in the Burbank Stage Company that could have put Clearwater on the map if some of the founders of the small community hadn't voted it down.

The company wanted to cut through some of the local cropland in the state to get to Cold Spring where, once there, they could make their way to the Red River and up to Canada for the exchange of fur and commodities. At the time, John Stevens had the ferry business that crossed the Mississippi at St. Anthony Falls. His business would start this venture by moving products from one side of the river to the other so these products could be sold up river.

Once the Stevens brothers became of age, they said goodbye to their parents and their birthplace in Canada and headed west for adventure and exploration. Both men made their marks on the state, but while John Stevens never minded the public life, his shy younger brother preferred to stay in his shadow. In fact, many surmised it would be years after their deaths before anyone would figure out how much they had contributed to the state.

When John Stevens stepped to the podium, Jennie noticed that he, like his younger brother Simon, leaned a bit, but neither of them were young men anymore. Stevens's gray beard formed a long V. His large black hat shadowed his eyes. Small in stature and almost frail, neither of the brothers looked like they could have played the part of adventurer, explorer, or hero. But that was many years ago, and their stories were legend.

Removing his hat, John Stevens began to speak. "My thanks for such a hearty welcome. I could return the praise to my brother for all he has done for Clearwater and Minnesota, but you aren't gathered to hear us sing each other's praise in our little mutual admiration society."

The audience close to the platform laughed. An echo of "What did he say?" swept backwards as those from the front started repeating the little joke. Row by row, the crowd began to laugh. Stevens remained quiet as the audience again directed its attention back on him.

He continued, "Ladies and gentlemen: We gather today to honor those who fought for freedom, equality, and justice. They are the real heroes of our country. They answered the patriotic call and sacrificed in discomfort far from the hearth of their homes so all of us could live in safety and peace. Whether a man fought to protect his countrymen from Indian uprisings, or traveled deep into enemy territory in the South, he needs to be honored.

"Today, I am going to let more eloquent men do the speaking, though. These are men who served faithfully and will be serving the state for years to come. Yesterday, friends, I had one last adventure before I hand in my raccoon cap. I wanted one last opportunity before I go to my good Lord to travel the Father of Waters, or as the Ojibwa call it, the Great River. I wanted to once again see the land and the water, like my brother Simon says, that he fell in love with because it reminded him of home. I am humbled, my friends. No matter how important I think I am, I realize the Mighty Mississippi is more powerful, more intelligent, and more honorable than any one man or group of men. I wanted to take one more journey to feel the lapping of the water against the bottom of the boat. When I told my wife what I was going to do, she didn't call me an old fool, but I bet she thought about it."

The crowd liked the joke Stevens told and chuckles erupted. "When I asked her if she wanted to come along, she gave me one of those looks. Gentlemen, you know what I mean. Our wives' wisdom speaks through their eyes."

Again loud laughter erupted from the crowd. With so many people and everyone so packed in between this little grove, Jennie could hardly see around her, but she heard Maude's distinct laugh. Standing a bit ahead of her, she noticed Orrin Dorsey looking down at Mary and winking. When she heard a cough, Jennie looked to her left. She recognized Sam and Maggie Marvin who also seemed to appreciate the colonel's joke. Dressed in a tan skirt and blue blouse, Maggie elbowed her tall gray-suited husband.

"My wife decided to come up on more traditional means and arrived here awhile ago."

Jennie and others stood on tiptoes to see if they could find Mrs. Stevens, but she too, was lost in the crowd.

"Being a bit hardheaded, I ignored her look and decided to take my little voyage anyway, so I set out to find the *J.B. Bassett*. As I headed to the dock, I bumped into an old friend. He told me he, too, had been asked to speak in Clearwater and was just then going to the train station. When I told him where I was going and how I was getting here, he said he would like to go on one last adventure. So we decided, instead of taking Jim Hill's choo-choo, we'd have a last rendezvous on the greatest river in the world. We departed early yesterday morning by hopping on the little steamboat that has traversed this area so many times, helping our loggers move timber down the river.

"As we passed by the towns on the way up here, Elk River and Monticello, I felt proud to call this grand state of Minnesota my home, and to know in some small part, I played a role in its development. These communities like most in this state are wholesome, with high educational standards, and profitable because of the roads, train systems, and waterways that are loaded with the bounty of God. Friends, this is the finest country in the land," Colonel Stevens declared, as he slapped the podium. "And that, my friends, is something to boast about!"

While everyone clapped enthusiastically, men, old and young, hooted and hollered. It was then Jennie realized why Colonel John Stevens had been called Minnesota's greatest salesman and booster. He knew how to stir up a crowd.

Once everyone settled down, Stevens continued slowly and more soberly, "Yet, my friends, we wouldn't have this great state without the sacrifices many of our men made to secure our land from a potentially dangerous national split and a few renegade Indians. These men are the ones we need to be most proud of. Some were able to come home to the waiting arms of their families, but others? They paid the ultimate cost and went home to the waiting arms of their Maker. All any of us can say to these gentleman is a hearty thank you!"

The crowd continued to clap until the former soldiers stood up and bowed.

"This next young man who is going to bend your ears for a few minutes is by no means a newcomer to Minnesota. Although he was born in another fine state, Vermont, he came to Minnesota after becoming a lawyer in Illinois. He has served as a Stearns County treasurer, was elected as a representative in the House, and finally, was appointed lieutenant governor under Governor Davis. Ladies and gentlemen, I give you a man who has been a guest in my home many times. I'm never sure whether he came to visit me or eat my wife's cooking, but I give you Lieutenant Governor Alphonso Barto."

So this is the man who was on the *Bassett* yesterday. Jennie had read about him occasionally in the newspaper, but she had never seen him. As the crowd clapped, she couldn't tell who they were clapping for—Barto or Stevens—but she surmised it was Stevens because he had a way with a crowd.

Dressed in a black suit, the former lieutenant governor was a short, stocky man, with a bulging stomach. With his hair and mustache groomed to a gray slickness, Barto looked like a stereotypical caricature in a political cartoon.

"Thank you, Mr. Stevens, for that fine introduction. I'm sure I don't have to comment much on this man's adventures, but a finer man in all Minnesota you'll never find. Despite this, he has put me in an awkward spot. If I say I came to visit him, I risk insulting his wife's cooking, and if I admit I came to get a good meal, I risk losing him as a friend. I'm in a no-win situation."

After the audience finished laughing, Barto continued, "Without the colonel's unique ability to bridge the conversational gaps on both sides, our Indian situation back in the sixties could have been more of a disaster than it was. I can't tell you how many times I saw smoke emerging from the tops of teepees scattered on his property down at the Falls. His ability to, excuse my choice of words, smoke the peace pipe with both the Indians and the government diverted many a problem before it erupted.

"I'm not here to babble about my own triumphs. I'm resting comfortably in near-retirement up in Sauk Center, another community always buzzing with activity. Today they are celebrating as well. Fat cats are praising each other."

Those in the front row started snickering. Soon people who couldn't hear very well asked what he had said. The words "fat cats" rolled backwards and more laughter erupted.

Barto continued, "The GAR is leading the events with salutes, the band is playing patriotic songs, and everyone is heading to the cemetery to adorn the graves of the dearly departed soldiers. They are thanking all our men who fought so valiantly for our country. Yet, the soldiers knew when they took off to fight for their country, they couldn't have done it without those who stayed behind. I ask all of you to join me in giving a round of applause to those who kept the home fires burning while they waited for their soldiers—husbands, fathers, and sons—to return to their loving arms."

The crowd followed Barto's advice. They clapped, turned, and nodded to those around them. Jennie joined in as well, but when she turned to her right, she saw the side view of Pitt one row ahead of her. As he straightened around to focus back on the speaker, he saw Jennie as well. He nodded and smiled. When she returned the smile, she recognized Professor Rankin standing next to him and the two young women, his niece and her friend, who he came to pick up in the store earlier in the week.

"My fellow Minnesotans, I want to tell you a bit about our speaker, Congressman Charles Towne. Raised near Pontiac, Michigan, he attended the University of Michigan to earn his law degree, and was admitted to the bar in 1885.

"The bug for adventure and a bit of wanderlust brought him to Minnesota where he settled in Duluth. His intelligence and spirit caused quite a stir. He became Judge Advocate General for St. Louis County and then accepted the nomination for and was elected to the Fifty-fourth Congress. He has been most instrumental in the development of the iron ore industry in northern Minnesota. Please, welcome the Honorable Charles Towne."

The audience did as they were bid, clapping loud and long. As the gentleman took two long strides to the front of the stand, Jennie surmised he was in his mid to late thirties. Tall and thin, Towne wore wire-rimmed glasses that gave him an intelligent air. His black tailored suit and black bow tie gave him a rich, polished look.

Towne began: "Thank you . . . thank you . . . thank you very much for such a hearty welcome." Soon everyone had quieted. He began. "Members of the Grand Army of the Republic, ladies, and gentlemen, an imposing spectacle this day meets the eye. From border to border of the Republic the customary haunts of men are deserted, ordinary duties are intermitted . . . while in sedate and solemn pageantry . . . the ranks of the living are moving to the resting places of the dead. Wherefore is this? It is because a generation ago, millions of brave men accepted in the name of civilization and humanity the insolent challenge of barbarism to fight to the death for the preservation of liberty and the last hope of self-government upon the earth. Today, the nation pays homage to their deathless victory. Hail! Auspicious and inspiring day, dedicated to reverent recollection and devout resolution. My countrymen, we are not singular in this remembrance of our heroes."

The congressman continued to drone on in a hypnotic tone, talking about communities not unlike Clearwater, but never really referring to their village, either. He talked about ancient tribes that lacked civilization and even gave credit to the Greeks and the Persians who were the "prototype" for their public display for their fallen Athenian warriors. His language was so high-toned and flowery, Jennie lost interest and wondered if she were the only one. Maybe because she had been standing so long that her feet began to hurt, she couldn't concentrate on his speech. Restless, she began to shift weight from one foot to the other. Of course, she reasoned, they couldn't have found enough chairs in the county to seat this large crowd, but sitting would have made listening a lot easier.

Maude bumped into Jennie and whispered her apologies.

Jennie wondered if Maude, too, were uncomfortable. Soon Jennie's attention focused on throats being cleared, whining children being shushed, and feet shuffling. No, she surmised, she wasn't the only one who wasn't following the speaker.

Soon a dark-suited man and a pink-ruffled woman with her arm wrapped around his turned and squeezed out of the crowd. Their action spawned repeated departures. Before long, Jennie had space to relax her arms that she had held so tightly against her sides. Free to move, she finally had an opportunity to see familiar faces.

As Congressman Towne continued to speak about the valor of those who fought for their countries, Jennie scanned the spectators in front and to her sides. She recognized a woman dressed in a familiar green plaid skirt with matching shawl and wearing a green hat. A few wisps of red hair escaped from where they had been neatly tucked inside. There was no mistaking her. That was Claire. Jennie could see she had recovered from her deep sleep.

After a few moments, the woman turned, apparently to see who was around her, as well. Jennie felt a pang of guilt for staring. Their eyes met. The young Irish woman looked beautiful. Her friendly smile aimed at Jennie brightened her whole face. Danny Higgins stood to Claire's left. Dressed less formally in his white dress shirt and gray pants, he was handsome and respectable. The young couple made an attractive pair.

Off to her right, Bob Lyons and three of his children stood respectfully at attention. Jennie recognized Minnie, who was getting married sometime soon, and the two teenagers, Frankie, who nearly ran the family farm by himself, and young Louisa, who only stood a few inches over four feet tall but had already turned into a charming young girl of thirteen. Then there was Charlie. Although he was handicapped, he was as rambunctious as any other seven-year-old. Bob had a large hand on the boy's head. This didn't seem to stop the little rascal because he turned and made a face at one of the small boys behind him. Jennie had a hard time controlling a giggle. She looked around but realized Louisa was nowhere to be seen.

Trying to concentrate, Jennie stared at the younger congressman. With his dark mustache and a hint of gray at his temples, Towne had a certain magnetism even though his oratorical skills were lost on her. When he started to slow his speech and enunciate more carefully, Jennie hoped he was wrapping up.

"Thus, martial heroism always had in it an ideal element . . ."

Unfortunately, the congressman's language was too highfaluting for Jennie. Again, she became distracted when someone bumped into her from behind. When she turned to see who it was, she noticed that Professor Rankin had moved in closer to the platform to hear, and Pitt had followed. As he slid in closer, their group formed an arc. Jennie could see better but she was taken back when she noticed Pitt arm in arm with the young woman who came into the store with the professor's niece. *What was her name again? Alice? Yes, of course, Alice.* Jennie remembered when she met the young woman, she had associated her name with the murdered Leonard girl.

Jennie quickly sized up the situation. The more she observed, the more she felt her stomach jump up and down. *Pitt and the woman seem to be a bit cozy. One day he proposes to me, and now he is playing love with another woman?*

The throng of clapping hands awakened Jennie. She looked around. She hadn't heard Towne's last words, but she was relieved he had finished. When he turned to go back to his chair, Donald Wolff went to the podium.

"Thank you, thank you. We'll close this part of our celebration with the Ridley quartette singing, 'We Are Coming Father Abra'ahm.' Immediately afterward, we'll commence to the Acacia Cemetery for the graveside services and the decoration of the graves. The band will lead the way."

The Ridley quartette was well-known around the area. The youngsters of Alvah and Mary ranged in ages from Effie who was twenty-four, and the only girl in the family, to Bill and George who were in their early twenties, down to Bert who would graduate from high school next year. They harmonized beautifully.

The song was over before Jennie remembered it had started, and again the audience was clapping. Almost immediately the band interrupted the applause to begin playing, "The Drum March of the Guards." Jennie could hear her father pounding the drums. As she turned around, she caught another glimpse of Pitt who had circled around with Alice's white gloved hand still encircling his arm. He looked at Jennie; she looked up into his eyes. They stared at each other. Pitt turned red. Glaring back, Jennie abruptly turned her back to him and walked away.

Having no desire to stick around and watch another display, Jennie felt as if she had to get away fast. She bobbed and weaved her way toward the main part of town.

"Jennie?" Maude hollered as they crossed the street. She grabbed hold of Jennie's arm. "What was Pitt doing with that young woman on his arm?"

Diverting her face from Maude's gaze for fear of losing control, Jennie looked straight ahead. "How could he, Maude? How could he?"

"I've got to admit it looks suspicious. That young woman looked proud as can be as she hung on to Pitt's arm. I've never seen such adoration in anyone's eyes before. If it's any consolation, Jennie, I don't think he was returning her admiration. Maybe he was playing the part of a kind gentleman."

"What I saw wasn't a kind response, Maude! He looked down and smiled at her. Then he covered her white gloved hand with his own and patted it."

Maude and Jennie arrived at the front of the Methodist Church. Carriages had lined up to head out to the cemetery. The streets became noisy again: people talking, bells jingling, and horses snorting and stomping. It was all too much for Jennie.

"If you want to go out to the cemetery, please go. I'm no longer in the mood. I promised Father I'd check on the store, anyway. I'll stay and help Mother and the other women get ready for the pie social."

"No, I'll stay back, too. When are they setting up?"

"After the picnic, maybe closer to two o'clock or so." Jennie answered, wishing she had a few minutes alone to herself. "Please, Maude, don't stay back on my account."

Not getting the hint, Maude said, "That's okay. I don't want to leave you alone."

The last of the buggies and horses made their way toward the bridge to cross over the Clearwater River and head out to Acacia cemetery. Everyone would be gone for at least a couple hours because they would leave for Cedar Point and potluck picnics. Reconciled to the fact she wouldn't be able to be alone, Jennie realized the next best thing was to keep busy.

"Should we find our mothers?" Maude asked. "Maybe they could put us to work."

With hardly a breeze blowing, the town had become eerily quiet.

"Jennie! Jennie!"

Jennie turned to see who was calling her. Running up the street, Marietta huffed and hollered. Alarmed, Jennie ran toward her mother.

"Ma? What's the matter?"

Holding out her hand for Jennie to grab, she hollered, "The drug store, Jennie." Marietta wheezed. "We've been robbed!"

Chapter 22
Aggressus
An Attack

"What?" Jennie hollered as she grabbed her mother's outstretched hand. She ran as fast as she could pull her mother back down the sidewalk and toward the family store. Maude ran close behind them.

Reaching the back door, Jennie stepped inside and inspected the whole chamber. The backroom door was wide open, and the door to the safe had been torn from its hinges. She couldn't remember exactly how much money her father had stashed inside, but she calculated the robbers had taken off with at least a hundred dollars.

Jennie stood on her tiptoes, trying to see if the burglars were in the front of the store. Not seeing anything, she crept in, carefully watching every step she took for fear of tripping over papers and broken objects she was too afraid to look down at to inspect. Hoping she wouldn't find anyone lurking in the shadows, she looked under the counters near the table dispensary. Relieved no one was hiding anywhere, she saw two cupboard doors wide open but didn't stop to check what had been taken from them.

She continued toward the front, tilting her head in every nick and cranny, "No one's here." As she waved for Maude and her mother to join her, she added, "Looks like the whole store's been ransacked, though."

She looked around from where she stood. Drawers were opened, and everything in them, papers, matches, pencils, clips, and tubes of various ointments, had been dumped onto the floor. The glass showcases stood wide open. As if it were sticking out its tongue, the gilded cash register drawer was wide open and empty of all its cash and change, probably no more than ten or twelve dollars that Jennie had taken in earlier in the morning.

"Ma, don't tell me you came in here all by yourself?"

"Actually, I didn't come in at all. As soon as I saw the door open, I saw the mess. That's when I came running for help."

"That's a relief," Jennie said a bit distractedly.

"Ruthie was being rambunctious. I knew she needed to be taken home for a while, so I sent her with Blanche before the congressman finished speaking."

"What's the matter, Ma?" Jennie asked as she looked over to her mother and read a panicked look on her face.

"Oh, Jennie, I realized! I sent the girls home before I realized we were robbed. I sent them out on the street by themselves. I have to go and check on them," she added as she backed toward the door.

"I'll go, Marietta," Maude hollered, turning around and running out the door without waiting for an answer.

Jennie watched as Maude raced past the front window and headed toward the Phillips's house.

"Ma, I'm sure they're all right. I doubt if they were taken hostage," she said, half hoping what she said sounded believable even though right then she wasn't so sure about anything.

"I pray you're right!"

Looking around the store, Jennie tried to plan what her next step should be. "Okay, now we have to think. Almost everyone's out at Acacia Cemetery. I don't know of anyone who'd still be around, unless Frank or Sarah Scott are over at the hotel or George Newell's at the depot." Walking toward the front window, Jennie looked left and then right before suggesting, "Do you think you could see if anyone is around to get us some help? I'll stay here and try to figure out what all was taken."

"Yes, I can do that, but I hate to leave you here alone."

"I'll be fine. Whoever did this won't return to the scene of the crime. I'm glad you're all right. I can't imagine what would've happened if you'd come upon the burglars while they were in the act."

"God be praised. I didn't!"

"Amen! And by the time you get back, Maude should be back with good news about the girls."

"Jennie, did you notice they didn't touch the pies?" Marietta said as she looked in the storage room. She started to giggle, then covered her mouth. "I'm shocked I can laugh, but it's kind of funny, in a way, they didn't destroy them."

"*We are* in shock, Ma," Jennie said as she smiled wearily. "It *is* ironic, almost as if the culprits knew and respected the work you women put into your pies!"

"Really! I guess it's true that no one is completely bad nor completely good. Anyway, I'll get back as soon as I find someone to help us."

Jennie watched her mother step gingerly toward the side door. Then she saw her cross the street and head to Hotel Scott. Once she grabbed hold of the door handle, she jiggled it for a few moments before giving up and heading toward the depot.

Obviously, Jennie thought. Mr. Scott, too, had closed up shop for awhile.

Not knowing where to start or what to touch, Jennie tried to size up what was destroyed or missing. One empty shelf shouted at her that two or three boxes of razors had been swiped. She noticed the humidor was opened and emptied, and the six boxes of cigars, which had been stacked in a pyramid on the front counter, had been taken as well. The clear jars of taffy and lemon drops were empty and tipped over. Bigger items, like leather bags, expensive perfumes, and shaving cups, were, apparently, unwanted and untouched.

"Jennie," Marietta said, her voice causing Jennie to jump. "I should've made more noise when I came in."

"I guess I'm still skittish."

"Well, the hotel's locked up, but the sign states he'll be back around one-thirty. I found George Newell, though. He said he'd saddle up and ride out to the cemetery. He promised to keep the news as quiet as possible, so as to not to disrupt the ceremonies or cause panic. He'll bring back your pa and young Wolff for sure. He didn't think he should leave us alone, but I told him we'd be fine and to get out and back as fast as he could."

Right then, both Jennie and Marietta heard George Newell slapping his horse's side to get it to go faster. Now all Jennie and her mother had to do was wait and be as calm as possible.

"Ma, I can barely stand it in here. I don't feel I can do anything until Father comes back anyway. Let's go outside."

As they rounded the corner toward the front of the building, Maude appeared and joined them on the front stoop.

"The girls are fine. They were feeding bread and butter to Ruthie. I told Blanche what happened and told her to stay in the house until you come home." Maude placed a basket on the ground. "Marietta, I hope you don't mind, but I helped myself to what I found. I reheated some coffee, too, but I forgot cups."

"Oh, Maude that was very considerate of you. I know we have some cups in the store," Marietta said as headed to the back door.

"Be careful, Ma," Jennie begged as she looked one way up the street and then back toward the other end of town. "I'm sick about this. I suppose we were pretty vulnerable, especially since we left the door unlocked for the ladies to drop off and pick up their pies. We've never had a problem before." Jennie nervously wiped her forehead with the back of her hand. "Now I can see it was stupid with so many strangers in town."

"Don't blame yourself. Whoever did this probably would have gotten in another way, breaking a window or something."

When Marietta came back with three white cups, Maude removed the towel she had wrapped around the jar to keep the coffee hot. She poured each a cup and handed each a slice of buttered bread.

Quietly, they sat on the stoop slowly sipping their coffee and nibbling bread. Jennie looked uptown toward the Whiting building. The town was eerily quiet. Suddenly, she felt a tight squeeze in her stomach. "Is someone riding this way?"

Maude stepped out onto the street and looked north. "You know, I can't be sure, but it looks like Doc Edmunds."

All three of them looked toward the man on horseback. As soon as he got closer, Jennie recognized the village doctor.

"Are you women okay?" Doc hollered as he came to a quick stop and slid off his horse.

"Yes, but we've been robbed," Jennie said loudly.

"So has Boutwell," Doc said. "I was the last of the crowd to leave. I'd been talking to Gilbert Tollington about the Hasty and Silver Creek rounds he's taking for me. Since he and his wife had parked across the street from the ceremonies, they offered to take Mrs. Edmunds with them to the cemetery because she and I had walked down the hill from our house. I told them I'd join them after I saddled up. I had ridden about halfway down the hill when I heard a blast. I thought it came from the Boutwell's so I headed there."

"Oh, no!" Maude exclaimed. "We heard nothing. That had to be minutes after everyone left for the cemetery."

"And, probably, just minutes after they robbed us here," Marietta added.

Doc looked at Marietta for a second. "By the time I got to the building, I wasn't sure what I'd find. The side window closest to the river was broken, but I could see the back door was wide open. I crept to the door and listened for a minute or so before I peeked inside. No one was there, but I saw Boutwell's safe had been blown open and emptied."

"Good heavens!" Maude proclaimed. "Was the whole town robbed?"

Jennie looked at Maude and her mother who were looking at Doc. Jennie read shock in everyone's face as they all seemed to acknowledge the ugly fact. "I'm glad you're safe, Doc. It's hard to believe you were that close to the burglars." She put her hand on her stomach that churned with pain. She added, "They didn't have to blast our safe because it wasn't that sound. But they created quite a mess for us to clean up." Jennie shook her head before looking across the street to the hotel and then a bit north toward the banks and kitty-corner toward Lyons's General Store. "I wonder if anyone else got hit."

"I was heading down to see if Newell was around. Thought we'd better telegraph the county sheriff."

"Ma sent George out to Acacia a bit ago to get us some help."

Marietta retold the story of how she came upon their own break-in and how Jennie had gone into the building and investigated everything. "I think we're pretty much alone in town, at least in the business community. "All I can say is *thank heavens* no one was hurt."

"Let's hope you're right about that, Marietta. Wish I knew if he telegrammed the authorities," Doc said as he looked down the street. "I'm afraid the man or men who did this'll be long gone by the time anyone gets back from the cemetery."

"I hate to admit this," Maude said. "But I really hope they're long gone."

"I agree," Marietta said. "I hate to think they're watching us."

"Oh, my," Jennie said, crossing her arms and nervously rubbing them as if chilled. "I don't even want to think about it. I hope the culprits are gone, too."

Doc stepped to the curb and looked in all four directions. He swiped his hand down over his mustache, circling his mouth. "You women think you'll be okay if I take a look around town? I'll stay within hollering distance, but I think I should investigate the rest of the businesses, maybe start with the banks."

"We'll be fine. George and the others will be back soon," Jennie said, trying to reassure everyone.

After a tip of his hat, Doc Edmunds walked across the street.

Jennie took the last swig of her coffee and put the cup in the basket. Hands on hips, she paced to the curb and back, staring in all directions like Doc had. "I feel so helpless. I wish there were something else we could do."

"And I hope the church ladies don't show up for their pies before the men get back and get to the bottom this," Marietta declared as she dabbed her forehead and reached for her fan in her apron pocket.

Jennie knew her mother was going through middle life and often had these intense hot flashes. She had tried everything, but lately, they had gotten so bad, she carried a small hand fan with her everywhere. The more excited Marietta became, the hotter she became and the faster she fanned herself. Right now, Jennie thought, if the woman could fly, she would.

Jennie kept a close eye on Doc Edmunds as he cut across to Shaw's bank. She watched as he looked through the front window, jiggled the doorknob, and walked around to the side.

Then for a few moments, she lost sight of him. Looking north, she saw no evidence of anyone heading into town. "What's keeping Mr. Newell? He should have been able to get out there and back by now."

Marietta grabbed her handkerchief again and dabbed at her forehead and the back of her neck before calmly answering, "I don't think he could've gotten out there, found your pa, and come back by now, Jennie. Probably hasn't been gone more than half an hour or so. I'm sure he'll be along soon."

Jennie, who now felt the temperature and humidity rising, wiped her neck as she paced. Doc re-emerged from the side of the bank and waved in their direction before removing his hat and wiping his forehead with the front of his arm. He replaced his hat, walked to Lyons's, and tried the front door.

Jennie was astonished when he walked right in. He wasn't in long before he stepped back outside. "Jennie," he hollered as he waved. "I need your help."

Jennie picked up her skirt and walked briskly across the street.

"What's going on, Doc?" she asked as she stepped inside the store.

As her eyes adjusted to the dimness, Jennie saw cans of fruit and vegetables littering the floor. Small and large boxes had been tipped over. A large cracker barrel lay on its side, spilled, with crackers smashed and scattered like sawdust. Then Jennie saw why Doc needed her.

She stepped gingerly as she followed behind him toward a body on the floor.

"I checked Louisa's pulse. She's alive, anyway," Doc said as he knelt and felt her wrist again.

Crumpled and lying sideways, Louisa looked more dead than alive. Jennie bent over and saw the woman's swollen face. She had been slugged. Jennie guessed that soon enough Louisa's eye would be turning black and blue, if the swelling was any indication. Her cheekbone was red, and a stream of blood drained from her lip.

"Her pulse is strong yet. That's a good thing." Doc gave Louisa's arm a gentle shake. "Louisa, Louisa. Wake up."

As the woman began to stir, she moaned as she tried to turn on her back. Then Jennie noticed that the bodice of her dress had been ripped open. Her breasts were exposed, and the front of her dress was above her knees.

"Oh, dear God!" Jennie cried, covering her mouth with her hand.

Doc Edmunds looked up at Jennie, alarm written all over his face. "It's okay, Louisa. Don't move too fast. If you hurt, don't move at all."

Louisa groaned but sat up. "What's happened?" She winced as she tenderly touched her swollen cheek.

Jennie went to the back room to look for a rag. She saw a bowl and pitcher along with a hand towel on a small table. She dipped the towel in the water and wrung it out. Gently, Jennie wiped the blood from the woman's face and lips. Then she patted her eye and cheekbone. Louisa had only been beaten on the left side, but it was as nasty sight.

"Louisa," Doc said. "Let's try to get you up and sitting in the chair."

Only as she tried to stand did Louisa see the front of her dress. "Oh, no! Robert, Robert." Once on her feet, she bent over in pain. She began crying and coughing.

"Is anything broken, Doc?" Jennie asked as she pulled Louisa's dress down.

"If she can walk, no."

Self-consciously, Louisa pulled her bodice together as she limped toward the chair. When she tried to sit down, she flinched in pain again. Returning to the back room, Jennie rinsed the towel in clean water. Louisa's shawl lay on the cot.

"Try to hold this on your eye and cheek. The coolness will help with the swelling," Jennie instructed Louisa when she returned. "I brought this to cover you up." Jennie wrapped the shawl around Louisa and then moved away so Doc could squat on his haunches to talk to the woman. Knowing Doc had to ask some hard questions, Jennie said, "Doc, I'm going to get Ma. I think she might help us the most right now."

He nodded, and Jennie left as she came, stepping over debris. When she joined Maude and her mother, she stressed that what she had to tell them had to remain a secret.

"Louisa's in there. She's alive, but she was beaten pretty badly, and it looks like . . .well, it looks like she's been molested." Jennie read the shock in their eyes. "We have her cleaned up as best we can and sitting down. Ma, do you think you could go over there and try to keep her calm until Robert gets back? I think she needs someone right now."

"Oh, that poor soul! Of course, I'll go," she added as she put her cup in the basket and walked across the street.

"Ma, be careful. The floor is a shambles. Walk carefully once you get in there."

"It's hard to believe all this could have happened this morning." Maude said, taking two deep breaths. "I'm surprised whoever did this thought he had the time to do what he did to Louisa, too."

"Oh, my Lord!" Jennie closed her eyes and bowed her head.

"What?" Maude asked.

"It could have been Ma. It could have been one of my sisters. It could have been any one of us."

* * *

MAUDE AND JENNIE WALKED to the middle of Main Street but said nothing. Both looked north but didn't talk. Any other time, Jennie would have appreciated the quietness, but now it had an almost supernatural feel.

She said, "Let's go back over there and see if we can be of any help. Maybe, if we could get Louisa outside, she could get some air and away from that scene."

Doc must have been thinking the same thing. As Jennie opened the door, he and Marietta had Louisa standing and were each holding one of her arms, leading her to the door. Doc kicked a pathway as they walked so no one would trip and fall. Jennie held the door open as they led Louisa outside. They all walked to the sidewalk in front of the drug store, where Jennie hurried inside for a chair.

When Louisa tried to sit again, she grabbed her stomach as she flinched in pain, but finally settled back in the chair. Only then did she ask, "Where is everyone?"

"They're out at the cemetery for the rest of the Decoration Day celebration."

"Oh, of course," Louisa said as she rested her head against the chair.

Doc asked, "Remember what I told you? It looks like the town's been robbed."

Jennie wanted to add, "Amongst other things," but she didn't.

Louisa shook her head and cried, "Robert. Robert." She sobbed, and shook so violently that Jennie knelt down and tried to comfort her.

"It wouldn't surprise me if she was going into shock," Doc said as he watched Louisa shiver, despite the heat and the shawl around her shoulders. "I'm going inside to see if you have anything I can give her to calm down."

Almost inconsolable, Louisa sobbed out her explanation for why she was in the store. "I didn't feel well enough to go with Robert and the children to hear the speakers. I took a swig of that bottle I bought the other day, Jennie, and I fell asleep. All I remember is waking when I heard a crash. I stood up and saw a dark shadow coming toward me. I remember the pain when I was hit. Not until Doc just told me what happened did I know . . ." and Louisa started crying again and wringing the hem of her skirt. "Robert is going to be so upset with me because I let the burglars destroy the store."

If Louisa hadn't remembered the attack, it might be a blessing in itself. Yet Jennie couldn't help but think there was enough sadness to go around. *Robert will feel terrible once he remembers he forgot to dilute the medicine Louisa purchased*, Jennie thought. *Both husband and wife will be sad when they realize what happened to Louisa. The town will have plenty to think about when its citizens understand that their community is as vulnerable as any.*

Marietta tried consoling Louisa. "I doubt your husband is going to be upset with you, Louisa. He's a good man. He'll understand."

Maude whispered, "I can't stand this. I've gotta do something. Jennie, Marietta, I don't want to desert you, but I think I'll drive out to see what's taking the men so long. I can also haul a couple more people back."

"I hate to see you go out there by yourself, Maude," Marietta said, "but it might not be such a bad idea."

Jennie watched her friend hike up her skirt and run toward her rig. Maude nodded at them as she urged her horse to turn left. It didn't take her long to get out of town. Jennie couldn't help but think Maude enjoyed being in the middle of the action and part of the solution.

Doc came back out with a bottle of the same stuff Louisa had been taking, Pastor Koenig's Nervine. "Here, Louisa. Now I want you to take a couple sips, not drink the whole bottle." He looked at Jennie and said, "It looks like it's about the safest stuff on the shelves. It'll probably make her relax. Too bad I don't go around with a bottle of whiskey in my pocket."

Any other time, Jennie could have read a bit of humor in the doctor's voice, but today she read sarcasm. With one hand patting Louisa, Marietta looked up the street, searching for help.

"Hopefully Maude will see what's holding some of them up," Doc said. "If you ladies think you can handle this, I think I'll head up the street to see if anyone else's hurt."

"We'll be fine, Doc," Marietta said with her eyes staring north.

A few minutes later, Doc walked back their way.

Jennie met him. "What did you find?"

"Whittemore's bank was broken into as well, but I don't think much was taken except what was in the teller's drawer. The safe seems solid, just a bit of smoke damage like they tried to blow it open but couldn't. It'd take a ton of dynamite to get into that. Cash drawers open and empty but the safe is still solidly closed. No one else around that I can see. I know I saw Laughtons leave for the cemetery, so besides taking some money, I'm sure they're safe. I don't want to leave you women to go up the street any farther. I'll wait until Newell gets back with help."

"Hopefully, Maude'll meet up with them as she heads out to Acacia. I just hope we can keep our visitors free of worry and still get to the bottom of this."

"I think I see someone coming now," Doc announced from the middle of the street. "Yep, I see two horses, and one of the horses is carrying two men. I bet Maude met them on the bridge as she crossed the river."

They all stepped out into the street to see the approaching riders. Soon, Donald Wolff and George Newell pulled to a stop, and Stanley Phillips hopped down from behind Newell. Jennie read worry lines across his forehead.

"Father!" Jennie greeted.

"Is everyone all right?" he asked, grabbing hold of Marietta's arm and putting an arm around Jennie.

"Yes, we're alive. Doc's been scoping out the town and believes the burglars are long gone," Marietta said quietly. Only then did Stanley notice Louisa Lyons. Marietta pulled her husband aside. Jennie looked at her father's startled expression.

After Newell and Wolff climbed down from their horses, Doc Edmunds related the story of how he heard the blast at Boutwell's Hardware Store and what he found there and at the banks.

"I wonder if these are the same men the Sherburne County sheriff telegraphed about earlier in the week," George Newell questioned as he proceeded to retell the story of the robbery in Elk River. Jennie could hardly believe that it had been only a few short days since Danny Higgins told Jennie and her father about the robberies. Doc Edmunds excused himself and said he would be back after he checked out the rest of the village.

Donald Wolff paced back and forth on the sidewalk. He looked ready for action, ready to start searching through every store in town. He didn't wear a gun and holster, but Jennie could picture the cocky man with pistols up, rushing his way into one of the village buildings as he looked for robbers.

"I'm going to look inside to get an idea of what's been taken," Stanley said to the small crowd. "Then I'll meet up with the rest of you to canvas the area. We've got to make sure the town's safe as quickly as possible before everyone comes back from the cemetery."

"You're so right, Mr. Phillips, so right," Wolff said.

Without waiting for Wolff to give him an order, Newell gave a backwards wave as he stepped down the sidewalk and walked toward his horse. "I'll catch up with all of you later. I'm going to telegram the Wright County sheriff before the afternoon train arrives."

Stanley walked toward the front door.

"Father, the back door's wide open. I think you'd be better off heading in that way. There is so much broken glass up near the front."

Wolff followed close behind Stanley. Jennie left the women and walked behind them.

"It's a mess," Jennie said, cautioning them as they stepped inside the store.

"I can see that," Stanley said as he tread lightly across the floor.

Donald Wolff, not as graceful as Jennie's thin father, plowed his way into the building, tripping on objects as he made his way behind Stanley. Jennie stood in the door jamb and tried to watch. Wolff, a large man, blocked her view of her father, but she could hear them talk.

"Donald, don't you think you should be taking notes for the sheriff?" Stanley inquired impatiently.

"Yes, sir, that makes sense. You got a pencil and paper I can borrow?"

Jennie figured her father could handle Wolff. She returned to the street where Louisa sat. She looked more relaxed. The Nervine must have helped. Marietta chatted about her garden and how well the lettuce and radishes were coming along.

Soon Jennie saw four fast horses heading down the street. They resembled the four horsemen of the Apocalypse, each heading in a different direction. She could see George Boutwell hop off the back of his horse and run into his hardware store, one horse and rider turned west, and another rode southeast.One horse headed toward them carrying Frank Scott, who owned the hotel. Maude came rolling in behind all of them and braked in front of the drug store. Robert Lyons and Charles Whittemore jumped down from her rig. Charles headed toward his bank while Robert, who towered over most men in the village, took two large steps to meet up with Louisa.

"Louisa, are you okay?" her husband asked, looking down at her in the chair. Robert had deep worry lines across his forehead. "Your face, what happened to you?"

Her hand went up to her eye and cheek, which had become even more swollen now. "I'm sorry, Robert. I feel terrible about the store being such a mess."

Robert looked at Jennie, who looked deep into his eyes to see if he knew anything. Apparently, he didn't know what else had transpired because he said, "Don't worry about the store. All that can be replaced."

Robert Lyons had the calmness of a saint. Despite all the challenges God gave him, the farm in the country, the store in town, four children, one of them young Charlie who was full of the dickens and handicapped, and an ill wife who couldn't always be by his side as a soul mate and helper, Robert's gentleness proved his greatest strength. Jennie recalled a phrase from one of Shakespeare's plays: "O, it is excellent to have a giant's strength, but is tyrannous to use it like a giant."

"Will you be okay if I leave you for a few minutes while I look over our losses? I promise I'll be right back."

Robert Lyons crossed the street as Doc Edmunds came down the sidewalk. They met at the mercantile door, Doc following Robert inside. Jennie could only imagine how the man was going to handle what the doctor was about to tell him about his wife.

* * *

IT TOOK AWHILE for the village to fill up again. Most headed out to Cedar Point to have a potluck picnic before returning for the afternoon activities. This gave the Phillips family time to start cleaning up the store for tomorrow's business. Marietta left to help the church ladies with the pie and ice cream social. As soon as Sammy, Blanche, and Carl had helped push a few boxes around and swept up the center of the floor, Jennie told them to go out and meet up with their friends.

"I'd ask the three of you not to mention what took place around here today." Stanley stood up with a full dust pan in hand. "Your friends will find out soon enough, but let's let the town people host these visitors in the style we planned. Tomorrow's soon enough for the news to get out."

His children promised him they would keep their mouths shut and walked out one by one. "What do you think, Jennie? Want to join in on the shindig? A slice of your ma's rhubarb pie would hit the spot about now."

"That's fine. I promised I'd meet up with Maude. In case she told Jeanette, Ella, and Gert what happened around town, I'd like to forewarn then about the necessity for secrecy at least until the town clears out." Jennie looked over the boxes heaped with broken items. "I suppose the rest can wait until the morning. But, I have to say, I've lost all interest in celebrating."

"I know. It'll be good for us to get our minds off this mess for a while. As I wander around, I think I'll check up on the other businesses to see how they're faring."

At least they could walk down a clear path to the back door without stepping on shards of sharp objects. Stanley closed the door and padlocked it. "I think that'll hold now. Not that there's much left to take, but no sense in inviting more trouble."

"You mind if I park my rig alongside your building here?" Maude hollered as she drove in from the west.

"Of course. Thanks for your help, Maude." Stanley waved before he walked across the street.

"I was going to look for you," Jennie said as she walked around the front of the carriage after Maude hopped out.

"I was helping Ma with her lemonade stand in front of the Masonic Hall. When some of the Eastern Star women showed up, I decided I could leave for a while. Pa's around town checking on the damages."

"Hard to believe any of this has happened in Clearwater," Jennie said.

"I know. Except for a few skirmishes down by Quinn's, our little village has never seen such action."

"Have you said anything to anyone about what happened?" Jennie could almost guess Livy Paisley had found out some way and spread the news.

"Pa told Ma. Honestly, I've been racing around since I last saw you and haven't had time to talk to anyone."

Jennie felt a bit relieved. "Have you seen the girls?"

"I saw Gert with her folks earlier, but we didn't talk. I'm sure we'll find them."

The middle of Main Street resembled a summer carnival. A crowd of boys and girls circled the front of Laughton's Meat Market as they took turns tossing bean bags into a mouth of a clown face painted on a sheet of plywood. Young voices hollering "whoops" and "ahhhs" were followed by laughter and clapping.

Hordes of people kept the church ladies busy at the pie and ice cream social. Men, women, and children filled all the chairs around the tables and overflowed onto the church steps.

"Good turnout. So many people." Jennie saw her mother at the table bending over a barrel of ice cream. She hoped she could take her mind off their recent troubles by visiting with friends and town guests. "Let's stop on our way back. Besides, a glass of your mother's wonderful nectar would taste good right now."

"Looks like some of the men are having a lively game of horseshoes." Maude nodded to the street that ran in between the church and Livy's house.

Jennie recognized a few of them who, with rolled up sleeves, took turns pitching and aiming to score a ringer. Standing under an elm tree in front of the Westcott building, Carl's friend, Waylan Woodworth, entertained six or seven young boys with his magic card tricks. Jennie had seen him perform before. He was crafty. Her eyes could never catch him at any of his sleight of hand tricks, especially the cups and balls trick. How he could make the little pebbles disappear and then reappear under one of the cups amazed her.

Down in the little gully behind Livy Paisley's house, a number of children stood in line waiting for a pony ride. "Look at that, Maude. I had no idea someone would haul in their Shetland and offer up rides."

"Look. A girl in the pinafore didn't let go of her lollypop," Maude and Jennie watched a few moments as a man lead the animal and girl in a circle. "I didn't know we'd have this much going on today."

Jennie could not believe how many people the town could hold. Main Street and the sidewalks overflowed. North of the drug store, every lawn, every side street, and every store porch had a vendor or activity taking place. Up until then, Jennie had completely forgotten about Pitt. For some reason—maybe all the excitement of the day—she began to feel nervous about seeing him. "Maude, I've about had it. I'm tired. Let's get some lemonade and then head back to the church."

The two fought their way through the crowd to the Masonic Hall where they managed to get two glasses. "Let's stand off to the side, Jennie. I'm afraid someone will bump into me and spill this."

Jennie turned her back to the crowd. "This is what I needed." She drained her glass and carried it back to Maude's mother's stand. "I'm sorry to rush you, Maude. I'm too jumpy. Ma'll be upset if I don't stop for some pie. I want to see Jeanette and the others, but I'm about ready to go home and put my feet up."

* * *

WHEN THEY ALL RETURNED the next morning, they continued filling up boxes with the products that had been broken, placing the salvageable items back on the shelves. Jennie started a list of everything that needed to be replaced.

"You'd better add two and a half bottles of laudanum to the list," Stanley said, as he searched the shelves.

"I suppose the burglars knew what they were taking," Jennie declared as she added the narcotic to her list.

"I'm not sure where these belong, Jennie," Sammy interrupted, holding up three purple boxes. "I opened them. The bottles in them ain't broke."

Jennie pushed a few stray hairs behind her right ear. She wanted so much to correct her younger brother's grammar, but she was way too exhausted and stressed to take the time now. She bit her tongue and patiently said, "Oh, good. Let's see. That's Wampole's Preparation and should go up on the third shelf."

At eleven years old, Sammy was already taller than Jennie. He was always such a good helper when he put his mind on what he was doing.

"We're going to have to order more shaving mugs next week. Almost every single one is cracked or has its handle broken off," Jennie told her father as she placed another in the trash box. "I can't get over this. It's like a herd of pigs stampeded in here. Who could have done this and why?"

"I don't know the mind of a thief, nor do I want to know it, but what I really don't understand is how anyone can destroy someone else's property," Stanley replied, placing his glasses up on his head. "Our place is in bad shape. I only had time to look in on the hardware store yesterday. I can't imagine what other businesses are dealing with."

"Why don't you go find out?" Jennie asked as she took the broom and started sweeping shards of broken glass into a pile near the front door. "We've got everything as back to normal as possible for today. Sammy and I can finish up here if you and Carl want to take a look around town," she added as she swept the last pile into the dustpan.

While the store looked neat, it also had a vacant look, almost too clean. Somehow she knew the other village business owners who had been burglarized had the independence and ingenuity to make it through, including Bob Lyons. On the other hand, she realized the only way Louisa would ever truly get well would be if women, especially her close friends, stood together to help her as much as possible.

Chapter 23

Extende super alutam mollem (Ext. sup. alut. moll.)

Spread upon Soft Leather

JENNIE FINISHED ADDRESSING her last envelope. She had a stack of orders to replace the goods stolen or destroyed by the Decoration Day burglars. She put them in the outbox on the counter. One of the family members would come down later to take them to the post office.

As Jennie stood at the counter, her back to the front window, the sun warmed her head and back. She felt amazingly relaxed, considering all she had experienced over the last couple weeks. Monday was usually a big delivery day. Even though the village had quieted down from the previous week's big events, she knew she would be busy soon.

"Is your pa around?"

Jennie jumped. It took her a minute to recognize Tom Porter standing in the door blocking the light. With his trademark coonskin cap sideways on his head, his long beard, and his large clear spectacles, Maude's father was easy to identify.

"I didn't mean to startle you, Jennie," he apologized.

"Oh! Mr. Porter! You *did* startle me!" she said as she raised her hand to her heart. "I was just thinking how relaxed I was, but I guess I'm still a bit nervy."

"You're not alone, Jennie. I think everyone in town's a bit on edge yet."

When the older man came more into focus, she noticed he carried a fancy leather satchel. For some reason, it looked very familiar.

"Father went with Donald Wolff, Doc Edmunds, and George Boutwell to Buffalo on the train. They think they caught one of the criminals," she added as she again looked at the bag the man carried. "What's that you're carrying?"

"I thought I'd better show this to your pa before handing it off to Wolff to add to his stock of evidence. It's a bag of burglary tools."

As Porter lifted the satchel onto the counter, Jennie heard the familiar clinking of metal on metal. All of a sudden, she remembered where she had seen the bag. "Goodness! I tripped over this the other day," she said, telling him the incident of how she bumped into a strange man in front of the Whittemore Bank. "Where did you find it?"

"It was in a pile of hay in the east pasture closer to the gate that leads to the river. I went out there this morning to get a load of hay for the cattle. I grabbed the pitchfork, stuck it in the pile, and jabbed into it."

"For goodness sake! The other day Maude and I took the path down to the river right there by your pasture. I saw fresh footprints and hay strewn around. I thought it odd because Maude said you hadn't been over there since last fall. Honestly, we got to talking, and I totally forgot about it. What's in it?"

"Tools of the trade for a burglar, Jennie. Tools of the trade."

"You've got to be joking!" she exclaimed, knowing he wasn't teasing her.

Tom Porter opened the bag and pulled out two short pipes, a couple lengths of fuse, some chains, and a bag of gun powder. Then he pulled out two items that caused Jennie to chuckle—a mask and a set of whiskers.

"You said you tripped over this the other day? Are you sure it was this bag?"

Jennie looked over the satchel. "I'm positive. I remember I noticed the style and figured a poor man couldn't afford something like this."

"Could you identify the stranger?"

"Pretty sure I could because the next day I saw him standing outside across the street at Scott's." Jennie recalled how the stranger also saw her and nodded. At the time, she couldn't help but think he had been flirting with her.

"I wonder if he's the brains behind this outfit that robbed the town?"

"He was so well-dressed." *And had a certain magnetism,* Jennie admitted to herself before saying, "I wonder if he signed his real name over at the hotel. Maybe, we need to talk to Scott about this."

"I suppose we'd better tell Donald Wolff. Sometimes we have to tell him what to do, but this *is* his job."

"Should we have Newell send a telegram to the sheriff's office in Buffalo?"

"Good idea! I'll head over there now. Would you be uncomfortable if I kept the bag here for a while?"

Jennie wished there were an alternative, but she answered in a brave voice, "I'll be fine." She hated to see him carry it all over town. "We don't need to advertise that you have it. Why don't we put it behind the back counter and out of the way of spectators?"

"I won't be gone long, and I'll take it home with me if we can't find another safe place for it."

"Before you leave, do you know if Maude is coming downtown today?" Jennie hadn't seen her friend for a couple of days. She knew she had decided to go out to Professor Rankin's cabin on Clearwater Lake with Jeanette Sanborn. Jennie had decided not to attend the literary discussion because she knew Pitt would be there. Because of their fight and his arm-in-arm companion at the Decoration Day celebration, she felt uncomfortable being in the same place with him. Even though she didn't attend, Jennie was still curious about how Sunday afternoon's get-together went.

"Maude wasn't up when I went out to the pasture, and I haven't been back in the house yet, but it seems to me her ma said Maude was going to run some errands this afternoon."

After Tom Porter left, Jennie turned her attention to her job list. She promised she would prepare an order for Doc Edmunds before he came back to town with her father. They had run low on some of their specialty items they made up for a few regular customers. She also promised a few village women that she would make up more jars of her recipe for cold cream. She had run out because of the special she had run in the newspaper.

Doc had ordered a double batch of Dalby's Carminative, his remedy for colicky babies. Although anyone could buy a patent medicine similar to what she and her father could make, Doc frowned on anyone giving an innocent baby any of that "quackery." The over-the-counter brand contained opium.

Jennie figured she had enough time to get started on one of the orders before business picked up. She pulled her father's recipe book from the shelf to make sure she concocted everything correctly, and grabbed the blue-and-white ceramic mortar and pestle, inspecting it to make sure it was clean.

After removing a small dropper from the drawer, Jennie set the heavy, brass scale on the counter. Every time she used the scales, she heard her father telling her of the importance of having a good scales. Stanley Phillips took pride in his profession and couldn't abide sloppiness when people's lives were at stake. A grains or two different from the recommended dosage of a medication could cause potentially serious problems, maybe even death.

Jennie grabbed the tea kettle off the Bunsen burner and poured hot water into a bowl. Lathering and scrubbing, she looked out the window and noticed Louisa Lyons cutting across the street. She dipped her hands in the water and wiped them on her apron. She'd have to come back to this job later.

"Good morning, Jennie," Louisa greeted her cheerfully. Her face, especially her left eye and cheek, were still black and blue.

"How are you doing, Louisa?" Jennie asked as she continued to wipe her hands on her apron.

Louisa shook her head. "Still stiff and sore. And of course my face . . ." she paused as she touched her eye and cheekbone. She didn't mention her personal attack.

Jennie felt like couldn't form the right words. She was nervous because it was Monday. Louisa nearly always came in on Mondays to buy some new curative after she read an advertisement about it in the Saturday paper. Struggling to come up with something to say, she asked, "Have you and Robert been able to clean up the store?"

"Bob had the place put back to normal that very night. He's a hard worker that husband of mine. We sent the children home and slept on a cot in the back room. He's a bit uneasy about leaving the store unoccupied until the burglars are behind bars."

Jennie thought Louisa appeared more alert than she had expected.

"Is there something you're looking for?"

Concentrating hard and scanning the patent medicines, Louisa didn't acknowledge she had heard Jennie. A few moments went by. Jennie wondered if she should suggest one of the specials of the week. She, too, turned her attention to the shelves in search of something harmless for Louisa to take. Jennie wondered if she should suggest Dr. Kilmer's Female Remedy or Dr. Guertin's Nerve Syrup.

"Can I see that Lydia Pinkham's product? Maybe, also Chichester's pills."

Jennie couldn't help herself. She started to say the products were dangerous but caught herself before she finished.

Their eyes met. As if she could read into her soul, Jennie knew why Louisa believed she needed these particular items. Louisa returned her attention to the shelves. Reaching for the green-and-white box and grabbing the red-and-silver tin container, Jennie pondered a moment before sliding them across the counter.

Louisa picked up the package of Pinkham's and read the side panel. Then she picked up the red metal box and read its claims.

"I'll take both of these. How much do I owe you?"

After she laid down two dollars and change, Louisa put the packages in her purse, patted her hat, and walked toward the door.

"Thank you."

Then Louisa was gone, leaving Jennie to wonder what she was to do about this visit. She and her father had made it a practice of talking to Doc Edmunds when Louisa came in and purchased an over-the-counter patent medicine. In turn, Doc informed Robert about his wife's latest purchase. Jennie knew this situation was different though.

Pinkham's products had been around a long time. Since Jennie starting working with her father, she had sold quite a few to the local women. Up until last week, she thought these same women were only using the over-the-counter medicines because they were too embarrassed to ask a male doctor about their monthly problems. The drugs were expensive, a dollar a box, and only a few town women could afford this luxury.

Jennie sold a lot of Chichester's Pennyroyal Pills as well. In fact, every month or two she had to reorder more of the little tin boxes. Until Maude told her what some women used the pills for, a type of morning after pill, she had considered them harmless.

Louisa wasn't stupid. She had been a straight A student, especially in science, and could have gone beyond high school if she hadn't fallen in love with Robert and gotten married. Jennie knew exactly what worried Louisa the most and why she purchased these specific products.

Scrubbing and lathering again before rinsing, Jennie hoped she'd have time to finish at least one order before she had another customer. She wished she had asked Blanche to help her, but because she doubted she would have that many interruptions this morning, she encouraged her sister to study for her finals. Before long, Blanche would get the experience she needed behind the counter when their father left for Eden Valley to open the new store there.

As she pondered being in charge of the Clearwater store, Jennie felt a tightening in her stomach. Time was near for all of the family to get along without their father during the week. Doc Edmunds had assured both Jennie and Stanley that if she had a question about anything medical or if she needed help concocting one of his orders, he would help her.

Despite all the help that was promised her, last night when the family sat around the table for supper, her father expressed his concern about leaving Jennie in charge of the business. "I'm struggling with our decision to start up the new store. Clearwater's been in a fanciful state, thinking nothing could happen to us. We were sitting ducks. What if something worse happens?"

"I'll be okay at the store," Jennie had said, trying to reassure him and her mother. "I think everyone in town had a wake-up call and will lookout for one another. Besides," she added, "we have Scott, Whittemore, Shaws, Barretts, and Lyons all around us."

Stanley still looked concerned. When Jennie looked at her mother, she recognized a bit of dread on her face as well. Why wouldn't she be concerned? Her husband, her partner, would be gone five days of every week; she'd be the only one responsible for her family.

"I gave notice out at Rices," Carl said, interrupting the conversation.

Jennie looked around the table, reading looks of surprise on everyone's face as they stared at Carl. They knew how much he liked working on a farm.

The most surprised was Stanley. "Wasn't necessary, Carl. We'll manage somehow. You were finally getting some farming experience out at Rices'."

Jennie agreed. "You can't do that, Carl. You've complained at times, but you love working outdoors. Besides, everyone's making too big of deal here." Jennie looked from her mother to her father to her brother and said matter-of-factly, "I'll be fine."

"Jennie, Pa," Carl answered firmly, "I left everyone high and dry last year. This's something I've gotta do. I've already given Rice a week's notice. I told him last Saturday after I talked with Barrett at the livery stable. He promised me some part-time delivery work. I'll be working outside, Jennie. If I can find another part-time job, I'll make as much as at Rices. Besides, I won't have to sleep there or come and go the two miles if I wanna be in town. I'll be out and about all day long, Pa, so I can keep a watch on the store and Jennie."

"And I'll be there to help out, Pa," Blanche answered.

Stanley Phillips studied his wife's face. Jennie could tell her mother looked more relaxed. She patted her husband's hand as if giving him permission to go ahead with his plans. Jennie could tell her mother was proud of her responsible children.

"If I can get this business going," Stanley said, "I might be able to sell it in a year or two for a nice profit. For once, we could face the future in the black."

Because Jennie was the oldest, she knew it had been hard raising their large family, but her folks seldom complained or discussed their financial issues in front of their children. It was settled with Stanley somewhat reassured that they would all look out for one another while he set forth on his new venture.

Jennie hoped she could fill in for her father and make wise business decisions. For over a year, he had taught her what he thought was the most important to know. He'd help her by going over the books or making other ordering decisions each weekend when he came home. She'd have to leave everything else up to chance and common sense.

"I'm back, Jennie," Tom Porter announced as the bell over the door rang, awaking her from her thoughts.

"Goodness," Jennie said, "I almost forgot about you, Mr. Porter."

"I had Newell send a telegram to the sheriff's department in Buffalo. I said you could describe the person who owns this bag. Do you know what time your pa'll be back today, or is he staying the night?"

"He took a few things with him, but he said he hoped they'd get back so he could sleep in his own bed tonight."

"I don't blame him. I wouldn't mind going with most of those men, but I'd hate to be sleeping with Wolff. Hopefully, your pa's there when the sheriff gets the message. I'll take the bag and keep it safe until our town constable gets back."

It didn't take much guessing to figure out that even Tom Porter, who was pretty easy to get along with, had little confidence in their local constable.

"Guess I wasn't as nerved up as I thought because I forgot it was here," Jennie laughed. "But, I'm a bit relieved you're taking it with you."

"I'd best get moving. I promised Abigail I'd be home to eat dinner, and I still have a couple stops to make."

"Pa! Jennie," Maude greeted as the screen door slammed. She started to close the front door, but Jennie stopped her.

"It's starting to warm up in here, Maude. Leave it open."

"How's everything at home?" Tom asked Maude.

"Oh, fine, Pa. Since Charlotte's been doing the wash, Ma's helping with our noon meal."

The Porter family could well afford hired help around the house and farm. Jennie realized her own mother, with the help of her sisters, would be finishing up wash because that's what a housewife did on Monday. Tomorrow her mother and any of the girls who were around devoted themselves to ironing the piles of shirts, pants, blouses, skirts, and dresses.

"I'll see you later then. You coming home for dinner?" Tom Porter asked.

"I'll be there. I think we're having boiled dinner. The pot's been on the back burner since this morning with the left-over ham bone."

Jennie loved her mother's boiled dinner. Marietta said her own ma put everything in it, leftover potatoes, carrots, onions, and bits of ham or corned beef. Most everyone in her family fought over the onions and carrots.

"So how are you today, Jennie?"

"Keeping busy, Maude, keeping busy. I have a few things to get done yet today besides waiting on customers, but I doubt it'll be all that hectic. I'm sure most folk are tired and cleaning up from the long weekend."

"You're probably right. Town's pretty quiet. You have this place looking like nothing happened," Maude said as she looked around the room.

"Everyone chipped in except, of course, Ruthie," she laughed. "It wouldn't take her long to make more of a mess."

Jennie wanted to say something to Maude about Louisa's latest purchase, but she knew she shouldn't. Every customer deserved privacy, her father said. It was one thing to tell Doc Edmunds and her father, but it was another to spread gossip, no matter how concerned Jennie was about the woman's health.

"So, Maude, I'm curious. Tell me how your Sunday went at Rankin's place out on Clearwater Lake."

"We had a nice time. The professor said he heard Mark Twain's coming to Minnesota in mid-July to speak. Apparently, he's on a world tour, starting in Cleveland then Minnesota, and moving westward toward the Orient."

"Wouldn't that be wonderful to see him in person?"

"Yes . . . sure would. Let's see if we can get tickets."

"So what else did you do out there?"

"The professor read a wonderful short story by . . . oh, she's southern. He said she's written a few of these little tales about women and their concerns."

"There are a few wonderful women writers. I wonder if I know the story. What was it about?"

"He said it was published in *Vogue* last year, but I don't remember the title. Anyway, it was about this woman who had a heart problem. Her sister breaks the news to her that her husband has been killed in a train accident."

"Sounds familiar. I can't remember the title or the author. She isn't well-known, but I think I know the story. After the wife finds out her husband's been killed, doesn't she ponder what it will be like to be free? Toward the end of the story, he walks in, and she drops dead?"

"That's it! I can only imagine what it would be like to be married to a man I no longer cared for."

"I know what you mean, Maude, but don't you think the story goes deeper than that?"

"Of course. A woman goes from her father's dominance to her husband's. That's still the case as I experienced trying to sign that lease at Whitings' on my own. Some men think they have to have complete control over their wives. I wasn't raised like that. My mother and father are almost always in agreement with each other on decisions that govern our future."

"Mine, too. Both encouraged us girls to think for ourselves. I suppose in a way that's why I couldn't give Pitt total control of our future together. I know I'd never be content being a housewife and a mother."

Maude walked to the window and looked out. For a few moments, she said nothing. Jennie thought that odd. Maude seldom didn't share her opinions.

"I'm glad you've resolved the matter, Jennie. What I have to tell you, hopefully, won't be too hard for you to hear."

Jennie stared at Maude.

"I'm sure you knew Pitt was going to be at Rankins's."

Jennie wondered what Maude was alluding to. "I told you Pitt invited me to go with him before we had it out. He even tried to get you to encourage me to come afterwards."

Maude nodded. "What do you know of this Alice? Alice Jacobs, I think her name is."

"The one Pitt was arm-in-arm with?" Jennie rolled her eyes and shook her head. "I think she had Pitt as a teacher at the Normal School. From what I gathered when she came into the store was that she recently graduated and will begin teaching in Annandale in the fall. Why? "

"Let's just say something doesn't make much sense." Maude bit the side of her lip. "I suppose I should be the one to tell you."

"Tell me, what?" Jennie took a sip of water from the dipper in the bucket.

"Like I said, this makes no sense. First, Pitt pleads with you to marry him, and then Professor Rankin announces Pitt and that Jacobs girl are getting married next summer."

Losing grip of the dipper, Jennie spilled water down her front. She grabbed a towel and dabbed herself hard, then harder and faster.

"Jennie?"

"I'm all right. It's only water." She turned her back to Maude.

Horse hooves, wood rattling, bells and chains jingling caused Jennie to look up and out the window. Danny Higgins hollered, "Ho!" Of course, now when she was a mess, she'd have someone who needed her attention.

Maude looked up as well, then back at Jennie. "Do you want me to see if he'll come back, Jennie?"

"No!" she answered abruptly. Then repeating a bit softer, she corrected her tone. "I'll be fine. It's probably good he came so I could get my mind off this."

"Do you want me to go?"

"Please don't, Maude. I'm glad you're here, and I'm glad you were the one to tell me this news. We can't talk about it again until Danny leaves."

Jennie wiped her eyes and sniffed.

"Morning, Jennie, Miss Porter," he greeted lifting his hat. "You want me to bring the boxes around the back or in here?"

Struggling to think, Jennie reasoned that if her father didn't return from Buffalo today, she'd have to leave the front of the store unwatched while she unpacked the crates.

"How about up front, Danny?" she said, trying to be cheery.

Danny brought in four crates, placing the last one on top of the counter. Taking out his log book for Jennie to sign, he commented, "Looks like you have most everything cleaned up. Hard to believe what happened!"

Jennie looked around the store front and replied, "I think Father and I got off lucky compared to others in town." Of course, she didn't mention what Louisa Lyons would have to live through. "From what I heard, because of the blast, Boutwell's had more damage than loss. I'm sure you'll be carrying in more boxes than usual for all of us in the next few weeks, to replace what we lost."

"Well, that's my job. The more business, the happier Newell is."

Jennie remembered she hadn't seen Claire for nearly a week. "What's Claire up to? I saw her Decoration Day but didn't have time to talk to her."

"When she's not workin' for Doc, she's out at our place in the country. Ma's helping her dig a garden. They got a little square cleaned up and raked. Apparently, her pa sent her some seeds from Ireland."

Jennie had no doubt the kind of crops Claire planned on growing. Danny gave no facial clue to knowing what his sweetheart was up to.

Would it matter? Claire wasn't stupid nor would love blind her to what she considered her obligations. On top of all that, she was wise enough to know she couldn't raise her herbs in Doc's backyard. It was obvious Claire O'Casey was determined to do all she could to help women who found themselves in trouble.

"Would you please send her my regards and tell her to stop in sometime soon? I'd like to visit with her."

Chapter 24

Percola

Strain through, Percolate

After Danny left, Maude turned back to Jennie. "I'm sorry I had to break the news about Pitt and that woman, but I didn't want you to hear about it on the streets."

"I can't lie. It's a shock, Maude. I suppose deep down inside I had a glimmer of hope we could make up."

"I thought he and she were a bit snug when we got there. Like what we saw on Decoration Day. She was hanging all over him, held onto his arm as if she'd fall over if he weren't holding her up. I swear I even saw her bat her eyes at him when he looked down at her. Such a typical female ploy." Maude grimaced. "Then, after we finished our literary discussion, we went into the parlor for refreshments. The professor asked us not to drink our punch until everyone had a cup in their hands. He announced that Pitt and Alice didn't know that he was doing this, but he was so excited he couldn't help it. He wanted us to raise our cups to congratulate the 'happy couple.' Apparently, Pitt had asked Alice to marry him on Saturday after having a brief discussion with the young girl's father who, along with his wife, had come up for the celebration."

Jennie grabbed the packing knife and turned her attention to prying open the wooden crate Danny had left on the counter. With super strength and a wave of grief, Jennie stabbed and stabbed at the box before dropping her head and saying, "I can't believe it!"

"I'm sorry, Jennie. Pitt turned as red as the heart of a watermelon. If I were to give him any credit, I'd say he was obviously surprised and embarrassed the professor would make the announcement at that time in front of us all."

"I have to get a grip here," Jennie cried, leaning over the crate and resting her head on her arm. "It hurts, Maude."

"I don't know what to say, Jennie. It's odd, almost like he knew this Alice was after him, but he wanted you first. I've gotta tell you, Jennie, Pitt didn't look overly excited when he greeted Jeanette or me."

"Why would he ask me to marry him, then turn around and ask her? This doesn't make sense. And what if I had come? We'd both be humiliated."

Jennie remembered how the two young women, Rankin's niece and Alice, acted a bit coquettish when they came into the store to wait for the professor, especially when Pitt's name was mentioned. Jennie hadn't thought much about it until she saw Pitt and her walking away from the crowd last Thursday. She figured Alice had been infatuated with Pitt. Jennie knew she wasn't the first or the last student to think she was in love with her professor. Still, she wondered what Pitt had done to encourage Alice's attention.

"I hope you don't confuse the message with the messenger," Maude said.

"I'm not mad at you. It takes a good friend to tell a person something like this." She wanted to run away, maybe go again to the river to wrap her mind and her heart around this bit of news. Jennie had been convinced Pitt loved her as much as she loved him. Now she felt like a fool.

Yet, she knew she couldn't desert her post, her duty, for emotion. She continued to pry open the crate, figuring it best to get back to work to get her mind off her problem. *This is what you wanted, your career. Now you have it!*

"If it helps any, Jeanette wanted to come with me to tell you, but I said it would be easier if I broke the news. She, like others out at Rankins, was shocked when the professor made his announcement. I know she, Ella, and Gert were flabbergasted. They'll be stopping by sometime today or tomorrow."

Even though she appreciated the thoughts and concerns, at that moment, Jennie didn't want company coming to express their condolences. She wanted to bury herself in her work and get her mind off Pitt.

"I'm sure I'll be fine. I can't run away this time, Maude. My father isn't here. He went to Buffalo with Doc and a few others to talk to the sheriff about the burglaries and other things," she added, nodding toward Lyons's store. I bet I'll be called over there as well because I might be the only one able to identify the person who owned the satchel your father found buried in the hay pile."

Maude gave her a look of surprise.

"You don't know about the satchel?" Jennie said, laying down the knife.

"What satchel?"

Jennie retold the story of how she tripped over the handsome, well-dressed man after she left Maude and the rest of the crew working down on the platform, getting it ready for Decoration Day. Then, after she recovered from the shock of nearly knocking down the stranger, she was about to leave to get back to the store when she tripped over his traveling bag, or what she thought was his traveling bag.

She told Maude what she had observed when they went down toward the river, about the hay pile looking like it had been disturbed even though Maude said her father hadn't been down in this part of his pasture yet this spring. And now today, Maude's father found a mysterious bag buried in his hay pile.

"I thought it looked familiar, but then, when your father set it on the counter here," Jennie tapped the glass countertop, "it jingled and clanged. Instantly, I recalled where I'd seen the bag and what I heard when the stranger hefted it into his buggy. I knew I could identify the man who owned it." She also wondered if he was the one who attacked Louisa Lyons.

"For a small town, we sure have had our share of excitement lately. Have you seen Louisa lately to know how she's doing?" Maude asked.

Jennie told her that Louisa seemed to be holding her own. She left off the part about her purchase of some of the female products. "I, for one, have had enough excitement for a while," Jennie answered, trying to smile. After a few moments, she added, "Okay, now don't take this wrong, but I'd better get back to work."

"That's fine. If you're all right, I'll take off. I'm heading uptown to look over the store in the Whiting building. I hope I can set up shop by September."

"Imagine! You'll be a business woman, too. I can't wait to hear your plans."

"I'll come down after supper, and we'll go for a walk."

Maude's sympathetic pat on the shoulder caused Jennie to choke up again. Before she lost control, she got hold of herself by swallowing hard and taking a deep breath. "I'll be fine," she promised, wishing she could be alone but knowing she'd be thinking way too much if she were.

Maude left. Jennie sighed before opening the crate. When she finally got through to the inside, she pulled out straw stuffing to find a dozen boxes of Lydia Pinkham's Vegetable Compound. *How ironic!*

She read the ingredients on the back of the box: Unicorn root, Life root, Pleurisy root, Tenugreek seed, Black Cohosh.

Jennie knew Unicorn root was sometimes used for a colicky, gassy stomach, as well as female problems. Doc prescribed it to be brewed into a tea for women who had painful monthlies or hard deliveries. He also had her father or her mix Life root into a tonic for a patient suffering from tuberculosis. Even though many died of the disease, some found relief from the coughing that led to bleeding of the throat and esophagus.

Pleurisy root—even though the name implied the obvious, Jennie thought she would do some research on it because she wasn't quite sure what else it was used for. She grabbed the *Handbook of Prescriptions* she and her father often referred to when they wanted to know what an herb or drug was used for. She opened the book to "Herbs" and followed her finger down the page until she came to the bolded "Pleurisy Root." She read that it was used to fight pleurisy, inflammation, and stomach problems.

Jennie couldn't figure out why Tenugreek seed was in the product. She knew it was used for women who couldn't nurse because they were dried up or couldn't release their milk. Maybe, it was included as an ingredient because it was a mild pain reliever.

Jennie knew women like her mother used Black Cohosh to lessen their discomfort from hot flashes. Marietta's mother's generation often went out and picked their own herbs and roots to make their own home remedies. Marietta would have done that if Stanley hadn't had a supply of almost everything she could find in the woods. He told her he'd make her a tonic. When she found out his concoction contained a great amount of alcohol, she decided against it. Instead, he brought home a small chunk of the root that she boiled in water, strained, and seeped into a tea. After adding some honey, she sipped a few teaspoons a day whenever she had an attack.

The box of Pinkham's claimed it would restore "female regularity" and "remove impurities." The ingredients were pickled in alcohol and had enough potency to give any woman an easier few days if she took it on a regular basis.

While Pinkham's product caused Jennie concern, Chichester's Pennyroyal Pills caused her more. The other day, Maude referred to them as the "morning after pill." Yet, Jennie had known many women who claimed the pills helped their monthly pains. Every month she replenished her stock.

She picked up a can and read the directions: "A day or two before expected menstruation take one pill before meals and at bedtime." Pennyroyal, which she knew could be caustic if not taken appropriately, was supposedly its main ingredient. As she flipped the can from front to back, she realized it didn't show a list of ingredients.

Jennie couldn't understand this. Why would women take this product if they didn't know what was in it? She had a good knowledge of concocting, of how important it was to be exact with all the components that went into a prescription. If she didn't remember or know how to mix up something, she looked it up in the recipe book or asked her father or Doc. She sure wouldn't suggest this product to anyone, but then none of the women ever asked her. Jennie was beginning to understand that her customers knew what they wanted before they came into the store. Apparently, either of the products could do what Louisa wanted them to. But both could spell serious problems.

Jennie wanted to know even more—what worked with what and why. The other reference guide she and her father used, *American Druggist,* tied together some of the gaps. Lost in her thoughts, she didn't realize her mother had walked into the store until she heard the ding above the door.

"Ma, what're you doing here?" Jennie looked at the clock. She hadn't even heard the noon whistle.

Carrying a basket, Marietta said, "I thought I'd deliver the mail for you, Jennie, and bring you a little lunch."

Jennie looked at the large basket that had a white cloth covering a large mound. "Ma, that doesn't look like a *little* lunch!"

Marietta laughed. "I'm also bringing some of my last year's dandelion wine over to Louisa Lyons."

"Ma! You're not going to give that woman a dose of your spring tonic—cod liver oil and wine," Jennie teased.

"Of course not!" Marietta said, laughing again, this time shaking her finger. She became more somber when she added, "It probably wouldn't hurt her, though. Louisa told me she'd never tasted dandelion wine so I promised to bring her a bottle." Marietta set out Jennie's sandwich, a jar of coffee, and a triangle of pie. "I told your brothers and sisters to leave the last piece of rhubarb meringue for you. I thought I should bring it now for lunch because someone might forget and swipe it before you get it. We'll all have to wait a couple days before I have time to bake again."

Marietta looked across the street at Lyons's store. As though she were directing her thought across the street toward Louisa, she absent-mindedly patted down her basket. She turned around to the mail outbox. "Is this what you want me to take uptown to mail, Jennie?"

Jennie thought her mother was acting a bit distracted, as if she wanted to say something. She definitely had something on her mind and didn't seem to be in a hurry to leave.

"Are you sure it's not out of your way, Ma? I mean, if it's too far to walk, I could run up and drop the stack off if you'd watch the store for a few minutes."

"Heavens no, Jennie! Doc says exercise is good for me."

"But, Ma, I bet you're tired. You've already put in a day's worth of work doing the wash."

"That I did! Blanche and the boys helped a lot by hanging some of the wash and carrying the laundry basket in and out. We're done. Si's helping fold some of the clothes as we speak." Marietta walked to the other window and looked south as if she could imagine what was going on in her house at the moment. "Tomorrow, we'll do the ironing. That'll be hot work. I'm glad that job is done now for another few days."

"Like I said, I could drop off the mail if you'd stay and watch the store."

"The outing will do me good. It's a beautiful day! I must say, though, I'm a little lonesome with your pa out of town."

Oh, of course! That's her problem today. "I'm sorry, Ma. Maybe he'll be home tonight."

"I'll go uptown first, and then stop at Lyons's on my way back." Marietta stuffed the envelopes into her basket, but she still dawdled.

As she began to leave, Jennie stopped her. "Ma, could you wait a minute? I'd like to talk to you about something."

"Of course, Jennie" Marietta turned and looked at her daughter.

"I thought you'd like to know I'm pretty sure I can identify one of the men responsible for the town's burglaries." Jennie proceeded to tell her about the man she bumped into, how she tripped over his leather satchel, then about how Tom Porter found the bag in the hay pile."

"I didn't know any of that."

"Ma, it's been so busy around here, I didn't even tell Pa. It slipped my mind."

"My gracious! What do you think will come of all this? Do you think the authorities will expect you to go to Buffalo to identify the man?"

"I suppose," Jennie answered, hoping she wouldn't have to make the hard trip over to the county seat.

"You know what else I've been thinking about?" Marietta folded her hands together as if she were praying and then brought them to her mouth. She didn't say much as she walked to the window and slowly looked left and right.

"What, Ma?" Jennie asked.

"Remember the other day when that shyster walked into the store and looked around? What if he were part of the pack?"

"Ma! You need to become a Pinkerton! I forgot all about him, too. Give me a second here. I need to make note of that, too." Jennie took a slip of paper and wrote down a summary of what had happened. "We had plenty of strangers in town last week. I suppose they all could have been suspects. Any of them could have done this. It's hard for me to visualize the person who took advantage of Louisa, though." Jennie thought of the man she had bumped into and the rough one who looked inside the store. She had a difficult time believing it was the better-looking man, but looks could be deceiving.

Jennie remembered a few other incidents. She jotted down the information about the man who bought cherry pipe tobacco and walked across to Scott's Hotel. He seemed to know the stranger with the satchel. He had hopped on a horse to follow him as he rode out of town.

"What else are you writing down?" Marietta walked over to the counter and looked over Jennie's notes.

"Listing a few people who might be suspects. How could any of us keep an eye on everyone who came in town last week?" Jennie thought a moment. "This could give the authorities in Buffalo something to go on, though."

"It's like the store has eyes. The big bay windows seem to look out on everything. It can see a person walk from the depot, get a room at the hotel, and ride into and out of town," Marietta said. "You sure you don't need anything else while I'm around today?"

Jennie could tell her mother was still stalling as she picked up the basket again.

"Ma, you do know that Pitt and I are finished for good now, don't you?"

Marietta looked at her daughter, sighed, and slowly answered, "Jennie, I know. I sort of heard about it through the grapevine."

"News gets around fast, doesn't it? Did Maude stop and tell you?" Jennie couldn't believe how calm she was. She didn't feel a tear coming on. She didn't choke up. She felt as though it was truly a fact that she could live with now.

"No, nothing like that. To tell you the truth, your pa told me first last week—the day you two broke up, but I figured you would patch it up. You usually do. Then, of course, last Thursday at the pie social, Livy Paisley felt it was her duty to inform me that you two had split."

Why, of course, Livy Paisley! She would have been able to observe the scene. "I'm sorry, Ma. I should have told you sooner. There's been so much going on, and I needed to stay as focused as possible. Really, there wasn't time."

"I knew something was up, Jennie. You've looked like you were carrying a world of cares. You're pale. You look like you have lost a bit of weight."

"Funny! I think I have too. My skirts are loose around my waist. I'm sorry I've worried you."

"Doesn't seem to matter how old a mother's children get, they can still cause her to lie awake nights."

"Ma, I'm sorry." Jennie looked at the pharmaceutical book she had opened. "I want to ask you something, but before I forget, I need to tell you Pitt is getting married, but not to me. He asked one of his students to marry him."

"Gracious! He can propose to this woman so soon after breaking up with you? I thought I knew that young man better than that."

"I know, Ma, but it's time to move on. He'll be married next June."

"You're okay with all this?"

"For some reason, I'm feeling calmer than I was earlier in the day when Maude told me." Jennie gave Marietta a summary of Pitt's proposal and ultimate breakup, the literary discussion she'd declined to attend, and Maude's version of the professor's announcement that caught everyone by surprise. Jennie looked down a moment, and this time blinked back a few tears. She knew now what she was feeling—a sense of betrayal.

"I'm sorry, Jennie. I thought you two would eventually get married."

"Maybe I did too, Ma," she said wiping her eyes before looking up at her mother. "I know I'll be fine. I have to keep busy, and I'll be busy enough when Father leaves for Eden Valley."

"You sure will, but everyone will chip in to help you and your pa." Marietta looked at her basket and then across the street. "You think you'll be okay if I head out? I must say I'm relieved to have had this talk, even though I'm upset with Pitt."

"Seriously, Ma, I didn't withhold any of this purposely."

"I'm glad to know what's been going on because we've got to get along with his folks and keep a step ahead of Livy. Sometimes that woman seems to take such pleasure in skimming the scum from the top of the water barrel." Marietta shook her head. "I know you're hurting, despite the fact you're putting on a brave front. But you're a strong woman, Jennie. If you can hold your head up high even with that woman pecking at you, I know you'll make it."

"I haven't been brave, Ma, believe me. Ask Maude and Pa. They've seen me at my worst." Jennie tried to give her mother a reassuring smile. "I think I'm now more angry than anything, but I know I have to get to the point where I can forgive him and give him and his future bride my best if we run into each other."

Of course! Anger and betrayal are what I'm feeling. I can't believe I almost agreed to marry him. All Pitt wanted was for me to give up my life for him, bear HIS children, forget myself and my dreams, and dote on him! How selfish!

"And don't forget, we've got to get along with Pitt's folks."

"You're right, Ma. The Colgroves are good people. Pitt's a good man, and I bet they're as shocked as anyone about his engagement to a former student."

Marietta walked to the door. "I'd better be off. I have a few stops before I head on home. I thought when I drop off the wine, I'd also pick up some canned fruit. We're almost out of the peaches and apples I put up last year."

She knew her mother might be able to help her with one of her biggest concerns. "Before you go, Ma, I need to ask you a personal question, maybe even a moral and ethical one. I'm really struggling right now for an answer."

"Jennie! You aren't?"

"Aren't what?" Jennie read her mother's shocked expression. "Oh, Mother, no! In the family way? Of course not! You should know me better than that!"

"Thank heavens! It's just that when a couple is so in love as I thought you and Pitt were, sometimes—" Embarrassed, Marietta turned her head. "What's the problem then?"

"I don't know where to start, Ma," Jennie said as she nervously moved closer to the window to check that no one would be coming in too soon. No matter how uncomfortable this was to talk about, she needed guidance. Who else could she really rely on? "Do you know why some women use some of these patent medicines?" Jennie grabbed the bottle of Lydia Pinkham's Vegetable Compound that she had taken out of its box and reached for a container of Chichester's Pennyroyal Pills and slid it across the counter.

Jennie's mother put down her basket and looked at the products. After a few moments, Marietta looked at Jennie and cleared her throat before answering softly, "I've heard some women use these for regulating their monthlies, but I've also heard they've been used for, well, for other reasons. Why do you ask?"

"I've recently found out that some women have used them to end their pregnancies or stop them before they begin. I've sold these products regularly and have to restock quite often. Seriously, Ma, I thought the women who were buying these medicines were simply too embarrassed to ask Doc for medical advice. I not only feel as if I've been caught in a triangle, but I feel responsible for Father's business—his reputation."

"All I can tell you is that your father knows what the products can be used for. And not all women use them in that way. We've talked about it. Both of us have come to the conclusion that even if he could do something about it, he won't."

"I can't believe you'd act so blasé about this," Jennie said, disappointed that her mother didn't see the issue like she did. "Don't you think this is murder if they are used the way I've heard they've been used?"

"Jennie, it's an age-old question. I don't know if there's an answer. You can't ask a woman why she's buying them. They're legal and available on the market."

"I know they're legal. But if a woman takes them incorrectly the baby could die," Jennie said, returning the medicines to the shelf. "To me this is a moral and ethical issue."

"Of course, I don't believe that it's right, Jennie. No one believes in aborting a child, *no one,* but I also don't feel as though I can judge. Some women have had a hard lot in life—too many pregnancies or men that are less than kind. Others may have created their own problems to begin with, but like I said, I can't judge because I don't know their circumstances."

"Ma, this morning Louisa Lyons came in and bought both products."

Marietta's eyes grew large as she looked across the street again. "Oh, dear!"

"Then you think the same thing I do? Father and I've made it a habit of telling Doc what she's purchased so Robert can deal with it. Usually, she buys only things that contain alcohol, and Robert tries to dispose of the contents. What she purchased today is different."

"If you're asking me what to do, I can't tell you. However, the last thing, *the very last thing*, that woman needs now is another child, and especially the way she *might have* conceived this one."

"I know." Jennie also turned to the window and stared out. "Do you see how hard this is for me?"

"I know, Jennie. It isn't easy," Marietta fumbled with the gold atomizer atop a green bottle of perfume. "I suppose you're old enough to know what I had to deal with when I was younger."

"What?" Jennie asked.

"It was a long time ago when I was single and still living in Maine. I had a friend who got herself in trouble. She couldn't bear to tell her folks. She went to this woman in the country known to help girls who found themselves in this type of situation." Marietta leaned onto the counter and covered her forehead with her hand as though she couldn't handle the guilt of remembering. "I don't know how the poor thing survived the walk home, but I sat with her in her bedroom, holding her hand. She bled so much. I told her ma she was sick with her monthly. She seemed to believe it and mixed her a tonic to help her sleep."

"You knew what your friend had been up to? I can't believe this!"

"It was hard, but the boy who got her in this predicament ran off, deserting her. She didn't want to bring shame onto her family. She said she had no other choice. What was she to do, Jennie? Some women think they have no other choices available to them."

"I can't believe you know about these things. How come you never told me before?"

"Most women know these things, Jennie. Those who say they don't are not being honest. I'm sorry we didn't have this talk sooner. I suppose the topic never came up. To be honest, Jennie, you're so smart I thought you'd figured it out already."

Jennie read the sincerity in her mother's voice. She probably should have known more about some of these products and what they were used for. "Oh, Ma! Now I'm even more confused. From here on in, when I sell some of these concoctions, I'll be suspicious they're being misused. And besides the issue of abortion, what if the woman gets seriously ill or even dies? What if Louisa dies?"

"It would be awful, but I really doubt the store would be responsible. Like I said, the products are legal, and it's a woman's free will to buy them." Marietta turned her attention back to Lyons's store across the street. "Sometimes we women have to help each other. Maybe you should try to ignore all this until you can wrap your mind around it."

Jennie leaned against the back shelves and wrapped her arms around herself. She was shocked her mother, a woman who quoted the Bible when she was trying to guide her children, would be giving her the same advice both Maude and Claire had given her—to ignore, to turn her back, to accept the fact that the products are legal, even if they could be lethal.

"All I could do, Jennie, was hold my friend's hand." Marietta picked up the wicker basket and walked to the door. Before she left, she turned back and looked at her daughter and said, "That's all I knew how to do at the time, but sometimes that's all that matters. The rest might have to be left to God."

Chapter 25
Pondere
Weight

JENNIE WATCHED HER MOTHER leave the store. Usually, Marietta Phillips had a smile on her face and held her head high. But after her conversation with Jennie, her head hung. Jennie wondered if her mother's memories had caused her pain or if she, like Jennie, was worried about Louisa Lyons.

The afternoon turned quiet. After pouring a cup of the now tepid coffee, Jennie bit into her sandwich. Could there be anything better than her mother's homemade bread, butter, and cold roast beef?

She decided to begin mixing up a batch of cold cream. Following her father's basic recipe, Jennie added other ingredients to make it her own product, which had become popular with many women in the village.

Carefully, she measured out sixteen ounces of oil of almonds. She sliced what looked like four ounces off a bar of white wax. After a year of mixing up the cream, Jennie could eyeball how much wax she needed, although it never seemed to matter if she were a little over or under. She placed chunks of wax in the top pan of a double boiler and poured enough water to fill the bottom pan about half full. She lit a match and turned on the Bunsen burner.

Once the wax had melted, Jennie pulled it out of the water bath. Using a little wooden whip, she beat in the oil of almonds before setting it aside to cool for a bit, yet not so long that it hardened. While she waited, she found the bottle of Tolu, her secret ingredient, which was sticky and smelled like balsam. She also needed rose water. All her sisters, mother, and Jennie had worked tirelessly last summer to grow roses and dry them so Jennie could use them in the cold cream and powders she made.

Soon the wax and oil had cooled enough to set up. Jennie measured out twelve ounces of rose water into a large, glass measuring cup. Carefully, she squeezed one drop of Tolu and poured one and one half ounces of water into the oil and wax, mixing well before repeating the process. Once she had all the ingredients incorporated, she whipped the concoction until it was fluffy.

The smell of sweet roses and the spicy balsam of the Tolu was intoxicating. Whatever remained after she filled up the eight, small jars for sale, she took home to share with her mother and sisters.

While she filled the last jar, Jennie thought about Alice Leonard. She wondered how many little frills like cold cream, perfume, or talc the girl had in her life. Obviously quite poor, she had to face one tragedy after another, her father's and mother's deaths, and then, as if the whole family were meant to be together, the girl came to her own awful end. Had no one in Irish Town tried to protect her from the person or persons who had taken advantage of her and eventually bludgeoned her to death?

Jennie couldn't figure out why she felt so responsible or concerned for this dead girl. She didn't know her or know much about the family until just lately. What was it that was nagging at her so much? Maybe it had something do with the fact that the case wasn't solved and her own supernatural encounters. Even in the dream, the apparition seemed as if it were begging Jennie for help. Yet, what could she do? Hopefully, if the spirit of Alice Leonard had been wandering the swamp, Claire O'Casey helped her find eternal rest. Jennie hoped she could talk to Claire soon.

Gathering the lids and metal clips to seal the jars, Jennie's thoughts wandered back to Pitt. This new revelation about him marrying someone else made her realize he wasn't who she thought he was. The man she had grown to love would never have betrayed her the way he had.

Pitt was smart, but so was she. Nevertheless, because he was a man, he had more opportunities than Jennie had. It truly was a man's world, and that was how he wanted to keep it. He wanted a woman to keep house, bear him children, and dote on his every word. How did Tennyson's poem go?

> Man for the field and woman for the hearth:
> Man for the sword and for the needle she:
> Man with the head and woman with the heart:
> Man to command and woman to obey;
> All else confusion.

She loved Tennyson, but why had she never thought deeply about the words of his poem before? She could not imagine obeying Pitt, or any other man, for that matter. Her parents had raised her differently. No, even though her heart hurt, she knew deep down she wouldn't be content being this type of wife. Perhaps Alice Jacobs was the right person for him after all.

She sealed the last jar, wiped all of them with a damp rag, and glued her own label, "JENNIE PHILLIPS'S COLD CREAM," onto the front of each jar. She felt a sense of pride as she lined them up neatly on the shelf behind the front counter that her father teasingly called "Jennie's Corner."

Returning to the dispensary counter, Jennie flipped through the recipe book until she found Dalby's Carminative. As she read the formula, she pulled one ingredient after another from the shelves, starting with carbonate of magnesia, oils of peppermint, anise seed, nutmeg, and tinctures of assafoetida, castor, and cardamom. She knew babies sometimes suffered from colicky gas. Almost everything in this recipe could give the baby some relief from the painful spasms.

What else did she need? Doc's prescription contained none of the opium or oil of poppies that were often included by other doctors or in patent medicines. She reread the list until she came to the last ingredient. *Pennyroyal?* How many times had she made up this prescription for him and not wondered why this was included? Over the last couple weeks, she had come to understand the full potential of this plant, which she thought was used solely to calm the stomach.

After washing her hands again in hot, sudsy water, and rinsing off, Jennie peered outside to see if anyone were coming. However empty the streets were on this quiet Monday, it all could change in a second. She hated to get started on Doc's special prescription for the baby with colic and then get interrupted. An accident, like forgetting one ingredient or doubling up on another, could happen and be serious if her mind strayed from her task.

Although the afternoon was coming to a close, Jennie noticed a few men still hanging around the hotel livery stable behind Lyons's store. One man dressed in bibbed overalls and a dark, wide-brimmed hat kneeled by the back wheel of his wagon. Another man with gray hair and beard stooped over the other man to observe what he was doing. No one seemed to be coming in the direction of the drug store so she decided to get busy with her biggest project.

Because the sun was hiding in the west behind the store, Jennie lit the overhead lamp to see more clearly. She set the scales on the counter at eye level. The whole contraption, the brass chains and the bowls, swung back and forth, flickering under the light.

Jennie placed one scruple weight after another until she added six in the center of the left brass bowl. She spooned carbonate of magnesia into the right bowl until both dishes balanced perfectly. She poured the powder into the mortar. Then as she finished measuring each ingredient, she placed a check by its listing in the book.

Next, she pinched the black rubber topper of the eye dropper into the oil of peppermint until it was nearly full. Carefully, Jennie counted each drop until she had squeezed eight into the mortar. After cleaning the dropper, she moved onto the oils of nutmeg and anise. She needed two drops of each.

She continued on to the tinctures. Castor, cardamom, and assafoetida helped with painful gas. She needed many drops of each so she pulled a larger dropper from the drawer. Once she had finished this, Jennie stirred the mixture into a cream.

Next, she needed five drams of syrup of poppies, but Doc had substituted tincture of viburnum prunifolium, which caused relaxation but was less addicting and less dangerous than pure opium. She calculated drams to ounces. She needed five drams, which was hard to calculate exactly because four drams equaled one-half ounce, and six equaled three-fourths of an ounce. In order to measure precisely, she poured the liquid into a small, clear beaker until it read 0.625 ounces. Then she measured two ounces of peppermint water, poured it into the mortar, and mixed it until it was smooth.

She moved onto her last ingredient, fifteen drops of pennyroyal. *Why in the world would Doc Edmunds allow this ingredient in his prescription for colic?* She wondered if there wasn't something else he could have used. While she began to add one drop after another, Jennie recalled the patent medicines that contained this ingredient along with other powerful herbs and roots. They were all disguised as products that helped women "become regular." She remembered what the beautiful, red-haired Claire O'Casey, her good friend Maude Porter, and now her very own mother had expressed—women need to help women.

Deep in thought, Jennie hardly heard the whistle of the incoming train until the screeching of wheels alerted her. Almost shocked that the afternoon had escaped her, she finished up the colic treatment by stirring it into a syrup. After pouring it into a clear bottle, she twisted the cap until it was closed tightly. She wrote Doc's instructions on the label: "Mix one tablespoon into a half cup of warm water. Pour into baby bottle. May be given to child up to three times a day." Then she glued the label to the bottle and set it on the counter for Doc to take whenever he came back from Buffalo.

Usually, they had few customers from the westward bound freight train, but she noticed a couple of men walking from the direction of the depot. One carried a small black bag. As they got closer, Jennie recognized one as Doc Edmunds. Both men had pipes sticking out of the sides of their mouths, but the other man looked a bit older and somewhat familiar, even though Jennie couldn't instantly place him.

"Hello, Jennie," Doc said as he stepped through the door with the other man following.

Jennie stepped out from behind the counter. "I'm surprised to see you already."

"The two of us hitched a ride from Buffalo to Monticello and hopped the train to get back here." He thrust his thumb backwards before adding, "This here's Deputy Sheriff James Lowell. He's been investigating the heists in Wright County."

"How do you do, Deputy." Jennie greeted, still trying to figure out where she had seen the man before.

"Miss Phillips, it's good to see you again. Not sure if you remember me or not. I came into your store last week."

A whiff of cherry tobacco stirred her memory. "Of course! You purchased some tobacco."

She quickly told the deputy about the man she had bumped into who had a leather satchel. She told him how she had watched him hop on a horse and race after another man as he headed south out of town.

"You're very observant, Miss Phillips, and I have to say I'm sorry, but I have to serve you a subpoena. Before we left, the sheriff's office received Mr. Porter's telegram about his finding the bag with burglary tools. His note said you could identify the man who had it in his possession at one time."

"I'll be glad to help, but if you know who he is why do I need to go?"

"I have my suspicions, but I lost him on his way out of town. We need your testimony and description."

The deputy handed Jennie a folded document. She opened it and looked it over. "How soon will I have to leave? I assume my father and the rest are staying the night in Buffalo?"

"You're right. The sheriff's office was taking the Clearwater businessmen and your constable's depositions when we left, but it'll be too late for them to get back tonight," the deputy clarified.

"I bet they'll be back on the late morning train, Jennie," Doc said. "I gave the authorities what I knew but said I had to get back home. I know Gil went out to Lynden this afternoon to check on Mrs. Frank. I hated leaving the town without a doctor. Been busy today?"

Deputy Lowell interrupted. "I'll leave you two to your business, Doc. Thanks for being such a good companion, but I need to check in at the hotel across the street and deliver another subpoena. Miss Phillips, as soon as your father gets back in town tomorrow, we'll plan our trip. I'll escort you and our other witness to Buffalo tomorrow."

"That's sounds fine. See you tomorrow morning."

Jennie looked at the doctor before answering his questions. "So who is he delivering another subpoena to?" she asked.

"Oh, I'm sure it's for Tom Porter."

"I forgot that he's holding evidence. But back to your question, no, it's been quiet. This morning, I had a few customers, but since then, it's been quiet so I made up your orders and took care of a few other small projects."

"Good. I see you got the colic medicine ready, too," Doc said as he tipped the bottle up to read the instructions. "Do you need help with anything? I promised Stanley I'd look in on you and help you if you needed something."

"I'm pretty much finished around here for the day. I was thinking since it was so slow, I'd close up early. Maude and I are going out for a walk after supper."

"You need a break. I doubt if anything so exciting will happen again for a while. Your pa and the rest'll be back tomorrow morning or afternoon for sure, as the deputy said. They needed to give a full account of their losses." He walked over to the window and looked out. "Speaking of Lyons's, I hate to say this, but I think the poor thing may get a subpoena."

"Oh, no. Hasn't she been through enough?"

Doc shook his head. "I agree with you. Even though I explained the situation, the authorities might insist she come. I better go over and explain it to Louisa. Have you see anything of her? I suppose she came over for her usual advertisement special."

Jennie also looked out the window at Lyons's General Store. She turned her back to the doctor and walked behind the counter. When she lifted the brass scales to place them back where they belonged on the dispensary table, the bowls clanged into each other.

"Nothing serious, Doc."

Epilogue

Aqueous Solution (aq. sol.)

Water Solution

THE JUNE AIR WAS CRISP as Jennie carried her morning coffee down to the river below the house. She tossed a rug on the ground. Sitting down, she noticed a stray log bobbing and rolling downstream and another rolling toward shore. Watching logs on the river had always been a game to her. Would this one keep moving? Would it get caught up in the weeds and eventually sink into the mud?

As she sipped her coffee, she thought about what had happened to her peaceful village over the last couple weeks—first the fire and now the burglaries and violent attack on Louisa. She hoped her town could get back to normal quickly. With the testimonies of everyone who had been victimized, Jennie felt confident the men would be apprehended soon and put behind bars for a long time. From now on, she promised herself, she would be more on guard, not so trusting, especially since she would be in charge of the store while her father moved to Eden Valley.

Although she felt a pang of guilt because she had withheld a bit of information from Doc Edmunds about Louisa Lyons's Monday morning purchases, Jennie felt some relief that Doc wasn't concerned with her purchase of Lydia Pinkham's product. All he said was, "Good to know she's only dealing with female problems, not a pregnancy." Jennie had no idea what he would have said if she had told him that Louisa had also bought Chichester's pills.

Both Jennie and her mother agreed that the last thing Louisa needed now was to have another child. But Jennie still had to rummage through the knowledge that some women were taking matters into their own hands concerning their reproduction issues. Many of the patent products were little more than quackery, yet they were legal and some apparently effective. Regrettably, these over-the-counter products also helped keep the store's books balanced.

Nevertheless, if she, one of her sisters, or her mother had been the one attacked instead of Louisa and ended up in trouble, Jennie would probably search the shelves for something to end the problem. In fact, she realized she now had the knowledge of how to mix up some type of concoction herself. The thought startled her.

Jennie had been glad to see Claire O'Casey yesterday afternoon. When Danny gave her Jennie's message to come see her, she told Missus Edmunds that she had to run a couple errands. When she reached Jennie, Claire apologized for not coming sooner. She knew that the two had a lot to discuss. After they talked about the burglaries, Jennie told Claire what they presumed happened to Louisa Lyons, because she knew if anyone could keep a secret, it was Claire. After shaking her head, she mumbled something in Irish before she looked across the street toward Lyons's store.

Brightening up, Claire told Jennie her plans for the garden she and Danny's mum were planting. Now, Claire told her, she would have fresh herbs to work with and wouldn't have to rely so much on what was on Jennie's shelves. Jennie wasn't sure if she felt more relieved or concerned about Claire's endeavors.

Jennie brought up the subject of what happened out at the Tamarack Swamp and told Claire that the next evening Doc Edmunds came looking for something to perk her up. Claire apologized for sleeping all the way home and regretted worrying the "good doctor and his wife." She explained her "gift," or so her priest in Ireland had called it, to settle a spirit, especially that of a person who came to such a tragic end. Sometimes, she explained, something flew out of her after an encounter, and all she could do was sleep it off. Even though Jennie knew that she, too, had experienced something out in Irish Town, she had to admit to herself that all of her rationality, her common sense, vaporized when she was around the charming redhead. For now, Jennie wanted to put what happened out there far behind her.

Nevertheless, over the last couple weeks, Jennie had come to understand that most women were vulnerable. Alice Leonard, Louisa, the woman Claire was helping . . . and so many Jennie couldn't name. Of course, she could do nothing for Alice anymore, but others? Jennie was sensing a new respect for the color gray. Pharmacology was almost always an exact science. Judging people's intentions and motives was not. Maude, Claire, and even her own mother echoed: *Women have only each other to rely on.*

Thinking of the apparition in her dream who beckoned her with crooked finger, Jennie pondered what she wanted her to do. She had no spiritual gift like Claire O'Casey. She knew if she decided to stay in this profession, she had to be as honest and ethical as possible. What was it her mother had suggested if Jennie suspected a woman was buying an over-the-counter product? Turn her head and leave it up to God? Admittedly, she realized that might be, for now, all she could do.

Jennie took a last swig of her now-cool coffee, dumping the remainder in the grass. The tranquility of the morning created a feeling of peace she hadn't experienced for a couple weeks.

She knew she had shed all the tears she was going to for Pitt. She hoped he had found in Alice Jacobs what he felt he needed—total dedication to him, his career, and a family. Without a doubt, Jennie didn't want to marry right now. Maybe someday, but not yet. She had to follow her heart.

A breeze had picked up. It was nearly time to open the drug store and she hadn't finished packing her bag for an overnight stay in Buffalo, where she would give her testimony and attempt to describe the person who owned the satchel she had tripped over.

As Jennie stood up to leave, she watched one of the logs change course and float downstream. All of a sudden, she felt eager to see where the new currents in her life would carry her.

Solvenda

Acknowledgements

First, I want to thank my mom, Winnie Frank, for loving history and bestowing this love onto me. She loved all history, but she had a great love for the town she and Dad raised my brother, sister, and me in. This book is about Clearwater's early days. She died in 2009, but she was one of the founding members of the local historical group and had a memory full of conversations with people who knew their history.

I could not have completed this book without the help of my sister Becky Frank. Her love for the historical village by the Mississippi River equals mine. She spent many years collecting, compiling, and documenting much of Clearwater's history, its historical records, and many of the biographies I used to create a few of the characters of the community. She and I made numerous trips to the Minnesota Historical Society, Stearns History Museum and Research Center, and the Wright County Historical Society. Here we pored over personal stories, newspaper articles, pictures, and stories that I used to write this historical novel. In addition, Becky has always been on the search for postcards and any other objects d'art she could find. Some items I have included or described in the story.

I want to thank Soderlund Drugstore in St. Peter, Minnesota. They have the most fabulous collection of historical drug store items that my husband Frank and I browsed through while I was researching for this book. I also want to thank the Watertown Regional Library in South Dakota for the use of their microfilm machine where I spent long, eye-spinning hours reading and copying articles from the Clearwater newspapers dated from 1880 to 1941. I couldn't have done this without the access to interlibrary loan and the collections department at the Minnesota Historical Society in St. Paul.

Book Club Discussion Questions

1) Identify the main characters.
   a) Define their personalities and inner strengths.
   b) How does the setting figure as a character in the story?
   c) What are their motivations, i.e., why does a character do what he/she does?
   d) What effects do the events (time, nationality, physicality) have on the characters' personalities, motivations, and beliefs?
   e) How do characters change or evolve throughout the course of the story? What events trigger such changes?

2) What is your general knowledge of the setting of the book?
   a) How do the characters educate you on women's issues of the period?
   b) How is Clearwater like many other small communities?
   c) How has this novel broadened your perspective about the times?
   d) What new ideas have you been exposed to or learned?

3) Discuss the structure of the book. Does the book tell only one story or are there a number of little stories that weave around the main one?

4) Discuss the theme. How is it played throughout the book?

5) What symbols are used to reinforce the point of the story?

6) How are the book's images symbolically significant? Do the images help to develop the plot or help define characters?